Fandango

Other Books by Linda Berdoll

Mr. Darcy Takes a Wife

**Foreword Magazine* Book of the Year Silver Award

From *Booklist*:

> "Austenites who enjoy the many continuations of her novels will find much to love about this wild ride of a sequel, especially Berdoll's depiction of the enduring, strong love between Elizabeth and Darcy."
>
> — *Kristine Huntley*

Chicago Tribune:
"A Breezy, satisfying romance"

Library Journal:

> "While there have been other *Pride and Prejudice* sequels, this one, with its rich character development, has been the most enjoyable."

Darcy & Elizabeth: Nights and Days at Pemberley

**Independent Publisher's Book Awards* — 1st Place Historical Fiction 2007.

From *Booklist*:

> "Although the florid prose is packed with the historical details, descriptions, and familiar characters fans appreciate, the plot trots along at a good pace. A frothy historical dessert following a meaty entree of a classic, suitable for fans of Regency romance who don't mind a little spice."
>
> — *Kaite Mediatore*

The Darcys: The Ruling Passion — Coming in 2011

Fandango

Linda Berdoll

 Published 2011

Well, There It Is
Austin, Texas

Cataloging in Publication Data
Berdoll, Linda Baker
Fandango: a novel / by Linda Baker Berdoll
— 1st ed. Well, There It Is

ISBN 978-0-9674817-2-2

Printed in the United States of America
at Ginny's Printing in Austin, Texas

— For Taylor

1

San Francisco—1850

It was dusk, and fog enveloped everything, giving a ghostly pallor to the familiar streets. Although she knew it wasn't a fit time for a lady to be out alone, Annabella Chase didn't care. She didn't notice the time or the threat of darkness. When she had her mind set on something, she didn't let anything stop her—be it danger or decorum. After all, if anybody dared meddle with her, she had her father's Pauly pistol.

Although she'd never admit it, she had been a bit apprehensive. Everywhere she turned, people had told her tales about just how wild San Francisco had gotten. It was said law-abiding men couldn't walk down the street without being interfered with by lewd women or gunfighters.

As she headed up from the wharves, she was greatly relieved. The streets looked quite respectable. Windows lit for the evening trade glittered like the eyes of one of those Chinese serpents. People could be heard laughing and music filled the air. The notion of needing the pistol seemed preposterous.

For all its progress, however, the streets of San Francisco were still just as boggy as ever. Some of if sunk knee deep in mud and dung. With money pouring into the town coffers, one would think that the city fathers would improve the thoroughfares. (The muck had always been the chief suspect when men or mules went missing.) Knowing how unsteady the tottering walkboards could be, she steeled herself to traverse them. Cautiously tip-toeing from one to the other, she still managed to trip. Fortunately, she caught herself just short of catastrophe.

Righting herself, she muttered, "Drat these blessed slippers."

She should have worn her boots. With all the new construction in town, it would have been dicey going in the broad daylight. Managing to arrive at the corner of Clay and Kearney without bodily injury, she recognized a placard that had been overlooking the intersection for as long as she could recall.

These streets aren't passable
Not even jackassable!

Vulgar or not, that faded sign meant she was but a few steps from home. She couldn't stop herself from giggling with relief.

As she did, her attention was caught by strange noises wafting from up the alleyway. It sounded like an animal caught in a trap. Narrowing her eyes, she stopped and peered into the darkness. The rustling and lamenting grew loud enough for her to recognize the intonations as human.

She gasped.

One of them was a *woman*!

It was an outrage above any other! A lady had been dragged from the street and was being molested even then! She remembered the pistol in her pocket. She withdrew it and took several steps in the direction of the assault. In the time it took her to make her move however, the utterances, which had been so obviously combative, altered.

Together, came simultaneous chants, "Yes, yes, yes, yes...."

"Eew!" Annabella burst out, "*Eeew*!"

Shuddering with disgust, she hurried on her way. Couldn't these people do their lewd business where decent people weren't privy to them?

"Eew!"

Unfortunately, her outburst alerted a trio of low men across the street. She did not think their stares were those of mere admiration. They were so menacing that the hair on the back of her neck bristled. Hurrying on her way, she tried to pretend that she didn't see them. The palm of her hand began to perspire, threatening to loosen her grip on the gun. When she saw that the men had begun following her, she didn't hesitate to turn around and confront them. Her fingers trembled, but her aim was true.

She hissed, "If you take one more step, I'll shoot you where you stand."

She didn't lower the gun until they faded into the fog. The sound of their retreating footsteps wasn't the consolation that it should have been. As she headed back up the way, she kept her pistol in her hand but hid it beneath the folds of her skirt.

She was angry, but disheartened too.

Meanness don't happen overnight—that's what Gus always said.

He was right. Real cruelty took time to marinate properly.

The San Francisco she recalled was a raucous boom town. Lawlessness had been limited to bar brawls and a little rustling. The streets had been safe as any back east—day or night. Now it was falling headlong into the arms of perdition. If she was to set things to right, she had a lot of work ahead of her.

In wanting to hurry to begin this restoration, she lifted up her skirts—just high enough to see where she stepped. Immediately, catcalls began. She tightened her grip on the pistol.

Someone, somewhere began to hoot. Another took up the call and hooted too. Then another. And another. In a matter of seconds, the hoots turned into whoops and the whoops into howls. It was such a cacophony that Annabella put her hands up to cover her ears. In doing so, she nearly conked herself senseless with her pistol but she didn't slow down.

Fear and humiliation made her pick up her skirts again and run for all she was worth. She ran so fast that she ran right out of her pretty, satin slippers. She didn't look back. Had she, she would have seen them sticking up like a pair of tombstones in the deep, wet muck of Clay Street.

2

Two Years Earlier

Annabella Chase had beauty and wit, but was far too rich to be truly happy.

Like any other young lady with elderly relatives and sizable inheritance, she was watched like a hawk. Sitting in the grand salon of her maternal grandparents' palatial home, she wore a petulant expression and far too much perfume.

Dousing herself with a cheap fragrance had been a pointless rebellion (one of many). Her grandmother had caught a whiff of her and returned her to her maid to scrub her neck. When she returned, she had plopped herself down on a brocade settee with just enough irritability that her skirt burgeoned around like a satin chrysanthemum. This left no room for a gentleman to join her, thus dashing her grandmother's hopes for her to form a courtship that very evening.

She was not without suitors. Young men circled her like wolves, fairly panting with desire. Usually that made Annabella happy as a clam in high water. This evening, however, was different. She was cranky and didn't care who knew it. Showing displeasure was frowned upon. (A young lady was required to wear a vapid expression at all times lest a potential husband fear that she might have an independent thought.) Annabella was unrepentant. There was no one at their little gathering she cared to impress.

When left to her own devices, she was quite vivacious. However, her own devices had a tendency to beg scandal. Indeed, the sole purpose of the party was to divert gossip away from her most recent misconduct. Despite the grandness of the soiree, talk of her expulsion from Miss Perry's Academy for Young Ladies had yet to die down.

Her grandparents had sent her off to school so that she would learn to be a lady.

The school's genteel halls were full of silly girls and tiresome instructors. They taught how to sit properly and pour tea when all she wanted to do was to learn French, study anatomy and read indecent novels. These pursuits were thought to have been the impetus for several of her misadventures—one of which involved making eyes at the butcher's son and the other running matron's drawers up the flagpole.

The one thing she abhorred was that her expulsion required a lecture from her grandfather. Her grandmother took to her bed in a paroxysm of moans. He accused her of being capricious and reckless with such vigor that Annabella was very nearly contrite. (She was saved from outright regret with the knowledge that her grandfather's keenest concern was not for her, but the Goodenow name.)

He intoned, "For the flesh lusteth against the Spirit, and the Spirit against the flesh: and these are contrary the one to the other: so that ye cannot do the things that ye would."

Quashing a yawn, Annabella responded, "It is well and good to have faults; without them we would have no friends at all."

Simon Goodenow took a dim view of such flippancy.

He lectured, "Wit in women invites violence. You have beauty. Nothing more is required of you."

She almost pointed out that the most beautiful things in the world were the most useless—like flowers and peacocks. But belittling her finest asset didn't seem to serve her purposes.

Her curiosity about passionate love, however, wasn't dampened by the butcher's son's blue eyes. She didn't care that her reputation was sullied. She was determined to offer her chastity to the first young man she fancied. Understanding that possibility, the Goodenows wisely decided that, despite her tender age, it would be necessary to find her a suitable husband forthwith.

Gussied-up like Christmas turkey, Annabella was put on display in every fine house in Boston. Such a move stunk of desperation. She was being sold off to the highest bidder—fast as spoiling milk—and she knew it.

At first she welcomed the alteration. In fact, when they first began to groom her for the marriage market, she was giddy with excitement. However, the rules about courting were rigid. There would be no furtive kissing or grappling in the garden. As a young lady of good breeding, she was charged with both waggling her allurements and slapping the hand of any gentleman who dared try to touch them.

The other girls her age seemed happy with their lot. They certainly looked at her warily enough. She knew they saw her as a rival. She might have disabused them of that nonsense except they were all a bunch of conceited twits. It was true that she could have any young man she wanted. This wasn't an arrogant presumption. It was fact. Despite her well-deserved reputation of an unrepentant flirt, she had quickly tired of playing with young men's affections. Their pubescent face hair and puerile ways had quickly disgusted her.

Lord Byron was right: *Society is now one polish'd horde, Form'd of two mighty tribes, the Bores and Bored.*

So far as she was concerned, marriage to a cultured dullard was only a tad less inviting than living her life out as a reproving old spinster. While the Goodenow's trolled the opulent ballrooms and neat boulevards surrounding them for suitors to throw in her direction, she pined for the broad shoulders and rippling sinews of a Grecian god.

She spent her days sulking, certain that somewhere in the world heroes and romance—real men and true love—abounded. Unfortunately, the Boston of her world was a bastion of constraint and disapproval. Her starchy grandparents' mansion was cold and mirthless as a mausoleum.

The Goodenows were stately people of strict morals and healthy regimens. They were among the finest of the Boston Brahmins. They were also humorless and vain. Her mother, now ten years gone and buried, was their only child. A painting of her hung above the mantle. With the same corn silk hair and brilliant blue eyes, Annabella knew she resembled her. She had no idea what traits she might have inherited from her father. He was but a faint memory.

It wasn't as if she didn't ask about her parents. Her Grandfather Goodenow just shook his head.

He intoned, "All you need to know, child, is that your dear mother now rests in heaven."

"And my father?" she asked.

"Your father was long ago consigned to hell."

This particular hell, of course, was languishing a continent away.

3

According to her grandparents, Newman Chase was an inebriate, a charlatan, an adulterer, a larcenist, and, no doubt, a horse thief too. When they gained her custody, they had saved her from a life of disadvantage and depravity.

As poverty and wickedness sounded astoundingly attractive to someone who had never experienced either, Annabella Chase was intrigued. Too idle for her own good, she was determined to learn why her mother and father married in the first place.

She quickly learned two important life lessons. First of all, digging up old hurts, rancorous banishment and general family dissension was the epitome of entertainment. Secondly, there was an easy route to uncovering this treasure trove of intrigue—one must make friends with the help. They knew everything and with very little encouragement, were happy to tell her everything.

Annabella liked to think of her parents had been star-crossed lovers, scarred by abuse and divided by death. After a few visits below stairs, she concluded that Newman Chase and Bella Goodenow were just two rancorous halves of an unfortunate marriage. Her mother was no saint and her father, no fiend. She was dead so Annabella couldn't hold that against her. Her father, however, went off and left his only child in the hands of her soulless grandparents.

She had every intention of personally point out his spurious dereliction to his face. Unfortunately, it took rifling through her grandfather's desk to find out where he was. He owned a mercantile out west. Escape was at hand. (If in kindling a little excitement for herself she could exact some revenge on her father, that would be fine too.) The first thing she did was find California in the Atlas.

A sea voyage would be necessary to get there. That was daunting even for a determined daughter. Annabella had never taken so much as a ferry ride. But the mystery of the unknown stirred her blood. She crossed and uncrossed her legs obsessively every time she thought of swarthy sailors, handsome sea captains, perhaps even pirates. The bored and the boring would soon part ways.

"Begone, you privileged boys with your stiff collars and wan smiles!"

It was difficult not to giggle with elation at what lay in store for her. The one thing she was certain of, it wouldn't be wise to let anyone know of her scheme in advance. At the very least, her grandparents would lock her in her room. A convent might even be considered. That said, she didn't write to her father to tell him she was coming either. No good would come from that. Once she was there, he couldn't make her leave. Silence was all for the best. However, it would be important for her to make some sort of report of her journey. She found leather-bound diary and flipped through its pages. There was not a single entry.

Carefully folding it open, she began to write, "I shall leave covertly and travel in stealth. Alone and unaided, I will brave the savage storms and audacious seas to meet my destiny."

She would not, however, travel without someone to see to washing out her dainties. (She was headed into the wilderness, but she wasn't a savage.) Her first choice to assume this rewarding position was a young kitchen maid called Adele. Annabella came to know her on her occasional forays to sneak contraband from the pantry. Aware of Annabella's often rash behavior, Adele was disinclined to leave a secure position.

"Yes, yes, I know. A bird in the hand and all that," said Annabella. "But think of what an adventure we will have!"

Annabella baited her lure with promises of lucrative employment and a picturesque trip. Traveling the world as special maid to genteel young lady of means would be quite an elevation in station. Eventually, Adele agreed. After that, Annabella did not waste precious time niggling about with the details.

She told Adele, "Gather your belongings for we sail with the tide."

Annabella had no idea about the tides, but that sounded as if she did to Adele. Annabella's biggest worry was not reassuring her servant, but stealing away with from the house with two trunks and a hatbox. Flagging down a hired coach, she had to pay the driver extra for her luggage and arrived at the wharf with barely enough time to board. They were standing on the pier when Annabella muffled a gasp of horror.

Their ship wasn't a sleek sloop, but an enormous square vessel with laundry hanging from her rigging. It was fraught with dry rot and teeming with rats. To her horror she saw also that the bow was in the shape of a naked woman.

"Don't worry, dear Adele," she said. "It has to be seaworthy or the crew would mutiny."

She wasn't, however, altogether certain she believed that herself. Regardless, she donned her bravest smile and her newest bonnet and handed over her precious baggage. A line of men, each brown as a beetle (and likely culled from the penal system), passed her trunk from shoulder to shoulder, up and onto the deck. There, a sailor put his foot on the end of it and shoved it into the hold. A rank, old seadog stood next to her. He wore a coat of blue pilot cloth and didn't have any teeth. He tipped his hat and gave her a gummy smile. In a pinched voice, she thanked him.

Clasping Adele's hand, they joined the crush of people pushing and shoving their way up the rickety gangway. Annabella held out some hope that the ship's captain might be more attractive than his crew, but was disappointed once again. He was brawny and had a full beard, but he issued the foulest curses she had ever imagined.

Somewhere along the way, she and Adele were separated. Annabella tried in vain to find her, but the wind fought for her attention. It was so ferocious that as she tried to tie her bonnet strings tighter, it was actually ripped from her head. She watched helplessly as it floated on the wind like gull before finally settling in a puddle back on the pier. Shrieking with indignation, she watched as someone took hold of it and trotted off. Recognizing the thief, Annabella was relieved. It was another moment for it to dawn on her that Adele had a change of heart. As the little maid retreated back toward the street, she tied Annabella's bonnet tightly onto her head. Annabella couldn't really blame her.

But she did anyway.

"Drat your hide, Adele," she hollered.

It wasn't just the loss of her company. It seemed a bad omen for what was to come.

Her spirit, however, was the irrepressible sort and she soon rallied, vowing that she would be damned if she would let one little set back thwart her. Once the ship had unfurled all sails, her priorities shifted. Without a head covering, her curls were quickly turning into frizz. So her first matter of business was to fight her way through the ship's hold to locate her hatbox. From it she withdrew a hat that had a brim as wide as a sombrero and wide, black ribbons to keep it on. It would keep her hair tamed and shade her nose. She didn't care whether it was flattering or not. There was no one on board she cared to impress.

Dicey company or not, it was a constant struggle not to chat idly. Worried that her grandfather would have detectives on her trail, she knew that it was important that no one knew who she was or why she traveled alone. So she allied herself with a seemingly dull-witted Irish girl who claimed to be responding to an ad for a cook in Galveston. Annabella was thrilled to be cavorting with the common element.

"We'll share a bed, just like the poor," she chirped.

Although she had many female acquaintances in Boston, she hadn't any confidants. This was not as it should be. (It was the young, predatory men—with suggestive leers and wandering hands—who were supposedly not to be trusted.) She hadn't been tossed onto the marriage market long enough for competition for beaus to become an outright, dagger-drawing melee. Still, she understood that when it came to female friendship, beauty had its disadvantages. Because she and Mary Catherine were of differing circumstances and no admirable men on board ship, they bonded famously. They were, quite literally, in the same boat.

Because she could tell Mary anything she liked about herself, Annabella grew fanciful. She told her new friend that she was going west in search of her long-lost love. Mary confided that she too had been crossed in love. They talked of nothing more than the deficiencies of the male sex. When Mary left the ship, Annabella was morose—quite overtaken with what she supposed was grief. Over their weeks at sea, Mary had become quite special to her. They kissed cheeks and promised to write each other faithfully.

When Annabella returned below to mourn the loss of her friend in private, she was aghast. For her fast new friend had not only left her with massive tears of farewell, she had absconded with Annabella's jewelry chest, two petticoats and a pair of her silk drawers too. She felt as defiled as had a man sneaked into her bed and ravished her. She didn't have long to mope about it. Soon enough, she had other, more pressing, concerns—those of the life and death variety.

Rounding Cape Horn scared the dear Jesus out of her. For the first time, she truly feared for her life. The roiling seas washed over the deck again and again. Drenched, she clung to the rigging, refusing to go below. The dank of the hold was befouled by the retching of the other passengers. There were some degradations just too great to endure.

Whatever the comeuppance facing her mortality gave her, it was soon lost in calm of the Pacific. With nothing to do but sit on deck watch the burnt skin peel off of everyone's noses, she thought she might just go mad with boredom.

Halfway up the coast of South America, they encountered an unprecedented attack. It wasn't pirates who clamored aboard, but prospectors. Much to her chagrin, she learned that they shared her destination. All of them were desperate to reach the gold strike on the American River. It was biggest in recent history. Every one of them chattered incessantly about the gold nuggets they would find.

Annabella turned a deaf ear. To her they were nothing but a bunch of reprobates—no doubt one step ahead of the law. When they made port at San Francisco, she had half a mind to repair to the local *penalidad* and report them to the proper authorities.

✧

It was four hard months before their ship finally skirted the fog-shrouded black rocks of Farallones, five leagues from entrance to Bay of San Francisco. Annabella didn't breathe a sigh of relief until they shortened sail and readied anchors. She was not only revolted by her fellow seafarers, she had come to hate the wind, the sun, the ocean, and the rotting bucket that carried her. Even if San Francisco was the wasteland of the western world, it would not be not objectionable enough to induce her to return to the stinking ship that brought her.

This, as all vows, was subject to reconsideration.

4

From a safe distance, San Francisco looked to be one pony short of paradise. As the ship slid through the brilliant waters of the bay between the square-toed whaling vessels and around a massive Chinese junk, Annabella was able to set all the travails of her voyage aside. All she longed for was a bath and to sleep in a proper bed. She had very nearly forgotten the mission that had sent her west — which was just as well.

The unity of adventure and spite that she had imagined did not quite crystallize. There wasn't much of a pier and they had to get to shore by way of a small boat. When she stepped on land, it was obvious that the town wasn't the bucolic wonderland she had envisioned either. It sat on a desolate little sand bar and was positively bleak.

There was no grass, no flowers, and no trees. All its structures were weather-beaten and dingy. The stench from a privy was everywhere. It was nothing like the Wild West she had imagined.

"It looks more like the Squalid West," she groused.

She gulped down her disappointment. There was no turning back. Her pride would never allow her to admit a mistake (especially when so many people would be willing to point a finger at her for it). In having a second thought or two, she had to remind herself of just how intolerable Boston had been.

As men swarmed around her, she tried not to look as disillusioned as she felt. Everyone else seemed to think San Francisco was on the cusp of great wealth. They predicted that the bay would soon be full of ships. That looked unlikely, but she was glad to hear it. Commerce would be a godsend for such a common place.

A tall, ruddy-looking codger wearing a hat with a tatty emblem introduced himself as Mr. Peet, the harbormaster.

"Avarice always spurs commerce. Mark my words, young lady, soon every man and his burro will be headed towards the American River and we'll know not what to do."

He told her that the United States government had set up camp in town—which gave her a sense of reassurance that would prove unwarranted. In fact, the only sign of authority was the American flag flapping from a spindly post in the middle of a vacant square. A raggedy man had climbed the flagpole and was waving about what looked to be a vial.

He hollered until his voice was hoarse, "Gold! Gold! Gold from the American Fork!"

He paid her no mind, and she was reluctant to ask for directions lest it be taken as a sign of weakness. She stopped just long enough to get her bearings. There were several streets fanning out from the shore. Steeling herself, she selected one and strode purposely up the hill. As she did, she attracted an odd-looking, ill-smelling entourage. They looked far different from anyone on the ship. She didn't know what they wanted, so she smiled gamely, opened her parasol and proceeded on.

As they appeared to be citizens, it occurred to her to ask if anyone knew Newman Chase. Besides the stink, they all shared the same odd look. Their faces twitched with excitement, but their eyes looked dead. She couldn't imagine what had made everyone of them daft.

There were no other women on the street and that made her uneasy. Surely a place such of this would have families, a school, or perhaps a church. It was a test not to run screaming back to the ship.

The further she got into town, the muddier it was. One rusty-headed fellow with a new beard and a dirty red shirt hurried ahead and straighten planks for her to walk on. As she trod by, men watching from other side of the street held their hats across their bosoms as if she was a deity of some sort. One man fell to his knees. She busied herself by reading the various street signs, hoping for something that made sense to her.

When she finally recognized a name on a building it wasn't "Newman Chase." It didn't read "mercantile" either. Gold-tinted lettering announced the place within to be "*The Bella Goode*." Beneath it was the single word "*Spirits.*"

Instantly, she realized what it was. Her father had named a saloon after her poor, dead mother. From the looks of the place, it didn't look to be particularly eulogistic. She shook her head. Whether that was in marvel or disgust, she hadn't decided. She supposed it was the thought that mattered.

She decided to say it aloud just to see if it sounded any better as it rolled off the tongue. To give it her very best effort, she mimicked a Boston matron with six generations good breeding behind her.

"*The Bella Goode.*"

That didn't make it sound any better.

The ornately-carved doors were half shut. Their grandeur was incongruous against the mud-stained wood of the rest of the building. A little sprucing up—perhaps a coat of paint—would do wonders for the place. As she pondered that, it came to her attention that some of her followers were becoming unruly. Mostly it was a bit of pushing and shoving, still it made her uneasy. A man stepped out of the noon-day shadows.

Touching the brim of his hat, he said, "Sorry, Miss. We don't see many ladies in town."

She refused to admit to being even a little frightened and gathered some bravado.

In an unnaturally breathy voice, she said, "Goodness, after Cape Horn, it would take more than a few daft strangers to unsettle me."

Shielding her eyes from the glare, she looked up at the man. As he looked back at her, his eyes narrowed. She noticed the alteration of his expression. It bewildered her.

Tentatively, she said, "I am inquiring after Mr. Newman Chase. Do you know him?"

The man quickly removed his hat and gave an awkward little bow. "I... I am Newman Chase."

She smiled broadly and held out a hand. Her father didn't take it however. He seemed confused.

"And who might you be?" he asked dumbly.

She lowered her hand, ready to fling her arms around his neck. As his confused look took a turn towards disbelief, he staggered a bit, but kept his footing.

At last, he managed to ask, "Annabella?"

"Poppa!"

5

Annabella Chase had happened into town just as the first swell of prospectors had played out.

News of the gold find had sent a good part of the population of San Francisco running stark, raving mad. Every able-bodied man in town had dropped what they were doing and headed for the gold strike. Preachers tucked a bible in their traps and drinkers stowed their bottles. A lucky few hit it big. Most spent every nugget they found on games of chance, hard liquor, and loose women. The vast majority came back with their tail between their legs, dead broke and looking for means to have another go.

Men wise in the ways of a getting rich stayed in town and sold provisions to those who weren't.

Newman Chase was one of the few citizens of who hadn't been beguiled to Sutter's Mill.

The thought of gold made his loins tingle as much as the next man's, but he had been around of the tree more than once. Crouching on his haunches daylight until dawn was not for him. Panning was a young man's game. There was surer money to be made off gold without the back-breaking work.

When the word of the strike first got out, he bought up every pickax, pie pan, and blanket in town and resold them by dusk.

Getting more merchandise wasn't easy, but he had been around long enough to know how to do it. After all, he made a go of selling dry goods store when the Hudson Bay Company couldn't.

However wretched Annabella thought San Francisco was, it had improved tenfold since Newman first stepped ashore. Back then there it wasn't more than a cluster of tents. It had a fine sign, but even the rest of the *Bella Goode* was makeshift. In time, both the *Bella* and town improved. With new capital, they might even manage to get a ditch dug to divert sewage. Progress was inevitable.

Excited at the prospect, Newman gushed, "I heard that claims at Sutter's Mill are so rich they're yielding five pounds of gold a day."

Gus Gerlache was always the voice of reason.

He said, "Before we go counting our eggs, my friend, we best recall what happened down in Los Angeles in the year '42."

Newman knew he was right. That find down south played out fast. It could happen again. Miners might go back home red-faced and empty-handed this time too. Still, this strike seemed different. Newman could feel it in his vitals. The air was thick with anticipation. Soon half of the known world would be elbow to elbow, scratching like chickens in the sand of Sacramento Valley—he could *feel* it.

Newman and Gus were friends and partners. They had been making a living out of the *Bella* but not much more. Newman had gone out on a limb ordering huge quantities of staples and gear on credit. Gus was fervently opposed to borrowing money.

Waiting for his merchandise to arrive made Newman jumpy and irritable. He was well aware that a shipment could go awry at any turn. Supply and demand was a twisty, troubling game, and he was out of practice. When he was younger, nothing flustered him. Back in Boston he had owned and operated several stores. That made him well-aware how often cargo was lost. Now, just thinking of such a possibility made his belly ache. Every delay meant money lost. Financial catastrophe was very nearly as likely as a windfall. Asher Price didn't look like a particularly sympathetic man. Few lenders did.

Like a soldier awaiting orders to charge into battle, Newman began to feel the need to settle his affairs. He vowed to write to his little girl.

Gus told him, "You're a day late and a dollar short for that, pard."

Newman knew he was right. Admitting it was hard. Self-pity intercepted his good intention.

He said, "I suppose that I'm no better father than I was a husband."

If he expected Gus to contradict him, he was in for a wait.

His life was an open book. Given a drink and an eager ear, just about anybody heard that he was the widower of a heartless wife and had been driven from Boston and all good society by his heinous father-in-law. He claimed to have a darling daughter—fairer than the evening primrose.

One thing he didn't talk about was a dream he harbored. He had always fancied that one day he would return to Boston and retrieve his dear little girl. It was the one promise he made her. However, in his mind's eye he would be dressed to the nines and carrying a wad of banknotes thick enough to choke a horse. Year after year he didn't get any richer, and that notion had all but faded away.

As he wasn't one for wrestling with his moral short-comings, he made himself think of another more manageable concern.

"What if pirates capture my cargo?"

Gus took a long draw on his pipe.

He said, "Don't you know that all the thieves are already on their way here?"

Newman laughed at that truth. Sure as fire, hoards of card sharps, pickpockets, loose women, and, of course, politicians would be following the miners. They best brace for that storm too.

When the weather was good, he and Gus usually claimed a couple of straight-back chairs under the portico of the *Bella Goode* and talked. They did that day as well. Taking a deep draw on his cigar, Newman decided to be pleased with himself. After all, he was a semi-dutiful father, successful businessman, and genial friend. What more could a man be?

Just then, Henry Butler darted by them. He was Asher Price's right hand man and he ran by so fast that he almost knocked Newman's cigar out of his mouth.

Something was up.

Mr. Butler headed straight towards Portsmouth Square. He stopped short on the next block. A sea of prospectors was filling the streets heading away from the docks. That commotion had come to be commonplace. This bunch had to be more than just a herd of miners. Newman was ready as the next man to have something more exciting to see than scores of shabby miners.

Over his shoulder, he asked Gus, "What did they do—offload an elephant?"

In the middle of a raucous throng of men was a pink parasol. He nudged Gus. Whoever held the parasol wore a white lace glove and a bonnet with feathers on it. Newman had been a long time gone from Boston, but he recognized the accoutrements of a real lady when he saw them.

He recognized his daughter too. She was the image of her mother.

6

Henry Butler knew Asher Price better than most anyone in San Francisco. That didn't imply that he knew much about him. Except for Mr. Butler, no one particularly liked Mr. Price, but all would agree one thing. Asher Price didn't look at all like a murderer.

Nothing about him was menacing. He was of medium height, middling weight, brown-haired, and brown-eyed. His face was plain, his features regular. He had the straight-backed, unflinching walk of an honest man. Back in Nantucket he was a Quaker and honored their ways.

The name Price was of importance in the whaling business. That meant it was of importance in the world at large. Whale oil lit every parlor and saloon on seven continents made it prosperous. When properly managed, a whale boat paid out better than interest-accruing money in the bank.

Asher was one of the few ship owners who had never lost a vessel. In an avocation where omens and signs were dearer than a wife's goodwill, this lack of bad luck carried a great deal of weight. They said that Asher Price was dependable as the sunrise. Of course, that kind of golden aura couldn't last forever. After The Tragedy, no one spoke a word about how fortune finally failed him. That was just too obvious.

The scandal of The Tragedy tracked Asher to the near end of the world—or at least to California.

He remained close-mouthed there as he had back home. Without any mitigating particulars, the story of his young wife's untimely demise was the victim of wild speculation. The farther the tale traveled, the worse it got. What was known was that he had given up Quaker pronouns and quit observing the Sabbath. By the time both the man and the saga arrived in town, his guilt was a forgone conclusion. No man left kith and kin—and his church too—so far behind without the devil fast on his heels.

He had an odd, haunted look about the eyes—like a man who had reminiscences that were not a comfort. Nobody out west noticed that about him though. It was so subtle that it would have taken a woman's sensibilities to recognize it. The few females in town weren't the sort to appreciate a man with a dark side.

Men, however, saw him another way—one not so peaceable. When provoked, Asher Price's eyes turned dark as coals and hard as twice-baked biscuits.

One thing both sexes were in agreement about Asher Price. In a town where buckskin was the height of sartorial resplendence, he was widely admired for his refined appearance. Some supposed that foregoing the plain ways of his church was the reason why he was so particular about his attire. Despite the mud, he wore fine leather boots, a low-crowned beaver hat, and a pair of spotless yellow, deerskin gloves.

Although he removed his hat when indoors, he never took off his gloves. He didn't take them off when signing papers or shaking hands. That didn't sit well with some people. Others didn't mind. The west was full of men with more lethal aberrations. Knives were drawn and fists swung with little provocation. Many men (and a fair share of women) were disfigured in some way. Seamen and trappers were carved up regularly, be it through recreation or occupation—what with skinning mishaps and thresher sharks slashes.

As for Asher, he appeared oblivious to all the talk. He made no move towards socializing. He had poured all his spare time into building a house overlooking the ocean. The dunes reminded him of the undulating sandbanks surrounding Nantucket Sound. His house was a replica of those back home. Nobody noticed that. All they knew was that the lacquer on red shingles shone in the afternoon sun like a beacon and that Mr. Price prowled the walkway circling the chimney stack. With spyglass to his eye, he searched the horizon for the sails of his returning ships.

Even after the gold strike hit, he didn't change his ways. Asher could still be seen up there, his ever-present yellow gloves shone from afar. They *were* fine gloves.

But they also served a purpose.

As it happened, dapper Mr. Price had his own scars. Beneath those fancy gloved were scarlet welts circling his hands like a serpent. They were the awful result of the burns he had sustained the evening his handsome Nantucket house burnt to the ground—with his pretty young wife in it.

7

The reunion with her father wasn't exactly fraught with loving emotion.

Annabella had hoped for more. She had thrown her arms around his neck. All he could manage was a self-conscious peck on her cheek. In the uncomfortable silence that followed, Newman hemmed and hawed. Annabella shifted her weight from one foot to the other, contemplating whether to flee back to the ship or slap him silly.

The crowd of men had moved back a little, but hadn't dispersed. They had followed her like she as a golden-haired piper and remained transfixed. The murmur of admiration arising from their ranks began to turn raucous. That lit a fire under Newman.

"Get away from here, boys!" he commanded.

Hats still in hands, the men allowed themselves to be shooed away. Then they reformed like a swarm of flies the minute he turned his back. Annabella's golden locks were as alluring as the gold they had come so far to find.

Newman asked her, "Where's your gear?"

Before she could answer, a horrifying thought occurred to him.

He whirled, asking, "You didn't come *alone*, did you?"

"Alone?" she lied. "Of course not!"

Fortunately, he didn't ask questions. Even Annabella knew that in some cases it was best to allow people to believe what pleased them.

Newman returned to the matter at hand, repeating, "Where's your gear?"

She looked at him blankly.

"Your gear—your dresses and bits," he said impatiently. "Your blessed trunk."

"Oh," she said, finally comprehending. "It's down there."

She pointed in the direction of the shore, apologizing, "It was far too heavy for me."

"Let's hope it's still there," he grumbled. "Couldn't you have got someone to pack it up here for you?"

Here he didn't pause, giving Annabella to understand that he didn't expect an answer.

He immediately called out, "Gus! Gus, get one them fellers who owes for their drink. I need 'em to fetch something."

Annabella saw a tall, ruddy-cheeked man with a mane of brown hair and neatly trimmed grey beard appear. He wore a muslin apron, but was in the process of removing it. As he walked towards them he wiped his hands with it and tossed it aside.

Observing Newman's oddly dazed expression, Gus asked him, "Did you get pole-axed or something?"

Newman didn't answer at first. He raised his hand and extended a trembling index finger in Annabella's direction. His powers of deduction were at least as keen as the next man's, so Gus concluded that the young lady must be Newman' daughter. An introduction, however, wasn't forthcoming.

Extending his hand, he cheerily announced, "Hello, dear girl. You must be Miss Annabella. I'm August Gerlache."

She curtsied and then gave a description of her trunk. Gus motioned to Rutledge Mayne to go get it. He was the resident saloon hound and was suffering from his usual midday hangover. He jumped at the chance to get a closer look at the little lady. He tipped his hat. Annabella recoiled. She had seen all sorts on her sea voyage, but Rutledge was especially repulsive. His features weren't any uglier than half the men in town, but he wore an ankle-length fur coat that stunk to high heaven. Females found him especially repugnant, so he was delighted to have the opportunity to repulse one. Daintily holding out the hem of his coat, he gave Annabella a little curtsy. Then he grinned.

His teeth were green. Annabella gasped with disgust.

Mayne was happy—but not for long. Gus gave Mayne a glare so searing that he tucked his head and trucked towards the wharf.

Gathering his wits, Newman finally asked, "How did you get here, little girl? Where are your people?"

"I came by that ship," she pointed at a mast towering over the others. Happily, she straightened her bonnet and announced, "I came quite on my own!"

Newman looked at her incredulously. "You are alone?" he repeated, his voice rising. "You are *not* alone?"

Here, a story would have been prudent. Even Gus knew that. However, Annabella looked back at her father defiantly, declaring, "Indeed, I am."

To his implied reproach, she merely shrugged.

"Baby-*girl*," he whispered.

"I believe I have proved that I can take good care of myself," she said defensively.

Yes. It was clear that she could take care of herself. That was not all her unyielding gaze said to him. It reminded him that she had to take care of herself because her father had flown the coop. It didn't matter that he wasn't the only derelict in California. It didn't matter that Captain Sutter himself had abandoned a wife and children back in Switzerland—or wherever the blazes he was from. One of the biggest advantages of relocating to California was that a man could reinvent himself to his heart's content. At least he didn't go parading about in a fancy uniform claiming the King gave it to him like Sutter. When looking into his little girl's big, blue eyes that was small comfort.

Guilt hit him like a fist in the chest.

He recovered quickly, extending his arm to lead her past the saloon doors. There was a side entrance. Several timbers served as a threshold. A small sign said "Office."

"After you are settled, I do not think you shall want for anything, Annabella," he said stiffly, "But if you need me, knock on this door and I shall be round immediately."

Here, he rapped on it as if she needed instruction on how to knock on a door.

His voice dripping with gravitas, he said, "Never, under any circumstances, will you come into this establishment."

Just as grave, she nodded.

"Perhaps you could put up a little bell-pull here," she said touching the door jamb. He looked at her blankly, as if such an object was unknown to him.

So she repeated, "A bell-pull—it would be easier for you to hear callers."

After a moment, he responded, "Yes."

Then he simultaneously turned the knob and hit the door with his shoulder to open it.

"It's the climate," he explained. "Sometime the wood swells."

"Happy days," she responded a bit insolently.

Ignoring that, he put his hand out for her to precede him through the door. It was a small room and Gus didn't follow them inside. Nimbly, Newman edged around her and began to move things out of her way, uncovering a straight-back chair. Seeing that it was for her, she primly seated herself. He turned on his heel and left.

The slam of the door made her jump.

Being absolutely alone for the first time since she left Boston was odd. Even odder, the silence made her nostalgic for her grandparents' home. That feeling quickly passed, however, when she spied a door leading to the attached saloon. She looked over her shoulder before quickly peering through the keyhole. With any luck, she hoped to see a lady of the night. They were supposed to be rife in such society. Seeing nothing, she began to snoop through her father's desk. She did not hesitate to do so; she might not get another chance at it.

Although an oil lamp sat on the desk, it wasn't lit. Most of the room was in shadow. A small window allowed a slice of sunlight to cross the floor. She shook her head, this time clucking in disgust. The state of the room told her one thing. He had not remarried. No lady would allow such a mess. She breathed a sigh of relief. The possibility that her father had replaced her in his heart had dogged her for years.

When Newman finally returned, he found her standing atop a chair.

Looking her up and down, he asked mildly, "Problem?"

"No!" she lied.

Nimbly jumping to the floor, she pretended nothing was amiss. Actually, her rustling amid his papers had disturbed some animal. It was probably just a rat, but she didn't want to chance it being something bigger—fiercer.

They both ignored the incident.

"I've let a room for you across the way," he said, thrusting his thumb over his shoulder. Well-pleased with his own efficiency, he added, "And I've got you a maid as well."

Then he motioned for her to follow him. It wasn't nearing dark, but spent of emotion, Annabella welcomed the chance to rest. After the travails of sea travel she had given in to the faint hope of a bit of luxury. She looked at her new home, however, with trepidation. It was called the Hotel Deluxe, but to her great regret, it wasn't even a little plush. The carpet in the lobby was quite worn and a spittoon sat in the corner. Both it and the wall were spattered with tobacco juice. A door in the vestibule opened to the restaurant next door. The proprietor had a thin mustache and introduced himself as Mr. Boomer.

A tiny Mexican woman stood at the bottom of the stairs. She had cropped hair and the frayed cuffs of a pair of men's plaid pants could be seen below her skirt. A wisp of cigar smoke circled her head like a crown.

"This is Lupe," Newman announced. "She'll see to you."

That seemed unlikely. Lupe was possibly the least hospitable-looking person she had ever seen—and that included the little brown man from Borneo that rode their ship's bowsprit for a week out of Valparaiso.

Although Annabella's trunk had been deposited at her feet, Lupe didn't make a move for it. Instead, she crammed her cigarillo into the corner of her mouth and folded her arms. Newman caught one handle and he and Boomer began to heave the trunk up the steps. Anxious to plop down on the bed, Annabella edged around them and took the steps two at a time.

Mr. Boomer called out, "Room 2!"

Seconds later she threw herself wearily onto the bare mattress. A cloud of dust and an unidentifiable odor emanated from it, but she was too tired to care. After dropping his end of the trunk on the landing, Mr. Boomer held his hand out, palm up. Newman counted out a few coins and gave them to him.

Making for the stairs, Mr. Boomer called out over his shoulder, "Clean linens are on the table. Breakfast at half-past seven."

Annabella didn't hear him. A soft snore emitted from the back of her throat.

Newman's hand caressed the door jamb for a moment before closing the door.

8

Newman tip-toed down the hotel staircase as if the least little squeak would wake the dead, and made for the door like the devil himself was on his tail. He was panting by the time he climbed onto a barstool in front of Gus.

Without being asked, Gus poured him a cup of coffee with a generous dollop of whiskey. Hands trembling, Newman blew on the steaming mug a time or two before managing a sip.

Half the cup was gone before he could say, "Thanks."

It took several glasses of pure whiskey before he could go to sleep. When he arose, he still felt unsteady. Squatting on his heels, he inhaled deeply until he could exhale without shuddering.

There were only two other occasions when he could recall feeling so muddled. The first time had been on his wedding day. (The thought of that debacle was only quelled by the memory of his bride, Bella, all lush and lovely.) The second time had been the day he set sail for California. He was quaking when he climbed aboard the dilapidated ship. Since Annabella arrived back in his life, however, his heart had seized on him every other hour. It was as if God was punishing him.

Looking heavenward, he asked, "We sow what we reap, eh Lord?"

It was possible he was simply jolted by how much Annabella favored her mother. There were differences of course. Bella had had skin so fair it was almost translucent. Annabella's complexion was olive like his—and no doubt tanned by her months at sea. But Annabella had her mother's eyes. They were blue as the Pacific and blazing as the summer sun.

He was not only stunned; he was also a bit bewildered.

Part of it was his little girl showing up so unexpectedly and being such a beauty and all. But was he to admit it, his pride was a bit injured too. He and Gus—and every other man he knew of who had rounded the dreaded Cape Horn—had done it with stomachs in their throats and their nuts shriveled to the size of acorns. The wicked winds were relentless and the food inedible. Sometimes beetles in hardtack were all they had. They were damned lucky to live through it.

And here came his baby girl, sailing fourteen thousand miles and stepping off the ship as if she had done no more than taken a stroll down Third Avenue.

"She must've gotten her grit from me," he decided.

That conclusion soothed his pride just a bit. Besides, nowadays the ocean was tamed by faster, sleeker ships. Back when he took to the sea, it wasn't for the faint of heart. Uprooting himself from all he knew and loved and heading for the frontier was the real test. It was doubly a courageous undertaking for a city man like him. No doubt about that. Just thinking of it all caused a line of perspiration to appear on his upper lip.

The fear of the Horn was so pervasive; he had been sorely tempted to cross the Panamanian isthmus to reach the Pacific instead. It was only about sixty miles to Balboa and a Pacific port. By the time they reached Cristóbal he became so anxious to shorten his trip that he went directly to the local bodega to inquire about a guide. There were men aplenty who would do the job for a nominal sum. The plan sounded simple enough. The problem lay in the details.

It was only sixty miles. The first forty odd miles of the trip would be taken paddling upstream via a dugout canoe. The rest of the journey would be by donkey. Newman's teeth hurt at the thought of all the jouncing, but the alligator-infested waters worried him more. Chagres Fever was an even greater threat. He considered his constitution rather hearty. His bowels, however, could be a source of aggravation. Death by diarrhea was not a particularly noble way to go to one's great reward.

There was also the problem with indigenous people. Some of them bore spears and were ill-disposed towards interlopers. He hadn't presumed that he would be carried in a sedan chair. However, his notion had been more along the line of slashing through the jungle with a machete. Alligators and donkeys were no part of it. Neither were murdering savages. A jungle panorama that included his head on a pike was highly distasteful.

For all he knew, Balboa might be the *beau monde* of the Pacific coast. But he wasn't about to lay money on it. He hied back to the ship as fast as his legs could carry him. He spent the night on the ship while some sort of festival commenced in Cristóbal. Whatever it was—family feud, military uprising, or some sort of celebration requiring sacrificial tourists—it was punctuated by gunfire. He kept his head down and prayed for the tide.

That's how he ended up hanging on for dear life through what they called a "Cape Horn Snorter." It gathered momentum of thousand miles of open water. The gale howled and the sea spray stung like bees. The boards of the hull groaned with the sea's pressure as the ship tilted near sideways. No doubt the newer vessels slipped through water without a bump. Back then there was no choice but to hunker down in the hold and pray. He wasn't the only one. It was every man for himself. He was clinging to his hammock when the ship yawed and a fellow passenger was thrown in his direction.

When they were face to face, the man yelled, "You scared?"

Spittle clung to his quivering chin, but Newman wasn't about to admit that he was afraid.

"*No!*" he hollered back.

When the man didn't look convinced, Newman got his back up.

"You got a problem with that?"

"No," said the man. "It's just that if somebody asked me that, *I'd* lie."

"So," said Newman, "you scared then?"

"Hell, yes," the man answered.

It was raw terror. The bedlam lasted for days. No one could eat and men fought for their turn at the slop bucket. Then, just as suddenly as it began, the storm ended and they had blue skies and white caps. Everyone crawled out of the stench of the hold and into the fresh air. Newman Chase and August Gerlache introduced themselves.

Gus wore a pea coat, but otherwise didn't look like a sailor. His face was genial and his hands were soft as a baby's bottom. Obviously, Gus hadn't done any more manual labor than he had. To Newman, he looked like the only person on board who wouldn't kill him in his sleep.

Gus asked him where he was going. Newman explained that he was headed towards a little town on the Bay of San Francisco. It wasn't until later that he told him that putting a continent between himself and his in-laws was a good part of his incentive to head west.

Instead, he said, "A man who owed me money told me about how *Californios* are desperate for necessities."

Then, conspiratorially, he added, "But the real money is in your luxury goods—Brittany linens and porcelain plates."

Gus looked perplexed, "I thought Spain refused foreign traders."

"Mexico's got California now," said Newman. "It still ain't exactly legal, but they owe so much back pay to their people, it's pretty cheap to buy 'em to look the other way."

Gus nodded, saying, "I heard Ol' Andy Jackson was trying to buy it."

Newman nodded in return. "It's just a matter of time before it gets made a territory. Of course, the real money to be made is from otter pelts and tallow. Take the shipment to Canton and make two, three hundred percent on your money."

Before the offer was officially extended, Gus announced, "I ain't got much, but I'm in for that."

They shook on it.

✧

Teaming up with Gus was the smartest thing he'd done. Together, they had weathered every hazard of the trade and flourished. Newman was proud of that.

Having settled himself enough to raise a blade to his whiskers, he looked at himself in his shaving mirror. Turning first one way and then the other, he lowered his head and raised an eyebrow. He didn't see where he changed all that much. His hair was grey at the temples, but he was still trim. That wasn't by chance. He had always been a little vain about his figure.

Gus opened the door and said, "Miss Annabella is having her breakfast over at the café. She'll come looking for you soon."

It was early and Newman was still not as composed as he wanted to be. Looking at his reflection wasn't a consolation. His coat was pretty worn.

"I used to have a diamond stick pin," he said to Gus. "Did I ever tell you that?"

"Once or twice," replied Gus.

"I only left Annabella in Boston so she wouldn't have to do without."

Without a change of expression, Gus said, "You are a noble man."

"I should have written her more than I did," Newman fretted.

"You're right as rain about that," Gus agreed.

Newman responded absent-mindedly, "Having little Annie come here after all this time is a hell of a thing, ain't it?"

Said Gus, "I think 'a hell of a thing' ain't the half of it."

As it happened, Gus was an optimist.

9

Seeing his lovely daughter brought back all the recollections of her mother Newman had stifled for years. When it came to women, he, like most men, had been his own worst enemy. After all this time, that failure still stung like a hornet.

He thought it was probably his father's fault. He had married above himself, so his son had to do better. His father was a tailor, on his knees every day measuring other men's inseams. He never understood why his dear mother married such a man. Newman intended to be a man of some consequence in Boston—wearing a silk hat and brocade waistcoats. (None of this kneeling at other men's feet for him.) To reach the pinnacle of commerce, he needed determination. To conquer society, he had to have the right kind of woman on his arm.

That was why no pert-nosed shopkeeper's daughter had been good enough for him. He wanted a real lady. All his considerable drive was put to into building a fortune worthy of such a woman. Once that little chore was done, he only had a short wait until he was overwhelmed with invitations to Boston's most elite soirées. His father's name did not buy him much respect, but his mother's people did. She had been a Newman, one of the most respected families in town. They had lost much of their fortune through bad investments, but their name still held some weight. If a man had the right connections and a hefty bank account, there was a dazzling array of damsels to court. He had only to choose one.

The moment he saw Bella Goodenow, his heart was stolen for good.

For a man known as a stickler when it came to breeding, her father had been surprisingly amenable to Newman's suit for her hand. Usually an acute business man, Newman chalked his agreeableness up to having an over-abundance of daughters and a shortage of suitors. Of his three daughters, Bella was by far the most beautiful. However, she was bad-tempered and impetuous. Her mother and father were willing to relax their standards in order to get her married and off their hands.

Even with their encouragement, Newman had his work was cut out for him.

He wasn't handsome in the slick-haired way of the swells that decorated the drawing rooms of elite families—he knew that. However, he had a direct gaze and a fine physique. Until Miss Bella, he had no need of employing any wooing skills. But a challenge had always been what caught his fancy—and Bella was quite a test. (She looked at Newman as if he was something she had to scrape from the bottom of her shoe.) He dogged her company with the same dedication that had made him very nearly wealthy, but without success. As it happened her heart wasn't cold, it had already been stolen.

It wasn't surprising that Mr. Goodenow guarded his daughters diligently. What Bella's two sisters lacked in beauty, they made up for in good sense. They reserved their affection until a ring was on their finger. Not so for Bella. Despite how religiously Mr., Goodenow guarded his daughters diligently from roués and fortune hunters, his stewardship of Bella's chastity was for naught. Bella had a body of a voluptuary, but the sophistication of a lamb.

She had been ripe pickings for the first man who took her in his arms and blew in her ear. While all the true gentlemen sat sedately in their parlor, she began a torrid backstairs affair with her dancing instructor. (She was clumsy on her feet, but quite willing on her back.) Unfortunately for Bella, the man wasn't who he said he was. In truth, he was a sweet-talking traveling man who had a wife and four children in New Jersey.

When Bella told him she was pregnant with his child, he quickly concluded that Mr. Goodenow would not be pleased. He made fast for the nearest road out of town lest Mr. Goodenow set the sheriff after him.

When this little calamity came to light, Mr. Goodenow wasted little time over what was essentially spilt milk. He had his priorities in order and finding Bella an acceptable fiancé as at the top of his list.

They had no further to look than their own front stoop. There stood the very determined Newman Chase—with flowers in hand and love in his eyes. As a lately come member of Boston society, he was a bit naive of its mores. That gullibility deemed him an ideal groom.

Mr. Goodenow believed everything to have worked out swimmingly. Newman was pleased as punch. His blushing bride, however, was fit to be tied about the turn of events. Understanding that she had little choice but to marry Mr. Chase, she sulked every day of their engagement. Newman hoped that she was just shy. Then, the many ways of love rarely included caution.

Their wedding was so hurried that more than a few mavens of propriety had begun their countdown calendars.

Before the wedding, Mrs. Goodenow gave her daughter some very sage advice, "You are fortunate that Mr. Chase is far too in love with you to question whether you love him in return. It will be a 'premature birth'."

The only thing in favor of a successful marriage was that Newman knew far less about lovemaking than Bella. What little experience he had prior to his wedding involved several episodes of groping and one investigation beneath the dress of an open-minded day maid. Therefore, when they came together for their nuptial night, the condition of her maidenhead—or even that she had one—wasn't a consideration. Afterwards, Newman was quite pleased with himself.

He unadvisedly gushed to his bride, "God be pleased, Bella! I'm happy as a puppy with two peters."

To which she responded, "Wot?"

Then she leapt from the bed and stuck her head halfway into her chamber pot. To Newman, this odd behavior meant only that something they had for dinner was suspect. Soon, the truth was apparent. His was the humiliation of a lifetime. He had yet to accept that his new wife was to bear another man's child when she miscarried. The loss wasn't mourned properly by either party.

Divorce was out of the question. That understood, he and Bella called a cautious truce. Newman threw all his energy into business. He had been a success before he met Bella and always prided himself on that. Soon, he wanted more and his father-in-law gladly footed the bill for the expansion of Chase Emporium.

Simon Goodenow showed himself to be a vain, petty little tyrant whose only gift was appropriating funds from elderly aunts and idiot cousins. It was foolish as well as degrading to become financially dependent on someone he despised, but at the time, Newman believed he was owed every penny.

Eventually he and Bella were lonely enough to resume their physical relationship. Even a baby as lovely as little Annabella couldn't mend their marriage. Soon it was a pitched battle of mutual abuse. Annabella's love was just another weapon they used against each other.

When Bella fell ill with fever and convulsions of chills, Annabella was whisked to her grandparents' house. No one knew Newman despaired for Bella's suffering and wept when she died. The Goodenows blamed him, rather than illness, for their daughter's death. Within the month Simon Goodenow called in his loans and Chase Emporium was no more. Newman let his employees go and rode home by hackney.

He knew that he had to leave Boston if he was to replenish his fortune—much less regain his self-respect. If he had to go to the ends of the earth, so be it. Because of that, Annabella had to remain with his despised in-laws. He was sorry to leave her behind, but he knew that few things salved the spirit like a good income. Money wasn't anything, it was everything.

Newman girded himself to meet with his daughter that morning in San Francisco. As he stepped outside, the bright sunlight hit him like a hammer. It was going to be a long day.

10

After a long, harrowing voyage, Annabella's first night on dry land was spent in a long, dreamless sleep. That probably accounted for how startled she was when a fist pounded on her door the next morning. She wasn't fully awake until she hit the cold floor.

The din didn't stop until she hollered, "Alright. Alright!"

She didn't chastise herself for that outburst. Even if there were gentry in this godforsaken town, she doubted they were within yelling distance of the Hotel Deluxe. Patting her hair, she crawled to her knees and attempted to stand. Immediately she was engulfed by an eye-watering stench. At first she thought it emanated from the night pot, but it didn't. It came from the mattress itself.

"Good Lord in heaven above!" she gagged.

Holding her skirt tail over her mouth and nose, she staggered over to the window and threw open the sash. She inhaled deeply. That was a great relief. If there was one thing in California's favor, it was its exquisitely brisk air. At least it was exquisite from the second story of the hotel. She didn't forget the fragrance at street level the day before. With that recollection, came another.

Scratching absentmindedly, she thought about her much anticipated reunion with her father. Now that it was over, disillusionment began setting up shop in the pit of her stomach.

In the quiet of that moment, she realized that her ankles and knees were under attack.

Louder than before, she screeched, "*Ooh! Ouch!*"

She began to scratch in earnest. But the more she scratched, the more she itched. Alternately leaping up and down and running in a tight circle, she continued to scream. When door to her room flew open she didn't notice at first. Approximately her third rotation around the room, she saw Lupe standing in the doorway. The little Mexican held a bowl containing foul-smelling concoction in one hand and a spoon in the other.

"*Lice*," Lupe announced flatly. "Bedbugs."

Extending the spoon, she motioned for Annabella to slather the potion on her extremities. Gingerly, Annabella took the bowl, but the putrefying odor of the muck was overwhelming. Shaking her head, Annabella tried to give it back. Lupe shrugged and went out the door.

Running after her, Annabella called, "What in God's name is this?"

Over her shoulder, Lupe replied, "Bear grease."

Under any other possible circumstances, those words (and the accompanying odor) would have caused a legitimate even obligatory, reason to swoon. As it was, Annabella's itch was of far higher priority. Her skin erupting into red contusions, she didn't waste any more time criticizing the remedy. But she did curse her luck to have survived four months as see in a rat-infested tub without such an indignity, only to be attacked her first night on dry land.

With no thought to ruining her stockings, she hastily began peeling them off. It was a considerable challenge however, to hold her nose while slathering the slime onto her ankles. Since her stockings were already ruined, she did what she could to keep the mess from fouling her fine under-linens too.

As she daubed, she groused, "Sadistic little pests."

There was one thing that was sure—with this bug calamity and resulting stench, she was in no hurry to go down to greet the glorious new day.

Holding her skirt as high as possible, she waddled back to the window and took a good look across the street. In the harsh light of morn she had a good look the front of her father's saloon. It appeared even more disreputable than it had the day before. Undoubtedly, it was a den of iniquity. She still didn't see lewd women, but that looked to be a good possibility. The opportunity to get a first-hand look at wickedness brightened her mood considerably.

"How astonishingly superb!"

It was early. The ornately-carved doors were still shut. They were very incongruous against the weathered wood of the rest of the building. Her initial appraisal appeared to be correct. A little sprucing up would do wonders for the place. Without actually leaning out the window she looked as far up the street as she could. Very few people were stirring. Most of the businesses were still closed.

Her dressing routine was constrained by having no maid to pulls her corset strings and the losing a layer of skin to the corrosiveness of her bedbug antidote. She tried to keep her complaints inaudible. At least the bear grease had done its work. There were welts, but she wasn't itching anymore. While she was still tidying herself, someone banged on her door again.

"*Alright*," she hollered. "I'm coming."

She didn't think twice about yelling this time. In a land of rusticity and lice, it looked like any number of niceties would go missing.

Sliding her toes into her good slippers, she stuck her head out the door to see if there were any slovenly creatures to avoid on the staircase. Seeing all was quiet, she sidled out the door and turned the key in her lock. For good measure, she checked the knob to make certain it wouldn't open. That was one good lesson she learned on her lengthy sojourn—one must keep all valuables secure.

Satisfied, she turned only to run squarely into little Lupe. Knocked back a half-foot, Annabella almost lost her balance.

"Pardon me!" she said, expecting the same in return.

"*Quizá*," replied Lupe impassively.

Annabella had picked up a little Spanish along the way, but it was more along the lines of greetings and calling for the local *policiá*.

"Ah, yes," she mumbled. "*Si.*"

Lupe grinned. She was missing a bottom tooth and a cigarillo was tucked into the opening it left. From the looks of the thing, Annabella guessed that it was the same one from the night before. Taking it between two fingers, Lupe withdrew it and blew a large puff of smoke directly in Annabella's face. Annabella tried with all her might not to cough, but she did.

The smell of bear grease gradually engulfed them both. Of the two odors, the cigarillo won. That too seemed a capitulation. Annabella would have liked to put Lupe in her place. And, for the merest moment she was moved to strike her. Even thinking of such a thing was abominable. Not because Lupe wasn't asking for it, just that a lady should have someone to exact such punishment.

Despite the fact that Annabella considered herself quite the little scrapper, some intrinsic sense of self-preservation kept her from reproaching Lupe. Instead, she sashayed around her as haughtily as possible and made for the stairs. All she could muster was a huffy glare.

Annabella was at a loss as to how to handle such impudence. Her grandparents had dozens of maids and none of them dared behave like that. But then Lupe had a wild look about her. No doubt she hankered for a fight. Annabella had seen a bitch dog like that once. If anyone dared look at her in the eyes, she'd attack. Word was that a boy teased the dog and lost his upper lip. She didn't know if that was true or not, but eventually the dog was found poisoned.

Once at a safe distance, Annabella said sagely, "Senorita Lupe might learn a lesson from that story."

Before she had the chance to decide whether to report Lupe's behavior or not, Mr. Boomer took her arm and seated her at a table in the far corner of the café, fawning enough for any ten servants. That settled her feathers. Still, she had no idea what might be considered a culinary delicacy in northern California. One had to retain some standards. She put up with enough gruel aboard ship. She gave an involuntary shiver at the thought of that.

To the establishment's credit, there was a clean, white tablecloth on the table. In the middle sat a brown bottle bearing a single yellow flower. That was the only nod to civilized dining. Obviously, table manners were optional. A man at a nearby table had stabbed his entree and was eating it from the blade of his knife.

Annabella spied her father standing at the door. His eyes searched the room for her. Sedately, she lifted a hand. With great nonchalance and pretty good aim, he tossed his hat on an empty hook on the hat rack. When he sat down, he did so carefully—like a man who had sat too long in the saddle.

He placed himself across from her. That suited her. She hadn't really gotten a good look at him the day before and was glad not to have to appraise him out of the corner of her eye.

As pleasantries were exchanged, she gave him a thorough inspection. Her general opinion was that he was an attractive man. A little rough around the edges perhaps, but he was freshly shaved. Although his coat could use a good brushing, his vest was brocade and looked new. Even in the stale air of the restaurant she could smell his tobacco. It was an aroma that was oddly familiar to her. At first, she didn't realize why. When she did, her reaction was visceral.

Like some fawn in the forest, she had recognized his scent.

That was unsettling. How was it that she could barely recall her mother's face and she could remember her father's tobacco? Newman looked at her with an odd expression—it was as if he knew. Straightening her shoulders, she smiled gamely. Just then a hairy man with an open collar set a plate before her. It was overflowing with strange-smelling sausage and fried potatoes. Swimming in grease, two egg yolks looked unblinkingly back at her. Her stomach churned. She pushed it away.

"Mind if I have that?" Newman asked.

She shook her head.

He pulled the plate of food across the table and snared her knife and fork. Taking the precaution of tucking a napkin into his collar, he pierced a link of sausage with the tines of the fork. Fat squirted out and onto the table cloth. Annabella blanched. Busy with his food, Newman didn't notice. Once he chewed the link into submission, he parked it in one side of his mouth and began to talk.

"Annie, dear, if you stay, I must set down a few rules."

Rules. Had she not already felt queasy, that word alone would have made her bilious. If a single word could encompass the reason she had fled Boston, it would be "rules." Still, if she didn't want to be sent packing, she knew it would be necessary to have her father's assistance. That was the other thing her voyage had taught her. A male protector was, if not essential, at least a prudent.

She smiled as prettily as she could and patted his hand. When she wanted to, she could seem very cooperative.

After all, the conditions he imposed weren't all that disagreeable. In fact, she was accepted them eagerly and with half-hearted sincerity. She promised him that she wouldn't ask questions. She promised to obey every demand without complaint. She vowed that she would never, ever, come through the front door of the *Bella Goode Saloon*.

Her only request was new batting for her mattress.

"Bugs," she explained daintily.

He nodded his head agreeably. She made a mental note to approach him about renovations to his drinking establishment. If she were to help operate a saloon, it would have to acquire some verve, some style. She believed she had the authority to make those demands. The *Bella Goode* was named after her mother. That made it her namesake as well.

11

Newman's instinct for business hadn't failed him when he relocated. The *Bella Goode* had steady business from the start. Half their customers were sailors enjoying a little time on dry land; the others were trappers who had come down from the Sierras to sell their pelts. He and Gus sold them liquor and brokered their goods.

Their patrons were tough men with simple needs. After their business was done, they liked to celebrate—with liberal libations and bit of female flesh. Liquor was easy to get. Every other shanty in town sold bottles of homemade brew. The *Bella* offered a genial atmosphere in which to partake, but at that time their little hamlet had just two open-minded women.

One was Ruby Gottwald, the town laundress, the other, Cattle Kate Sweeny. Ruby was sweet, but Kate was dried as beef jerky and mean as a snake. After the strike, Ruby was busy as ever but they didn't see much of Kate. Every new saloon came supplied with card sharps and loose women, giving men looking for love a wider array of women to give it to them.

Newman thought that Kate left town due to more discriminating customers. Gus disagreed.

"She's probably just making more money trading livestock," he said.

Lord knew pack animals were in short supply. Lewd acts, however, were becoming more commonplace by the day. Newman had given little notice to all the unsavory activity as he was far too busy trying to cash in on it. The minute Annabella showed up, it suddenly became appallingly obvious. Generally speaking, such acts were still after dark, back-alley trysts. If he kept his daughter to a strict sundown curfew, she should remain unwitting of it. Another problem loomed larger. His biggest concern was not concealing lewd conduct from Annabella—it was to concealing her and all her blonde glory from the riff-raff that hung around day and night.

Much to her father's dismay, people of all sorts came by the *Bella* to get a look at the girl who rounded the Horn all by herself. Annabella had the good sense to pretend modesty. She put on quite a show, affecting the perfect blend of innocence and disinterest. He shooed them off, but they never entirely lost interest.

With squalid hoards of prospectors pouring into town, keeping her out of sight would be an ever-increasing task. Her golden curls cascaded down her shoulders like the richest vein that was being picked, panned, and washed out of the placer mines above Sutter's Mill. It was imperative to find her proper companionship, but San Francisco wasn't known for its tea parties. By the time they reached Annabella's age, daughters of the town-folk were married off or put to work. As the days of her stay turned into weeks, her future worried him more and more.

It took her far less time for Annabella to break every promise she made to him.

She continually asked questions and complained constantly. The one promise she kept was not entering through the enormous teak doors of the *Bella Goode Saloon*. She sneaked in through side.

Once she had settled in, Annabella didn't give any thought to returning to Boston. There she was just another of society's young ladies. In San Francisco she was very nearly a celebrity. Most important of all, however, she was generally free to do as she pleased. She just had to be inconspicuous. Learning subtlety was a remarkable feat for anyone—especially Annabella.

Each day she traversed the mud-caked streets, artfully dodging mongrels and flea-bitten men-folk as she did. First she brought her father his lunch like a good daughter. Then she sneaked into the *Bella* while he was busy with his food. Gus was already behind the bar and it became her custom to drag a barstool around so she could keep him company. After a while she didn't have to drag the stool over, Gus had it waiting for her.

He enjoyed her company. To his mind it was better to keep her in sight than risk her wandering the streets. Every day she sat on the stool swinging her legs like a child. Her eyes, however, didn't miss a thing. Every colorful curse, vulgar story, and caressed knee—she eagerly (if surreptitiously) soaked in. At first she thought they were all the same sort, soon her eye became more discerning.

They were all a dirty, foul-smelling bunch, but she came to see that some of the prospectors were actually educated men. To a man all the trappers were extremely uncouth. The sailors were too loud, singing coarse songs and the like, but they were well-muscled and tanned. They were all a far cry from the fops she weathered back home.

Annabella took measure of these men out of the corner of her eye. She was smart. She knew instinctively that it was important to pretend that she disliked them all. She also pretended not to understand the bad language and foul jokes. If anyone tried to talk to her, Gus glared at them as she painstakingly inspected her fingernails.

Gus wasn't fooled by her pretended disinterest, but others seemed to be taken in by her big, blue, guileless eyes. He didn't see her eyeing the taut muscles of the sailors, but he did realize that she fostered a dangerous misconception of youth. Because she didn't see those around her as her intellectual equals, she believed that they were less cunning too. That was a calamity in the making. It was just a matter of time before Annabella tired of being a mere observer. He prayed when she took the leap it wasn't into the lap of some rogue.

Newman was oblivious to the potential problems. But then he harbored the notion that Annabella and Lupe should be fast friends. They had absolutely nothing in common except an independent nature and avid dislike of condescension. As time went on, they developed a bond far richer than that of mere friends. Annabella and Lupe were contentious as a pair of jays and never tired of fussing at each other.

One would think that the well-bred and very determined Miss Chase might have had the upper hand. This was not the case.

Guadalupe Concepcion Alfonsa Escobar's occupation may have been a maid, but she refused to be at anyone's beck and call. When Annabella tried to give her orders, Lupe spat out Spanish invectives.

Used to finagling and maneuvering others at will, this kept Annabella fit to be tied. From her perch behind the bar, complaining to Gus about Lupe's perceived shortcomings became one her very favorite pastimes.

Annabella complained, "She wears men's trousers under her skirt! Have you ever heard of anything so appalling?"

Having once known a man who kept his money in a bag made out of another man's scrotum, Gus chose not to answer that.

Finally, he said, "I reckon that she wears them to stop male interference."

Having read her share of scandal sheets, Annabella knew that had to do with a man doing some indelicate business with a woman. She wasn't convinced that was what the issue was either.

"Lupe smokes vile-smelling cigarillos. Those alone should thwart any man bent on "interference."

Gus shrugged his shoulders, saying, "If anybody has the lay of the land, it would be Lupe. It wouldn't hurt you to be a little more cautious."

Annabella wasn't listening. Her mind was busy appraising the Bella's large, front window. Lace curtains would be a wonderful improvement.

12

It would be unfair to lay Miss Adelaide Perry's downfall entirely on the incorrigible Annabella Chase. But she had her share in it. Mr. Simon Gooodenow had the rest.

Adelaide Perry hadn't waited for the sheriff to tack a notice of foreclosure on her school's door before notifying the students' parents its failure. She had hoped to head off what looked to become quite a scandal.

In this she would fail.

It was a relief, however, to give up her complicated subterfuge. Always looking over one's shoulder and anticipating strangers on the doorstep was no way to lead a peaceable life. Keeping the secret had been her second occupation—one almost as trying as keeping two dozen adolescent girls in check.

As a woman, Adelaide had accomplished a considerable sleight of hand. It had lasted for as long as it had by her burying her father's dead body, but keeping him alive so far as the bankers were aware. She hadn't engaged in pecuniary hanky-panky. She was his legal heir. His will was quite clear on that point. That, however, was one of the few times that the law was on her side.

Teaching was the only suitable occupation for a lady. Adelaide had many fine attributes, but patience wasn't one of them. Her mind was more suited to accounting than tutoring. Still all went far easier than she would have guessed. She had leased a building, hired a staff and issued advertisements all under her father's name. Once she got the hang of it, she took a liking to bureaucratic folderol.

"I see how the world works now," she noted. "Women can do anything a man can—save urinating standing up. We just have to do it twice as well to be thought half as good."

Through sheer perseverance she had just managed to keep the school solvent. It had taken late hours and a careful accounting, but she had succeeded in fending off the numerous wolves circling her door. Until Miss Annabella Chase absconded without a by your leave and Simon Goodenow wanted blood to be let because of it, no one had cause to question whether A. Perry was Adelaide or Amos. A dozen years of dealing with people of his ilk led her to understand why Mr. Gooodenow felt compelled to bring her and her school down. It was simple, really. He had to find somewhere else to blame lest it land at his own feet.

It didn't take much snooping from a detective of the Hairsbreadth Investigatory Agency to uncover her ruse. By the time Mr. Goodenow was through, the notion of a single woman owning and operating an academy without benefit of a male overseer was tantamount to reckless endangerment of impressionable young ladies' minds. He was not alone in this opinion.

Upon the revelation that Miss Adelaide Perry was not only the headmistress and its namesake of Miss Adelaide's Academy for Young Ladies, she was the owner and operator, mothers then swooned and fathers gnashed their teeth. They were unable to decide which they despised more—Miss Perry the Liar or Miss Perry, the Usurper of All That is Holy to a Man. Why, everyone knew that females were flighty and indecisive. It was unnatural for them to be in charge of their own finances. To do otherwise flew in the face of God's grand design. They also agreed that it was most fortunate to learn of Miss Perry's peculiar predilections before all their daughters put on trousers and headed towards the wild frontier doing God-knows-what with each other like Annabella Chase.

Opening a school would have been an enormous gamble had the deck not been stacked against businesswomen. Insolvency among fashionable boarding schools wasn't exactly unprecedented. Had she known these odds beforehand she might have chosen to open a piece goods store. In the fiscal morass of surrounding such situations, at least that kind of inventory couldn't up and leave (and exchange unfounded rumors as they did). Refunding tuition fees didn't have to be her chief concern. She could have just walked away from it all herself. But to Adelaide it presented a troubling conundrum. On the one hand, to keep their money would have served those misogynistic twits right. But that would have left her (and thus her sex) open to further denunciation. To her mind, that was unthinkable.

"They'd say, 'Just like a feeble-minded woman,'" she harrumphed.

Her good friend and lawyer, Mr. Dutton oversaw the closure of her school. After the outstanding bills were settled, there was nothing of her inheritance left. By the time Mr. Goodenow had finished sullying Adelaide's name, her teaching days were behind her as well. Her prospects were few. She couldn't cook and she couldn't sew. She didn't really know how to please a man. But of the three, the last one looked like the easiest one to learn.

13

Gus's prediction about Annabella becoming bored came true soon enough. She began making forays into the iniquitous San Francisco streets as soon as she was certain that she wouldn't be missed. To her they weren't menacing, just colorful.

The heart of all the bawdy activity was Portsmouth Square. The flag was still flapping on the flagpole, but that was the only thing she recalled from the first time she walked up the hill into town. The man who had been screaming about the gold strike was gone.

Although she wasn't supposed to be there, she didn't skulk down the walkway. If caught, she intended to say she was looking at the shops. After all, new businesses were opening right and left. There dry good stores, but they largely carried gear for the mines. A few, however, had bonnets displayed in their windows. She had to be content with that.

The square was a hive of activity day or night, but it was easier to go mid-afternoon. Then ruffians weren't lolling about on the walkway making vulgar remarks. On the upper side of the square was a large adobe structure with wide steps. That was the favorite spot for street preachers. They railed against the evils of drinking, gambling, and consorting with loose women. It was an ideal location to sermonize. Annabella had seen the gamblers and the women. They were easy to spot. The women wore boas and abundant décolletage; the card sharps had fancy suits and conspicuous waistcoats. She wondered where they shopped.

The El Dorado was the first real gambling den. It was only a tent with rough board floors. On warm days the canvas was thrown back. There were streamers and buntings hanging everywhere and an elevated platform—either for musicians or some sort of performances. She thought the streamers looked garish. Music, however, would improve the Bella. She vowed to speak to Gus about that.

Every upright plank was sporting a placard. She stopped and looked at a sign tacked to a post advertising the appearance of a Mexican quintuplet featuring two harps, two guitars, and a bass drum. It had been so long since she had heard more than a banjo, she was entranced. She wondered how one went about engaging such entertainments. Unfortunately, as she went on she wasn't really watching where she was walking and collided with a man walking the opposite direction. She was knocked off of her feet by the impact. Only her parasol cushioned her fall.

"Oh, I do beg your pardon," said the man extending a gloved hand.

Naturally, everyone in the street stopped in their tracks not to miss a minute of her mortification, so she had no choice but to accept his help. She tried not to look at him directly, but he had a piercing gaze. She thought him a bit rude for it.

Straightening her bonnet, she tried to regain some semblance of dignity. It is presumed that any collision was always the gentleman's fault. She had half a mind to give him a small what-for. But his air was so refined that seemed out of the question. Besides, in San Francisco gallantry was in far too short a supply. She didn't want to put a damper on it.

She held up her ruined parasol, saying, "I believe the only true injury is to this."

"Allow me to see to it," he replied.

She shook her head, giving him a little chin-ducking curtsey instead. He touched the brim of his hat and walked purposely on. She did too. But after a half-dozen steps, she stopped and turned to look back at him. It was a daring thing to do. He might have looked back at her too. She was somewhat disappointed that he didn't. All she could see of him was his hat as it disappeared into the crowd.

Normally after her furtive strolls over to the square, she went to her hotel room. That was only because she didn't want to have to lie unnecessarily. This time she was so intrigued by her chance meeting with the stranger, she went straight to the *Bella* to see if Gus knew him.

However Newman rambled in at the same time and before she could ask anything, Gus made an announcement.

"Well, hold on to your hat, Newman," Gus said. "The gold strike is being written about in Baltimore and Boston."

The *California Star* was published weekly. Annabella first recognized Sam Brannan on one of her perambulations around the square. He was easy to spot, always flailing around like one of those barkers hawking tickets to a show.

She had never had much interest in the news or newspapers, but on hearing "Boston," Annabella's ears perked up.

"The Courier?" she asked.

"Mmmm," Newman stroked his chin, and asked Gus. "When was that?"

"Judging from how yellowed this newsprint is, I'd say a while back," Gus replied. "They're still talking about making California a territory, but they're hung up on slave-holding."

Gus leaned against the bar and rested his chin on his fist. Annabella was already atop a bar stool, one leg tucked beneath her. The sun was getting lower. Before long she would be expelled. While they talked, she idly claimed a half-drunk glass of beer left on the bar and took a sip. Newman and Gus both saw her. Gus grabbed it before she could take a second swallow. As he did, it sloshed on his hand and onto the bar. Sighing, he pulled his ever-present bar cloth from his shoulder to wipe up the spill.

But it was Newman who said, "Not only are you too young to drink spirits, you have no idea who has spit in that glass!"

Unhappy to be reprimanded in front of Gus, she retorted, "It is my understanding that distilled products are curatives."

But the idea that one the vile patrons of the *Bella* might have spat in the drink made her blanch. For a moment she attempted to look untroubled by the notion, but quickly a spasm of nausea overtook her. She leaped from her stool and made for the door. Gus and Newman watched her leave.

Finding that event unremarkable, Gus returned to their conversation.

"Just you watch, this Manifest Destiny sounds all highfalutin, but it's nothing but a land grab. Sure as the day is long, if land gets worth stealing, some government will be standing at the head of the line to do it."

Single-minded as always, Newman wasn't of a mind to argue politics.

"We better start buying more land before someone else has it all."

"Yeah, like Sam Brannan," said Gus.

"Yeah," agreed Newman. "Or maybe Asher Price."

14

Like every other sinner, sneak, or scalawag running from the long arm of the law, Patrick Aesop Bowles headed due west. He intended to run until he was stopped by the sea. There, he would make his peace.

There were vast members of humanity to join on his urgent trek west. They sought to make their fortunes, but not all of them intended to find it in the bed of the American River. They headed to Oregon, and they aimed to stay. They claimed that it was heaven and they would do anything to get there. These immigrants spent months readying for such a journey. No one was less prepared than Patrick to bear the rigors of the trail. He had left St. Louis so fast that he had only taken a few minutes to jam his smalls and a few books in a bag and be on his way.

Kansas City was where settlers gathered until they had accumulated numbers large enough to cross the plains. That was where he headed too.

They were hardy people, and Patrick looked out of place. He was tall and ungainly, with narrow shoulders and hands soft and white as bread dough. Nobody mistook him for a frontiersman. When asked, he claimed to be a teacher looking for a new start. It was plausible lie. Music was his forte, but he supposed he could teach spelling to a passel of over-grown farm boys if it saved his hide.

So far as he knew there wasn't a handbill out on him, but his features were the sort that would make him easy to spot. He kept a wide-brimmed hat on and his head down just in case. In time it all might blow over. Certain accusations died when they were kept from the light.

The trail across the plains wasn't yet well rutted and it was rough-going. Their guide wore buckskin and the fur of small, dead animal on his head. He was laden with weaponry, although the only threat was not to them but to the local wildlife. Due to careless target shooting, carcasses were left festering with flies in their wake. Every time a gun went off, Patrick jumped. And every time he did, he wished he had more padding on his buttocks.

He sat in the back of the last wagon in the caravan and ate dust most of the way. The only good thing about it was when they descended a hill he could look ahead and see the white-tops of the wagons laid out before him like cotton bunting.

Their biggest worry was to make it through the mountain passes before winter hit. That was a relief. Stories were rife of the Reed and Donner parties who got waylaid by a snow storm and ended up gnawing their toenails and the feeding on the frozen corpses of their lately dead neighbors.

The only thing that slowed their own trek west was word of the gold find on below Sutter's Mill and the American River. That incited a two-day palaver over whether they should allow some members to splinter off to go to the strike or not. In the end nearly half the wagons headed directly to Sutter's Fort.

The tedium of the wagon train convinced Patrick to tag along with them to the fort. It was what passed for civilization and he figured he was better suited to that than to the wilderness of Oregon. By the time they arrived, Patrick had just convinced himself that he could pan for gold as good as the next man.

Once he got a good look around, Patrick realized that western society left a lot to be desired. The fort was swarming with miners. The only entertainment was a large group of men gathered around the cook pot swapping tales, so he joined them. At first he stayed on the periphery, but he was gradually taken in by stories about grizzly bears encounters and attacks of marauding bandits. A time or two he even spat into the fire as he listened to tales of the infamous Mexican bandit Jose Carrillo, who was more feared than all the desperados in the Sierras.

"Who's ever even seen Carrillo anyhow?" asked a man called Buster. "I bet he ain't even real."

"Oh, he's real, alright, my friend," said a man they called Knoxville.

Everybody hushed. Knoxville kicked an ember back onto the fire with the toe of his boot.

Then he continued, "Jose Carrillo would kill a white man as soon as look at him."

"Why white men?" gulped Patrick. Even with months on the trail, his skin was extremely fair.

Another man butted in, "White men stole Carrillo's claim, that why."

"There's as many Mexicans who claim-jump as white men. That's no reason!" said somebody.

Crouching by the fire, his face glowing in the light, Knoxville said, "Yeah, but these claim-jumpers raped his wife, hung his brother, and left Carrillo for dead."

He broke some kindling and tossed it on top. Two dogs circled just outside the firelight, waiting for some dinner scraps.

Knoxville turned reflective, "I think the law looked the other way while he killed off them that done his family wrong—even if it was a Mexican killing white men. His band is more than eighty guns now—and one is his wife."

A few men thought the notion was titillating. One even giggled.

Knoxville looked up, and continued, "She was an ugly little brute of a woman, but was said to be a crack shot. They both got taken by sheer blood-lust, torturing men just for the fun of it."

"So you've seen him?" Patrick asked reverently.

"Naw, but Buster's cousin did," answered Knoxville. "Besides his wife, Carrillo rode with a feller named Three-fingered Jack, tying coolies up by their pigtails and settin' 'em on fire."

First cannibalism and then torturing the poor Chinese? Shivering, Patrick was sure he wasn't meant for the frontier. A dog came and sat next to him and began to lick its privates. Patrick scooted away. Then and there he decided that he would be on the next ferryboat leaving for the metropolis of San Francisco. Captain Sutter sent his twenty-two ton schooner, *Sacramento* from his landing at Sutter's Fort to San Francisco regularly. If the wind was with them, a one-way passage took less than ten days.

Patrick admired the idea of San Francisco. There they would have hotels with mattresses and linens. There would be bathhouses and barbershops. It was a place where picking ticks off of dogs and popping them between the fingernails wasn't considered a cultural event. It was Elysium. It was Utopia. It was nirvana, Shangri-La, and the happy hunting ground all rolled up into one.

He couldn't wait.

15

Unsurprisingly, Adelaide Perry had been a precocious child.

Although she was the apple of her father's eyes, she knew that like all men, he still wanted a son. When her mother became pregnant, it was difficult not to look upon the coming child as a rival for her father's affection. Hearing their carefully crafted reassurances that the new child would bring even more love to their already happy family, she didn't believe it for a minute and snorted indignantly. They could all just go hang themselves. Once they had their pretty new baby—whatever its sex—she would be consigned to the attic with grandmother's trunks and broken furniture. It pleased her to brood about that inevitability. In fact, she whiled away hours thinking about how she would run away when the baby was born. That would show them.

When feeling particularly insignificant, she tromped up the steps to the garret. There she sat before a long, oval mirror she had propped against the wall. It was so old and warped that it barely reflected her image. But it was enough for her to practice a variety of put-upon expressions to later exhibit for her mother. Her mother, however, was too busy embroidering pillowcases for the new baby to notice her. In disgust, Adelaide plopped down on the piano stool. Her mother asked her to play a piece for her. That request only reminded Adelaide that she had been ignoring her music lessons. Petulantly, she began to plunk out the notes with her elbows.

"Please, dear," her mother said, "Mummy has a headache."

With a melodramatic sigh, Adelaide repaired to the kitchen wherein their cook, Mrs. Stackpole could usually be counted on to feed her muffins. Squat and full-bosomed, Mrs. Stackpole looked as a cook should. Her conversation was as dull as her culinary skills, but she kept a jar of hard-rock candy in the pantry and that made up for her lack of wit.

The kitchen was always warm. Steaming cabbage had turned Mrs. Stackpole's face so red that her freckles were indistinguishable. She didn't look up when Adelaide came in and edged into the pantry to scrounge some sweets. It would have suited Adelaide to be scolded her for such thievery, but Mrs. Stackpole didn't oblige her.

"I hate them all," Adelaide announced with the candy rolling around her mouth. "I hate them and the baby they want instead of me. I hope they all die."

"Vengeance is mine saeth the Lord," Mrs. Stackpole finally scolded her.

Adelaide was amused. So far as she knew, church was not where Mrs. Stackpole went when on her day off. That meant her opinion was not, as they say, to be taken as gospel. Still, Adelaide knew she had wandered from mischief into blasphemy and hushed herself. She would be banished from her home soon enough. When her mother gave birth, Adelaide was to be consigned to stay with her aunt and albino cousin in Plymouth.

She was all set to be unhappy about that when her mother went into labor prematurely.

The household was in such a thunder, Adelaide was totally forgotten. With her heart pounding with fear, she hid behind her bed. Listening to her mother's ever-increasing moans, she had plenty of time to worry that this horrible turn of events was all her fault. No doubt God intended to make her pay for every flippant word she had uttered. She began to pray, not only for her mother and the baby, but her own wretched soul. Fingers steepled against her forehead, she crouched in the darkness and begged forgiveness.

Suddenly, her door was flung back. It revealed a silhouette of someone holding a knife. The Angel of Death coming to demand its due no doubt. Cowering against the wall, Adelaide smelled the sickly scent of liquor. She was fairly certain that angels didn't partake. Still, she remained where she was. One couldn't be too careful. A voice boomed out—one was ear-splittingly familiar.

"Child!" Mrs. Stackpole demanded. "Come here."

With a determined grimace, Adelaide shook her head. Then she shrank back against the wall. That was useless. Adelaide's eyes were so big with fright that the whites showed all the way round them. Even to the cook's bleary eyes she was easy to spot. Mrs. Stackpole continued to weave about, flailing a bread knife. It wasn't clear to Adelaide if she intended to do murder or was calling her to supper. Adelaide's teeth were chattering so badly she could hardly talk. Instead, she just shook her head emphatically. There was no way in creation she would come to that knife-wielding....

"Foolish girl!" the cook hissed. "I need you to put this under your mother's mattress."

"Why?" Adelaide asked incredulously.

"It will cut the pain."

In desperation, Adelaide shook her head again.

"You must," Mrs. Stackpole insisted. "Do it for your dear mother."

With surprising logic under the circumstances, Adelaide asked, "Why me and not you?"

"I'm not family," the cook insisted. "Do it, dearie—to cut her pain."

Even Adelaide knew that was a worthless wives' tale, but decided to use it as an excuse to see what was happening to her mother. Taking the knife between finger and thumb, she scurried up the hall like a mouse. She meant to just take a peek, but some sort of sordid curiosity drew her into the room. Withdrawing to a darkened corner, she was struck dumb by the ordeal taking place right in front of her eyes. Her mother wailed, the midwife called for someone to summon the doctor, and everyone else washed linens. But it was all for naught.

In time, her mother's cries stopped. Still in a corner, Adelaide heard a small bleat. After that, there was nothing.

The slash of blood and the newborn's gray, slug-like corpse was much too ghastly for her young eyes, but no one, not even Mrs. Stackpole, was there to lead her away. So she finally made her legs move on her own. As she fled down the stairs in her nightdress, the silence followed her like a train.

The next day, the lifeless baby boy was swaddled and laid out in the coffin in his dead mother's arms. They would be together for all eternity. The coffin was set out in the parlor where her father stoically accepted condolences as they were offered by the sympathetic neighbors and grieving friends. Adelaide sat with him for a while, but when it came time for the burial, she ran away. Once again, she hid behind her bed. There, she shuddered uncontrollably. She knew she should cry, but she was too terrified. Any moment God would strike her dead for her sins.

Covering her head with her hands, she squeezed her knees against her chest. As young as she was, even she knew that the smaller the target, the harder it was to hit.

16

Annabella wasn't especially precocious, but she was always a fast learner.

Having made it to her room without the beer causing a gastrointestinal incident, she vowed never to sully her innards with intoxicants of any kind again. Lying back on her mattress, she enjoyed the smell of fresh batting and waited for her stomach to settle. It gave her time to ponder what was fast becoming a new infatuation.

"The Gentleman"—as she began to think of him—was unlike those sweaty-pawed boys back in Boston. His hand was strong, his voice, virile. He had lifted his hat, so she knew he had all his hair. He was well-dressed and well-mannered. Although it was difficult to gauge his age, she doubted he was married. She had no rationale for that conclusion other than that his collar wasn't pressed. What wife would allow her husband out the door like that?

She mooned about their suitability for the better part of an hour.

There was no rush to return to the *Bella* once the subject was business. The only thing that interested her about increasing commerce was her quest for a new gown or bonnet. Those fancy women who came into town had to get their accoutrements somewhere. Perhaps there was a seamstress about. She must give them a run for their ill-gotten money lest The Gentleman got his head turned by the wrong sort.

Newly invigorated, she rummaged through her trunk for more ribbons and lace. Nothing improved the spirit like new trimming and she congratulated herself for thinking of bringing them. The lace was wound around a wooden spool; the ribbons had been pressed between the pages of several books. She removed them all and tediously replaced her belongings. Since Lupe seemed to enter her room at will, she then re-locked the trunk.

She climbed back atop the bed and removed the ribbons one by one. She was pleased. They were in remarkably good shape. They would be a great improvement to her straw bonnet. If Lupe didn't know of a seamstress, she would attach them herself.

That monstrous botheration resolved, she cast about how next to occupy herself. She idly perused the titles of the ribbon-bearing books. At one time she enjoyed a good read. (When she set to packing, weighting down her trunk with the classics hadn't seemed wise.) She looked at what she had. One book was *Don Quixote*, the other *The Prisoner of Chillon*—by *Lord Byron*. The third was her-long abandoned diary. It had a single entry. She had written it on the day she left Boston—when her trip seemed all full of promise and excitement. She sighed at her naiveté.

Choosing which book to read first wasn't a difficult decision. Just running her palm across the gold lettering of Byron's name was provocative and she savored the moment. She hadn't actually read any Byron, just a book of quotations. But she had heard about him. She decided to save *Don Quixote* for another, more industrious day and opened the Byron carefully. The humidity of the ship's hold had compromised its binding.

She turned up the lamp light and didn't stop reading until she reached the end. After she finished it, she held it tight against her bosom and thought about The Gentleman with the piercing eyes. When she looked at the book again, she saw that some of the gold leaf had rubbed off and clung to the bodice of her gown. Perhaps that was an omen of love to come. It was a nice thought.

Looking at her diary, she decided to take it up again. After all, few ladies had endured the travails of western travel. She was literate as the next woman and her memoirs of California might be publishable. Of course she knew some used pen names so as not to ruin their reputations. As her reputation was even more sullied by running off like she did, that wasn't really an issue. She would not, however, call her book a diary. Here forth, it would be a journal. That sounded far more sophisticated.

"*The Memoirs of Annabella Chase*!" she thought gleefully. "How *exciting*!"

Of course, she would need reminisces. Obtaining them would become her new objective. Having a possible inamorato in her sights improved her chances of that considerably. Moreover, she needn't limit herself to just her own stories. Every person who entered the *Bella* was a potential chapter. No telling what she might learn about that enigmatic stranger she bumped into in the street.

The very next morning, she tucked her journal under her arm and headed for the Bella. Her first order of business was to ask about The Gentleman. However, Gus and Newman exchanged glances and claimed ignorance. She allowed them their little folly, knowing sooner or later she'd see him again.

That line of discussion at a dead end, she was unwilling to waste a perfectly good morning. She decided to embark on a campaign to find out about someone else. Gus seemed to be the easiest target. She decided to find out all about how August Gerlache came west. In this, he was also uncooperative.

She was left to a few deductions.

Although his hair was barely speckled with grey, Gus's whiskers were growing whiter by the day. With his red ball of a nose, he looked like a cross between Father Christmas and the town sot. He was neither. He was a no-nonsense teetotaler. Even to someone as unworldly as Annabella, a man who sold booze for a living and drank nothing but coffee looked suspiciously like a man who didn't trust himself to drink. All she could find out from her father was that Gus had quit whiskey before he showed up in California.

"Liquor had led to some sort of bad business—bad enough that he didn't talk about it—and neither should *you*," her father said pointedly.

The more she thought about it, she realized how little she really knew about Gus.

Strictly speaking, he tended bar. In actuality, he was part a romance counselor, part medical expert, and often, a father-confessor. On occasion, he could even be seen writing a letter for the illiterate. Annabella admired him in all these pursuits. Unfortunately, he wouldn't answer any questions about not only where he was from, but even if he had ever married.

"If it's a tale you want, you should ask your father."

"Oh, please," she huffed.

What could her father possibly tell that would be of interest? He and her mother didn't get along and he took off. End of story. She looked around the room for any other candidates. Her eyes came to rest on Rutledge Mayne. He was still drunk from the night before. Although he was bleary-eyed, he spied her watching him and grinned like a possum.

"Hello, darlin'," he purred.

Quickly, she leapt from her stool and made for the door. She was willing to sacrifice a lot for her literary career, but even she had her limit.

"Buh-bye," Rutledge called after her.

A shiver made its way down her spine. "Eww," she whispered. "What a rodent."

Gus looked her way, a silent offer to accompany her across the way. She smiled and shook her head. She could manage the fifty feet by herself.

"See you in the morning," she called.

Indeed, she would return later. Gus had stories to tell—really, really good stories—if only he would tell them. As she stepped outside, the light from the window was cast across a moaning figure in the alley-way. That wasn't particularly unusual. A few over-imbibers were often thrown out to sober up on the streets. This one, however, seemed different.

"Who is it?" she called.

"To be or not to be?" said he. "Is that not the question?"

"Goodness me!" she yelped.

She didn't know much Shakespeare, but she knew that. The last person she would have expected to be sitting in a puddle in front of the Belle Goode that time of night was an educated man. There had to be a tale in that. She walked towards him, pencil in hand.

17

With three streets—California, Broadway and Clay—fanning out from the beach, it took Patrick less than an hour to realize San Francisco was the least civilized place he had ever encountered—and that included the night they spent under siege by hostile Indians. Filthy prospectors were everywhere—either coming from or going to the gold fields. Women, who clearly were not ladies, offered to perform indecent acts upon his person in exchange for money. Men wearing side-arms were under the influence of intoxicants and shot randomly at the sky. Thieves and pickpockets crowded the walkways, and the streets were so muddy as to be impossible to cross.

His nerves were frazzled and he was also almost out of money. He would have sold his watch, but it had been stolen the first day he arrived in town. The only bright spot was that there was work for musicians. Several establishments had signs out. Unfortunately, his piano was sitting in a boarded up room at the Excelsior Hotel back home.

The last of his money was taken by a thug hiding in the shadows. He was beaten almost senseless. When he awoke, he was sitting in the middle of a puddle (the unmistakable stench of which confirmed that it was not rainwater). He had no money for food and no place to go. He wanted to be dead and began to wail. It was a wonder that he had heard the voice.

When he stopped crying and looked, he saw a girl smiling at him. Her teeth glittered like pearls. She was nothing less than an angel descended from heaven. She extended her hand.

"Come," she said. "I'm Annabella."

"I'm Patrick," he replied. He was up and fast behind her when he said, "Pleased to meet you."

The first thing Miss Annabella did was to take him to the Deluxe Restaurant's kitchen and feed him a plate of stew. He crouched over his food like a mongrel dog. She knew not to interrupt. Just talking to an itinerant could be dangerous, much less questioning him. When his spoon slowed down, she thought it was safe to get his tale of woe.

"Dear Sir," she crooned, "how was it that you came to San Francisco?"

A bit of cornbread spewed as he said, "I am by trade, a pianist."

"Truly?" Annabella gasped. "A *pianist*?"

Little by little, he told her the story of his trip west. (His version was heavy on the tribulations and minus the legal difficulties.) Before he was finished—both with the stew and his story, she grabbed him by the sleeve and tugged him to his feet.

"You must see my father!" she squealed. "A piano is just what the *Bella* needs!"

Still holding his spoon, he licked it like a lollypop as she dragged him out the door.

"What can you play?" she asked urgently.

It dawned on him that he was meant to audition. Franticly, he tried to think of a suitable piece of music. All he recalled was a bit of Chopin. It was highly unlikely that many of San Francisco's citizens would appreciate that. There was, however, a lively tune that he had heard by the campfire. Now what was it? Oh, yes.

"I know '*Oh, Susanna*'."

"Wonderful," she gushed.

When they reached her father's door, the napkin was still in his collar and she grabbed it. In a vain attempt at tidying him up, she brushed it across his lapels. Then she thrust him into her father's dark, dusty office. Newman sat at his desk and raised a disputatious eyebrow at the interruption.

"It's me, Poppa," Annabella said. "And I have a great treat!"

Newman sat back in his chair and raised a lantern. The wick was low, but it had enough oil to cast a flickering glow on Patrick's moon-shaped visage. Mr. Chase didn't like what he saw. Slowly, wearily, he shook his head. Patrick began to wring his delicate hands, apologizing for the intrusion. (He also prayed that his coat didn't still stink.)

"What in the hell did you drag in, girl?" he blared at Annabella.

She, however, was undeterred.

She announced, "He is a musician, Poppa! A real *musician*!"

Newman rolled his eyes, and steepled his hands in supplication. "Why, Lord? Don't I have enough useless sots lying about that we have to go out and recruit them?"

Annabella wrapped her arms around her father's neck and said, "He's just what the *Bella* needs, Poppa! We must keep up with the Portsmouth Square proprietors."

Newman conceded the point.

To Patrick, he commanded, "Sing!"

In the dim light of the lamp, Newman Chase looked like a he-lion, ready to have him for dinner. This scared Patrick spit-less and therefore unable to wrench out a note, even if he had been, in fact, a singer.

"No, Poppa," Annabella explained. "He isn't a singer. He's a musician."

"What in the hell is this, little girl?" Newman roared as Patrick's stench finally caught up with him. "He smells like horse piss!"

Unfortunately, that was true. Patrick gathered himself, shrugging apologetically, he said, "I admit that I have met with some misfortune."

"Poor man," Annabella clucked.

"Poor man, indeed," sighed Newman. Then he demanded, "What songs do you play?"

Patrick knew what to answer, "What I can't play by heart, I can play with sheet music."

"Harrumph," said Newman wearily.

Fearing she was losing the battle, Annabella burst out, "He has references—good ones!"

Patrick looked at Annabella, aghast. He hadn't presented references because he didn't have any. She had told her father a bald-faced lie. Bless her.

Apparently, Annabella Chase knew what she was doing. It was late. Butting heads with her would cost her father a great deal of aggravation and lost sleep. He came to a swift decision.

"Take him to Gus. He can work for tips."

Fortunately, Gus was more amenable to the scheme than Newman. The first thing the next morning, he rolled an aging spinet out from the back. It had been taken for a debt and was badly out of tune.

Shoving a table aside, he made room for it. Annabella was pleased as punch, but a bit worried that their patrons would be too rowdy for Patrick. It was obvious that he was a man of refined tastes.

"Can you bear it, Patty dear?"

Although he was ten years older than she was, she petted him like a child.

Closing his eyes like a contented kitten, Patrick said, "I was dead not twenty-four hours ago. Being at the mercy of a rabble of inebriates I consider a personal triumph."

It helped that Annabella sat next to him on the stool as he tinkled out tunes with no beginning, and seemingly, no end.

"Can you really play the classics, Patrick?" she asked.

"These little tunes we play for our keep," he nodded towards his hands. "But the concertos we play for our soul."

The first real song he played, he dedicated to her. That night he began accepting requests and gratuities. And with that, his reincarnation was complete. He was no longer Patrick Aesop Bowles, instructor of music to the finest young ladies of St. Louis, but Patrick A. Coffin (after his mother's people), purveyor of musical entertainment to the semi-finest drinking establishment in San Francisco.

18

Asher Price. Asher M. Price. Mrs. Asher *Per*-ice.

She said the surname as if it were two syllables. She tried to trill the 'r's" like Lupe, but couldn't manage it.

Although Gus and Newman weren't forthcoming, between then and the day the she collided with The Gentleman in the street, she had found out just about every thing there was to know about the infamous Mr. Asher M. Price. A lot of what she learned had come from Lupe. Who would have guessed that such a bad-tempered little *bruja* would be such a fountain of gossip? A shared interest in other people's business very nearly made them friends.

As for Mr. Price, people said that he had murdered his wife in Nantucket and that because of it he had been cast out by the Quakers. He had to travel all the way to California to escape the law and carried a gun beneath his coat in case the authorities came for him. And he owned a flotilla of ships. Her father was his business partner—or at least owed him money.

"Asher M. Price," she repeated.

Did the "M." stand for murderer? It didn't matter. He was rich, nefarious, and gallant—how could any man be more intriguing?

She hurried to her father to confront him, but all he wanted to know was if she came through the teakwood doors.

"Did you come through the teakwood doors?" Newman repeated."

He knew she did. There was only two ways to enter his office. One was from the side door that opened directly into the room. The other was from the saloon itself. She only actually came through the side door when she carried him his lunch. Regardless, he asked her the same question every day. Instead of arguing, she ignored it. There were other things on her mind—so much so that she had temporarily set aside her memoirs.

He was not to be put off, asking again, "Well, did you?"

It was clear that Newman Chase wasn't a pretentious man. In fact, in most ways he was remarkably sensible. However she had reached the end of her tether about his preoccupation with her not coming through his blessed Malaysian doors. When she asked why she had to skulk through the back door like a domestic, he mumbled something about "unfitting of a lady." That was complete claptrap of course. Everything that went on was easily seen from her perch behind the bar.

"Jehosephat's brother! If you're so ashamed of being a saloonkeeper, Poppa, why don't you close down and open a haberdashery? Lord knows the gentlemen in this town could use some tailoring."

His glare was withering enough to peel paint. But she knew it was coming and turned her back. She had already deduced that being ignored drove him batty. (No doubt that was how her mother must have got the best of him too.) It didn't matter whether his look scolded her for her language or her disrespect. Neither was the point. He was a bit late when it came to fathering her and she didn't mind reminding him of it. This day, she didn't care to argue.

"I believe I ran into your business partner the other day near the square."

"What? *What*?" he yelped. "When were you at the square?"

Without answering, she flipped her curls and flounced away. He didn't get up. His stomach had been bothering him and he silently wondered if he might do better to walk up the thoroughfare and take his meals at a new restaurant. The Deluxe was too free with the peppers. Annabella had said there was a new Italian place. Perhaps, he thought, he should take her there.

Directly, he went out to the bar and found his daughter long gone. Gus sipped chicory coffee and poured him a cup. He told him about Annabella's excursion to Portsmouth Square. Gus didn't look surprised. It seemed that more and more of their conversations weren't about how to make money off the strike, but how to keep Annabella out of trouble.

"How am I gonna get her to stay put?" moaned Newman. "She's just a girl. She's too young to be looking for a suitor."

Behind his cup, Gus shook his head. "Wishful thinking ain't gonna keep her that way. Besides, she could do worse than Asher."

Gus thought maybe a husband was the answer to it all. He liked Mr. Price—his secrets notwithstanding. Most of the men in town were either miscreants or on the run from their past, and that included him and Newman. So far Annabella's boredom caused them only a small price beyond consternation. Her openness was how they came by their new piano player. Patrick Coffin was a hair more trouble than a sick hound. He wasn't a rogue, so he had to be trying to escape from something. He claimed delicate health. Gus suspected he had attained a preference for absinthe, but he wasn't one to butt in. Although Patrick came in to play long after Annabella went back to the hotel, the first thing out of his mouth was always to ask where she was.

If he missed her, he sighed, "We sure as hell don't deserve such a divine treasure, do we Mr. G?"

Patrick's vernacular was an idiosyncratic work in progress. It had become an odd blend of the profane and the correct. Although he had watched Annabella swirl around like the Queen of May, he had nothing but admiration for her and her ways. To him, Gus and Newman attempt at curbing her wild streak was blasphemous. He was happy to join the conversation uninvited.

"Leave the child alone, she is a goddess," he said.

Newman leaned on the bar and sipped from his coffee cup, lost in memories, "You should've seen her mother..."

Seeing an opening to make a point, Gus asked him, "Was she as smart as Annabella?"

"No, Bella's charm was in her face."

Gus took a breath and said, "Smart ain't the same thing as wise, Newman."

"Well of course it ain't," retorted Newman. Now he realized they were not just in a conversation, but a philosophical discussion. Newman learned his scriptures at his dear mother's knee. Gus's education was more informal. As it was his forte, Newman relished any opportunity to quote the bible.

"She don't need to be wise." Girding his memory, he added, "Ecclesiastes says, 'In much wisdom is much grief: and he that increaseth knowledge increaseth sorrow.' All that little girl has to do is listen to her Poppa."

Gus was getting tired of listening to a man—who hadn't stepped foot in a church for twenty years—quote the bible. He shrugged though and took another sip of his coffee. That wasn't Newman's only irritating inclination. When it came to women, he thought his failed marriage made him an expert on them too. So far as Newman was concerned, no female should be smarter than a man. It wasn't God's plan. He said Annabella would marry a man of his choosing and produce a half-dozen grandchildren for him.

"All of this, of course," Gus deadpanned. "Would be without engaging in sexual congress?"

Newman snorted.

As Gus saw it, that harebrained fantasy was only half the problem. The front door of the *Bella* wasn't the problem either. Once the sexes were in sniffing distance, trouble was a foregone conclusion. Sooner or later Annabella would be attracted to one of the whalers, gamblers, or opportunists who were crowding into port. Compared to them, Asher Price (dead wife and all) was positively a saint.

Gus hoped the heat of amour would happen later for Annabella rather than sooner. The men around the Bella were ignorant, crude, and hygienically compromised. Fortunately, she despised ill-kempt men. So it stood to reason that the first smooth-talker who didn't stink to high heaven would seduce her. Annabella read way too much of that bloody Byron for him not to be worried about that. That memoir business wasn't much help either. There were too many blank pages. They lay there all white and empty, just taunting her to fill them.

Unfortunately, Gus wasn't actually behind the bar when a confusion of lust and love really struck Annabella, so he didn't even have a chance to issue a warning.

It wouldn't have helped.

19

Few people would have faulted the Goodenows if they had washed their hands of their reckless granddaughter for running off to her cursed father like she did. But they had their reasons. First and foremost, she was a Goodenow. Her father was a scoundrel who lured his poor innocent daughter to come to his side. Simon Goodenow all but hissed when he spoke the name of Newman Chase. Even when he was married to their dear Bella, all the haberdashers in Boston couldn't make him gentleman. Their granddaughter was flighty, but Simon Goodenow refused to concede her to him yet. Give her time and she would come home to good society.

Annabella wanted to keep that window open too. Although she had no intention of returning to Boston, she was not about to burn such a lucrative bridge. The west was barbaric when it came to the latest fashions. It wasn't easy to get work boots, much less those lovely little niceties necessary to soothe a young lady's furrowed brow. When the first shops popped up, they would no doubt carry garish corsets and Spanish shawls. Annabella had her standards and set about mending the rift with her grandparents as soon as possible.

For a flighty girl, her letter to them was a cunning piece of work. It dripped with contrition and oozed self-reproach.

When her letter arrived, Mr. Goodenow huffed a bit. Her grandmother, however, was just happy to learn that she was on semi-American soil and not a slave in some Turkish potentate's harem. To celebrate, she immediately sent off a batch of dresses. Frontier or not, one must be properly attired. If Annabella wasn't well-dressed, how would any of the locals recognize her as quality?

That first package arrived approximately the same time as the town's first postal agent. Mail couldn't be delivered beyond San Francisco, so stacks of mail accumulated at an alarming rate. It was absolute luck that the name Chase was recognized and sent over to her.

The box contained a blue poplin dress and a pink shawl her grandmother had crocheted herself. Under usual circumstances, Annabella might not have liked the shawl. But it was soft and warm and therefore a surprising comfort from the cool evening breezes.

The dress was a triumph. It was cornflower blue and the bodice was far too small. She was delighted at the cleavage it produced. The pink shawl she threw across her chest until the time was ripe for the great bosom unveiling at the Bella. Although she was tempted to send Lupe over to make certain there was a proper audience, she was too excited to wait. She scurried across the street and was disappointed that the place was all but deserted. Patrick and Gus were not to be seen. The sole occupants were a quartet of men sitting at a table playing cards.

They were sailors—or from the looks of them—whalers. Only months before the Bella's customers were almost exclusively seamen. She watched as prospectors overran the place. It was easy to tell the difference. It was all in the eyes. Those looking to pan for gold had wide, excited expressions. In their dreams they had already spent a fortune of nuggets. The seamen looked all the same—besides muscular forearms. They had scorched skin and crinkled, blistered eyes.

One of the men sitting at the table was tall and extremely well-built. His enormous biceps bulged from a sleeveless shirt. It was bleached white by the sun and the armhole had loose threads surrounding the opening almost like fringe. He was heavily tattooed. Perhaps he was Maori, they had handsome skin decorations. None of the sailors noticed her.

She boldly tossed her shawl aside and looked in the mirror behind the bar. From that angle, the dress was a little too revealing, so she tucked a lace hanky in her cleavage and inspected the effect. As she arranged it, she happened to see the reflection of several pairs of eyes staring at her. Because she had been so engrossed in the one whaler and his huge biceps, she had not taken much notice of his companions.

Newly self-conscious, she busied herself by rearranging a few glasses and wondered where Gus and Patrick had wandered off to. Soon a voice called out to her.

"A new dress is it, lassie?"

Their usual patrons wouldn't dare speak to her like that. It was important not to encourage such foolishness. As she lined up a row of whiskey glasses, she ignored the inquiry. It was useless to try to teach a bunch of whalers some manners. Like other sailors, they were coarse and rude.

The man spoke to her again, "I say, that is a lovely dress, lassie."

Frowning, her cheeks began to blaze. Where was Gus when she needed him?

"Oh no, boys," said the voice, "I fear I've riled her. Heaven help us all if she takes a mind to come this way."

Try as she might, she couldn't help but look in his direction. Although she glared, he smiled back at her. His were the most arresting eyes she had ever had seen. They were at once fiery and translucent. Stunned, she looked back down, silently damning all men and their impertinent eyes. As she did, she heard the sound of a chair legs scraping back and the footfalls of soft boots as they scuffed across the wooden floor in her direction. Although she knew she should just leave, her feet seemed glued to the floor.

The rush of color spread to her ears. Suddenly, she couldn't recall whether her bosom was covered or not, so she stuck the end of Gus's bar rag into her cleavage for good measure.

The man with the opalescent eyes stood so near her, she could hear him breathing. Heat—of the sort she had never encountered—emanated from him. Perspiration formed on her upper lip. Without thinking, she dabbed at it with the end of the bar rag. More deliberately, she looked at him out of the corner of her eye. He wore an ankle-length coat cinched at the waist with a thick leather strop. The buttons on the placket of his shirt were undone, exposing a deep golden vee of skin.

Softly, he said, "With apologies to the rose, but I do not believe that I have seen anything quite so exquisite in all my days."

By then, she gave up a semblance of indifference and look at him openly. A leather string was around his neck. A shark tooth hung from it and nestled at the base of his throat. It was fastened so tightly that it bobbed up and down with his Adam's apple as he spoke. This transfixed her, holding her gaze like a vise. Still, she managed several deductions. The first of which was that his voice was a cultured one. He was unusually tall, with wide shoulders. His sleeves were rolled up, so she could even see that his forearms were strong and even more tanned than his neck.

Finally wresting her eyes away, she returned to fussing with the whiskey glasses, turning them first one way and then the other. The man gave her a low, almost theatrical, bow. The red and white stocking cap that had been riding on the back of his head was then gallantly swept across his midsection. Her knees felt weak.

"Forgive my manners, for I am too long at sea to remember them as I should."

Annabella could not stop her eyelashes from fluttering. She might even have giggled. He said something else to her, but she could not hear it for the roaring in her ears. He extended her his hand and she took it following him wordlessly to a table on the far side of the room. She felt herself beguiled—as if he had a flute and she had no will.

After some time, Gus returned. Annabella didn't see him. She was still sitting with the sailor, listening raptly to his every word. He sat back in his chair, one ankle hooked nonchalantly across the other. Gus had seen him in the *Bella* before. He always came with a group of his mates. It was clear that he was the big dog of the pack. They all vied for his attention and approval.

Gus stood watching them for a moment. Then he did the unlikely. Looking skyward, he issued a fervent prayer.

"Lord have mercy on us all."

20

The evening rush was beginning and Gus had filled a half dozen beer glasses before Annabella saw he was back. With studied nonchalance, she rose and walked over to the bar. Her new friend had introduced himself as Aaron Ainsworth, first mate on the whaling vessel, the *Mary Thayer*. When she left, he returned to the table with his mates. He said something and they all laughed. Then, simultaneously, all of the whalers stood and Aaron led them out of the door. If Gus noticed the defection, he didn't say so. Instead, he looked at Annabella's bosom.

Pointing to the bar rag still hanging down her mid-section, he asked, "What the blazes is that?"

Realizing that she had forgotten about it—and that it was there all the while she talked to Aaron—she was temporarily flustered.

"Oh, that."

Grabbing the end, she pulled it out and plopped it back on the bar so swiftly that she very nearly gave herself an odd kind of rope burn. She winced, but Gus didn't see that. He picked up the cloth by a corner and eyed her bulging bosom. Turning sideways, she put an elbow on the bar and tried to change the subject.

Pointing towards where she had sat with Aaron, she asked. "Did you see that gentleman just there?"

"Gentleman?" Gus repeated still a bit confounded.

She ignored him, saying, "That was Mr. Aaron Ainsworth."

Gus nodded.

"He is a fascinating sort."

"Oh," said Gus uneasily. "Looked like a whaler to me."

"He isn't a mere sailor, but from New York City and its society."

She related every bit of his biography to Gus, employing a breathy whisper so as not to be overheard. With great deliberation, Gus poured himself a cup of coffee. Annabella wasn't pleased with his lack of enthusiasm.

"This man is not just a *whaler*! His ship is the *Mary Thayer*. Can you imagine someone of his sensitivity and breeding daring to engage in such a dangerous occupation?"

"Can't say that I have."

She gushed, "He does not sully his heart with thoughts of gold! No! He loves the sea!"

Gus was unmoved by Mr. Ainsworth's aesthetic sensibilities.

"His mother is still living, but his father is dead. He had three sisters. He contracted scarlet fever as a boy. The disease took his only brother who, poor child, was but *three years old*. An uncle was so impressed with his keen mind that he funded a year at Yale College, but he was determined not to waste his youth and work himself into an early grave like his father."

She paused, but only to catch her breath.

"He vowed that his own career would be one of romance and danger. It would not do for him to be a commodore or captain—for both of which he is highly qualified. He said he has always known himself to be 'something of a salt.' But he forgoes the distinction of such offices to those who covet them. He calls himself a gypsy of the sea!"

Gus had heard enough.

"No one but an educated man who escaped from a family of substance could describe himself like that with a straight face," he harrumphed.

"He could have claimed a captainship," reminded Annabella.

"As if bragging about it makes him admirable," snorted Gus.

Ignoring that, she leaned closer, "In truth, he says he is a *novelist*! He hopes to make his way in the world by his pen alone!"

"I see," Gus said. "He's unpublished..."

Annabella gasped incredulously, "Do you see? Do you, Gus? I too am a writer!"

Seeing his sour expression, she knew enough not to waste further thoughts of destiny, instead she confided, "Aaron doesn't fancy those respectable employments that lesser men enjoy. He must be free in thought and spirit."

"Admirable goals," replied Gus, expressionless.

"When he has no money in his purse, he doesn't throw himself on his knife as did Cato, but takes to the sea! Can you imagine anything more romantic?"

"Yes, I can," Gus said, "But then I didn't just fall off the turnip wagon."

Annabella bristled, "Nor have I."

"Listen to yourself, m'love. You might have a different opinion," advised Gus.

"Do you know why the Persians believe the sea is holy?"

"Can't say that I do," replied Gus honestly.

With pinched self-righteousness, she retorted, "I thought not."

Taking a sip of coffee, Gus said, "I shall never forgive myself for my ignorance."

Annabella gave him a dour look, but couldn't stay angry.

She said knowingly, "He admires *you*, Gus."

"What?" Gus spat out before he could stop himself, "I never spoke a word to the feller before!"

"He says you are a man of knowledge and wit."

"I'm not one to argue with conclusions I happen to agree with," smiled Gus. "He didn't also remark on what a handsome bugger I am did he?"

"Well, not in so many words," Annabella hedged.

"Lucky me, if he finds me all that attractive," Gus said with a raised eyebrow, "Perhaps his predilection does not favor the feminine sex."

"Gus!" cried Annabella with frustration.

It looked as if she might come to tears. Momentarily, Gus thought it was a ploy. But he realized that Annabella never cried. It was a matter of pride.

Taking her hand affectionately, he crooned, "Ah, Annie, my sweet, you know that I'm only looking out for you. Don't fall for this feller. A sailor is gone years at a time—even the sweet-talking ones."

Gathering her dignity, Annabella replied, "I am not in the market for a lover. I merely admired his pluck."

"His pluck," laughed Gus, "His *pluck*! Is that what they call it these days?"

Miffed, she said, "I think you need to see to the real miscreants in here,"

"Yeah," said Gus softly, "there are larceners enough. If you don't want to get robbed, you gotta sit on your money-roll and hang onto your heart."

But she was gone.

✧

Although he wasn't personally acquainted with the sailors of the *Mary Thayer*, Gus still knew them. Their lives were not their own. They belonged to the right, the sperm, and the bowhead whales. Their souls, however, belonged to the ship's owner, Asher Price.

"Take care of this ship, she cost Mr. Price five thousand dollars to build," said her captain, Mr. Weeks.

Most American whalers were Cape Cod boys. Those who had proudly served on the *Thayer* had done so since they were adolescents. Others were just desperate for work. Those were the ones most likely to jump ship the minute they caught sight of a bare-breasted native girl. Lust wasn't always behind such mutiny—it was merely the most face-saving reason. A whaler's life wasn't for everyone.

Aaron Ainsworth was the only man aboard ship who was truly in command of his own fate. The others both envied and admired him for that. That wasn't why he was their de facto leader on shore too. To a man, the shipmates were virile and perspicacious. They followed behind Aaron like so many ducklings anyway. Command wasn't an easily definable trait. Either a man had it, or he didn't. Aaron Ainsworth was a man of considerable sway.

In a pantomime that was becoming a familiar street theater, Aaron and the rest of the crew had scurried ashore and scattered excitedly up the street as soon as they weighed anchor in San Francisco Bay. Not a dozen steps up the way, they slowed, astonished by the changes. They had heard that it wasn't called Yerba Buena anymore and an American flag could be seen flapping atop the flagpole on the square. But seeing all the new saloons, gambling dens, and wanton women in such a familiar setting was startling. These masters of sea beasts wanted, even needed, to collect themselves before confronting the changes and looked for a familiar landmark. As they walked up Clay Street, they were relieved to see the *Bella Goode* still in business.

The place had been empty, but Aaron grabbed a bottle from the behind the bar and they all took turns swigging from it. It was several hours before they relaxed enough to want to shuffle some cards. No one put money on the table. Theirs wasn't a game of chance. It was a pretense of normalcy. They knew they weren't like other men and prided themselves for that. After all, they gambled more than their pocket money every day of their lives.

They hadn't even begun to be drunk when Annabella Chase arrived. No one was a bit surprised that Aaron made for her right away. When it came to wooing women, he took the lead. He walked as if he was the finest-hung man who sailed the Seven Seas. That wasn't true. He proved what every man, even Gus Gerlache, knew. The size of a man's phallus wasn't what really mattered.

It was balls.

21

"Did you come through the teak doors?"

Rolling her eyes, Annabella said, "What if I did?"

Newman hadn't meant to begin with a confrontation. If she hadn't come to him, he would have gone looking for her. Both had harbored innocent airs and ulterior motives. But that bone of contention reared its ugly head before either could put their schemes into place.

Her tone hadn't been respectful. Before Newman could rebuke her, she turned her head quizzically.

"Who has been here?" she asked bluntly.

"What?" asked Newman, buying time to think of a defense.

His unease provoked a small cough.

"I mean exactly what I said," she said irritably. "*That odor*. I smell tobacco and it isn't yours or Gus's."

"Since when do my visitors have to answer to you?" he snapped.

Then, he rethought his belligerence.

Mildly, he said, "Mr. Price happened by is all. It was a social visit, nothing more."

He knew his denial was premature before it left his lips. Under his breath, he cursed his slip.

"I thought," She said curtly, "that you were *business* acquaintances."

Asher Price had been seen coming in and out of her father's office for days. Although she did not look in that man's direction, she could feel his eyes on her as he passed by. Compared to the other ne'er-do-wells in San Francisco, Mr. Price was an attractive man. The very thought of his infamy had been a titillation. Who wouldn't be drawn to the romanticism of a tragic past? But that was before she had met Aaron Ainsworth—in all his erotic glory. Now she was immediately suspicious as to why her father would misrepresent Mr. Price's visit.

"He's a murderer, you know," she announced.

"He is *not* a murderer," Newman responded wearily.

He was already tired just thinking of the row they were about to have.

"The man is a poor widower's all. We should offer him our pity and Christian charity."

Shuddering theatrically, Annabella said, "I've seen him up on that parapet. It's as if he guarding against his wife's ghost."

Newman's voice remained even. "Everything I know of him shows him to be a kind and good man."

Annabella snorted, "Are we speaking of the same person? Is this the same poor widower who walks these gentle streets wearing a side-arm? Surely you jest!"

With a defensive clip to his voice, Newman replied, "Mr. Price has never once drawn it on anyone."

She raised her eyebrows, "Do we truly know that?"

"We would have heard. San Francisco is hardly the badlands," he answered. "We have a newspaper, fergodsake."

"Mail doesn't come regularly."

Newman ignored that. "This country is thick with claim jumpers and such. Now if it's murderers you want, I can tell you of Jose Carrillo..."

"They say Mr. Price has never spoken of his wife," said Annabella quietly.

"What if he hasn't?" he retorted.

Wives and whether or not their deaths were mourned was a touchy subject to her. Her father named his bloody saloon after her mother, but never said a word about her. It was not an omission easy to overlook.

"That means nothing," insisted Newman. "Asher Price is a sensible man and far and away more suitable than that riff-raff you been sittin' with out there."

Newman tossed his head in the direction of the bar room. Immediately, Annabella stiffened. So, Gus *had* told him. She should have known better than twitter away like she had. That would teach her. Drat. A more prudent person would have beat a hasty retreat, but she did so like to have the last word.

"Mr. Ainsworth is not riff-raff. If you must know, he is a man of education and culture," she said defiantly.

"He's a harpooner on a whaler. I don't care how many books he's read!" spat out Newman.

She wanted to correct the notion that Aaron was a harpooner

rather than first mate, but she didn't dare. It had been a tactical error to show her cards so early. The last thing she wanted was for her love life to become the fodder for bar room chitchat. She mentally stamped her foot that it was just that. A dignified withdrawal was called for, but her parting salvo was an outright lie.

"Aaron Ainsworth holds no interest for me."

"If not, do think of Mr. Price. He's not really a bad fellow at all," Newman suggested.

By obtaining a denial of her feelings for the whaler, Newman thought he had done quite well for Mr. Price. It took him a while to realize that by the time their conversation had ended. Mr. Price's worth as a suitor had slid from a fine, upstanding business man to a wife-beating murderer with a short fuse. Her interest in him was history.

"He is not all that bad a fellow" is hardly a glowing recommendation," she snapped. "I know you, Poppa! I know what you are up to!"

What was a responsible father to do? To allow her to remain in these increasingly wicked surroundings in an unmarried state was unthinkable. Gus had won him over on that point. The gold strike was not letting up. There were veins far richer than anyone's imagination. Aureate hysteria had turned once rational and civil men into little more than jackals. Had Annabella arrived more recently, he would have sent her back to Boston on the first conveyance in that direction. But it was too late for that. The very thought of sending her away gave him a catch in his throat.

"But Annie darlin', I only have your best interest at heart," implored Newman.

She snorted again.

Newman shuffled a bit in his chair. He decided he would wait her out. That was folly, of course. Folding her arms, Annabella jutted her chin belligerently. In the face of this overt hostility, he pushed back his chair and stood.

"You will do as I say, young lady," he announced. "San Francisco is too wicked for you to remain here without a husband. I have *decreed* it."

"I do not *choose* to marry," said she. "And when I do choose to marry, it will be to a man I love."

"A man you love!" he spat. "Like that bloody sailor?"

All the color first drained from her face, then made a sharp turn upward once again.

Newman was a very savvy businessman. He knew when time was to pack his wares and make tracks. Ergo, conjuring a wounded expression, he decided it was time to cajole.

"Annie, my dear Annie. Can you not grant your poor, aging Poppa this last request?"

"Next thing I see will be you clutching at your chest and keening!" she huffed. "Since you have introduced the subject, let me be perfectly clear—even your dead body won't make me marry Asher Price!"

With that she strode angrily from the room.

To Newman's mind, a union forged by nothing but silly romanticism was the road to disaster. It had left Bella with another man's bean up her spout and him with a wife who never learned to love him. But he didn't dare invoke poor, dead Bella's name. He'd tried hard to keep sentimentality out of his search for a son-in-law. Since Annabella wasn't about to listen, he made for Gus and explained his reasoning carefully to him.

"I didn't just consider Price's social and financial situation," he said. "Moral turpitude is essential for a husband."

Gus puffed his pipe, silent.

Newman continued, "Granted, some say that Asher quit the Quakers. But then, who among us is in a position to criticize a man for falling away from the church?"

Gus nodded.

"Annie has to be kept in luxury. It's all she knows. I can't let her live off a whaler's portion, now can I?"

Gus shook his head.

"Price'll build her a house up on the hill. We'll sit in her parlor with a teacup balanced on my knee and watch my grandbabies frolic around my feet."

Just the thought of the grandchildren sure to come cheered Newman. His eyes glazed over as he thought of their golden-haired beauty. They would be boys. Surely God above would not burden him with another female's capriciousness. Besides, by the time Annabella had her family, all this gold rush business would be over and done with. They would all have made their fortunes and San Francisco would be peaceful again. The *Bella Goode* would be an emporium of fine liquors and wine.

Coming back to his senses, he whispered, "We gotta nail this deal down. If we don't strike while the iron was hot, Asher might send for a wife from Nantucket."

"What do you mean 'we'?" retorted Gus.

Newman ignored him, "Plenty of men do that out west. Nice New England girls are bringing top money. Why at this very moment the

Price family might be interviewing prospective wives."

Gus raised both eyebrows, "I think you're jumping the gun, old pard..."

"Time," Newman hissed, "is of the essence. We have to nip her infatuation with this weasel before they ... they ... get carried away."

Nothing Gus said could sway him. If anything, Newman picked up a head of steam. At the very first chance, he cornered Annabella. She had been leaning dejectedly against the bar, her chin resting against her right fist.

"You still mooning after that damned Algerine?"

The words had no more than left his lips than she bristled. However, she had no idea what he meant by "Algerine." She only knew that it was an aspersion against Aaron Ainsworth. So without altering her position, she turned her eyes towards Gus for him to interpret.

Gus obliged her, explaining, "He means 'Algerian." You know, Algeria—where all the pirates come from."

Annabella rolled her eyes once more, but didn't waste a scowl on her father. Rather, she patted Gus's hand in silent thanks and regally walked away. As she left, Gus looked grumpily in Newman's direction. A more obtuse man he had never recalled.

Pouring another cup of coffee, he said, "I know three things for sure, Newman."

"Oh, yeah," Newman said smugly, "What's that?"

"You never slap a man who's chewing tobacco."

"Oh, yeah," Newman counted one.

"Never kick a cow chip on a hot day."

That was two.

"And never," here Gus paused, "*Never* try to teach a pig to sing."

Newman then narrowed his eyes, readying himself. "And why is that?"

"It wastes your time and annoys the pig."

22

Fire was every family's greatest fear. Such disasters were prevalent in all climes, but a particular threat to wood-shingled New England homes. They began in a flash and were well nigh impossible to extinguish.

No one knew what actually caused the one that demolished Asher Price's home. The fireplace was always a chief suspect. Had Asher still lived under Quakerism's tenets, no one would have questioned that probability. (As his household was under the influence of a Congregationalist, many people believed it was not run with frugality.) Gossipers concluded that the culprit in this fire had been a flagrant overuse of whale oil lamps.

Regardless how it began, the blaze had moved so quickly and burned so completely, there weren't many clues to draw on. A line of men attempted to quell the flames with buckets of water from the horse trough. But it was no use. No one realized that Asher had been beating on a rear door—or that it disintegrated as he did. When he was found, his hands were charred and he was left stupefied by the horror. At the time, his trauma was not a surprise. It was only later when the whispers began.

All three stories of the handsome house had caved into the cellar. It was impossible to really know who was where when the fire broke out, but neighbors testified to hearing screams. Granted, in such a catastrophe it was not unusual for recollections to be muddled, but the possibility of victims being burned alive was too awful for loved ones to contemplate. A gold signet ring identified Cora Price's body. Another body was found in the rubble near hers. It was never identified and was buried unclaimed. Who he was and why he was there was the topic of many backdoor conversations.

Asher's hands were slathered with salve and wrapped with gauze until they were the size of melons. Amputation had been a serious consideration. He refused that solution just as he refused laudanum to ease his pain. When he declined to attend his wife's funeral it was excused—poor man had to be half-mad with grief. Although he was welcomed, he didn't accompany his parents to church meetings in the future weeks. All his days were spent sitting in a chair offered by a kind neighbor. He sat there looking out the window, staring sullenly at the ashes of his home. His nights were filled with nightmares so persistent that he soon refused to lie in bed at all.

In time it was expected, even demanded, that he show public signs of sadness, he refused. Friends and family were at a loss to account for it. A formal investigation absolved him of any fault, but unkind innuendos began to make the rounds. Marital misconduct was not ruled out. Through it all, Asher remained mute. Although he had inhaled smoke and coughed up smut for weeks, his voice was unaffected. It wasn't that he couldn't speak; it was that he wouldn't.

Asher walked sullenly down the streets of Nantucket as if daring to be accused. Some saw that as courage. Others thought it was an ugly sort of audacity. No one, however, put a question to him. He wasn't a large man, but his path cleared with remarkable speed. His flinty gaze kept any confrontations at bay.

Asher Price's people were what others called Quakers with a Vengeance. He had always had the purposeful gait of a man who carried the weight of a hundred old annuitants and fatherless children on his shoulders. Old Mr. Price's true love was the sea. Asher had always been the bookkeeper. It was under his stewardship that the Price family fortunes improved from merely comfortable to very comfortable indeed.

So when Obadiah Price said, "Fighting whispers is like pounding sand down a rat-hole, son. Time to begin anew."

Asher realized that his father was right. A change of scenery would do him good—and the farther away, the better.

23

Adelaide Perry did not have the gift of a father's wisdom.

Not that her father wasn't wise. He had been a kind man—and wise in his own way. Adelaide had adored him. Had she been older when her mother died, she might have been able to look after him like her mother had. Unfortunately, her mother's untimely passing left Mr. Perry quite lonely and rudderless. That meant he had been susceptible to his friends' badgering that he remarry as soon as possible.

"Fill the gap," they said.

After all, he had a daughter to think of and she was but a child.

Everyone agreed. Neighbors, relatives, and even the pastor—they all said that Mr. Perry was obliged—even *required*—to take another wife. Little Addie had needed a mother. Mr. Perry couldn't argue the logic. His daughter was growing up and he hadn't a clue how to raise a young lady. Yes, everyone was right. There was no sense putting it off. He would remarry as soon as possible.

Mr. Perry was a sensitive, loving man, but unused to making pragmatic decisions. Therefore, it was bad luck all round that the very first time he did, he bungled it.

Not that it was noticeable to anyone else. After all, second marriages were often ones of convenience. It wasn't unusual for a man to look within his household for someone to run it. The only woman handy in the Perry house however, was their cook, Enid Stackpole. She was friendly with Adelaide and knew what he liked to eat, so she seemed to him like a reasonable choice.

Mrs. Stackpole had been widowed for a dozen years—or at least she hadn't seen Mr. Stackpole for that long. (General thought was that he was swept down the swollen Merrimack River one extraordinarily rainy spring.) In her youth she was buxom, red-headed and good-natured. Generous with her charms, it was no surprise that men had flocked to her. Time, however, had faded her hair and widened her hips. She couldn't command the attention she once could. There were few situations for a middle-aged woman with a poor reputation. Although her culinary gifts were a bit wanting, she sought work as a cook. Fortunately, the Perry's had not been demanding employers. The only one hard for her to please was that dratted girl, Adelaide. Since her mother's passing, she had become even more ornery than before.

When Mr. Perry up and asked her to be his wife. Mrs. Stackpole had been astonished. She had believed that her charms had left her. Indeed, she was shocked near speechless (no small feat for a person of her loquacity). Thinking he might change his mind at any moment, she spent no time on coquetry. Grasping the good man's lapels, she enthusiastically blubbered her consent.

That little deed completed, Mr. Perry happily toddled off to tell Adelaide the good news.

Enid Stackpole was taken completely unawares that Mr. Perry secretly coveted her person. She celebrated by grabbing the cooking sherry and taking a generous swig. Wiping her mouth with the back of her hand, she tossed aside her apron and emitted an eructation long and loud enough to call in the cows. Then, she was ready as any other lady to take Mr. Perry's hand in holy matrimony.

Adelaide, however, was unexpectedly under-whelmed by the whole project. Mr. Perry tried to explain that he wasn't marrying Enid because he hadn't loved her mother. It was that he *had*. She couldn't be replaced in his heart. But his daughter didn't understand that. She believed that he was not only replacing her mother, he was replacing her. That was why she did everything she knew to stop it, alternately screaming and sulking. This only led her father to believe that it was even more urgent to have a female in charge of her.

Although Enid was about six-foot this side of cunning, she knew that it was important to win Adelaide over. She didn't realize that in this she was at a distinct disadvantage. For every time poor Adelaide looked at the cook, she was reminded of the night her mother died—and Enid's hand reaching toward her, urging her to take the knife.

"I don't see why you have to marry my father," Adelaide complained to Enid. "You already live here anyway."

"No, you don't understand," Enid Stackpole smirked. "Men have their needs."

Adelaide soon realized that Enid was right. It was an inescapable truth—even for the kind and dutiful Mr. Perry. Men did have needs. Once the marriage took place, Adelaide heard Mr. Perry's needs being met six nights a week. Her walls reverberated with every rhythmic bounce of the matrimonial mattress. And with each bounce, the new Mrs. Perry squealed with delight.

It both scandalized and confused poor Adelaide. Mashing her face deep into her pillow, she cried the impotent wails of the truly deserted.

Was that bedroom folderol not insult enough, Adelaide soon learned that along with a new mother, she also gained a stepbrother. Actually, the stepson came as a bit of a surprise to Mr. Perry too but he didn't tell anyone that. He was too embarrassed for anyone to know that his position of master of the house had been overruled so quickly. So he allowed the boy to move into room above his daughter's and pretended he had not been duped.

To Adelaide, it was just one more betrayal. Her father finally had the son he so wanted.

And Eduard Stackpole was a big, strapping boy, indeed. As he was four years older than Adelaide, Mr. Perry suggested that Eduard could be his new sister's protector. Mr. Perry knew his daughter must be fearful, for he had seen the knife she kept under her pillow.

That was undeniable. Adelaide did have a knife under her pillow. As her father suspected, it wasn't a ghoulish souvenir of her mother's death, but a weapon. Yet it wasn't there to ward off some nameless assailant. It had a specific purpose. Still plagued by self-condemnation for her blasphemous raging against her dear, departed mother and baby brother, she was wanted to be prepared for retribution. She kept the knife there long after she knew it would be useless against God's vengeance. She realized that the Lord had other plans. He did not intend to smite her directly; he sent minions to do it for him.

✧

At one time, the kitchen, with its reassuring aromas, had been Adelaide's favorite place to read. That changed when Eduard Stackpole moved in. He spent most of his time at the kitchen table knuckle-rolling a quarter and showing off his handsome head of hair. Despite Mr. Perry's hopes, he wasn't the protective type. His nature leaned towards the predatory.

Nor was the new Mrs. Perry interested in mothering the issue of the old Mrs. Perry either. She, however, was not as overtly predacious as her son. She simply ignored Adelaide. In return, Adelaide despised them all. She felt that way for quite a while, hating Enid Stackpole, Enid Stackpole's spawn, her father and God (in that order) with a single-mindedness rarely seen of one so young.

Most inopportunely, a pair of perky little breasts popped up on her chest. When they did, she was very annoyed. It attracted very unwanted attention. Eduard took such heed that someone might as well have poked him in the ribs with a stick. Suddenly, homely, bookish Adelaide Perry became quite arresting to him. He hovered around her like a hummingbird, plying her with compliments and vying for her company. In time, the under-appreciated and naive Adelaide surrendered to the handsome young Master Eduard—he with the golden locks and exotic name.

Whether Enid Perry knew what was going on right under her nose was a question that would bother Adelaide in years to come. At the time, however, evading her stepmother was her all-consuming passion—well, second to Eduard.

If Enid did not see, it was by design. She was very busy herself wrenching all the money she could from Mr. Perry before he up and died on her. On the short side of fifty, Mr. Perry was becoming feebler day by day. He had fallen mysteriously ill soon after their wedding. He lost weight and his complexion turned sallow. Had anyone been around to notice, they might have found something sinister in the timing. But as the second Mrs. Perry turned callers away, claiming Mr. Perry was merely the victim of a particularly nasty head cold, no one was there to protest. Especially blind was Adelaide. She was far too busy to notice her father hunched in a rocker.

She had embarked on a torrid little affair that was just this side of incest.

She had been wrong about one thing. God didn't send these minions; they came straight from the devil.

24

It was as if every daydream Annabella Chase had enjoyed back in Boston had come true.

Once she had Aaron Ainsworth in her sights, she didn't waste any of her time worrying about her father's disapproval or Asher Price's gaze. She was more concerned with the bevy of indecently clad women arriving daily to ply their mercenary charms on the Bella's customers.

One of them was more aggressive than all the others combined. She had dark red hair and wore a bright blue feather boa wrapped twice around her neck. She had shown up only a couple of days before, introducing herself as Mrs. Gaspard. But Annabella had heard men calling her "Dovie." She had half a mind to have Gus run her off. Aaron wasn't there, but he could come in at any minute.

Having been a beauty all her life, Annabella was used to turning heads. All she had to do was come from behind the bar and she had every man in the place licking their lips. But Mrs. Gaspard could steal her thunder by merely taking a stroll across the room. Her walk was a masterwork in seduction—half sultry, half guileless. Annabella had never seen such a provocative promenade in all her born days.

Unhappy to be one-upped, she glowered at her.

When Dovie threw the end of her blue boa over her shoulder and plopped her bosom on the bar, Annabella knew she had lost the battle. Even Gus gawked.

Miffed, Annabella went to complain to Patrick, "I swear, if that woman gets her bosom any higher she'll smother herself."

Patrick let her talk. She might not like the competition, but Dovie wasn't truly a rival. She had nothing on Annabella but mileage. He was convinced that if Annabella devoted herself to making a man hers, the others didn't stand a chance. Perhaps she didn't exactly know what she would do with him once she got him, but watching harlots meant she was learning fast.

Once Annabella left, Patrick went to the bar and held out a collapsible pewter cup for Gus to fill.

"Our Annie's got her a new love-interest, Patty," said Gus.

Rattling the cup, Patrick said, "Do you think Mr. Price really murdered his wife?"

"That was yesterday, dammit," said Gus.

Preoccupied, Gus poured, and then slugged down, a shot of rye for himself before he realized what he had done and tried to spit it out. If nothing else, such a slip pointed to just how ruffled he was. Patrick arched an eyebrow, waiting for Gus to fill him in on what had been happening. Taking up his pipe, Gus began to pack it. Nothing was better for deep ruminations than a smoke. He struck the match on the back of his trousers and touched it to the bowl of the pipe. It took three deep inhalations to get it going.

Patrick poured himself a shot of whiskey, but before he could get it to his lips, Gus took it from him.

"You know what Newman decreed..." Gus clucked.

Digging into his pants for the small bag he kept tucked in his waistband, Patrick picked through the coins until he found the correct ones.

"There," he said, "Happy now?"

"It's not my orders, Patty," reminded Gus. "Newman says everyone has to pay up front."

That didn't soothe Patrick, who said, "Lately that man's been tighter'n the bark on a tree. A body can't even have an anti-fogmatic for his aches and pains without laying down for it. He can take it out of my wages."

"You don't have wages, remember? You play for tips."

"A minor point," snapped Patrick.

As Gus flipped the coins into the pay drawer, he shrugged once again, "I just work here."

Even Patrick knew that wasn't true. And although he talked gruff, Gus was a soft touch. If his reluctance to give him a drink had mostly to do with the green dribbles decorating Patrick's shirtfront, neither said anything about them. Absinthe was a bad habit to try to lose and, of the two, Gus figured whiskey was the lesser evil.

Changing the subject, he asked Patrick, "You know anything about that gent over at the corner table?"

He nodded his head in that direction. Squinting to where Gus pointed, Patrick corralled his spectacles dangling from one ear and gave a hard look towards the now empty table.

Mystified, he turned back to Gus, "Sorry?"

"He's not still there you fool," fussed Gus impatiently.

"Oh," said Patrick. Then conspiratorially, he asked, "Did he steal something?"

"I hope to God not," Gus replied cryptically. "Annie was talking to him. He's a whaler."

"Oh, yeah?" marveled Patrick. "A whaler, huh?"

"So it seems."

"Just yesterday..."

Gus nodded, "She was asking all about Mr. Price."

"Was he a handsome bastard or what?" Patrick asked.

"How the bloody hell would I know that?" blustered Gus. Then he capitulated, "I suppose he was, in that cow-eyed way that the ladies like. And some silver-tongued devil to boot."

Patrick saw immediately, "A bean-counter like Asher Price didn't have a chance up against that."

It had been their silent opinion that Asher Price might be a good match for Annabella. Gus had seen all kinds of men come through the Bella—murderers, vagabonds, thieves, cannibals, Mormons, and Quakers—those who had nothing to hide and those who had nothing to lose.

"An honest business man—his past notwithstanding—might be a good, steady influence on her."

It remained unsaid that not much else in town would. Whatever was transpiring on the Sierras was having a dramatic effect not just on San Francisco and its citizenry, but a good part of the known world. Along with that came scuttlebutt that sperm and right whales were getting scarce.

A revolving cast of whalers had sat woefully around tables in the *Bella* and bemoaned the decimation of their livelihood. It wasn't just the diminishing whale population. Everybody saw that whaling ships were being abandoned in the harbor—half the sailors fleeing with a pan and a blanket up the Sacramento River and to the diggings. Not only were they jumping ship, those who stayed would face longer voyages and shorter port stays. Ainsworth would either be heading for the hills or soon back to sea.

Patrick already knew the score. "The one thing you can count on for a sailor—sooner or later they always leave."

"I hope sooner than later," said Gus. "As it is they're pulling apart those old whalers plank by plank so they can go to the gold fields."

Patrick couldn't quite believe it. "What'll people use to light their lamps without whale oil?"

Gus shook his head. Lord only knew what lay in store. The saloon certainly had its own changes. It was a challenge to avoid peddling flesh. That took a certain kind of management style and neither he nor Newman had it. Even so, that Mrs. Gaspard had already staked out the *Bella* as her territory. She took a table in the back, but she wasn't exactly inconspicuous. She was a bit long in the tooth and Gus figured that was why she added flipping cards to her repertoire.

"I'm a simple man, Patrick," Gus said wistfully. "This easy money and loose women are going to be the end of us all."

Not only were women prowling the streets, actual brothels were setting up everywhere. It was no secret that big-city women would steal you blind and leave you for dead. As for Mrs. Gottwald, she had all the laundry she could handle.

"I don't wish her ill, but I wish Newman would run this new tart off. She makes me uneasy."

Patrick figured anything in favor of the Bella's business was good for him too. His tips were better than ever. More and more customers were paying in gold dust.

"Face it, Mr. G, she's just a harbinger of things to come."

Gus sighed.

Whether or not whaling would remain lucrative, he couldn't say. But he knew one thing. Seaman Ainsworth would be back.

25

Asher Price actually hadn't been informed that Newman Chase was campaigning for him to marry his daughter. Asher certainly wasn't looking for a wife.

Not that Miss Chase wasn't pretty. She was. Her father was a bit of an eccentric. But then that could be said of just about any citizen of San Francisco—even himself. Cautious people weren't prone to wander all the way out west. Chase wasn't afraid of change, he'd say that for him.

All hell-fire broke loose once traveling time caught up with the other Argonauts. It wasn't just good fortune that Asher was financially well-positioned. What he lacked in affability he made up for in objectivity. He knew that befriending a personable man like Newman Chase would be an asset to them both.

Other than street traffic, nothing else changed for Asher. His regimen remained Spartan. He rose with the sun and ate two meals a day. He didn't have a housekeeper for the same reason he didn't consider taking a wife. A pervasive little problem haunted him.

No matter what time he took to his bed, his sleep was broken by wailings. The reverberation from these sobs was so great that he thought he could actually see the walls pulsating beneath the wallpaper. But then, that was impossible. The walls didn't really throb. Likewise, it was impossible that blood seeped through the floorboards, squishing up between his toes when he walked. Thick, choking, rancid smoke made him gag and cough just like he had that dusk back in Nantucket. At its worst he could actually see his flesh melt and drop from his bones like blubber from a whale.

The culmination of the nightmare was always the same. A pair of blackened skulls would appear in the midst of the flames. Both were cracked from the heat and a wisp of smoke curled up from each cavity. Convinced each night that the fire was real, he swung his arms wildly to keep from being consumed by it too. But no matter how hard he fought, the flames gradually overtook him. He would awaken only to realize that the cries were his own.

His windows were nailed shut and curtains were drawn to muffle his screams. After dark, sound carried. People talked enough as it was. He couldn't have armed men breaking down doors to see what murder was taking place. Murder enough was already done.

Instead of getting in bed, Asher began to sleep sitting up in an uncomfortable arm chair. He had thought that if he didn't fully submit to sleep, he could stave off the nightmares. He wrapped a wool shawl about his shoulders like an old woman, but he sat in the chair like a child, arms wrapped around his knees. Still, month after month he awoke drenched in sweat and frozen in place. The cold panic, the dread, the fear was spanking new each and every time it happened.

When he awoke, it took him a while to recognize the panicked weeping for what it was. He would only have a week or two of respite—just long enough to fool him to thinking they had ceased.

When it happened again that night, he was—literally—at his wit's end.

Tossing the shawl aside, he carefully stretched out his legs and placed his feet on the cold floor. The perspiration that ran down his spine and soaked his hair made him shiver. He took the oil lamp from the table next to him and walked across the wood floor to a narrow dresser on the far wall. Looking down at his toes, he made certain that there was no blood. He hadn't put a wool rug down in his bedroom for that reason. It would have been a capitulation to his nightmares.

Standing before a small bachelor cabinet, he looked into the attached mirror. It was the right height to make a good shaving mirror, but he didn't use it. He never looked at his image even to shave. When he did that, he used a smaller one—one that would only reflect exactly what he needed to see to trim his side-whiskers. He kept that small one in the top drawer resting among his woolen socks.

He opened the drawer then, but not for the socks or the mirror. He rummaged a bit before locating an amber bottle. Without bothering to use a glass, he pulled the cork and took a long, gulping draw on it. He gave the bottle an admiring look, and then drank until it was empty. Instead of being pleased with the sensation of light-headedness, he was angered. He slammed the empty bottle on top of the bureau. It clunked and then tottered over, skittering off the edge. He caught it before it dropped and was pleased with his reflexes. Replacing the cork, this time he carefully set it upright on the top of the chest. It wasn't in the exact middle, so he moved it slightly. That didn't suit him and he moved it a little more. He gave the bottle another good long look—this time not so admiringly.

Suddenly, he grabbed it. Then, with all his might, he dashed against the wall. It hit the corner of a framed watercolor of the sea. The picture was sent askew, but it didn't fall. However the bottle shattered, scattering shards of glass all the way across the floor to where he stood. Lifting the lamp so it could expose the glass, he turned up the wick. When he did, lamp light suddenly emblazoned his image in the mirror. His own image was so unrecognizable that it startled him. Clearly, he had aged. Nightmares, he ruefully acknowledged, were not a restorative. He hadn't had a good night's sleep in years.

Instead of going back to bed, he searched the sideboard for another bottle. Finding one, he held it to the light. He flicked his middle fingernail against the side. A thin ping indicated the bottle was nearly empty. He drank what was there.

When he was sober, he liked to think that emptying a container of whiskey was just another attack against the abstemious principles of his long-foredone faith. (Oh, those great, gray Quakers—their forgiving eyes were inescapable.) His drinking was still a secret vice, however. He found it a great joke on himself that when it came to drink he still couldn't bring himself to defy his parents publicly. (How to rationalize the hand pistol he tucked in his belt everyday would be saved for another day and time.)

Awake, but not really sober, he walked over to his bed. He was newly determined to sleep properly. His bare feet picked up a half-dozen slivers of glass on the way. He thought it served him right. As he picked them out one by one, he was reminded of one of his father's favorite sayings.

"A clear conscience is a restful pillow," he repeated to himself.

Then in answer, he spat out, "*Hah!*"

He didn't care to marry again, Annabella Chase or no. What woman would put up with his terrors? Besides, if Miss Chase was put to him as a wife, he just might demur. He wasn't certain the daughter had her father's amiability. At a distance she had seemed vivacious and sweet. But on recent encounters she appeared a bit cold. Perhaps she had heard the talk. It was something he had come to accept. People talk—and other people listened. As for himself, he seldom thought of what happened back east any more. His father was wrong. His heart hadn't healed.

It never would.

26

When Annabella Chase happened upon the *Mary Thayer's* crew that first afternoon, all had been quiet. Everything the shipmates had to say to each other had already been said. Their stories were old. If they were to swap them, they needed new blood to listen. Not surprisingly, Aaron was the story-teller. He was superb at explaining the exhilaration of the chase without the gore of the kill. He told it as all nice and tidy—and a big, fat lie.

That was what most folks wanted to hear anyway—the myth, not the truth. They didn't want to know how blood spurted from the blow-hole as the whale died, drenching them all with gore. They wanted to hear of the excitement, the bravado, the fight. Truth was that a whale ship was both a floating sarcophagus and a stinking, sail-propelled tub of whale oil. It took hard men to man it.

He may have been glib, but even he didn't talk about what troubled them most. It wasn't the life they had chosen. Every man had made peace with that a long time back. The trouble was that the *Mary Thayer* was meant to be fitted with four whaleboats and to carry twenty crewmembers. When they left Maui, they were down to sixteen men. Four more mutinied the minute they anchored, stealing a boat and heading for the American River and its gold.

Before long, the *Mary Thayer* was to sail again. Their hold wasn't near full and if they were to chase bowheads up the coast, they had to get more men. If they didn't, they would be suicidally shorthanded. That wouldn't stop them from going. Nothing would stop the hunt. They would go and they would chase the spermaceti and, if the spermaceti won, there would be would be no tales to tell. Whalers might complain about the food, the lack of winds, or each other's company—not one of them would dare admit to fear.

Instead of drinking, their first order of business should have been finding replacements. Captain Weeks knew enough not to interfere with men bent on raising a little hell. Besides, Second Mate Owen Drucker was morose and wanted to drown his sorrows not just get stewed.

His father, old Josef Drucker was sixty-eight and still pulled his weight aboard the *Thayer*. Or at least he did until he was found dead in his hammock five days out of the Sandwich Islands. Josef was tawny and strong as any of them, his eyes red from squinting into hard gales. They gave his body to Davy Jones with a few scriptures and a half-hearted hymn.

Owen cried, "I just can't bear for Pa to have been fed to the fishies."

As usual, it fell to Aaron to cheer him, asking, "You heard about old Nelson and the battle of Trafalgar didn't you?"

Owen shook his head.

"With victory at hand, he caught a musket ball in the spine and died. But was such a hero they were determined to bring him back to England."

Aaron paused dramatically to be certain that everyone was listening.

"To get him home without stinking, they put him up in a cask of grog. They pickled the bastard!!

Laughter broke out and even Owen smiled.

"Can you imagine? Ruining a whole cask of brew for one rotten Admiral! But that was the British for you. They think their arses don't stink like other men."

The laughter had just petered out when Annabella Chase walked in.

She was the prettiest girl any of them had seen in some time. It was no surprise that Aaron claimed her. Watching him do his magic, his mates were glad to enjoy his triumph secondhand.

Aaron didn't tell Annabella Chase about fear. He told her about how they hung on for dear life as a whale towed them like a stone skipping across the wide, flat ocean. He told her that the Maori was their harpooner and her how strong a man had to be to lob a one into a leviathan's body. Miss Chase certainly didn't ask about how it was butchered once it was killed. That was a monstrous, nasty job.

Even Aaron, the poet couldn't find the romance in that.

27

His Pa used to tell him that the brave weren't without fears. They just went on despite them.

During the toughest spells, Tucker McFee reminded himself of his father's wisdom. He didn't let the Sierras get him—nor the snow, nor the cold, nor the isolation—none of it.

He had left St. Jo so young that he couldn't grow a decent mustache. The mountains had stripped him of every ounce of fat and hardened what was left. The brutal wilderness had made him a man.

He had seen plenty of people who didn't make it. Big, fleshy brutes of manhood were felled like fawns from the cold, but the frailest female could last for weeks. He didn't make note of life's little ironies often, but when he was all alone in the woods at dusk, it was hard not to think of that.

If there was a living to be made in the high country, Tucker didn't know how. Trappers were said to live there all year and come to town only to sell their pelts. He always wanted to kill a bear. But he hadn't any luck. He did scavenge a rotting grizzly carcass for the claws. But he wasted precious ammunition by shooting game to feed himself when he knew he should conserve his gunpowder in case he was jumped by Indians.

He lost his long gun in a snow slide. Sheer loneliness, however, was what drove him to the lowlands. Snow was beginning to dust the higher elevations and he couldn't bear the thought of enduring another winter alone. When he made his mind up, he didn't wait. He steered himself due west by way the sun—and a little luck.

When got out of Indian country, he allowed himself a big sigh of relief. His greatest fear hadn't been freezing in the mountains or frying in the desert. Absolute terror had been reserved for the possibility of being accosted by hostile natives. He had seen for himself what Indians could do. Every Sunday of his life he could recall Deuteronomy Beacon sitting in the second pew at church wearing a doily on his head. In the year '35 he had been scalped and left for dead. He had managed to stagger home and his wife had knit him a cap to cover his skull. That, of course, had happened in Comanche country, so you couldn't put much store in it recurring locally. Still, it had made an impression on Tucker at the time.

Like a lot of other restless youths, the tedium of trying to make a living off farm land had made him yearn for adventure. Land-locked all his life, he read and reread a cousin's copy of the *Arabian Nights* until his head was filled with dreams of sailing the Seven Seas. The likelihood of finding his Scheherazade while in Kentucky was, admittedly, remote. When his family packed up to head west, he put his gun on his shoulder and stuck the book in his shirt. By the time he had crossed the Rockies, the book was disintegrating. That didn't really matter. By then he had it memorized.

Although he didn't tell them so, Tucker didn't plan to stay with his family once they settled on some land. The lure of the sea and its magic was too intense. He knew that he had everything against him in trying to get hired on as a deckhand. He looked barely out of short-pants and never set eyes on a body of water bigger than the stock pond back home. He had hoped they would run into the Great Salt Lake, but they missed it by a hundred miles.

Somewhere along the trail he had picked up a runt of dog. At first he saw it as a bad omen. It spooked him the way it had just showed up like some phantom. Tucker figured it was a stray from an Indian tribe. That first evening, the dog lay on the ground next to the fire like he had done it every day of his life. He lay still as a stone, but if Tucker made any movement, the dog's eyes flicked open. The pup was a walking skeleton and Tucker couldn't keep from feeling sorry for him.

"Here," he said peeling off a bit of dried deer meat, "See if this is to yer liking."

Tucker meant to toss it at the dog's feet, but the dog sat up and caught it in the air and gulped it whole.

"I bet you jumped outta some Indian's stewpot."

"Not that you would be worth eatin'," he continued, "Yer meat'd be too stringy, I imagine."

Tucker's plans did not include a pet. But the name, Stewpot, stuck. So did the dog. He was still there the next morning and every day after.

He sat next to Tucker as he looked out over San Francisco Bay. At the magnificent sight, Tucker's heart leapt into his throat. The sheer magnitude of blue sea lay before him like an extension of the sky.

"Will you look at that, Stewpot!" he said.

Stewpot sat at his heel, licking a burr caught in his hindquarters. Tucker just shook his head. He knew they were both a sorry sight.

28

Annabella found romance in Aaron Ainsworth's every utterance. When he left her that day, she was breathless with anticipation waiting for him to return. He had said that they would return to the *Bella* the next day. She took that as a promise, but knew enough not to look conspicuous when she watched for him.

Perching on the windowsill of her room, she invented a method using two mirrors to watch the walk up the way. Lupe saw exactly what she was doing and gave her long, disapproving looks from the hallway. Annabella didn't care so long as Lupe didn't blab it around. There were more important things for her to worry about than Lupe and her indiscriminate asides—such as the number of saloons in San Francisco. Annabella knew there were far more enticing establishments up the street. She had seen them herself. Wenches hung around their doors like bats waiting for the night.

When she finally spotted him and his mates coming up Clay Street, she let out a shriek. Cramming her fist in her mouth to stanch any further eruptions, her hands shook as she watched the reflection of their progress, fearing at any moment they would veer in another direction. When it was certain that they were heading for the Bella, she made herself wait what she believed was a decent amount of time before making her way across the thoroughfare. She had taken the precaution of placing boards for her to cross the mud, but they had been tromped down by other passersby.

"Drat!" she muttered, trying to keep her balance. "Drat, drat, *drat*!"

Her hem was a mess, but that didn't stop her. By the time she came through the teak doors, she was so anxious that she almost propelled herself into the room. Breathlessly, she caught the door post and settled herself. After a few deep breaths, she strolled across the floor. It wasn't with the sexual gravitas of a Dovie Gaspard, but she held her bosom high enough for notice.

Circling around behind the bar, she looked to see where Aaron and his friends had lit. She wished he was alone, but he was surrounded by the same odd bunch as before. A ferret-faced, middle-aged man named Ernie sat on his left. The Maori sat on the right and next to him was a new man. He was no more than a boy and looked green as a gourd. She knew they needed replacements for what Aaron euphemistically referred to as "attrition."

Although she eyed them, the only one looking back at her was the greenhorn. He looked no older than fifteen. She decided she had to be less inconspicuous. Collecting empty glasses from the tables would be her new career. Gales of laughter pealed out from the crew, but Aaron didn't seem to notice her. She returned with a tray of dirty mugs and tossed them down with disgust.

"Want to make it a permanent job?" Gus asked.

She would have retorted, but her attention was caught by a pair of harlots who began to circle Aaron's table. One of them had a deck of cards and shuffled them rhythmically back and forth in her hands. Seeing Annabella watching them, she stopped shuffling and reached out with her index fingered and deliberately overturned a glass of beer. The harlot looked at Gus. He untied his apron and held it out to Annabella.

"I am the mistress of this establishment, not a serving wench."

Just then she noticed that the painting on the far wall was askew. She swung her hips as much as she dared as she walked. Once in front of said painting, she reached out with one finger and carefully adjusted it. When that did not meet her exacting standards, she readjusted it. To determine if it was then symmetrical, she took several steps backward, finger and thumb stroking her chin thoughtfully. Not unexpectedly, her shoe bumped Aaron's chair. Like a poof of smoke, both the hovering harlots withdrew.

She turned around, saying, "*Do* pardon me."

It hadn't been Aaron's, but another's chair. The Maori looked up at her with his fierce brown eyes wide with surprise. Startled, she had to check herself not to back away.

"Well now," Aaron called to her. "Do you remember me, pretty lass?"

She answered him in an odd, unnaturally nasal tone, "Why, yes." Then she hedged, "Perhaps."

This time, Aaron wore a faded calico shirt with his canvas trousers and thick, black belt. The buckle was brass. That was different. Rearranging her features into a genial, if slightly wide-eyed, expression, she tried to look at him dispassionately. The mood, however, was lost when she had to stifle a nervous giggle. Putting the back of her hand to her lips, she made herself cough.

"You do look a bit familiar, what is your name again?"

Clearly courting his mates more than Annabella, Aaron said coyly, "You've forgotten me so soon? And here I have thought of nothing but you."

She narrowed her eyes. Nothing made her less happy that being the brunt of a joke—anyone's joke.

"I truly doubt you recall my name," Annabella said curtly. "But I care little one way or the other."

Before he could respond, Patrick appeared carrying his sheet music under his arm. Everyone's head turned in his direction. Annabella's did too. It was early, but he had found some new sheet music that he wanted to practice. His audience all waited expectantly as he carefully took his place on the stool and arranged his music. Leaving Aaron Ainsworth leaning on the back two legs of his chair, Annabella walked to the piano and pressed against it.

"Bless you, Patrick," she whispered.

Playfully, she ruffled his hair. He smiled contentedly and began to play. The first notes were poignant and he closed his eyes as his fingers slid across the keys. Truly mesmerized, Annabella drew her fingers lovingly across the top of the piano. Waggling his shoulders happily, Patrick gazed up at her with adoring eyes.

That would show smug Aaron Ainsworth.

As she looked in his direction to make certain he knew just how uninterested in him she was, the late evening sun shone through the windows, casting an golden halo around his sun-bleached hair. He realized that she was staring at him before she did. In a flash he had removed his sock hat and tucked it in his belt. Whether it was a recollection of manners rather than a move to improve his back-light, she didn't know. It was a ploy that she would have used to her own benefit if she had thought of it first.

Aaron smiled impertinently at her. Just then Patrick realized that he didn't have Annabella's complete attention and checked to see who did. He was well-impressed. Seldom were such fine aquiline features seen out west. Just then Aaron stood and held out his hand to Annabella.

To her ever-lasting disgust, she took it.

"Ah, lassie," he crooned, displaying her for his fellow sailors, "Shall I compare thee to a summer's day? Thou art more lovely and more temperate.'"

She recognized the quote, but she didn't realize that Aaron had used and perfected the lines countless times on countless girls before. She was far too enraptured by his gaze. It penetrated her very soul. Leaning on her elbows, she hung longingly on to his every borrowed word.

He came back every day for a week.

Every day Annabella watched for him. And every day Gus and Newman stood behind the bar, watching helplessly as Annabella lost her heart to a rogue.

Patrick thought it was all quite romantic, but knew that his was the minority opinion and kept his mouth shut. Flushed with rage, Newman chewed mercilessly on an unlit cigar. Gus claimed he wasn't worried. But Newman didn't buy that.

Out of the side of his mouth, he whispered, "If you don't quit sucking on that pipe you're gonna summon those Miwoks from the other side of the bay."

They watched suspiciously as Aaron magically plucked a tiny seashell from behind her ear. With a flourish, he offered it to Annabella as a gift. Had he bent on one knee and asked for her hand in marriage, it could not have looked more like a betrothal.

She ran to the bar to show it off.

"It's from Samoa," she said proudly.

Through all of this Newman had kept himself remarkably civil. But he couldn't stomach the shell business.

He moaned, "Take me, Lord—just take me now!"

Ignoring him, Gus decided it was time to talk turkey to Annabella.

He said, "The *Mary Thayer* needs more whale oil. Any day they'll be following gray whales down south."

She didn't know much about whaling, but she corrected him, "Aaron says the Sea of Okhotsk on the Siberian coast is thick with bowheads. That's where they shall go."

Shaking his head, Gus said, "If they go north they'll winter in Japan. If they go south, it'll be a Pacific island. Either way, they won't be back here for better'n a year."

Annabella looked at Gus closely before walking off. What he said clearly had made an impact. He just wasn't sure if he cooled her little romance or lit a fuse.

29

When the dull shadow of the winter sun had almost reached the edge of the bed, Adelaide said, "It's getting late."

It was unduly wet that year. As the days grew shorter, the minute darkness fell, a chill set into her bones that inconsolable. She didn't tell Eduard that. He didn't like for her to tell him anything, true or not, so he ignored her. Clenching her teeth to keep them from chattering, she reached for her chemise. As soon as she put it on, he grabbed her from behind and emitted a long, low growl—one that began at the back of his throat and was released through his nostrils. It wasn't meant to be funny, but she couldn't stop herself from giggling.

"I don't know why I waste my time on a child," he said.

She may have still been a child, but she certainly was no longer an innocent. Her fingers were long like her mother's, but even at her tender age, not as delicate. Still, his easily engulfed hers. Being so much smaller than he was made her feel more feminine—lest ungainly. In the past year, she had grown several inches and it had all been in her long bones. She likened herself to one of those colts frolicking at her cousin's farm—all loose legs and flailing neck.

Coltish or not, she was not strong enough to escape his grip. It had become almost painful, but she hesitated to squirm away. He had told her that once a man's fever aroused, there was no stopping. As persistent as he was, she could believe it. Once he was engaged, well, there was no stopping him.

Like then.

She supposed he would let go if she insisted, but not knowing that for certain stirred her in a way that she despised. She didn't ask and he didn't stop.

He seized her by the hair and twisted it, using it to pull her to him like a handle. Trying to deflect him, she arched her back like a cat wanting its back scratched. When he grabbed her by the hips, she pulled away. He told her all lovers did it from behind, otherwise things would get monotonous. She wanted to enjoy it like he said his other lovers did, but the entire procedure reminded her of a pair of feral dogs.

Catching the edge of her chemise, he flipped it up. She gave in. Sometimes it was better to let him have his way. As he performed, he pinched her buttocks. Whether that was part and parcel of copulation, she didn't know. She slapped his hand to make him stop, but that only seemed to encourage him. With his final thrusts, her face was mashed into the mattress so deeply that it was all she could do to breath. Fortunately, he finished the deed as quickly (and with less finesse) than one of those back-alley strays. As usual, he fell on top of her and then rolled to the side. The moment was quiet except for his gasping.

This collapse onto the musty mattress released a cloud of dust. It permeated her throat and nose. She sneezed twice.

"Get dressed," he commanded.

She did as she was told.

Looking at him, she waited to see if he would help. Sometimes he liked to roll her stockings up, but he didn't that day. He buttoned the placket of his shirt and began tying his tie before he put on his pants. As she tugged on her shoes, she turned her head so she wouldn't laugh. His legs were white and spindly as table legs.

She hastily tied a ribbon at the neck of her dress, but didn't bother to straighten her stockings. They were black wool and sagged no matter what she did. When she turned sixteen she could wear her mother's pearl brooch. Eduard said that would be a waste of good jewelry. It was the only opinion of his she chose to ignore. She could never be as beautiful as her mother, but the brooch would make her feel closer to her.

✧

Adelaide Perry was younger than Annabella Chase when she first fell in love. In some ways Adelaide was intelligent beyond her years. It would be some time before she realized that a good mind wasn't worth a nickel if she didn't use it. Once her libido was turned loose, all her other faculties came to a screeching halt. The furtiveness was what excited Adelaide most. It was exciting and titillating at the time. Just hearing Enid Perry's voice wafting up the staircase made her heart beat furiously.

"Child!" the woman demanded. "Come here."

Adelaide's hands began to tremble, fearing at any minute she would burst in on them. But Eduard was in no hurry. He leisurely donned his trousers, snorting with disgust at her fear. She would be happy when she was older. Then she would overcome her girlish ways and he wouldn't criticize her so much. She left the room on the fly—the buttons on her shoes not quite fastened.

Hearing Enid's nasal call again, Adelaide hustled down the staircase. She worried constantly about getting caught *inflagrante* by her stepmother. Recently come to mind, however, was whether or not it was legal for her and Eduard to marry.

So far, her father hadn't noticed either Enid's pilfering of the household accounts or his daughter's little affair. He was far too sick.

At first Enid said that he suffered from a case of the shingles—the location of which it was not proper for a daughter to see.

"My special poultice will do him up fine," she said wisely.

Massive quantities of laudanum were called for to counter its symptoms. That left Mr. Perry spending his hours moving only from his bed to his favorite high-backed rocker and periodically nodding off. Sedentary as he was, pneumonia was a constant threat. In what time she could spare him, Adelaide entreated him to rally. Despite his new wife's ministrations, Mr. Perry did not shuffle off life's mortal coil with any dispatch.

Although she wouldn't admit it to herself, her father's incapacitation saved her quite a bit of grief. Should he discover what she was doing, he would have gone apoplectic with revulsion and shame.

Perhaps it was the fear of discovery; perhaps it was her conscience bothering her. Somehow in the back of Adelaide's love-addled mind, she realized that she was playing a dangerous game. What she and Eduard were doing was forbidden—in more ways than just simply fornication outside of marriage. But Eduard's attention gave her flutterings of power that were intoxicating.

Eventually, she admitted that she was no longer a privileged young lady of distinction. She was nothing but a compromised female, self-respect in the gutter along with her good name.

If father was to learn of it, she must at least have a promise of marriage. It took her a while to screw up her courage to tell Eduard that. When she finally said something, he guffawed so violently that he choked on his own saliva.

"What?" he asked once he regained his speech. "Marry? Who, me?"

"What if I become pregnant?" she asked feebly.

He told her that the possibility of pregnancy hadn't crossed his mind. Surely she was too young for that worry.

"If something happens," he said earnestly. "I will take care of it."

The pronoun he used should have alerted her to his true intentions, but it passed unnoticed. She didn't know that marriage had been a consideration—at least initially. But as Mr. Perry's death loomed on the horizon, it occurred to Eduard that the mantle of stepson was preferable to that of Mr. Perry's son-in-law. Was he married to Adelaide, his other liaisons would be scrutinized. As stepson, he could carry on in his preferred occupation—that of the local roué—without the any serious finger-pointing. In either case, he would inherit.

"I can't marry you," he told her. "That is preposterous. I have my reputation to uphold."

Flustered at his reaction, Adelaide whispered hurriedly, "I don't mean that we must marry now—but in the future." Her cheeks burning, she added, "Just so that we have an understanding."

"Oh, yes," he sneered. "We *do* have an understanding. But it hardly includes promises of any kind. I would be a fool to agree to such a laughable engagement."

Every despicable action she had engaged in, every disgusting operation she had allowed—all of it—flickered across her consciousness. For a moment she thought she might swoon. Before she could stop herself, she said the most pedestrian thing imaginable.

She blurted, "I'll tell my father!"

Making such a ludicrous threat was even more humiliating to her than being seduced in the first place. As soon as she said it, she realized that there was no way in perdition that she wanted Eduard Stackpole for a husband in this life or any other. She was too mortified to say anything else and she slunk away. When she caught sight of herself in the mirror, she saw that her cheeks were the approximate shade of Enid's after a day tending to her stove. Eduard had a choice of being kind or not. He was not kind.

He followed her from room to room, demanding, "Did I force you? Well, did I?"

"Get away," she hissed, tears seeping into her eyes. "You liar! You snake-in-the-grass!"

She despised her tears, but she hated more that he saw them. Besides, he was right. She hadn't been forced. On the contrary, she had looked forward to each illicit encounter.

"Oh, don't be a baby," he said, laughing. "I am only teasing!"

Both knew that was just another lie.

"I care little for the opinion of someone who doesn't know how to spell 'Edward,'" she sniffed.

They both knew that was a lie as well.

By the time that she realized Eduard was born a bounder and a scoundrel and no amount of time would make a man of him, she no longer cared. Despite that, shame set in. It caused her to walk with her shoulders hunched and dress in clothes so dark and unflattering that strangers often took her to be in mourning. Her only consolation was that her father was too sick to notice. Her greatest fear was that Eduard would realize that he still had that to hold over her head. She would have done anything to keep him from telling her father what sins they had committed. She needn't have worried.

After their confrontation, Eduard only came around long enough to remind Mr. Perry who he was. But he soon tired of fetching tea for him and set off for other souls to conquer. Although Mrs. Perry stood over her husband like the grim reaper, he wouldn't give up the ghost. Impatient with the process, she went to visit her sister.

"Do call me, dearie," she told Adelaide, "if there is a turn for the worse."

But Adelaide didn't send for her when Mr. Perry left his rocker for his bed for good. Happy to be rid of outsiders, she ladled him a potion of gin and molasses and tenderly tucked the quilt around his feet. When the fever and chills began, she still didn't send for Mrs. Perry. She saw Enid as his wife in name only.

"I hear it, my little Addie," her father whispered.

Adelaide strained to listen, but heard nothing but the chirping of crickets.

"What do you hear, Papa?" she asked a bit condescendingly. Fever could make the sick hallucinate.

"I hear the sound of a trumpet," he whispered huskily. "It must be the Angel Gabriel calling."

She was only momentarily puzzled. From deep within his throat came a hiss. It was such a deep exhale that she steeled herself for the gasp to follow.

But it didn't come.

Edward Stackpole, however, did.

30

Tucker's clothes were nearly a scruffy as Stewpot's coat.

Worn and ragged, all his trials had merely steeled his resolve to follow his far-fetched dream. There was no way he could pay for his passage to the Orient. He had to hire on. If these ship captains got wind that he was a lowly landlubber, he didn't stand a chance.

As he got closer to the bay, he saw that it was studded with masts. He was too ignorant to tell a merchant ship from a man-of-war. That worried him.

When he got closer, he could see that some of the ships were not moored. They were a ways off shore and appeared to have been sacked. Scores of flatboats were unloading crates from anchored vessels. It was easy to tell the dock workers from the actual sailors. The sailors wore striped shirts and woolen hats. To a man they all had a swagger and were as weather-stained as the decks of the ships.

Once he scrutinized all he could, he headed for town. There was some old saying about avoiding any new endeavor that required new clothes, but he pushed that to the back of his mind and headed for the first dry goods store he saw. Circling down around the town he saw several set up out of a trunk on the street. Figuring the low overhead would translate into cheaper prices, he approached one. At first the proprietor acted put out that Tucker didn't have any ready money. But when Tucker pulled out his string of bear claws and plopped them on the counter, the man's manners improved. Tucker figured that he thought he had killed the bear himself. He didn't tell him otherwise.

"A bearskin will bring you a bottle and some company," declared the man.

He knew what kind of bottle he meant, but was stumped about the company he could buy.

All he could find was a tent to hide behind to try on his sea-faring duds. They included a vest had brass buttons shaped like a bell. Those were easy to master, but he hadn't a clue as to what he should do with the leather straps at the bottom of his canvas trousers. He tied them the best he could and strutted down the street like a cock of the walk. He didn't get far before the straps at his ankles began to flap. But on the whole, he was pleased with the effect.

It was the noon hour by the time he found a ship to approach. Work had been suspended for a meal break, but a group of sailors were standing around talking. They stopped mid-sentence when they saw him. At first he thought they were admiring his getup. A bit of snickering suggested otherwise. Mortified, Tucker considered running away, but figured he wouldn't get far before his leggings tripped him up.

Stewpot sat down on his left foot. Then he then proceeded to hump his leg. Without looking down, Tucker tried to shake him away with the side of his boot. Stewpot, however, wouldn't budge. Tucker decided if the dog wasn't going anywhere, he wouldn't either. He had endured every danger the mountains could throw at a man and survived. So he threw back his shoulders and stuck his chin out. But the surly bunch of seadogs still put the scare in him. When they all took a step in his direction, he ducked his head a bit. Stewpot let go and trotted off.

A quick glance over the lot of them showed that to a man they were all brown as coffee grounds. They looked just like the pictures of the Arabians in his book. Perhaps they were from Persia or the like. He did what he could to facilitate the conversation.

"I want," Tucker pointed to himself, then to the ship, "to hire on."

The beginning of laughter could be heard and Tucker wondered how else to confront the language barrier. From the rear of the group came a singular voice.

"Cocksure, aren't you boy?"

He quickly reassessed just who had what up on whom and sprang to attention.

"N-n-no, sir!"

"Come here, boy. I must interrogate you to see if you are fit for a ship such as this."

Had he known that his employment was a foregone conclusion, it would have saved him some humiliation. As it was, he didn't know that the *Mary Thayer* was desperate for help. He also didn't know that every new sailor had to endure a bit of ribbing. As the ship's wit, Aaron Ainsworth did the talking. As always, he wore his red and white stocking cap.

"Are you mute or just stupid?" asked Aaron.

"Uh, stupid, I guess. At least I'm not mute."

A bit of laughter came from the onlookers.

"What position do you apply for?"

"Sailor, sir—I guess."

"You certain you're not a pirate then?"

"No sir!" Tucker answered indignantly.

Aaron turned businesslike. "Well then, you must have some expectation of your lay."

"Lay, sir?"

"Yes, your lay—you know, man, your share!"

"I expect nothing more than a day's pay for a day's work," insisted Tucker.

"We don't get whales, we don't get paid—simple as that," replied Aaron.

Tucker nodded as if he knew that, but shuffled his feet uncomfortably.

"You may not see your mama again for three years—if at all," Aaron added. "You think you can bear that?"

"My mother's dead, sir," said Tucker, "All of my family is gone—got by an early snowstorm up in them mountains."

Nobody knew what to say then. Even Aaron was quiet. Fortunately, Hosea Weeks's head popped out of his cabin door.

He called out, "What we got here, boys?"

It took Tucker a second to realize the man in the stove pipe hat was the ship's captain. When he did, he pulled his hat from his head and clasped it to his bosom.

He called out, "Me, sir!"

"Why, you're just a whelp," Weeks responded.

Captain Weeks, being a self-respecting native of Nantucket, was distrustful of anyone who didn't hail from there. This boy was clearly a landlubber. Still, they had to make do with what could be found. As Tucker McFee was a living, breathing male with two good legs, he would have to do. Hell-fire, he would be happy with a peg-leg. But he didn't tell Tucker that.

"I'll give you a 700th lay," Weeks announced, "Take it or leave it.

From behind Tucker came Aaron's voice, "Don't settle for anything higher than 300."

Another, even more authoritative voice called out, "Give him 275."

All heads turned to that last voice. Just above them stood Asher Price. No one recognized him save Captain Weeks.

With fingers touching the brim of his hat in salute, Weeks tried not to sound too submissive.

"Yessir."

Asher said, "Thank you, Mr. Weeks," and to Tucker, he spoke shortly, "See that you earn it, boy."

His glare was so sharp, it hurt.

Aaron took the sting out of his words by saying, "Got your traps? Chests have to be on board by nightfall, no telling how soon we'll sail."

Tucker only had a small roll, but he held it up. Aaron nodded to a mountain of a man who held out his hands. Without a pause, Owen Drucker sent the roll sailing over the belaying pins and onto the deck. With unfathomable precision, it slid end over end and plopped into the hold. With that done, Captain Weeks disappeared back into his cabin. Asher turned and began walking up the hill in the direction of his home. Tucker, surrounded by his new shipmates, felt elated. As they walked away, a murmur erupted. Speculation was keen on the identity of the mysterious man who interceded on his behalf. General consensus was that the man was main shareholder in the *Mary Thayer*. His name was well known, but no one really knew the man. He had been a source of speculation for some time.

"A failed Quaker, I'm told," said one.

"A wife murderer, I've heard," said another.

"A tinker, a tailor, a candlestick maker," laughed Aaron. "He's owns us."

With that, they repaired to the Bella. Tucker was thrilled to suddenly become the owner of so many friends. Someone began to sing a vulgar song. Tucker didn't know the words, but he did a good job of humming the tune. They pushed up the hill to hoist a drink in his honor.

No one noticed that Stewpot trotted right behind them.

31

Like most Quaker newborns, Asher Price had been given a scriptural name. Called after the founder of the Asherites, one of the Twelve Tribes of the Israelites, Asher's name meant "happiness" or "luck." When he first set eyes on Cora Hicks, he thought himself a very fortunate man indeed.

Cora was much prettier than she realized. As a child, she had been teased mercilessly for her red hair and freckles, so the single vanity she had was to wash her face in cream hoping to fade them. The remedy (or simply time) worked quite well. By the time she was twenty her skin was pure alabaster. She was very demure and just bookish enough to hold up her end of a good conversation. Her figure was almost boyish, but Asher found nothing else about her to be so. She always spoke in a breathy, earthy way. It wasn't often that they could speak privately, so her voice was doubly provocative to him.

Their engagement did have one great hurdle to leap. Cora wasn't a Quaker. He would have married her without his father's blessing, but wanted it all the same. With a mane of white hair, his father always looked to him like old Neptune himself. Surprisingly, old Mr. Price had been the more pliant of his parents. Mrs. Price was apprehensive. But all of Cora's family had been born on Nantucket and as the elder Mr. Price saw it, one's birth place is written in stone. The different faiths part was curable.

"There is something of God in us all," he observed, "even Congregationalists."

With his father's approval, Asher reassured Cora, telling her that Friends believe every soul as a vessel of God. So long as she followed Quaker principles of sincerity and truth, she was a Friend.

Quakerism was an easy fit for her. By nature she was soft-spoken and plainly dressed. She began to attend twice-weekly prayer meetings and her own parents couldn't have been happier. The Prices may have been Quakers, but they were rich Quakers. Like most Nantucket ship owners, as they became richer, the strictures of Quakerism were relaxed enough to include a few modest displays of wealth. By all standards the house Asher built Cora was handsome. It had three stories with three bedrooms on the second floor and an enormous attic on the third. They intended to fill it with children.

What proved to be a greater problem for Cora was not the Quaker faith, but their insular existence. Asher spent his days at his office going over business ledgers. His mother visited her regularly, but other church members never seemed to lose their reserve. It was as if there was some coda that no one told Cora about. She dutifully attended the silent services and contemplated her inward light. At home, she swept her own floors and beat her own rugs. As she listened to the clock tick, she tatted and crocheted. Her finest piece was a lovely needlepoint of their names, intertwining their initials with swirls that would have been unwelcome in some households. Although Asher's mother pursed her lips, Cora had it framed and placed it across from the dining room table.

The isolation eventually began to take its toll. When once she was merely cautious, Cora became absolutely unnerved. She attributed it to the quiet, but rarely complained. Asher knew, however, that her biggest fear was staying in the house by herself after dark. They could have afforded it, but Asher's simple roots made him decide live-in help was an extravagance. Occasionally, Cora visited her mother on the Vineyard, but she didn't want to admit to anyone that she was frightened to be alone.

The only concession to her fear was the use of lamps throughout the house—whether the rooms were in use or not. The oil bill was their only disagreement. Asher could afford oil—and he was quite proud that he could. So he hushed his complaints. All they needed to make their happiness complete, Cora insisted, was to have a baby.

"One with your looks," she quickly added.

He believed that she was far too modest—even for a Quaker. To him, she was as beautiful as any porcelain doll. But he never told her that. He meant to. He meant to a hundred times. But a hundred times he didn't have the time.

Each morning Asher kissed her goodbye on her forehead. To him, it was an immoderate display of affection. But the morning light illuminated Cora's lovely face like no other time of the day. Sometimes on the way to work he was overtaken by salacious thoughts. He imagined taking his sweet wife right there in their sunlit kitchen. But he didn't have the courage. It might make her turn away from his affections altogether. They had never made love by the light of a lamp, much less in the daytime. He only knew her body by touch. Surely her tender crevices were pink, but he really didn't know.

He vowed one day he would take her to bed before dusk. But in the winter, days were too short, and in the summer, too busy. Well into their third year of marriage, they had not conceived a child. It had embarrassed and emboldened Asher when his father had told him—rather bluntly—that if wanted to have any children that he was going to have to spend more time with his wife.

"Thy wife dost not beget a child whilst unattended by her husband," said Obadiah Price.

Asher had taken that admonishment to heart. One fine autumn day he decided to rectify that. If he hurried, he would be home before dusk. By the time he arrived home, he was all but taken over by anticipation. Night had not yet fallen. It was a moonless sky, but he saw no sign of lamps burning. He intended to rectify that. He would whisk Cora into their bedroom and light a dozen lamps. He would place them in a semi-circle around their bed like an altar. Just the thought of it stirred his desire. Would she respond passionately? That question hurried his step.

Cora often sat and did handwork in the front window on the third floor. The room had a good view of the road and he flattered himself that she sat there to watch for his return. He loosed his horse from the harness and turned him into the paddock. As he made for the back steps, the darkened house looked forbidding. Striking a match on the wall, he lit a lamp and with it in hand walked through the mud room, the kitchen, down the hallway and into the back parlor. Lifting the light to illuminate each area, he saw no one.

"Cora," he called. "*Cora*?"

Curious and a little concerned, he carefully checked each room on the first story; went up the staircase to the second floor and did the same there. She was not to be found. All that was left to check was the attic rooms. As he took the first of the ten or so steps of the staircase, he heard scuffling sounds above him.

He didn't have enough time to translate what the sounds meant before he rounded the newel post and burst through the door. The room was dark and it took a moment to adjust his eyes to the light of his lamp. It cast a glow on the floor boards, and as he raised it higher, it lit the far corner of the room as well.

The very first thing he saw was his wife's naked back. Her white skin glimmered in the light. The sight was compelling enough for him to gasp. His was not the only breath that was heavy however. At first he thought it was Cora and he was half right.

The rest of it came from the man who stood next to her

32

The first wave of those following predatory professions into San Francisco was followed by another, then another. Unlike some saloons, the infiltration into the *Bella* remained unobtrusive. It was as if Dovie Gaspard had staked the place out for herself. If an unaffiliated woman entered, she settled into a darkened corner recess—a chimney-nook, or beneath the stairs. Soon, she either aligned herself with Dovie, or left. If she stayed, she commandeered her own table. Any financial arrangement between the women remained between the two of them.

Dovie lit her little inequity, even midday, by a small whale oil lamp. This was meant to illuminate not only the laying out of cards, but a generous décolletage. The others followed suit. Those younger, and therefore more agile, offered a generous gander at fishnet hose. This stacked the deck against customers who were already liberally served. On those occasions when the men won at cards, their winnings negotiated for payment other than gold dust. The most popular defrayal was exchanged down a side-street and in a vertical position. The decks of cards were stacked neatly and perched on the edge of the oil lamp as a sign that the table was only temporarily vacant.

When the rains came, it forced commerce indoors. Newman's decided it would be a good use of their resources to rent out space upstairs. A room with a bed could be let out for a hundred dollars a night. Newman knew that renting out rooms in the daytime for increments of twenty minutes at a time would more than triple their money. Gus wanted nothing to do with the scheme.

"Go to hell," Gus said with finality. "My Mama didn't raise her son to pimp women."

Actually, Newman was opposed to anything that meant unequivocally that he was a brothel-owner too. He had a daughter to think of. A compromise was in order.

He said, "We won't be renting them rooms out, we'll charge an occupancy fee."

"So, as long as it isn't called whoring, they ain't whores and this ain't a whorehouse—is that it?" snorted Gus.

"What people do on their own time isn't my business or yours," sniffed Newman. "Besides, they stay out of sight."

"If we don't look, it ain't happening, huh? Glad to hear that," responded Gus.

Gus knew it was useless to argue with Newman when he had a mission. His objective was money and he had undertaken getting it with awesome single-mindedness. It worried him that Newman's deep interest in marrying Annabella off to Asher Price had more to do with Asher's new bank than Asher's respectability. It didn't really matter. Annabella remained intractably opposed to him. She was just as sure of her love of Aaron Ainsworth—and she wasn't a bit fooled about the chicanery about the upstairs rooms.

Annabella wasn't completely ignorant of the rites of amour. She saw that men could be turned into little jam-jars of jelly at the sight of a woman's ankles. So the steady stream of filthy men accompanying garishly made-up women upstairs held her spellbound.

"Look, Gus. All these women have to do is to lift their skirts and she has men lining up to take her upstairs to play poke-the-pucker."

At that little euphemism, Gus squeezed the glass he was polishing so hard that it shot out of his grasp. Fortunately, he caught it as it came down.

He demanded, "Where the blazes did you hear such a term?"

She stuck out her lip, saying, "I'm not deaf—or blind."

"What would your new friend think of you talking like that?"

Annabella opened her mouth to retort, but shut it immediately. She turned her back to Gus and flippantly kicked one foot against the bar stool. She tried to disguise the fact that exposing such a carnal inclination to Aaron was very much on her mind. In fact, it had become a preoccupation. When she wasn't sitting next to Aaron, she was daydreaming of cavorting in his muscular, tanned arms. Her legs virtually trembled at the thought being stroked into submission. At night, she dreamed of nothing else.

The bumps and moans she heard wafting down from above stirred her blood. When Gus wasn't looking, she touched her aching temples, despising her unsettling feeling of need. What she disliked most was that she couldn't quite give it a name. It certainly couldn't be what passed for love upstairs.

She was still suffering from inertia and a strange funk when she heard that the *Mary Thayer* was to sail. Fear and near despair overtook her, but no one noticed. The crew didn't come to the *Bella* again. They were jittery with expectation of getting back to sea and passed a bottle between them. When once they skulked around the *Bella* like kitchen rats, now they hovered down at the wharf talking of nothing but their impending voyage.

The very thought of losing Aaron sent Annabella into a near panic. Here Aaron was about to leave and she had yet to be alone with him. It was time to fish or cut bait. If Aaron was to return to the sea for who-knows how long, she had to give him reason not to forget her. If he wouldn't come to her, she would go to him.

Running all the way, she only stopped when she reached the path just above the bay. Red-faced and out of breath, she knew she looked like some waterfront hussy, but she was too determined to see Aaron to care. From her tip-toes, she could see that the *Mary Thayer* and its riggings were crawling with activity. The sun was high and the glare off the water made her put her hand up to shield her eyes. Sailors climbed like monkeys over the masts and she thought she saw Aaron coiling a rope as thick as a man's arm. It was difficult to decide whether to go down to the ship or stay up on the ridge hoping to catch his eye. In the end she concluded that loving words and needful embraces required privacy.

In time, she saw an arm rise to her. She held up her hand and almost waved back—until she realized it was that snub-nosed boy that followed Aaron around like a puppy.

"Hell's bells!" she muttered. "Not you, not *you*!"

After what seemed like an eternity, Aaron lifted his head towards her. The wind had ripped and tangled everyone else's hair, but his locks ruffled handsomely around his cap. It was as if the four winds worked towards the glorification of his personal good looks. From his sun-kissed ringlets to his noble profile, he was nothing less than a sea-going Adonis.

Impulsively, she tore her bonnet from her head and held it aloft, allowing the ribbons to flow in the wind like banners. Once she had done that, she turned on her heel and walked further up the path. It was done. Either he followed her or he didn't.

The wind didn't quit. It whipped her bonnet strings into a frenzy, wrapping them around her body as if it was a maypole. The sun which had just shone so brilliantly hid behind a growing cloud. Just off-shore a squall was kicking up and huge drops of rain began to fall. Frantically, she looked for shelter. In all her contemplation of their union, she hadn't expected the heavens to open up so literally. The only cover she saw was the remnants of a tent. She didn't look back until she was beneath it.

Her heart in her throat and her hair was stuck to her forehead; she struggled to look for Aaron's figure through the growing downpour. As if a misty vision, she saw him cresting the hill. She called out to him. In an instant, he was in her waiting arms.

"My love!" she gasped.

There was no time for any bandying about. Her shawl hung over her shoulders like a drowned danseuse and she slung it aside. She wrapped her arms around his neck with all her might. This was a moment she had been preparing for since Boston.

Whatever his reaction, she didn't see it. Her eyes were tightly closed. But she felt it as he let his fingertips draw lightly across her collarbone. With that, she gave a nervous little shudder. It was just as she had imagined. She knew what came next.

At last their lips would meet.

She murmured, "Aaron, dearest love, I am yours."

Her words were not the ones she had practiced. Those had been full of wit and sophistication. It didn't really matter. Aaron didn't seem to notice what she said. He wasn't much interested in her lips either. All his attention seemed to be on her heaving bosom. It took her by surprise when he clutched her breasts, kneading them like dough. She was positively speechless when he finally buried his face into her cleavage.

She wanted to protest, but only squawked in astonishment. His hands slid behind her and cupped her buttocks. Then he began caressing her in places she didn't know she wanted to be caressed. Only seconds passed before he dropped to his knees and then slowly laid her back. Rainwater had seeped through the tattered canvas of the tent, and dripped on their heads. The ground was wet as Market Street on an October day, but she didn't notice the mud.

"Aaron, Aaron," she gasped.

At last, he smothered her lips with a deep, long kiss. It was what she had spent her nights longing for and she wasn't even a little disappointed. (His tongue tasted salty and—possibly—of sardines.) Sighing and writhing, she trembled as his fingers began to prod between her legs. It was a thrilling sensation, causing her to clutch at him wildly. The moan that she had choked back for weeks finally erupted. It was if she had lost control of her senses. She was mortified that it might be a swoon. She didn't want to miss one blissful second of their encounter.

Just as she arched her back in blissful surrender, he let her go. It was so sudden that it left her gasping and her mouth puckered like a fish flopping around on the deck of a boat.

"Wha-a-t?" she wheezed at last.

She sat up, confused and mortified—and still in the throes of passion. He, however, clasped her by her shoulders and drew her to his bosom. She tried to kiss him again, but he smothered her face against his neck.

He crooned, "Oh my dear sweet, innocent Annabella! I am a beast!"

Her insistence that she was not at all innocent was muffled. So much so, that she almost couldn't breath. Then, as quickly as that, he slipped out of her arms. His figure receded into the misty rain and he was gone.

"But, but..." she began to blubber as she reached out for him.

It occurred to her, she should follow him, but she feared he would reject her and she couldn't bear that again.

She intended to flee back to town. But her legs were wobbly and sand was everywhere. When she tried to stand her knees buckled. There was an odd sensation radiating down her legs. Agitated, she slumped to the ground and wrapped her arms around her knees. Keening silently, she rocked gently until it passed.

Gradually, the rain let up and she began to set herself to rights. All the gobbling Aaron had done to her bosom had exposed them. Quickly grabbing her soaked shawl, she began desperately tucking herself back down into her dress. It was odd how mercurial such concerns were. While in Aaron's arms she wouldn't have been stirred by Odysseus himself. Now trying to right herself, her fingers were trembling with hurry.

When she stood, she saw a silver chain slide from the folds of her skirt. She picked it up and looked at it intently. The clasp was broken. Had it been for her? She chose to believe that it had and pressed it to her lips. She would treasure it always. It was a far greater symbol of their love than that little sea shell.

The entire episode proved an undeniable truth. Aaron Ainsworth was the most honorable of men. That was why he left her. He would not sully their love by taking advantage of her. They would have all eternity to be together. Theirs was a union as sacred as any marriage.

Let no man put them asunder.

33

In the months after Aaron's ship left port, Gus and Newman watched anxiously as more streets were cut into the sand hills adjacent to Yerba Buena Cove. They were not only uneven, but they weren't properly graded. One building on the same street could be fifty feet higher than its nearest neighbor. It was a relief that Clay Street was finally packed hard from traffic, but the wet months caused the new streets to be nothing but mires. If a prospector went missing from town, no one could swear whether he had gone back to the mines or had simply slid off the walkway into the abyss.

A sign hung at the corner of Clay and Kearney that read: *This street is impassable; not even jackassable.*

Rutledge Mayne spun a wild tale about a team of mules that had been sucked into the mud like quicksand. Everybody laughed. But nothing was done by the city fathers until the tally of missing livestock and lushes hit triple digits. Several cart-loads of brush were gathered and thrown into the muck. It wasn't much, but it drew a crowd.

The town was simply overrun with miners. Rudimentary shelter became far harder to find than a willing woman. Consequently, tents were a luxury and a real bed was priced far beyond the common man. The more resourceful landlords rented out table-tops, billiard tables, benches, and rocking chairs—blanket not included.

In some ways San Francisco was becoming a sophisticated city. On the other hand, army deserters and failed prospectors like Rutledge Mayne and Ezekiel Hardy still hung around town like vultures, looking for a way to scavenge someone else's earnings from them. Hardy's specialty was escorting greenhorns to the strike and then stealing their poke. General thought was that he had blood on his hands too, but there wasn't any proof of it. When miners turned up dead in the Sierras, it wasn't always of natural causes. When that happened, it was usually blamed on bandits like Jose Carrillo.

"I seen that *diablo* in the flesh, right here in town!" Mayne claimed.

It was a name that got everyone's attention. Men with clean hats and shaved faces shuffled a bit, uneasy that a bandit like Carrillo really existed.

"Quit your yammering, Rutledge," Gus snapped. "That wily ol' bandito ain't ever come down out of the mountains and you know it."

Recalling other, similar tales, Patrick was one of those caught up by Rutledge's claim. Spying Lupe passing through, he called out to her. It was unusual to see her in the Bella. Like most rare occurrences, the root of this one was money. It was payday and she was looking for Newman. Lupe disliked Patrick less than most Americans, but as she was on a mission dear to her, she tried to ignore him. He called to her again.

"Guadalupe! Can you spare me a *minuto* of your time?"

She allowed him that, but no more.

Furrowing his brow, he asked, "Aren't your people from Sonora?"

Cautiously, she nodded her head.

"Jose Carrillo is from Sonora," he prefaced. Then he asked, "Would you happen to know him personally?"

Lupe responded, "Are you an American, *Senor* Patrick?"

Patrick nodded.

"Andrew Jackson is an American," she said. "Do you know *him*?"

Gus guffawed and Lupe went regally on her way.

Waggling his head a bit in surrender, Patrick was defensive, "Actually, Andrew Jackson has passed on, so it wasn't a fair analogy. Besides, I thought she might know more about her countryman than we did."

"You meant well," agreed Gus. "But then, the road to hell is paved with good intentions."

Looking around at the prospectors crammed into the Bella, Patrick observed, "It doesn't look as if bandits have slowed down gold fever, now does it?"

Gus agreed. Fact was, wagon trains were streaming across the prairies, through mountain passes, and into the Sacramento Valley. Hardly anyone was weathering Cape Horn anymore. They sailed only as far as Colón and crossed the isthmus to the Pacific and connected with a steamer heading north. Both passages cut travel time. However the terrain and early blizzards took more lives than bandits or Indian war parties in the overland route. Passage through Panama took less than six weeks, but illness and hostile locals were becoming an increasing problem to the swarm of American prospectors.

A good many men who survived either trip fell prey to the lure of San Francisco's shady gambling dens and even shadier ladies. As the town continued its descent into greedy pandemonium, the streets became evermore dangerous. Once Aaron Ainsworth was gone, Newman renewed his efforts to marry Annabella off to, if not Asher Price, someone respectable. Therein lay the problem. Marriageable men were few and far between.

At first Annabella argued with him. Then she refused to speak to him at all.

Everyone—most of all Annabella—concluded that Newman and Asher Price had an agreement. Although Mr. Price gave no indication of it when their paths crossed, she wasn't fooled. He was no different from every other man in San Francisco. They all directed lustful looks and longing glances at her when she passed, he was merely more guarded in his gawking. It might eventually have occurred to her that he had little to do with her father's scheme, but she wasn't inclined to question her personal allurements.

Word had gotten around, however, that she had been in the arms of her lover the very day he left. Gus was surprised that Newman didn't pitch a fit about it. But to his mind, the Algerine was gone and whether she kissed him before he left didn't matter. He was certain that absence wouldn't make her heart grow fonder—she would forget him. Just how long it would take her to wake up to that fact was a problem.

Someone swiped the little seashell Aaron had given her. Certain that it had been Dovie Gaspard, Annabella trudged around the *Bella* like a martyr. Grateful that she had the silver chain, she wore it as if it was a wedding band. Gus thought it imprudent to wear any jewelry on the street lest some thief knock her in the head. To Newman, knocking her in the head could only improve the situation. He was very impatient. If he couldn't get the romantic stalemate moving, he claimed that he would roll her in a carpet, tie her with a rope, and, silver chain and all, throw her on the next ferry.

Annabella ignored her father's impotent threats. She had her own problems.

A day didn't pass that she didn't watch for her love's return. As it happened, Clark's Point just northwest of town had the best vantage point for viewing the vessels arriving at Yerba Buena Cove. It was the site of the first fulltime brothels, populated by *chilenos* from points south. Annabella had staked claim there to stand watch for the *Mary Thayer*. Sometimes she was driven away by the rain, but more and more often the spot was invaded by a bevy of screeching women who did business in the nearby shanties.

They too were waiting for incoming ships, but weren't looking for returning lovers. They were on the lookout for fresh clientele. Annabella couldn't complain to anyone, she had no business being up there all alone.

It wasn't that Annabella didn't have sympathy for the women. Talk about town had it that many of them had been abandoned by men who had gone to the gold fields. Left alone, they did what they had to in order to survive. Amenities in these bagnios were scare. A wash-bowl and a straw pallet were considered frills. Its reputation for carnality and excess did little to dampen trade. Annabella had to stay to a path on the far side of the hill to avoid their patrons. But that wasn't the only reason she kept her jaunts up to the point to herself. She didn't want to have to defend where she was going or to hide her disappointment when she returned.

Added to her suffering, close quarters and general filth throughout the town invited all sorts of vermin. Lice had been common when Annabella first arrived, but careful hygiene kept them at bay. Eventually they invaded everything that touched the miners. Their hair, hats, privates, and bedrolls—all were infested. Parasitic insects were insidious, but rats were worse. They attacked sleeping men who hadn't the good sense to cover their heads. Gus regularly roused drunks before they awakened with chunks missing from ears or nose. Even the Hotel Deluxe wasn't immune. Annabella merely yelped when she saw them. Lupe tucked her trousers into her boots, so she didn't worry about them running up her legs. Annabella began to think that trousers weren't a bad idea.

It didn't help that Patrick intoned, "For every one you see, there are forty more."

In this war against rodents, Stewpot had come to earn his keep.

When the *Mary Thayer* sailed, the dog had been expected to go along. As they cast off, however, he had taken a flying leap off the ship and landed hard. Although Tucker hollered for him again and again, the dog made a beeline up the street and never looked back. When he turned up at the Bella, Gus didn't run him off. He was a flea magnet, but an excellent ratter.

Annabella had time on her hands, so she spent several afternoons petting him. When she tried to corner him for a bath, he made for the door. He was down the block before she could stop him. Sitting morosely on a stool next to Gus, Annabella felt like a scorned lover.

"Leave him alone, pet," said Gus. "He'll come back."

Glumly, she replied, "That's what they all say."

When he came whining back about supper time, Annabella scooped him up and hauled him off before he could run. She took him to the hotel's kitchen to find a tub. Although she had looked for Lupe, she couldn't find her anywhere. (Lupe was always secretive, mostly to irritate Annabella.) Reluctantly, she pulled out a wash tub herself and began heating some water in a kettle while Stewpot hid under the table. Trust evaporated abruptly when she plopped him into the tub. Ears down, he flailed about trying to escape. Water sloshing everywhere, the dog finally gave in and sat in a soggy, pitiful heap as she took the scrub brush to him.

Just as she pulled him out and threw the blanket on top of him, he had begun a barely-audible whine. But she ignored him and, taking a pink ribbon from her own hair, she wrapped it around his neck and tied it in a bow. His ears lay back and his head hung with a pitiful look specific to canines who must suffer their owners' grandiosities. Just when she had the bow perfected, he stopped wriggling and stood taut. His flews fluttered as he emitted a low-pitched growl. Initially so forgiving, the change in the dog's disposition was startling. It was ominous enough for her to let loose of him and stand.

The growl muted into a harsh bark and he lunged for the door leading to the alleyway. Annabella quickly put her hand on his snout, shushing him. Then she turned down the oil lamp so she could peer outside. But before she could, the door flew open and hit her smack in the nose. She let out a howl.

With the sound of hooves retreating up the alleyway, Lupe stepped in, offering no apologies to Annabella.

"I believe you broke my nose!" Annabella accused.

"You too nosy anyway," retorted Lupe.

Eying Lupe suspiciously, Annabella reopened the door and looked out. All she could see was dust. Whether it was one rider or two, she couldn't tell.

"Were you with a man, Lupe?" she asked incredulously.

Although Annabella plotted her own rendezvous, she clucked at the idea of Lupe secreting away for immoral purposes and was unable to keep the look of disapproval from her face.

"Que?" Lupe snapped. "You got something to say?"

"No," said Annabella defensively.

Annabella wanted Lupe to stay and talk, but she was long gone up the staircase. Stewpot trotted after her, stopped and came back. Annabella sat down and idly patted the dog's head. Soon, she was stroking his head, pondering Lupe and her man. It made her both curious and jealous.

"What good is a halo anyway?" she asked the dog. "It's just something else to polish."

34

Ships entering the Golden Gate were so commonplace that Annabella rarely listened for the call anymore. Going up to Clark's Point every time a vessel was spotted was an exercise in futility. She resigned herself to the unhappy probability that a year might pass before the *Mary Thayer* would be back in port. Despondent and bored, she holed up in her room reading a few old fashion magazines and writing odes to her absent lover.

Gus had a bad feeling about the whole business from the beginning. He didn't tell her that. She wouldn't have listened.

✧

Most afternoons shopkeepers in clean white aprons strolled down to the water to have their own look at what ships had arrived. They all hoped for a merchant ship, not more miners. Shovel and axe stock always needed replenishing. A few harlots showed up, waving brightly colored scarves. The duteous harbormaster, Mr. Peet watched each ship as they tried to avoid abandoned vessels now littering the bay.

Seeing an odd-looking ship approach, he withdrew his trusty spyglass and took a look.

It was a whaler, so the shopkeepers dispersed, leaving room for the oil traders. They watched with interest as the ship inched its way closer. Whale oil was getting sparse. What they saw wasn't reassuring. Even with the naked eye it was clear that something was amiss.

"Broken spars and shredded sails—the mainmast is gone!" reported Mr. Peet as he peered through the glass. "How could she have been under way with such as that!"

"May I?" Asher Price asked Peet.

He held out his hand for the spyglass.

Peet was startled. He hadn't seen Mr. Price arrive. Adequately deferential, he gave it to him. If it was Mr. Price's vessel that had met with misfortune, Mr. Price would bear the loss.

With the efficiency of a man who had peered through a thousand telescopes, Asher took a look. Quietly, he corrected Peet's assessment of the damage.

He said, "The mainmast is there, but it is splintered. Mizzenmast is intact."

Enraptured by the disaster, a crowd gathered to watch as the ship dropped anchor and came to a halt. Asher returned the spyglass to Peet.

"What ship, sir?" Peet asked.

"The *Mary Thayer*," replied Asher.

It had been at sea less than a half year. One good look and Asher determined that she was riding too high in the water to have much whale oil in her, but was salvageable. Ever the pragmatic, he began thinking of how to board the ship and see to injuries or illness. One of the traders called a question to him, but before he could respond his attention was caught by a figure on the ship's bowsprit.

Whoever it was took a flying leap into the water. The figure then swam to a lighter bobbing on the waves and climbed in. Asher had made it his business to shake the hand of every member of his ships' crews; he also prided himself on never forgetting a face. Reclaiming Mr. Peet's spyglass, he took a good long look. Stone-faced, Mr. Butler stood next to him as he did.

"Is that Ernest Braithwaite, Mr. Butler?" asked Asher, pointing in the direction of the man who had commandeered the boat and was paddling for all he was worth towards the other side of the bay.

"Could be," answered Mr. Butler.

Realizing that they were watching a mutiny to the gold strike,

Mr. Butler awaited his orders. Asher thought of apprehending Ernie. However, with his ship in a shambles and what looked to be a crew lost to the sea's vengeance, he hadn't the heart. He also didn't have a chance to board the ship. Right away he saw another light boat making for shore. In it was a lone figure. Behind him, the ship exploded and burst into flames.

Even before the explosion, word had spread that something unusual was afoot. When the ship erupted, the onlookers began to jam the pedestrian boardwalks and then the thoroughfare. They all had a commonality. They wanted to know what the hell had happened. As in most cases, the more a story gets passed around in town, the less it resembled the truth. This time embellishment wasn't worth the trouble. What they were watching unfold was tale enough.

By the time word hit the Bella, all was said was that a whaler had moored. Instinctively, Annabella knew that what was afoot was not just any whaler mooring. Trembling, she wanted to go to see who it was first hand, but fighting through the harlots would simply take to long. She went to the Bella's new rococo-framed mirror and saw what she already knew—her hair was a muss. She didn't have to redo it, so she pinched her cheeks and tried to calm herself. With that, she ran back to door and out onto the street and was astonished that people had gathered and were all looking at her. Stunned at the sheer size of the assemblage, she shrunk back through the doorway.

Someone was coming and it had to be Aaron.

She had spent too many days and nights at prayer not to know they had been answered. She closed her eyes in thankfulness that she wasn't doomed to wait three years—or even one—for Aaron's return. It was as predicted. The whales were hunted out and her love had returned to her. Penniless, perhaps, but she didn't care.

By then, Stewpot had come and sat at her feet—still washed and brushed and smelling of French perfume. Both anxious and happy, she picked him up and held him against her bosom. Her mind was already making wedding plans. Returning to Boston for the event had been a consideration. She would just have to see what Aaron wanted. He might want to go to New York. The one thing that she was sure of was that they wouldn't stay in San Francisco.

They would buy a sloop and sail the seas and visiting each and every exotic port. Aaron would man the wheel and she would cling to him—her arms wrapped about his trim waist. The vision was so strong, she felt faint with anticipation. The roaring in her head was overwhelming. Inexplicably, she ran behind the bar. When she opened her eyes the glare from the street obscured the figure at the door, but she had no doubt who it was.

Stewpot knew him too.

35

San Francisco saw plenty of threadbare men. As Tucker McFee marched down the street, he looked bad enough to turn heads on that count alone. Long gone were his bell-buttons and leather straps. All that clung to him were tatters. His expression was oddly dazed. Yet he put one foot in front of the other with great deliberation.

"Where's your mates?" someone called out.

Looking in the direction of the question, Tucker didn't answer. He walked unflinchingly down the thoroughfare. A single misstep and he would be engulfed in mud, but he didn't heed warnings of that either. He walked so purposefully that a silent collection of the worried and the curious fell into lockstep behind him. It was as if he was a messenger from beyond.

In a way he was.

That wasn't a conscious thought. He was simply on a mission and he wouldn't let anyone or anything stop him. The very fiber of his being was intent on that. At first all he could see were dust motes floating in the sunlight. Gradually, hoards of faces converged with his consciousness. The instant comprehension struck his expression; he was peppered with question after question. They all wanted to know what had befallen the *Thayer* and its crew. The din nearly overwhelmed him. Mr. Price was even there, his face creased with concern. But Tucker shook the men and their questions off and continued resolutely up the street. As they all crossed one street and then another, his destination became apparent.

Tucker had a ghastly tale to tell. He only had it in him to tell it once, so he intended to tell it to the one person who needed to know the most. How he would find the words to explain it all to Miss Annabella had troubled him for a thousand miles of rough sea. Aaron was the smooth talker. Tucker tried to imagine what Aaron would say, but it didn't help. His only hope was that once he was before her, the words he needed would come to him.

Before he went through the teak doors, he took a big gulp of air and held his breath.

Like most saloons, it was dark inside, and he had to wait a moment for his eyes to adjust. He didn't see Stewpot right off. His eyes were riveted to the halo of gold surrounding Annabella Chase's angelic face. She was as exquisite as he remembered her. Just being in her presence warmed his bones. The sun-burned crinkles at the corners of his eyes visibly softened. She wasn't looking at him, though—she was looking anxiously over his shoulder.

In the past months, he had learned how to drink like a sailor. Had he any money, he might have bought a bottle and downed it first. Such oblivion would have been welcome. In fact, he would have gladly shot off a toe—even several toes. Any pain would have been preferable to telling Annabella what had happened.

When her eyes ceased their search and settled on him, his visage should've told her all she needed to know. Hope, however, wasn't abandoned. With steps that seemed to float, she came around the end of the bar. A flush appeared on her neck, but her face had turned white as snow. Stewpot whined at his feet, but Tucker still didn't notice him. All he saw was Annabella standing before him like saint.

The murmuring mass of humanity that had followed Tucker up the street gradually surrounded him inside the Bella. One or two of the spectators sensed calamity and withdrew. For them, such a tragedy deserved privacy. But they were in the minority. Everyone else had the decency to be quiet—if only for the better to hear it.

In the spotlight such as he was, Tucker's manners suddenly seized him and he quickly grabbed the hat from his head. It was the one thing on him that was in one piece. His feet were bare and he nervously rubbed his big toes together. After an awkward pause, it was as if his voice was finally uncorked. It was barely above a whisper, but shot out of him like a cannon. As if a spell was cast on him, the words spewed forth in bone-chilling clarity. Although everyone was transfixed, Tucker spoke only to Annabella. She however, wasn't actually paying attention to what he said. She was oblivious to everything but what was in his hands.

It was twisted, but there was no doubt that it was Aaron's striped sock hat.

The sight of it stunned her and she staggered a bit. Disappointment crossed her face like a knife. Just like that—a heart rent in two. She didn't swoon, but Patrick saw the hat also and let out a wail. It was enough of a distraction for her to reach out and clasp his arm. By then, Gus had come round the bar. He hadn't called to Newman, but the ruckus had roused him from his office. He stood right next to Gus stood and held his breath.

Gulping, Tucker continued with his story. Only a word here, a phrase there was audible to everyone. As he continued to speak, huge tears began to roll down his face. Some of the men in the crowd murmured and shuffled their feet. A weeping man was more than they could take. Silently, they began to disperse. For all the repugnant behavior that was a daily feature of life in San Francisco, this sudden distaste for attending another's misfortune was remarkable.

"An island... no folks around... fires left burning... huts deserted... smoke was like a blanket everywhere... scared the tar out of me... bedded down... couldn't sleep. Skeeters ate us up. Others slept like babies... ate the food as well... not me... too blinky... We found their secret the next day."

Here he stopped, then hissed again, "We found out their *secret*."

Unsurprisingly, Tucker said that Aaron had been the leader as they went about combing the island for inhabitants. They had to hack their way with machetes to locate the source of the smoke.

"It was a pit," Tucker said, his voice stronger. "A pit six-foot deep and yonder. They all just stood and looked at us like we were demons—but they didn't run. The grandpa had a stick and was stirrin' the pit like it was a pot of soup."

It was, Tucker claimed, a mass grave.

"We knew they were dead cause of yeller fever and we pulled foot and ran," Tucker said. "I think we was hollering—at least I was hollering. We jumped in our light boats and headed for the ship. It had been sacked while we were gone... Cap'n Weeks was dead."

"No one bothered to check for bites," he continued. "We were all speckled with them. Four days out we began to get sick. First it was chills, then fever. Bleedin' out came next."

Gus asked the inevitable question, "How'd you make it and the others didn't?"

Tucker's nose was running and he wiped it with the back of his hand.

"Ernie was too gamy I guess," he said. "Me, I'm just lucky."

The expression on his face at that time supposed that he didn't feel all that lucky. He was looking at his feet and did quit them until he heard Annabella's voice. She needn't ask the question. Everyone knew the answer.

"And Aaron?" she asked softly.

In a manner that suggested it was physically painful to do so, Tucker shook his head side to side. The tears that had run down his cheeks and dripped from his chin began anew. It quivered. He pressed Aaron's hat against his lips to smother the sob that threatened to escape.

Gasping, Annabella thought of her poor, lost love committed to the ever-lasting deep.

It was an awful, if inescapable conclusion. Drownings, dismemberments, even murder was done during those vast, endless quests for sperm. When a man died at sea there was no grave to place flowers on, no kiss good-bye. Annabella's fingers went to her neck and fingered her precious silver chain. Every trace of Aaron was gone save that.

Although everyone expected it of her, Annabella didn't cry. She didn't gnash her teeth or rend her garments. Many onlookers were quite disappointed in that.

She only asked, "Did my love have any last words?"

"None that I recall, Miss," said Tucker earnestly.

"I see."

Annabella gave a perfunctory nod in his direction. Impulsively, Tucker reached out a comforting hand, but she shook it off. Rather, she held on to Patrick's arm too as tears were troubling him. He emitted a keen so high-pitched that at first only Stewpot heard it. Despite that, everyone was looking at her—as if gauging her reaction. As the seconds passed, people grew increasingly desperate for her to leave. When she finally did, she passed by Gus who was standing stone-faced in front of the bar. She didn't see her father, possibly because he looked quite unlike himself. In fact, he looked quite stricken—with guilt most likely. He hadn't actually willed the catastrophe, but he might as well have. Under the weight of that culpability, Newman decided his best course was to pass the blame.

Rather grandly he pronounced, "Such are the vicissitudes of life."

As soon as Annabella was gone, the usual street sounds began immediately. Lubricated by rum, the discussion of the disaster continued inside the confines of the Bella. That being the case, it was really difficult for Newman not to look upon everything about Aaron Ainsworth's demise as a complete boon.

Speechless with disgust, Gus just shook his head.

36

Fortunately for Newman, Annabella didn't hear his parting remark or the gaiety that ensued. She was bullying her way through the throng of people crowding the walkway in front of the Bella. When she broke free, she ran to the hotel. Inside, all was quiet and she ran up the stairs. She saw no sign of Lupe. Dropping to her bed, she kicked off her shoes and buried her face in her pillow.

Her voice was muffled as she screamed, "Where is that blessed girl when she's needed most?"

She kicked her feet wildly at the injustice and screamed a few more times into her pillow before coming up for air. She lay still for a moment, gauging if her weep was spent. Because her eyes still burned, she knew she hadn't quite given vent to her rage and despair. Just as a sob erupted, a figure appeared at her door. She looked hopefully in that direction, but it wasn't Lupe.

It was Asher Price.

What a foul beast! Her brow furrowed and her lip protruded pugnaciously at his impudence. Although she was affronted, she was also strangely happy to have someone to rail upon. So she grabbed the heel of her mud-caked shoe and threw it at him. Surprisingly light on his feet, he ducked. She couldn't tell if she hit her mark or not. Regardless, he drew her door closed.

Through it, he said, "If I can be of no other service, please allow me to see that your door is secure. It isn't safe."

"Go to hell!" she shrieked.

Apparently baffled by being cursed at for his trouble, he said mildly, "Of course. I just wanted to see to your well-being."

Annabella didn't bother issuing any more invectives. Heaping abuse on a man of rank like Asher Price was very nearly exhilarating, but she couldn't smile. She could hear his footsteps going down the stairs and was pleased. As he passed Lupe on the staircase, he nodded to her. Lupe could hear Annabella's crying from the landing and figured it was his fault. She placed her hands on her hips and glared at him accusingly. Although he really didn't think he should have to answer for his actions to her maid, her demeanor made him do so anyway.

With great formality, he said, "Miss Chase did not find my offer of consolation to her liking."

"No, *senor*," replied Lupe. "She is in grief.

It looked for a second as though Asher intended to defend his actions, but, wisely, he didn't. As he went on his way, Lupe rapped quietly on Annabella's door.

"Who is it?" Annabella asked harshly.

No doubt Asher Price was making another play. Taking off her other shoe, she went to the door and flung it open. Seeing Lupe standing there, she looked menacingly over her shoulder for Asher.

"Has that *bastard* gone?"

Lupe frowned, "That no way for a lady to talk. And look at the mess you made of this floor! I should make you clean it yourself."

The floor was a muddy mess. Annabella knew that she should have taken her shoes off before she ascended the stairs. Lupe was particular about the floors. She would never admit to that though.

"My father pays you good money and you do little enough to earn it," Annabella accused.

Taking the shoe from Annabella's hand, Lupe retrieved the other one next to the door. Annabella walked to the side of her bed and slumped down.

"He's dead," she said wanly.

Nodding, Lupe dropped the shoes and came and stood in front of her. Reaching out, Annabella wound her arms tightly about Lupe's waist. At first Lupe didn't respond. Then she began to stroke Annabella's hair. Reminded of her mother, Annabella was soothed. The smell of Lupe's cigarillos didn't seem vile at all.

"Thank you," she said.

Enormous tears formed in the corners of her eyes and flooded down her cheeks.

Annabella began to cry in earnest too.

37

In retrospect, it was a foolish decision. But Asher consoled himself that a man must do the gentlemanly thing whether it was well-taken or not.

Like others on the street, he had been drawn to young Tucker as he told his tale. Not only had he been there when his launch touched shore, Asher himself had tied it to the pier. The boy looked to be on his last legs. But once on land, he gathered himself miraculously. Everyone asked him questions, but all he would say was, "I must report to Miss Chase."

To that end, Asher accompanied him up the street and over to Clay. After all, it was his duty to notify the loved ones of the disastrous end to the *Mary Thayer*'s crew. Weeks' widow came first to mind. She was the only family of the crewmembers that he had met. So far as he knew, there were no wives living in San Francisco. All interested parties—save Miss Chase—were back east. As the owner, he could have demanded an accounting up front, but he was disinclined to do that yet. As he saw it, it was his duty to do what he could to ease the suffering of any and all survivors.

Clearly, Ernie Braithwaite had his own plans.

When the *Mary Thayer* exploded, Asher didn't even flinch. There would be nothing left of the ship. Any telling of events leading up to the loss of crew and vessel would be left to Tucker McFee. The crowd formed so quickly behind him, Asher did well to keep up with them. Fortunately, he knew where Tucker was headed.

At the Bella, however, Asher didn't go in. He was as curious as the next person, but innate decency told him that to go further would be insensitive. Moving to a covered walkway across the way, he waited patiently as each tidbit of the story was passed person to person and then to him. Young Tucker's story wasn't weighted down with minutiae, but it could still be edited down to two things—Yellow Fever and stolen provisions. If the ship hadn't blown, he probably would have done it himself. No one would board a ship tainted by the yellow curse. It was difficult enough to get crewmen without them worrying that the ship was contaminated.

The whispered report of the crew's demise had barely made the rounds when young Miss Chase appeared at the door. Although the crowd parted before her like the Red Sea, she did not acknowledge anyone. To Asher's mind, she was remarkably self-possessed. Hearing of her lover's death—particularly in such a public manner—would have sent most young women into a swoon. But Miss Chase didn't swoon. She did look dismayed, but she trudged majestically through the mud to the hotel. Her father didn't follow her. Gus Gerlache didn't either. The only one who appeared at the door was the spindly piano-player. He looked confounded, but he didn't follow her to the hotel. No one went to see to her distress. It was just as well. Under delicate circumstances, men usually proved to be quite useless.

It troubled Asher's sense of fittingness to think Miss Chase was unconsoled. It bothered him nearly as much as the thought of the tortuous duty that lay before him. There were many letters that he must write. He must apprise the portion-holders of the *Mary Thayer* that it would not sail again. That would be a financial setback for a number of families. It also fell to him to send his personal condolences to the relatives of the crew members. It wasn't required, but Asher intended to send a stipend to each wife and child. That would never recompense the loss of a loved one, but it would help in the cold northeastern winters ahead. He would do his duty as he saw it without hesitation. That meant seeing Miss Chase was not alone in her hour of grief.

Not surprisingly, Miss Chase was not open to a stranger's consolation. He didn't fault her any more than he faulted himself for making the attempt. Men *were* useless in some circumstances.

As he turned to walk back toward the bay, he heard the crowd issue sympathetic rumblings for Miss Chase's misfortune. By the time he'd walked down Washington Street to his office, the tide had turned. As Asher heard it, the general consensus was that Miss Chase was young and therefore her attachments were not as deep as a lady of some maturity. She would love again.

It wasn't much of a surprise either how quickly opinion turned from sympathy for her to dispassion. It had been his experience that people generally believed that which troubled them the least. Handsome people were given even less pity than those who were plain. He struggled not to grimace at such mean-spiritedness.

Although she wasn't family, Asher knew he had been right to offer Miss Chase his personal sympathies for her loss. Her romance with Mr. Ainsworth hadn't been a lengthy one, but there was little doubt that she loved him. Young love may flame fierce and bright, but that didn't mean it would burn itself out. His love for Cora certainly hadn't been fleeting

Not a day went by that he hadn't wished that it was.

38

Certain in the knowledge that Mr. Perry wouldn't dare die without her, Enid Perry didn't hurry home that last winter of his life.

In that time, Adelaide Perry grew up in more ways than years.

Enid took advantage of her trip to visit the seamstress. For she had grown too, but had less to do with moral enlightenment than that she had little to entertain herself but eat. While she awaited her new dresses, she partook of sweets and thought about her coming windfall. That and the oleaginous meals taken with kin in the wilds of Northern New York were unkind to her waistline and demanded several re-fittings before she set off for home.

When she reached the Perry house, she was astounded when she stepped from the coach. The house looked vacant. She was even more surprised when a man stepped from the shadows and introduced himself as Mr. Dutton, the Perry family lawyer. She all but collapsed in a swoon when he told her that Mr. Perry had died and his estate was left to his only offspring, Adelaide.

"Miss Perry did see to it that you would receive this settlement."

"What?" she shrieked, snatching the check out of his hand.

Looking at it incredulously, she howled, "This measly sum? I cannot live a year on this. I owe a seamstress!"

"If you are unhappy with it, Miss Perry would be happy to keep it," observed Mr. Dutton.

He, however, made no attempt to retrieve the check that she had cast on the wet ground. Like a turkey hen, every time he began to talk, she began to shriek.

"But she cannot have it all! What can a mere girl do with such a sum?"

"We can only ask such a question, I fear," said Loyal Dutton.

"But she cannot have it all!"

"It was as her father wished."

"But she cannot have it all!"

Finally, the second Mrs. Perry began to cut her losses, "My poor Eduard! He has nothing? You must do something!? Am I not Mr. Perry's legal wife?"

"Indeed," Mr. Dutton agreed, "But Mr. Perry's money came from the first Mrs. Perry and it was not his to pass on."

Stamping her feet in place like a horse in the cold, Enid realized there was nothing she could do except take refuge at a tavern down the road. Fortunately, it was one in which she was well known. They were happy to allow her to run a tab until she could turn her bequest into cash.

Adelaide had watched the goings on between Mr. Dutton and the second Mrs. Perry from her upstairs bedroom window. As Enid re-boarded the coach, Mr. Dutton had turned his head upward in her direction. As she could only hear when Enid squealed her indignation, he nodded to let her know that their business was complete.

Mr. Dutton had been the executor of her mother's estate. Adelaide had been unaware that she even had one.

"Oh, yes, Miss Perry. Your mother's people were well-situated," Mr. Dutton assured her.

Sitting in the Perry parlor, Loyal Dutton's large waistline caused an unattractive gaping between the buttons of his coat. He was younger than her father, but looked more tired than distinguished. Known as a man who took good care of his clients, his legal reputation was impeccable.

Mr. Dutton told Adelaide that he had heard rumblings that things might be amiss. It took him a while to gain her confidence, but his kind manner won her over. For the first time she unburdened herself about her father's unsettling disintegration.

"There is little doubt that your father's second wife (for he couldn't quite call her Mrs. Perry) was systematically poisoning him. Perhaps with rat poison...." Mr. Dutton mused.

Here Adelaide interrupted, "We had a cat that happen to eat poison. It was an ugly, quick process—only lasting a few hours."

The recollection brought tears to her eyes.

"If administered in small enough quantities, it can take months, even years." He looked at her evenly, "When do you recall the onset of your father's symptoms?"

Adelaide opened her mouth as if to answer and then suddenly clapped a hand over it. Her father was being slowly murdered and she stood by without protecting him—part of the time diddling one his killers. There was little doubt that Eduard had a hand in it. Both of them—Enid and Eduard were murderers of the worst kind. They didn't kill in the heat of passion, but with deliberation and planning. Thinking of the agonizing pain her father suffered, she couldn't contain her sobs.

"There, there," soothed Mr. Dutton.

Mortified to the quick, it took longer for Adelaide to confide in him about Eduard. To her mind, the affair was her fault. She allowed it—even enjoyed it. That, however, she couldn't bring herself to tell Mr. Dutton. Somehow, he understood. He also saw it quite differently, both legally and morally.

"You were but a child, my dear," he assured her. "It is called seduction and it is against the law."

Because Mr. Perry was dead in the ground, proving that he was poisoned seemed fruitless.

"You could live quite well on what has been bequeathed to you. But if you would like my advice..."

She nodded her head.

"You might even want to purchase a business or a farm—something to give you a living."

Due to her expression, Mr. Dutton back-tracked, "Well, perhaps not a farm. But perhaps a piece goods store, or a school—finishing schools for young ladies are all the rage in the *monde*."

"I know even less about teaching than I do fabric."

"Trust me, Miss Perry. Academics have little to do with such schools. Girls are expected only to learn how to walk, speak a little French, and keep up with the latest fashions. If they obtain any learning, it is a lucky coincidence."

"I know Greek and Latin, but not much French," she mused.

He reminded her. "You can hire a French teacher."

"Surely, I need to know more than that. I am clumsy as a pig on ice."

"You are a lovely young woman and there is but one thing to remember about presenting yourself as a lady of good breeding."

She arched a brow.

"You must conceal how well you think of yourself and how little you think of them."

A laugh erupted from the back of her throat. It was a long time since she had laughed. It felt good.

With that Mr. Dutton took his satchel and tugged himself into his gig. Taking the whip in his hand, he cracked it lightly, just above the horse's head. The horse bolted forward so quickly that Mr. Dutton nearly lost his seat. Adelaide didn't laugh then, but she could have. She saw in that just another of life's lessons. In his own way, Mr. Dutton was quite brilliant.

She was extremely grateful to have an attorney able to rid her not only of Enid, but of Eduard Stackpole as well. She would sooner have done murder herself than allow that wretched swine to have dominion over her again.

As if a test of that resolve, Eduard Stackpole presented himself to her.

✧

Adelaide Perry's future plans to open a school were in their infancy the afternoon Eduard knocked softly on her back door. The minute she saw him, she realized that she should have vacated the property in a more timely fashion. But she had dragged her feet. Packing wasn't just a chore; it was a goodbye to all that she knew in the world. She had to decide what of her mother's jewelry and her father's books she would take with her, so trunks were sitting about half-full in various rooms.

Apparently, word of being left out in the cold in so far as Mr. Perry's will was concerned sent Eduard on a direct course to his beloved stepsister's side. Within seconds of seeing his smirking face, she realized why he had come. He intended to renew his seduction. This time she was certain she could deflect his advances. However, her face went ashen when she saw him. He was already letting himself in before she could even say hello—or lock the door.

"Addie, *dearest*," he gushed.

With hands extended, he walked towards her. She put out her hand to keep him at bay. But he grabbed it, first to kiss, then to shove against his own bosom.

"Hear my heart, Addy? It's beating like mad—all because of your beauty! You know, don't you? You have become a devastatingly beautiful woman. To think that I might once have had your affections brings me to tears. *Tears!*"

With that he grasped her by her shoulders and drew her to him for a great, big, wet kiss on the lips. She took the back of her hand across her mouth, wiping off his saliva.

"Surely, you don't hold that little tiff we had as children against me?" He kissed her again.

Wrenching her mouth from his, she demanded, "Unhand me!"

Eduard was the sort whose greatest vanity was how expertly he could woo a woman. Adelaide lack of enthusiasm was taken as a personal affront. Still, he was too sly reveal his pique. Doubling his efforts, he smiled charmingly. She believed she saw the flash of a gold tooth.

"I realize that I did a great injustice to your honor," he cooed.

"But in truth I must point out that I was just a boy myself. Young men rarely have dominion over their desires. I was a boy who was in the throes of deep, abiding love and I did not know how to express that properly. I took terrible advantage of you. Can you ever forgive me?"

Humility was the last thing Adelaide expected. Disconcerted, she looked at his eyes with a hard stare. If they were the window to his soul, she wanted to see it. Usually so glib, she didn't know what to make of him just then. At the very moment she began to relent, the old Eduard returned—with a vengeance.

Clasping her in an enormous bear-hug, he planted another kiss on her increasingly uncooperative lips. To her disgust, she could feel his tongue thrusting against her teeth, waiting for her to gasp for a breath. They both knew it was inevitable, so when she finally did, he slid it expertly to the back of her throat. As he did, he moaned. It was that sound that brought her completely to her senses. It was all she could do to keep from gagging. Unaware of this, he ground his hips against hers.

She chomped down on his tongue as hard as she could. She tasted blood. He did too.

"Ptat ith a thowwy thing tho do, Mithy!"

Wondering how long he would be talking with a lisp, she giggled. Eduard, unfortunately, was most unamused. Taking a step back, he slapped her with all his might across her cheek. It knocked her from her feet. When she came up, there was a carving knife in her hand.

39

She wanted not to be judged. Annabella had wanted to mourn in private. In her ear, Patrick's high-pitched little keen on her behalf grated her nerves. She couldn't bear any more. If she didn't escape, she knew she would either join his lamentations with a plaint of her own—or slap him to his senses. That was why she made such a hasty retreat through the door.

She really hadn't cared to listen to Tucker's telling of the tragedy. Because in truth, it really didn't matter how it came about—only that it did. Perhaps she should have grieved for Aaron's suffering. Yellow Fever was a terrible death—she had heard every gory detail during her own ocean voyage. She knew that it was best to leave it alone. Had she allowed herself to think of it, she was sure that she might just run mad.

Annabella couldn't quite forgive her father for not at least pretending that he was sorry Aaron was dead. Just imagining his self-satisfied expression kept her in her room. It also played a large part in a difficult decision.

She *was* suffering.

There weren't even any last words of love. (Actually, there weren't any words of love at all, but sometimes the memory doesn't observe these fine points.) The thought of living without Aaron wrenched her heart in a way she never thought possible. Being surrounded by those who didn't respect her loss was doubly unbearable. She didn't eat for several days. Fondling the silver chain she fancied he had meant for her, she scribed a long, tear-stained, and punctuation-free chapter of her memoirs.

Annabella lay in bed so long that people had begun to suspect she was touched. Newman didn't have the Scotch to approach her face to face. He sent Patrick as his emissary instead. He bore badly-penned entreaties and placed them on the blanket beside her. Wadding up each and every one, Annabella tossed them in the corner. Patrick returned to the *Bella* and shook his head dolefully. As Gus saw it, sorrow needed solitude.

He told everyone, "The girl needs to be left alone."

Lupe might have agreed with him, but no one knew for certain. The little woman was nowhere to be found. Some figured that she was spooked by the mention of yellow plague. For whatever motive, she had packed her belongings and didn't say goodbye. It was days, however, before Annabella admitted that she was likely gone for good. Up until then she hadn't told anyone about Lupe's late night trysts with a secret lover. But in light of her mysterious disappearance, she finally revealed that secret to Patrick.

"Never in all my born days would I have guessed *that*!" he exclaimed. "I wasn't even sure she liked men...

In a fit of self-pity, Annabella asked, "Those all around me find love. Why am *I* alone denied?"

Not a day later, she made the decision to face the world and its unkind inhabitants.

The only black dress she owned had huge, tiered sleeves of lace. It was a beautiful gown—probably too low cut for a girl—or for mourning weeds either. That made it perfect for a San Francisco bereavement. Practicing her most wan expression, she tied on her straw bonnet and headed for the Bella. As she crossed the street, she was more intent on what she was going to say than where she was going. Her head down, she pushed her way through the men, mud, and oxen in her way. It completely took her aback when she all but slammed into Asher Price. To her, he was still her father's co-conspirator.

There was a brief dance as each tried to decide which way pass, but then they went on. It wasn't much of a tribute to her dead lover to care about her appearance, but she was aware that she didn't cast a very striking figure as she tromped across the muddy street. Perhaps her bonnet had obscured her face. She hoped so. Her eyes were red from weeping. It occurred to her that she should have checked his forehead to see if it bore an impression of her shoe. But it was best to forget that business.

When she stopped at the door of the Bella, she was framed beautifully by the afternoon sunlight. But no one saw her. So she "ehhemmed" for attention.

That given, she announced, "I have come to a decision."

After her father accepted that she was actually gone, he did his duty by sending off a letter informing the Goodenows of their granddaughter's return. It arrived four weeks after she did.

40

Asher still had the horn-handled knife.

Very little else survived the inferno that had once been his home. He had picked the knife from the ashes because it was unfamiliar to him. Had he offered it as evidence, might another conclusion have been drawn from the investigation? He couldn't say. But he reminded himself every day that two bodies, not one were found in the smoldering ruins of his house.

Although there was an official inquiry, its conclusion didn't sit well with the folks who most enjoyed discussing possibilities that put people of consequence in an unfavorable light. No one believed that the body that lay in Potter's field was a woman. An unidentified woman would have been of interest only if it had been Asher burned along side of her. He knew that the best sweetener of anyone's tea was scandal.

Before the fire he had been quite personable—an asset to his father's business. In the aftermath, words seemed pointless. People heard whatever they wanted to hear and saw what they wanted to see. When Asher decided to handle the family business from a western office, society gave him their full approval. It was a test over which party was most relieved.

No one but Asher knew what actually happened the evening of the fire. At the time, he didn't know whose reputation he was protecting. He told himself it was Cora's, but eventually he admitted to himself that any face-saving was his own. The fire wasn't caused by the overuse of whale-oil lamps—at least not directly.

No one in Nantucket knew that the day of the fire he had come home early. In a scenario as old as time, he did not find his dearest Cora alone. He found her in the arms of another man. Every time he closed his eyes, he saw the glow of her cool, white skin as it was revealed in his lamplight. Her chemise had fallen down and that man's tanned hand spread across her backbone to her shoulder. Two of his fingers (Asher recalled this detail particularly) were beneath the eyelet edge of her top. When the door opened, Cora looked over her shoulder and gasped. Her face was stricken. Asher could only suppose that his own expression mirrored hers.

She turned around to face him; her brown eyes were wide as a deer's. The front buttons of her chemise were undone and hung open, lewdly exposing her breasts. Under any other circumstances he might very well have fallen to his knees in adulation of them. Whatever his reverie, it was abruptly interrupted when a sun-tanned forearm came around and clasped her possessively across the chest. It was a well-muscled arm, burnt brown from day work. No doubt a face belonged to the arm, but it was hidden in the dark behind Cora.

Huge tears filled his wife's eyes.

Plaintively, she called out, "*Asher...*"

Asher shook his head hard.

"No," he said, shutting his eyes against that which he could not bear to witness. "*No.*"

At one time a single tear from Cora would have cut him to the core. Using such wiles then, in defense of the greatest betrayal a wife could make, was more than he could bear. With precision, he set the oil lamp down on a table and turned to leave. The need to put the sight behind him was so great that he hastened out the door. In doing so he bumped into another lamp hanging on a hook.

Asher didn't see this, nor could he have guessed what followed.

The room, and the only means of escape, went up in flames before Asher had slammed out through the back door. He hit it so hard that it bounced back open. That wasn't something he noticed then either. But it came to mind later. If he had closed it, that might have stemmed the air flow that fed the fire up the stairs.

It would have been interesting to know what he would have done had he been aware that he had inadvertently caused the fire that had begun to devour everything in its path. But he didn't. He had been intent on the ground under his feet and putting as much of it between him and his faithless wife as he could. Regardless, when a half-dozen members of the fire-brigade came clanging by, all clinging for dear life to the water wagon, it didn't register that the fire might have been at his own house. When it did, he raced there as hard as he could, running in long, desperate strides.

In a seeming frenzy, Asher tried to enter the flaming ruins. It was far too late, but he banged on the door as the house collapsed around it. He had to be drug away from the inferno. Burnt skin hanging from his hands, he stood over the wreckage of his former life without visible emotion.

"Poor man," they excused him, "It is a shock to his senses."

His father assured him, "Not a single voice at the meeting is critical of thee, Asher."

"No doubt," said Asher, "I never heard of a church-goer who couldn't bear another's misfortunes perfectly."

If pushed, Asher would have added that what Christians and heathens liked least was another man's success. But his father wasn't much of a philosopher. The poor man's brow was still knitted trying to determine if there was an insult in his son's last remark. Asher's mother didn't want him to leave. The depth of her comfort had only begun to be searched. But she knew Nantucket had nothing left for him but hurtful memories. His father hoped that work would be its own reward.

But then everyone knew that hell is full of good meanings and wishings.

✧

He kept the knife in a metal box. In the wee hours of the morning, he would bring it out and turn it over in his hand. The cold steel of the blade tempted him. With only the barest of pressure he could put an end to his suffering. But the suffering itself had become his reason to live. What other reason was there for life but to torture his soul?

For the longest time, he had no doubt about what had happened that fateful evening. Lonely and anxious, Cora might have been easy prey for some wayward lothario.

But time worked on his memory, asking again and again if he had seen what he thought he saw. The expression Cora bore remained with him every waking hour. It was what woke him each night in terror—frightened not that she had betrayed him, but that she had not.

It was years before his nightmares revealed that when he fought the flames that it was with a knife. It hadn't been at night, however, but in broad daylight when the significance came to him. It hit him like a thunderbolt. Pale and sweating, he rushed to his house and locked the door behind him. Only then, in the still, stagnant air of his bedroom, he saw what he had not been able to bear. Closing his eyes tight, he buried his face in his hands, both begging the image to remain and crying for it to go. He flung himself back on the bed and stared unblinkingly at the ceiling.

For what ever reason, the images were finally distinct.

The knife had been at Cora's neck. The point made the merest indention against her throat. As he stared numbly into the air, all he saw was her neck—and the single pin-prick of blood that appeared like a tear. His heart beat so hard he feared it might leap from his chest.

Cora had not looked at him with guilt. *It was sheer terror*.

She looked to him for her rescue. And he had turned his back.

He couldn't sit up or stand. His limbs felt as if weighted with rocks—boulders.

Another truth assaulted him. He realized that it wasn't the public's damnation that had followed him—it was his own.

Whose knife was it? A handyman or an itinerant? It would have only been a guess. Had he not been so taken by the sight of his wife's bare breasts, might he have realized the knife was there? Was he that much of a fool?

The answer was unequivocally, yes.

41

Not surprisingly, her grandparents were astonished to see their loving granddaughter.

Simon Goodenow was particularly pleased. Securing Annabella from the hell-hole she had been held hostage was a relief, but not his primary concern. He was most pleased that she had returned to Boston of her own accord. She had chosen the Goodenows over her father. Mr. Goodenow visibly preened to have triumphed over his god-damned-son-of-a-bitch son-in-law.

Coldness had always surrounded Simon Goodenow, so Annabella gave him a perfunctory peck on the cheek. Mrs. Goodenow's delight was more than enough for both of them. Grasping Annabella's hands, she held them wide, admiring the beauty she had become. Her grandmother's only complaint was the state of her complexion.

"Why, dear Annabella, you are brown as a bean!"

"I *did* try to use my parasol, Grandmother. But the wind and sea are simply treacherous!"

It was nothing short of miraculous how quickly Annabella regained her upper-class diction.

Mrs. Goodenow trilled, "As a Goodenow girl, a glowing complexion is your birthright, my dear. You mustn't take it for granted."

Her grandmother's first order of business was to call her seamstress. It pleased her no end to have Annabella fitted for the finest and newest of fashions and corsets in which to meet society. Annabella watched as everything she brought back from San Francisco was quickly consigned to the fire.

"Do get rid of that tatty shawl," she beseeched Annabella.

"But, Grandmother, it was you who made it for me and it has comforted me in all my tribulations."

"Oh, alright," Mrs. Goodenow conceded. "But you shan't wear it in company."

With maids flitting around seeing to her every wish, Annabella quickly recalled how exquisite it felt to be pampered. Truth was, although she thought of her long lost love every day, she retook her previous life with great enthusiasm. Somewhere along the way she had decided that she would tell no one of her broken heart. She placed the silver chain in a heart-shaped box and was content to go about with a mildly afflicted expression. As for parties, she reluctantly agreed to her grandmother's urging without much cost to her conscience. She was indeed in great need of cheering.

At an afternoon social reintroducing her to society, a lady she hardly knew asked, "How did you find San Francisco? I hear it is quite the frontier."

Annabella answered sedately, "In some ways it is that. The weather is magnificent—nothing like the winters here. Every day sees new refinements in society."

Much to her surprise, Annabella heard herself blurt out, "I only left because I lost the man I loved. I couldn't bear to stay there without him."

That piqued the lady's interest, she asked, "Did you return to Boston to remember him or to forget?"

It was an odd question—one Annabella couldn't answer. Soon, a headache bothered her. She bid goodbye as quickly as possible and returned to her waiting coach without her grandmother. She attributed her indisposition to a small storm that had passed overhead. It left the usually smooth road at bit rough. The carriage wheels hit chuckhole after chuckhole.

"Not even jackassable" came to her out of the blue. The thought made her laugh.

Once the fetes were set and her gowns ready, Annabella was left largely to herself. It didn't take long, however, before Mr. Goodenow began questioning her about the exact nature of her father's business ventures. Annabella was careful to say that he was in trade—hard goods and the like. But Mr. Goodenow interrupted her evasive answers with impertinent asides about him to Mrs. Goodenow.

Annabella fiddled with her sleeves and pretended that she didn't understand his remarks. She was insulted (on her father's behalf, and that her grandfather thought that she was so much of a dunce that she didn't know what he was talking about). She may have been mad as Jehosephat at her father, but she didn't much cotton to hearing him being slandered. So she sat in seemingly slack-jawed incomprehension, thinking about the expression on her grandfather's face was she to tell him that her father actually ran a saloon with a whorehouse on the side.

The time under her grandfather's roof proved that he was as overbearing as ever. If anything, he had grown even more insufferable. Annabella knew that if she were to remain in Boston, she had best stay out of his way. Nothing tried his disposition like a presumptuous female—that much was evident.

She also finally realized that she was fraternizing with her father's sworn enemy. She didn't like that, but to her mind she had backed herself into a corner. After leaving San Francisco in an angry snit, she couldn't just go crawling back. And even if she marshaled courage to eat crow, she had no money of her own to buy a return passage. Blissfully parading from one coast to the other, she finally grasped that money was a finite commodity. The jewelry she wore wasn't hers. It belonged to the Goodenows. She couldn't part with the chain Aaron gave her had it even been valuable.

In Boston or San Francisco, it was the same. If a woman didn't have her own resources, she was doomed. The only lady of her acquaintance with any semblance of individuality was Miss Adelaide Perry, of Miss Perry's Academy for Young Ladies. She hadn't left the school under the best of circumstances and believed it would only be polite to apologize for her transgressions. Woman to woman, bygones should be bygones. She set a day aside especially to see Miss Perry and sent her card announcing her visit. It was returned to her the next day.

Astonished, Annabella asked her grandmother what had become of Miss Perry and her school.

"Why your grandfather saw to her," she said knowingly. "We never blamed you, my dear, for running away. We had no doubt that your conduct was a direct result of Miss Perry's improper influence."

Annabella looked at her blankly.

"You certainly did not learn such behavior in our home," she hissed sweetly. "Mr. Goodenow saw to it that she was cast out from good society."

If Mr. Goodenow would take revenge on an innocent bystander just to keep his standing from suffering, it was no wonder her father wanted a continent between them. She was never able to locate Miss Perry to offer her sincerest apologies—and ask for forgiveness. The same was true of the poor little kitchen maid, Adele. A rich girl's bonnet was a poor substitute for a reliable position. Annabella inquired below stairs about what happened to Adele, but no one would speak to her. The invisible door that she had once entered at will had been slammed shut. That censure stung.

Under such malaise, parties gave her no pleasure; young men were a bore. Now that she had come to admire men with callused hands and sinewy forearms, none of her peers held any allure. Her future yawned before her a barren plateau. No hills, no detours, no laughter—nothing to distract or plague her. After several weeks of mooning about the vast rooms of the Goodenow mansion, an odd caprice struck her.

She decided that the only thing left to her was to have a baby. The very thought of a baby boy cheered her immensely. She would name him Aaron. (If it was a girl, she would call her Amy—for no particular reason other than that she liked the name.) Although she didn't really want a husband, she knew she must marry first. It was simply a matter of convention. The time she had spent in the lap of luxury persuaded her that she liked it there. Her grandparents—and Boston society in general—wouldn't stand for her having a child out of wedlock. She had heard whispers about young women who shamed their families in that manner. They were either shipped off to distant relatives or married off to someone inferior.

With a reputation for wildness, she had crowds of suitors. So deciding on a groom was merely a formality. She was so set on a wedding that she had the seamstress making the dress before she had narrowed down the field to a manageable number. Her grandmother gladly took it upon herself to sort out the wheat from the chaff husband-wise. (Both her grandparents thought getting her married forthwith was the safest course for them all.) All Annabella hoped for was that her husband-to-be wasn't a complete fool. When she looked over the crop of bachelors vying for her hand, she realized the chance wasn't encouraging. As her future looked quite dismal, her memoirs were abandoned altogether.

She had been weighing the strengths and weaknesses of various marriage proposals when a letter from Patrick arrived. It was long on hysteria, but a bit short on content. All she gathered was that her father had gotten himself in Dutch financially and had taken to drink.

"Good Lord, Poppa," she muttered to herself.

She didn't hesitate to head back to San Francisco to set things to right. This time round, however, she put her ducks in a row. She announced her departure to her grandparents in advance. Although her grandmother called for her salts, Simon Goodenow looked at her sourly. He continued to look at her sourly when Annabella asked for enough money to pay for her passage west.

"I will repay you promptly," she announced.

That was a bit of a bluff. She couldn't be certain that there would be any ready cash to be had if her father was financially compromised.

With great finality, her grandfather said, "I wash my hands of it."

After a small curtsey in his direction, she kissed her grandmother's tear-streaked cheek. As she left their house, she didn't look back.

42

In the months leading up to Annabella's return trip to California, the fevered quest for gold had triggered improvements in all methods of traveling west. It was no longer necessary to weather the tumultuous Cape Horn to get to the Pacific. However, Annabella had seen enough of the ocean altogether. To her, its depths were her lover's tomb. Just thinking of it made her melancholy.

Overland would be a grand, new adventure. There would be no sea spray, salt grit, nor roiling seas to plague her. She could see herself, wearing a fringed jacket and astride a painted pony. She would lead a column of prairie schooners through rolling grasslands. At night, the children would play and laugh by the crackling fire. Wrapped in the warmth of conviviality, she would fall asleep beneath a blanket of twinkling stars. All in all, it would be a jolly time.

Unfortunately, the joyous excursion she envisioned did come to pass. There was no fringed jacket or painted pony. There wasn't much conviviality either. Half her trip across the plains was spent squished between a squabbling husband and wife—sometimes with their squalling infant on her lap. Their wagon was lugged across the endless grassland by an enormous team of groaning Durham steers. When she couldn't stand the bickering couple or the stink of the oxen any longer, she walked. But nothing stopped the trail dust from engulfing her. It coated her hair and settled into every crevice.

By the time they struggled into the Sacramento Valley, Annabella didn't despise the ocean quite as she once had. She prayed that she would never have to cough up dust again.

Half of their number had dispersed into mining camps before they arrived at Sutter's Fort. The morass surrounding the fort was oddly familiar to her. There was a trading store operated by Sam Brannan, but filthy miners were everywhere. Some looked thoroughly beaten; others looked ill. She avoided them all. It was quite apparent that there had been no improvement in sanitation. Holding her nose, she couldn't quite conquer the stench of cesspools. That didn't slow her down. All she cared about was getting herself and her remaining belongings to the ferry landing. It was a two and half day trip down the Sacramento River and across the bay to San Francisco.

Four-legged ferry passengers outnumbered people two to one, so

Annabella was happy to claim a bench away from the livestock. (It had been her experience that it was important to remain upwind from the cattle.) She wanted nothing more than to be left alone to contemplate what disorder she would soon encounter, but the other passengers talked incessantly about the real possibility of being waylaid by bandits. Although she tried to ignore the talk, Annabella couldn't help but listen to the story of Jose Carrillo and how he plundered American miners' camps seeking vengeance for his dishonored wife.

She had heard from many sources that, especially in the area of the southern mines, Mexicans killed at will and rounded up horses, wild or not. So anytime any one came up missing, they were the chief suspects. One story had it that Carrillo disguised himself as a friar. Others said he fought in the Mexican War and wore a coat of mail. A wanted poster pictured him a mean, sanguine sort, quick to anger and fast on the draw. Nobody cared to confront him—least of all Annabella.

Still, robbery wouldn't be a catastrophe for her. She had little money in her purse and the only jewelry she had was Aaron's chain. It had broken long ago and she sewed it into her hem so as not to lose it. All that gave her a premature sense of well-being and led her to stow her father's Pauly pistol in the bottom of her trunk. Content, she recalled how naïve she had been when she first came to San Francisco. Now she was a woman who was wise in the ways of the world. Her heart filled with admiration for the lady she had become, she looked at monotonous river scenery and sighed.

Such complacency begged a comeuppance.

It was a common event for the ferry to be accosted. Had they been anonymous thieves, it would have been nothing more than an exciting tale to tell. However when someone spoke Jose Carrillo's name, the episode escalated from notable to outright extraordinary. They were on the last leg of their trip and she was the only passenger who thought they were in safe waters.

However commonplace, Annabella's heart raced when she actually saw all the guns.

The bandits had climbed onto the ferry so quietly, that all them were aboard—armed to the teeth—before anyone noticed them. When they did, a short-lived chaos ensued. The screams (some even from women) were quickly squelched by guns shoved in the offenders' faces.

Like members of some militia, the banditos all looked the same—wide hats and serapes across their shoulders. Brightly-colored scarves covered their mouths and noses, but it was easy to see that one man was the leader. No one called him by name, but he emanated some force of energy that enveloped them all. It was presumed that it must be none other than Jose Carrillo. When the name was hissed, Annabella believed it to be him too.

Dark and sallow-complexioned, Carrillo was muscular and tall—taller than anyone else. He was surrounded by a shield of menace so great that no one dared to put up a fight. One man was so scared that when Carrillo himself put his gun to his face and demanded his watch, he suffered a fit of incontinence. Urine spattered on the wood boards of the deck. It was such a humiliation, no one, save Carrillo's accomplices, laughed.

A man standing next to Annabella fingered his sidearm. She believed him to be mad and edged away lest she be caught in the crossfire. Spying an axe propped against a wall, she wondered if she had the courage to wield it.

Just thinking of standing up to Carrillo made her hands tremble. She was infuriated with herself for being too intimidated to pick it up. She told herself that if she had her pistol she wouldn't have hesitated to shoot. (That such heroics would improve her memoirs didn't occur to her until later.) One of the Carrillo's fellow bandits went around to the passengers one by one, grabbing their watches and demanding gold. Annabella had a black velvet reticule dangling from her wrist. There wasn't anything in it but a handkerchief. Still, she didn't much want it to be stolen. When one of the robbers came around to her, he didn't grab her bag. Instead, he reached out and knocked her bonnet from her head with the gun butt of his rifle. All that did was expose her blonde locks which seemed rather purposeless to her. At least it did for a moment. Then it suddenly occurred to her that she might be in danger of molestation. She grabbed for her bonnet and gave them all a reproving glare.

"Don't you touch me you sorry piece of trash!"

The expression on the bandit's face suggested that he didn't much care what she thought. Carrillo picked up her bonnet and handed it to her.

He looked at her face so closely that she feared she had provoked him in some manner.

"*Estupido,*" he said.

With that, he disappeared over the side of the ferry. To her great fortune, a swift escape was more important to the banditos than ravishing impertinent women. They all slipped away as swiftly and silently as they had come. Just as they disappeared, a motley group of actual militia came up from below. They had spent the majority of the crossing sitting in the cargo bay playing cards, their weapons across their laps. That was a monstrous dereliction of duty. She had half a mind to write to the proper authorities and complain.

She would have too—if she didn't have more urgent business to attend to in San Francisco.

43

Annabella pouted about the entire bandit business until they were so close to Yerba Buena Cove that she was forced to truly address why she had come back. What unseemly alliances that might have taken place in her absence came immediately to the forefront of her thoughts.

She needed a plan of action, but she didn't have one. She had been content to tell herself that there would be hell to pay without regard to just who would pay it and how it would be exacted. If, as Patrick wrote, her father was now a sot and that the *Bella* was in financial ruin, she had no idea how to put a stop to any of it. All she knew that so long as there was a breath left in her body there was no one who would get away with doing her father wrong.

She had begun to recognize a number life's lessons. One was that blood was thicker than water—and some blood thicker than others. Another was that, as an avenging angel, one had to dress the part. Her ferry-wear was inadequate for just about any pursuit.

She hadn't opened her trunk for a thousand miles. As the ferry bucked and swayed across the bay, she climbed into the baggage hold and dragged it clear. Her things were in remarkably good order. (She was a careful packer.) Withdrawing each article of clothing with precision, she held each of them up for inspection. Her blue gown was too wrinkled, but her red one would do quite nicely. It took seeing her slippers and silks once again for her to realize just how sick she was of wearing muslin.

When the ferry docked, she was the last person to disembark. Dressed to the nines, the stares she received were a reward for her efforts. Unfortunately, by the time she headed out, she realized that she had been so intent on her costume that she forgot to retrieve the pistol. In a last minute panic, she went back for it and secreted it in the folds of her cloak. It wasn't just Carrillo who had put a new fear of God in her heart. There was an odd sense of danger about. In the brief time that she had been gone, decency seemed to have taken a holiday.

As she trekked up the walkway towards the square, it was after dark and the pistol was a reassurance. Even in the murky light of the wharf, she could see that the town had changed in more than just manners. The façade was altered substantially. It wasn't so different however, that she couldn't find her way to the Bella. She knew that by heart. The indecent activity, however, had given her a start. As fog filled familiar streets, the pressure of ominous eyes weighed on her nerves.

Thinking better of walking right into the Bella, she decided to accompany her trunk to the Hotel Deluxe first instead. It had taken her last coin to get a wharf rat to lug it up the hill. That much hadn't changed in San Francisco. Prices were exorbitant and derelicts still drank. If she had to make another settlement, inducement, payment or bribe, she had no idea what she would do. She hadn't another dime.

Going to the hotel was a good choice. She had been so spooked by the denizens of the dark that she had run right out of her slippers. She had run so fast and the mud was so deep that she had realized she had lost them until she stepped onto the boardwalk. Nothing would have made her look more foolish than barging into the *Bella* in her bare feet.

Once inside the hotel, however, her breath caught up with her. It was reassuring to see Mr. Boomer. Of late he had done his best to keep up with the city's titivation by improving the caliber of his guests as well as gussying up his own wardrobe. He looked quite dapper in a satin brocade vest front. He looked absolutely astonished, however, to see her. When she asked for the key to her room, he was flustered. Beds, he said, were still extremely scarce.

She batted her eyes at him, asking, "Isn't there something for me?"

"For you, Miss Annabella, I do the impossible," Mr. Boomer trilled.

Someone, no doubt, would be evicted. It was a reassurance that the town wasn't so barbaric that coquetry didn't have its place. She was surprisingly unembarrassed to employ her feminine wiles. It was a gift she supposed—one God granted to certain earthly vessels at will.

Actually, Mr. Boomer had plenty of reason to be happy. He was getting paid twice for the room. Newman had paid her rent regularly. He had re-rented to a gambler who had a nasty cough. Mr. Boomer didn't scruple to throw that man out now that Annabella had returned. In fact, he was happy to have an excuse to evict him before he expired in his hotel. Sometimes newly dead bodies weren't claimed and if that happened, he would be left to foot the bill for removal. Like everything else, burial expenses had catapulted too.

As he showed Annabella upstairs, she told him, "You look quite handsome, Mr. Boomer. I take it your hotel is still prosperous."

She was simply making conversation with the man since he had done her a favor. But he genuflected his way out of the room before she could ask him about Lupe. There was still no sign of her. It occurred to her that Lupe might have gone to one of the mining towns that had cropped up on every other gorge. But Annabella couldn't quite imagine her dealing three-card monte or serving drinks. It was more probable that she had returned to Sonora. San Francisco had grown like gourd since she had been gone—and the changes were clearly not all improvements. No doubt Lupe disapproved.

Annabella didn't spend any time at the hotel after she dug out another pair of shoes. It was dark as midnight out. She knew that wouldn't breathe a sigh of relief until she cleared the Bella's teak doors. She took her father's Pauly with her. The Bella's patrons were a rough bunch, but she'd rather face them any day than these lurking miscreants in the shadows of the streets. She scurried as fast as she could across the way.

Her steps, however, had slowed and then come to a halt as she approached the open doors. The music wafting onto the sidewalk sent the tasseled toe of one of her dainty suede slippers tapping furiously. Clearly, it wasn't Patrick playing the piano. Someone must have commandeered it from him.

"Holy crimminy," she muttered under her breath.

Outrage overtook her and she managed to clear the door way in three steps.

Once inside, she placed her hands on her hips and bellowed, "What in Blazing Hell is this?"

Her father would have been fit to be tied if he had he heard her curse, but at that instant she didn't much care. Her indignation spiraled out of all proportion. She intended to set things to right and she might as well begin with Patrick's overthrow. It wasn't exactly the way she had intended to announce her return to town, but it would do. She didn't dare let her eyes drift towards the bar, Gus was probably there. Just the thought of seeing him gave her a lump in the throat. It was too soon for that reunion—she might cry. So she aimed directly towards the scoundrel making the racket at the piano. Because she heard the clap of her own footsteps, she realized just how quiet the room had become.

As she glared at the man banging away on the piano, she suddenly recognized the muskrat coat. It was Rutledge Mayne.

He hadn't noticed that the place had gone quiet. When he finally looked up, his fingers only gradually quit their plinking. As the last notes hung gratingly in the air, he turned around to see what had caught everyone's attention. He wasn't really worried—Gus always kept any violence in check. But anything could happen at any given time anymore. A card sharp could be called a cheat, someone's mother insulted, or a woman's affections contested. More and more often guns were drawn, but it was mostly threats. Still, the chance of danger was just great enough to keep patrons on their toes.

Mayne's eyes lit up with a mixture of excitement and fear at the thought of a fight.

In the silence, the squeak of the stool when he turned around was very loud. He blinked his blood-red eyes several times. It took him a moment to glean a single image from the several swaying before him. By closing one eye, his gaze steadied. A pretty, slip of a girl stood there. (She looked familiar, but he wouldn't put a name to her face just then.) His logic being under the influence of a half bottle of rum meant all he saw was s halo of blonde curls as she headed towards him. Anticipation attached a smile to the corners of his mouth. Simultaneously he began tugging at his crotch and let out a giggle.

"Rutledge Mayne at yer service! Sit here, my sweet nubbin."

Irked at all bumptious men (the bandit incident still uppermost in her memory), Annabella gave Mayne a smack up-side his head—one strong enough to send him flying. Several shrieks rang out from the crowd when she hit him. They reminded her of the robbery and she had to gather herself.

In the brief interim Mayne landed in a heap on the floor. Brought to his senses, he came up blinking—uncertain whether to fight or not. Laughter swelled and whoops rang out. With that, the realization of just who hit him sunk in. Judiciously, he slunk several feet away and then collapsed.

Annabella turned on her heel and walked as briskly as she could towards Gus and the safety of the bar.

She saw Patrick, but didn't swerve from where she was headed. Instead, she greeted him with a slight nod of her head. He didn't respond immediately—he was almost as surprised to see Annabella as was Mayne. She hadn't bothered to answer Patrick's letter, assuming rightly that she would overtake the mail. After returning Annabella's nod, Patrick daintily stepped over Mayne and made for his piano without looking down.

Someone yowled, "Aye Patty, play us a jig!"

Determined to regain his stolen piano stool, he scurried over. But he did take the precaution of removing a pocket-square from his sleeve and dusting any distasteful residue from his stool. (History told him that when drunk, Mayne sometimes soiled himself.) After everything was in order, Patrick sat down with his usual aplomb and watched Annabella out of the corner of his eye. The members of his new little orchestra took their places behind him. They had only recently been recruited. The *Bella* had to keep pace with other drinking establishments.

Positioning his spectacles, he arranged his music and commenced to play what was always a crowd favorite. The other musicians chimed in and as the notes of "My Bonnie Lies over the Ocean" rang out, a resultant cheer of recognition erupted. Patrick gave a theatrical nod. He was, after all, the star of this particular show—even in minds other than his own.

44

After he came to the realization of just what part he played in the horrifying events that occurred back East, Asher Price went on a long, difficult exploration of his soul. He finally concluding that he wasn't the man of caution and good sense he always believed himself to be.

He was a big fat fool.

Moreover, he still continued to behave like a fool. In the midst of the tragic incident overtaking the *Mary Thayer*, only a fool would think that it was a wise move to attempt to console an empty-headed twit like Miss Chase. As he chastised himself, the pharisaic in him could not accept all the blame for that fiasco. Even a fool should not be cursed for his trouble. *That* was inexcusable. Apparently, Annabella Chase was either too immature or too obtuse to recognize gallantry or compassion.

To him, the sole benefit of the incident was that it exposed Miss Chase's true nature. It was a long-held truth that a man's character could be determined by how well he shouldered life's difficulties. It was startled him to think that he might have wound up married to that silly girl. Such a ghastly mistake would do no service to his dear Cora's memory. Of *that*, he was certain.

After Miss Chase up and left San Francisco, Asher had turned over a new leaf. Although it coincided with her departure, he didn't see that the two events were in any way related. He had simply decided that drinking himself into a stupor each night did not bode well for his health. Although he was unlearned in healing professions, he knew that spitting up blood was a bad sign. If he didn't quit quaffing back a pint of whiskey each night, it was likely that he would not only die an untimely death, but that it would be a protracted, painful one as well.

He had seen it happen.

Whether highborn or low, drink got the best of plenty of men—especially after years at sea. Grog was like mother's milk to sailors. Most made a show of how much liquor they could drink before they retched. Some needed that sort of fortification just to sign on for another go. If the ship's hold didn't have a sufficient store of grog, mutiny was a certainty. Asher didn't fault them for that. When it came to employing spirits to ward off fear, the only difference between him and the men who sailed his ships was that he had tried to hide it. His bender had taught him one thing—the blinding morning-after headache equalized all men.

The night of Annabella Chase's return, he had gone to the *Bella* for... he couldn't really say why. Had he been pressed for a reason, he would have said that he was just trying to occupy himself. (Now that he quit liquor, he often found himself at loose ends after dark.) He always managed to find an unoccupied table and would sit with his hand guarding a sarsaparilla. Amongst a throng of merry-makers, he fancied himself a part of the conviviality. Once in a while he was spoken to; otherwise he felt awkward and looked aloof. He really didn't like to drink in public, but the management of saloons generally didn't look kindly on the abstemious taking up table space. Sarsaparilla was too sweet for his taste, so he defended it only because of the cost. (Buying one drink he didn't like rankled his principles; buying a replacement was absolutely untenable.) His chair, however, had been a perfect spot for watching everyone else.

From the perch he had claimed on the moral high-road, Asher had watched astonished as everyone else as Miss Chase appeared from out of nowhere and lambasted Rutledge Mayne. Asher roundly disapproved. It was behavior unbecoming a lady. Still, he had a very odd—even disturbing—reaction to the event. He had become aroused.

God have mercy.

From the hoots he had heard, he wasn't the only one who had his privates whipped into a frenzy by the sight Miss Chase flailing away on Mayne. But that was hardly a comfort. He had always thought that, in his public conduct at least, he was a notch or two above the other men. Becoming sexually stimulated by an act of violence was not just another example of his moral failure, it was almost a depravity. Inwardly, Asher shook his head in disgust. How long would God allow him to fall short on these tests before he withdrew him as life's little vanguard?

His eyes followed Miss Chase as she invaded the men at the bar. It looked as if she had already forgotten knocking Rutledge Mayne silly. He had to admit it. That girl was still a pistol.

Making a big show of checking his watch, Asher determined that he had spent enough time amongst his fellow citizenry. He must keep to his schedule—and that demanded he be in bed and asleep no later than eleven. So he tossed back the remainder of his drink. The taste was so cloyingly vile that he had to keep himself from gagging. In the future he would stick to lemonade. Either that or he would just have to scandalize himself by ordering a beer.

Working his way through the writhing morass of miners and lewd women, he remained determined to reach the cool night air so he could enjoy his cigarillo in peace. A few steps from the door, he leaned against a pillar so as to strike a match on the back of his trousers. There was just enough of a breeze to make him cup his hands around the flame. Small Spanish cigars had become one of his few pleasures. Like just about every other luxury in town, they were becoming scarce. He would only allow himself a few puffs at a time. Then he carefully put it out on the door post. Anyone who noticed him might think him just another miser. He didn't care. He had to make the one box he had last until he had another in his hand.

With Patrick Coffin once again manning his piano stool, fine music wafted out the teak doors. Outside, the notes were better appreciated. Asher tapped his foot a bit as people hurried past him and into the festivities. He looked back through the door and peered at the crowd. He wasn't tempted to return. For him the Bella's evening entertainment was over. No other performance could surpass Annabella Chase's extravaganza *du jour*.

Wetting the end of his middle finger, he carefully touched the end of his cigarillo to make certain it was out. It was then that he noticed Rutledge Mayne navigating out onto the walkway on all fours. A few obscenities were thrown in his direction for blocking the entrance. Asher extended him a hand. Mayne took it. After a bit of grunting, he got to his feet. Because he was swaying ominously, Asher slapped him good-naturedly on the back, then steered him down the walkway.

"You need some air, friend."

"I don't need no air," Mayne insisted, yanking his shoulder away.

Swaying, Mayne dug beneath his coat for his knife. When he found the handle, he pulled it out and swung it wildly in Asher's direction.

"I need to cut that little girl—show her what's up is all."

It was an enormous knife, but Asher's voice remained calm.

"Put that thing away, friend, or you'll answer to me."

Mayne wasn't certain who he was talking to, but his voice sounded as if he meant business.

"I ain't your friend," he whined.

Although it was a distinct possibility, Mayne managed to replace his knife back without stabbing himself. Tottering to the side of the building, he slid to a squatting position. It looked as if he would stay that way a while, so Asher moved on. But before he went too far, he looked back once through the window of the Bella. He couldn't see Miss Chase. She had been engulfed by the crowd and its mayhem.

The thought of her returning to San Francisco hadn't pleased him. In his memory, she had looked fresh as the morning dew. Perhaps it was the dull glow of the oil lamps, but this time she looked different. She hadn't been gone long enough to look older. Perhaps it wasn't the years, but the miles. There was no easy way to get to San Francisco and she had come twice.

"Not my problem," he reminded himself.

Tucking his snuffed cigarillo into his vest pocket, he turned and walked on. He whistled as he made his way up the uneven walkway. Then a most unlikely thing happened. Asher Price burst into song.

"Bring back; bring back; oh, bring back my bonny to me."

45

After Tucker McFee had told his momentous tale of the *Mary Thayer* to Miss Annabella the previous year, he had been set adrift.

For a while, he was such a celebrity, someone was always there to slap him on the back and buy him a shot of whatever he wanted. He didn't know who found him some clothes. He thought it was probably Mr. Gerlache. Once he realized he was very nearly buck-naked, Tucker put them on without a fuss. But no one seemed to have an extra pair of boots. After scuffing around in his bare feet for a while, he bought some for himself with the money he got for bringing in the *Mary Thayer*.

It was well and good that the ship arrived when there were plenty of witnesses. It was even better that he was long gone before she went up in flames. That good ship rested beneath the briny deep like fifty others in the harbor. If anyone took the time to look, they would have found his named carved just below where the mainmast had broken off. He wasn't the only one who had done it. That had been a ship tradition. His name, however, was at the highest point—and it would be for eternity.

Despite the unhappy circumstances, being a luminary—even a temporary one—was fine and dandy. Of course, a luminary's shine fizzles when the next calamity or misadventure comes along. Fortunately for him, Tucker didn't really like the limelight. So when it flamed out, he wasn't particular bothered. He was glad as grapes to claim his lay from Asher Price himself. He had intended to use it in some way as to divert Miss Annabella from her grief. He fashioned a bouquet of flowers and tried to give it to her, but he was told that she was holed up in her room at the hotel and didn't want to be bothered. Although he watched for her every day, she left town before he even heard about it.

Bereft, he tried to tell himself that it was just as well. He couldn't afford to keep her in a fine manner on the pittance he received from Mr. Price. If he wanted to have her, he had to earn his fortune. He was still pretty green, but he wasn't stupid. The only way he could do that was panning for gold. He didn't know anything about the gold game, except that it was a sight easier than winning at cards. He knew enough to quit poker before he lost all his money.

After that, Tucker kept his funds good and stowed. Even with all the fine ladies asking for him to buy them a drink, he wasn't tempted to carouse. He didn't drink and he didn't whore. Once he set his mind on something, he stuck to it. He had survived two separate disasters—starvation in a snow-bound pass and the ravages of sun and sea adrift on the ocean. That he persisted when others died, he saw as a sign from above that he had a higher calling. He didn't misconstrue it as a call to the good book, he interpreted it that he was meant to win Miss Annabella Chase.

One lesson he learned early on was to keep his mouth shut about that. Dreams should be kept stowed tighter than money. Still, he didn't see winning the hand of a lady who was half a world away any less plausible—or noble—than any other prospector's motive. Most claimed to be seeking gold for the folks back home. But Tucker knew better. He saw it again and again. Once miners grubbed out a little dust, they spent it on cheap liquor, fast women, and slow horses. Then they returned to their claims to do it all over again.

As he contemplated panning for gold, Tucker admitted that mining didn't look to be his favorite occupation. But anything beat out hunting whales for a living. That had worn out his insides. It certainly hadn't been the much-vaunted profession he'd been told. The only good thing about it was in the chase. Once the whale was killed, it was both monotonous and gruesome. After his ordeal on the *Mary Thayer*, he had no intention of setting foot on another ship—particularly a whaler. The only whale oil he wanted to see was in the base of an oil lamp.

Dogged perseverance was what would pull him through. When other men gave up, he alone endured. He alone had taken Holy Communion.

"This is my body. This cup holds my blood"

He had no choice. It was either that or end up like Jonah. No, he wouldn't go to sea again.

After a providential meeting with a man who desperately needed to sell a gold-producing mine, Tucker took his shot at glory. Armed with a wash basin, a fire shovel, a few yards of jerked meat, and his semi-faithful dog, Stewpot, he arrived at his dearly bought claim full of hope. Annabella Chase was all he thought about when awoke each day and the last thing on his mind when, dead-tired, he collapsed into sleep each night. To maintain his self-imposed regimen, all he needed was to believe that his purpose was higher-minded than that of the rabble sifting silt in the Sierra ravines.

Within a month he was out of grub. He was also lonesome. On the ship, the quarters were close and he kind of got to liking talking to people. So he and Stewpot packed up and went to Sutter's Fort. It was a big letdown. Makeshift stores were lined up outside the gate. Some consisted of nothing but a plank suspended between two barrels. As far as civilized drainage went, Sacramento City couldn't hold a candle to San Francisco. People who knew said that the smells and outrages were above those found in New York City. It stench rivaled anything he had smelled on the *Mary Thayer*.

A line of women grinding cornmeal piqued his interest. So much so, he spent half a day watching them patting the cakes into tortillas. Their heavily-padded hips gyrated in unison, making it was the most stirring sexual experience of his young life. Before long, a man in a tall hat took notice of him. So as not to be taken for a deviant, Tucker traded some gold dust for a half-dozen Mexican johnnycakes. It was a steep price, but as the miners all learned, the going rate for anything was what someone would pay.

Because prices were so steep, Tucker vowed the next time he came for supplies he would go all the way to San Francisco. If he didn't have money for the ferry, he would paddle across the bay in a dugout canoe. The rate of exchange would make it worth his while. Getting Annabella's Boston address was not his primary reason to go there, but it was major a consideration.

✧

When it came time to head for San Francisco, he was down to deerskins. Even then, he carefully tucked a long knife in his belt. If a man looked dangerous, he was taken more seriously. He certainly had his fill of being taken for a kid. His garb made him look like many other prospectors—skin tanned dark as the bark on a tree and hair bleached blonde by the sun. No one was around to remark on that, or the stink from his groin and armpits. So he went forth unencumbered by the knowledge of just how curious he looked or badly he smelled. When it came time he forked out a dollar to cross the bay on Mr. Sutter's ferry. Wherever he stood, passengers moved away.

"Maybe they think we got fleas, Stewie," he said.

He said that in jest, of course. Joking relieved the tension he felt at the thought of crossing the bay. Since the *Mary Thayer*, he hated even the smallest bodies of water. When he looked over the side at the ripples, all he could see were dead men's faces floating in the foam. It didn't help his nerves when the ferry became mired on the mudflats and they all had to disembark fifty or so yards away from the shore.

Others waited for a skiff to rescue them, but Tucker was too impatient to be on his way. So with Stewpot under his arm, he crawled onto the beach. Unfortunately, that left him caked with a sloppy mixture of mud and sand. His boots came apart before he made shore.

He had wanted to slip into town, get re-supplied, and obtain Miss Chase's exact whereabouts without a fuss. Early on he had decided to buy a mule. But after months of small finds, he realized that he was wasting his time by manning a long tom and panning all by himself. He still believed the claim was rich, but he needed more manpower to uncover it. More and more men were joining their claims and working them together. He saw as many as thirty men chopping into the hillside of one ravine. Of course, they would have to split the bounty thirty ways. But then, one-thirtieth of something was a lot more than one hundred percent of nothing.

He was startled flat-footed by San Francisco's alteration. Now it looked more like a picture he had once seen of Chicago. There were fancy men and women everywhere. High-toned carriages near ran him off the avenue and opera houses were on every corner. So he laid low the first night just to get his bearings. All the rooms were taken in even the cheapest hotels. That was just as well. He didn't dare waste his money.

Stewpot went missing right away. It must have come back to him where the best handouts could be found. At first light Tucker set out to see what his dust would bring. After that, he wasn't surprised that he and the dog had the same destinations in mind. It shouldn't have been unexpected to come across Rutledge Mayne lying in the alley.

Their reunion wasn't particularly celebratory.

46

Annabella Chase hadn't come back to San Francisco just to knock Rutledge Mayne sideways. He was dismissed from her mind before he hit the floor. With him in a moaning heap, she headed straight towards the bar. There had been big changes in the *Bella* while she was gone. The rowdy crowd was testament to that. They parted like the Red Sea to make way for her, so she didn't take much note the new decor.

✧

Although Annabella didn't notice it, the Bella's renovation had come about because of her. It cost a small fortune, but Newman needed something to take his mind off of her abrupt and angry departure. Of the two, Newman had always been the visionary so Gus didn't complain. His first move was to rid the place of every piece of whale ivory. Next, the two crossed harpoons that hung over the doorway were put out back with the trash. Newman said they were rotten, but general thought was that he wanted to rid himself of any reminder of Aaron Ainsworth.

"In the new San Francisco," he announced, "No one wants to look at such quaint objects any more."

Nautical relics certainly didn't fit with the improvements he had in mind for the place. From the very beginning he had envisioned the *Bella* with brass rails and baroque mirrors. Now he wasn't content with just that. He had a new bar fashioned of the same teakwood as his precious doors. It was stained dark and lacquered to a glossy sheen. Gus was proud as a peacock over it. Newman wasn't content to leave it there. As if to celebrate his independence from fatherhood, Newman purchased a piece of erotic artwork that he would never have considered had his daughter been there to see it.

Other saloons had bawdy paintings, but his was twelve feet long and was very nearly a work of art. That was not to say it wasn't provocative. It was adorned with a dozen unclad women, all in poses immodest enough to make the average miner blush. The work was entitled "Turkish Bathers." Gus, Patrick, and Newman had stood before it once it had been set into place. It was a moment before any of them spoke. When the spell was broken, it was by Gus.

He said, "I never seen so much flesh since winter hog-killing."

"Aren't the figures a bit too ... billowy?" asked Patrick.

Gus replied quite testily, "How the blazing hell would I know about how fat a naked lady's supposed to look? Ask him! He's the bloody art lover!"

He pointed at Newman—who had turned beet red and made tracks for his office.

Patrick continued his critique, stroking his chin, asking Gus, "It's meant to be after Rubens' bacchanals. But tell me, where is the vibrancy, the tumult?"

Gus answered, "I guess it's where ever them women's clothes are."

The Bella's bedecking became a victim of its own success. Newman had intended the place to cater to a wider (and more prosperous) spectrum of customer. His plan was only semi-successful. Business did pick up. However, the monde didn't exactly clamor for admittance. The *Bella* prospered without them. Smoke from gamblers, drinkers, and assorted denizens of vice was so thick that the fancy new ornamentation was largely obscured.

✧

That was how Annabella found it. She didn't notice the voluptuous nudes on the wall—at least not at first. She was too aware that every eye in the place was on her. She did, after all, strike a fine figure. Admiration was part of it, but many of the onlookers craned their necks to get a good at her weapon.

When she slung the pistol on the top of the bar, she said, "Can you give this back to Papa for me?"

Gus had watched the entire fracas. It was a surprise that Mayne's head hadn't broken it. He was glad that she hadn't used the other end of it. Although he did his best to appear unperturbed, he was not. Seeing little Annie again—looking like a lady rather than a girl—gave him pause. He doubted, however, that she got more worldly sitting in a parlor in Boston. While she was gone, San Francisco had turned into little more than a showy hellhole. To survive and thrive, a man needed guile and grit. A girl was just another lamb for slaughter. Annabella needed to grow up—and fast. As it stood, he doubted that she realized that all Mayne's digging at his privates wasn't attending to an itch.

He didn't much like it that she clunked that pistol down on his newly varnished bar either.

Annabella's dander was still up so when Gus frowned and pursed his lips. From her expression he could tell that she thought his look was criticism of her unladylike behavior.

With artificial gaiety—and as if she had seen him just that morning—she said, "Gracious, can you imagine the gall of some men?"

Just as he would have had he seen her that morning, Gus didn't answer, he merely grunted. He knew why she had come back.

"Damn that Patrick," Gus muttered to himself. Why did he have to go write to her about this mess?

"Good to see you, Gus," she said.

He nodded, "You as well."

"Wait until I'll tell you how Jose Carrillo and his band attacked our ferry! Where's Poppa?"

Gus tossed his head in the direction of the huge mirror hanging behind him. Without a word, she went straight to the door.

He called after her, "He's in an ornery mood, Annie."

"When isn't he?" she retorted.

Knowing the unerring truth of that, Gus shrugged agreeably as she disappeared into her father's office. Only seconds later she was followed Dovie Gaspard.

"So it begins," Gus sighed.

47

Although no one saw him, Newman Chase had seen his daughter's dramatic entry into the Bella.

As usual, he was holed up in his office. Not much had changed there. If he was doing his accounts, he usually spread them out on the bar first thing in the morning. His exquisite little desk was now used as a catchall and heaped with the minutiae of his life. Without Annabella to fuss about it, his office was twice as cluttered as before. These days, no one, not even Gus, was allowed in. Before, he had had nothing hiding beneath his mountain of debris. Now his mess shielded the evidence of a weakness that he would just as soon keep to himself.

To find room for his coffee, Newman had to shove a mass of old newspapers to the side. That was important. It needed doctoring—lots of doctoring. With precision, he withdrew a small bottle of whiskey from a pigeonhole above the desk and emptied it into his cup. Hunching his shoulders, he blew on it. It was still scalding, but he took a gulp anyway.

He tossed his empty bottles in the opposite corner. He smuggled them out every few days, carting them under the cover of darkness and blending them in with trash from out front. That was easy enough. On a good day the *Bella* went through scores of every type of liquor. He could hardly appreciate the success. His constant state of intoxication had sneaked up on him. He thought he was fooling everyone else too—even Gus. Business was so good that men were often three and four deep at the bar.

So when he retired each evening, he said, "Don't bother me, Gus. It takes a lot of time to count all our money."

There had really no reason for suspicion. As a rule, Newman had always been a man of few vices. His success at being a saloonkeeper and avoiding that pitfall fell to adhering to a single maxim. *Whether gambling, inebriants or running women, the purveyor of vice must never, ever fall under the power of his product.* He had known more than one proprietor who pissed away their business.

Now, he had gone and let it happen to him.

Suspicious, Gus warned him, "You better watch it, pard. When you least expect it, you'll have a bitch-dog attached to your nuts."

Some mornings he had to take a swig of whiskey to ward off the shakes. With business concerns pressing him more every day, Newman didn't look to get loose any time soon. Sometimes he longed for the days when there weren't enough customers in the place to start a good argument. With all the mean drunks and card cheats, hardly a day went by without someone's head getting bashed. It was nothing to find a dead body in the alleyway.

Only a year ago the commonest prostitutes were only found at Clark's Point. Now they were housed on every block in town—and a few of them sitting in their saloon. They could be had in every way possible, sometimes for the price of a drink. Even Newman had to admit that his grand scheme to improve the *Bella* had fallen short. The more elegant bagnios were well up the way. Their purveyors of sexual pleasure called themselves courtesans and charged exorbitant prices just for their company. They strolled down the street in Parisian finery and were carefully rouged and heavily scented.

Had one of those numbers entered the Bella, Newman wouldn't have looked at them twice. He had once been married to a lady. Everyone knew that had ended badly

"Once you've smelled the finest perfume, nothing less will do," he said time and time again.

Newman came up with a plan to add a third story to the Bella. Of his schemes, Gus thought better of this one than others. A third story was a good use of real estate. The rooms they had were always kept let. Lots were selling for $40,000 a piece. Gus didn't see the books, so he hadn't realized that there was more money to be made selling women than their other ventures combined. When Newman finally admitted to Gus what he intended the new rooms to be used for, Gus pitched a fit.

"I told you, Newman," Gus reminded him, "My mama didn't raise her son to pimp women."

What business of that nature they had galled him quite enough. The "renting out the rooms" hypothesis had run its course, so Newman tried a new one.

"These women don't work for us or the Bella. They are what you call 'freelance.'"

"Free-lance, huh?" Gus asked. "You want to explain the particulars to that to me?"

With an expression of unparalleled earnestness, Newman explained, "They are freelance—like freelance soldiers in the Middle Ages. Mercenaries. You know, one who acts independently, or are without affiliation."

"How long did it take you to come up with that justification?" snorted Gus.

Ignoring him, Newman added, "As we have always done, we merely let rooms. It is not ours to question who rents them—nor our business what they do once in them."

Gus glared, "I see, you're renting rooms with women in 'em, not renting women in rooms."

"You just see to the bar," replied Newman as he walked away, "I'll see to the hotel."

"Hotel?" called Gus, "What hotel?"

Both knew that other gambling houses had partitions right there next to the new poker tables for gamesmen to take a little time with their temporary inamoratas. That was appalling. Newman believed a place should at least harbor the *pretense* of respectability. Patrick witnessed the entire argument. He was more shocked than Newman when Gus called it quits.

"I'm out," Gus called after him. "I'll run this bar, but I'll have no more of *that*."

Gus knew he should have walked out completely—but couldn't quite leave Newman high and dry. The man needed looking after. Something wasn't right. Newman had been behaving peculiarly for months. It was more than just pining for Annabella, but Gus couldn't put his finger on it. None of it made sense to him. Barmaids, however, he consented to. He thought they would make his job easier. As it happened, it only made his job more difficult, what keeping the customers from fondling the barmaids and the barmaids themselves from stealing him blind.

Patrick looked on his friends with an unbiased eye. He had been the one who first suspected the truth about Newman's trouble. To

Patrick, he behaved like a man confounded by love. Newman talked of his dead wife's fine perfume so often that everyone was sure there was no room left in his heart for anyone else.

It never did occur to anyone that drink wasn't the bitch-dog Gus warned Newman about. It was beyond everyone's wildest imagination that Newman Chase would have taken a harlot to his bed—let alone make one his wife.

48

Annabella took a deep sigh before rapping softly on her father's door.

"Go away, you bastards," he half-shouted.

It didn't much sound like Newman's voice. It was deeper—and less coherent. Patrick had written that her father had set to drinking, but she wasn't ready for what she saw when she opened the door.

When he turned towards her, he had a coffee cup was in one hand and a near-empty bottle of whiskey in the other. But she didn't notice that at first. In the glow of the oil lamp, she only saw a bloated face. It was familiar, yet anomalous. A sagging apostrophe of fat surrounded each eye. They were glassy, and his lower lip protruded like a bulldog's. Although he sounded bellicose, he didn't look it. He looked beaten, but fearful too—liked a treed animal.

"Poppa?" she said tentatively.

Standing, he blinked repeatedly, asking, "Who is it?"

"It's me, Poppa," responded Annabella, removing her bonnet.

The amber light was reflected in the bottle in his hand. From there it glanced across his cheeks. They were wet with self-pity. Pushing himself unsteadily to his feet, he held out his arms to her even before he called her name.

"Annie?"

She ran to him, leaping into his arms like she had as a child. But she wasn't a child and her weight caused him to fall backward and onto his chair. It creaked as if it might splinter, so she slid to her knees and clasped his hands in hers. His were cold and trembling and she tried to warm them. But he escaped her motherly grasp and cupped her chin in the palm of his hand. Looking lovingly at her, he took several of the blonde tendrils that she had so carefully arranged along the side of her face and tucked them behind her ears. For that moment she allowed herself to be a child again. After the trip she had endured, she would have been content to be cosseted by her father for hours—whether he mussed her coiffure or not.

She had too many questions to ask him to be still for long. It also occurred to her that she should have taken the time to catechize Patrick before she got her father's prettied-up version of events. Before she could ask him anything, she heard the soft, heart-breaking sound of her father crying. Thinking that he wept for her alone, she couldn't help but do the same.

She lay her face against his knee as he stroked her hair, crooning, "I thought I'd never see you in this life again, Annie."

"Oh, Poppa..."

They were both startled by a voice that boomed from the doorway, "What the bloody hell is this?"

Placing a protective hand on his daughter's shoulder, Newman tried to stand. As he struggled, Annabella sensed danger and scrambled to her feet anyway. A figure filled the doorway and cast a shadow across the room. Annabella had to step to the side to see who was there. She recognized the boa. It was Dovie Gaspard

Dovie repeated her question, this time even louder, but her inquiry wasn't directed to Annabella.

"What the bloody hell you think yer doin' husband?"

Annabella placed her hands impudently on her hips and gave Dovie a good look up and down. Then she asked a single-word question at her father.

"*Husband*?"

Dovie was the first to recognize the other. Granted, Annabella was at a disadvantage in that. To her, painted women were only discernible by their hair color. Since her marriage, Dovie had changed hers to a bright—almost iridescent—orange. Her blue boa, however, was quite memorable.

"Dovie Gaspard," Annabella said with uncharacteristic sarcasm, "Can it be you?"

"Ha-haw-ha-haw-ha-haw!" cackled Dovie.

Her vulgarity was quite an alteration from the sultry siren Annabella recalled. Aghast, Annabella looked at her father incredulously. He had absolutely no defense so he shrugged.

Holding out her arms and waggling her fingers, Dovie gushed, "Give us a kiss, sweetie!"

Uncertain if the offer was made to her or her father, Annabella played it safe by taking a step backward. Newman made no move in Dovie's direction (and looked like he might turn tail and run to boot). Dovie thought this lack of takers was enormously funny and she let out another guffaw. Without another word, she threw her boa over her shoulder, turned heel, and disappeared out the door. Only a few bits of blue feathers wafted in her wake.

Seeing her father's situation so tellingly in the flesh took a bit of punch of out of her. Setting things to right might be a bit more taxing than she thought. One thing she knew, it was time for some frank talk with Newman Chase.

What he told her didn't improve her mood.

Even in Boston it wasn't unheard of for a man of substance to marry an unvirtuous woman. Granted when they did, they spent a great deal of time and money covering up past indiscretions. Dovie, however, apparently only put her profession behind her long enough to take her wedding vows. It was a difficult thing for Newman to admit to anyone—especially his daughter. Being a cuckold always was. It was good that he didn't look at Annabella as he related the events leading up to his predicament. As he talked, the revulsion she felt was apparent on her face.

It was his position that he had been hornswoggled. All his worldly goods had been stolen out from under him and were in the hands of a lewd woman through no fault of his own. When it came to how he caught her in bed with another man, he was less direct. Perhaps, he said, she had merely returned to her previous profession. The Bella's new calling as whorehouse he put off on Dovie too. Adding another story to the *Bella* had been all her idea. Why, she even put up some of the money. At the time it had seemed only gentlemanly to put her name on the deed as well. He *should* have known better than trust a lawyer of hers—and to co-mingle funds. By the time he realized he had been rooked, she saw to it that she was the majority owner in all of his holdings. Her plan, he surmised, was to run him off from the Bella.

Annabella agreed with that. It looked like Dovie did mean to run Newman off—through sheer mortification. From the looks of things, she was well on her way.

Newman at least had the good sense not to tell Annabella that he held her responsible for the mess he was in. To his mind, if she hadn't up and left him when she did he wouldn't have been so lonesome—nor would he have turned to Dovie for consolation. Annabella's conscience, however, wasn't any better used than his. So far as she was concerned, he was a grown man and should have known better. If anything, she was embarrassed for him. However, if they were to address their present predicament (and Annabella did consider it a family problem), they had to set all that aside. It was time for her to be blunt.

"How can we rid ourselves of her?" Annabella asked. "Supposing, of course, that *we* want her gone."

That she had used the plural pronoun was reason enough for him to forget any impudence in the question.

"Yes," he said, clearing his throat. "*We* do."

Tossing debris from a side chair, she pulled it up so she could sit down to think. As she did, a stack of papers and several bottles slid to the floor. The place was such a mess, she didn't even consider picking them back up.

Ignoring the avalanche too, Newman reluctantly said, "I've really got my tail in a crack, Annie."

"Truly," she agreed. "Has Gus any ideas?"

Gus had always been a port in any storm—but not then.

"Not unless he has a rich relative that's on the brink of death," Newman said miserably.

She said, "You must divorce her, Poppa. You have just cause."

It was obvious that was a sore subject—and a delicate one. Neither of them wanted to pursue where and how many ways Dovie had betrayed him.

Newman said softly, "She doesn't want a divorce."

"No doubt. The *Bella* looks very profitable," Annabella replied.

With a degree of pride, Newman said, "And so it is—sometimes a thousand dollars a day."

To her raised eyebrows, he added, "That's not profit, you understand."

"It is gross, not net," she said reasonably.

Surprised that his little daughter knew the difference, he suddenly felt like the child.

With a deep, pitiful sigh, he said, "She dug in deep, I'm afraid."

As Annabella soon found out, "Dug in deep" wasn't the half of it.

But if there was more to the story, he wasn't forthcoming with it. Newman busied himself with a few papers. That only dislodged a mound of others and he gave up the pretense of doing bookkeeping. With papers cascading around her, Annabella remained deep in thought.

Even Dovie Gaspard had to have an Achilles heel. If anyone knew it, it would be Gus.

49

Knowing that he always had a fresh pot of coffee brewing, Annabella went to retrieve a mug for Newman. Time was at hand for him to sober up. Gus was busy, but he was looking for her. They needed to talk too. But first, she carried a fresh cup of lucidity to her father. She didn't leave until he had taken a few sips. Hands on her hips, she silently dared him to doctor it. He looked back at her with eyes wide and innocent as a child.

"It's time, Poppa," she announced.

He nodded once. It wasn't enthusiastic, but at least she had his agreement. When she returned for a cup of coffee for herself, Gus had it waiting. Out of the corner of her eye, she saw Dovie was flirting with customers from behind the bar. So did Gus, so he led the way to the storeroom where they could parley without fear of her swooping in on them. Annabella was glad for that. Suffering Devil's Sister once that evening was quite enough.

Annabella nodded in Dovie's direction, "Your new co-owner is a gem."

"Ah," he said. "She is a gem. But I don't have the clout around here I once did."

Annabella frowned.

"When Newman brought her in, I cashed out."

Incredulous, she said, "And Poppa let you...."

It wasn't really a question, so Gus ignored it. There was more urgent news.

"Dovie came by just now and relieved the cash box of its contents. That's hardly the first time—but her doing it so early in the evening looks as if she was marshalling her resources."

"You think she intends to go?"

To her that was tremendous news, but Gus didn't look to be particularly elated.

"A quick escape perhaps—most likely back to New Orleans. She won't do that until the Bella's well is dry."

Gus didn't have to tell Annabella that in making such an ostentatious reappearance, she had made a colossal blunder. She had put Dovie Gaspard on alert.

"You could've told me what was going on...." she said defensively.

"Water under the bridge," Gus muttered, then changed the subject. "Braining customers ain't good for business, Sis. Patrick should take care of himself."

"Rutledge Mayne is a slimy piece of work and you know it. Patrick can't take care of anything, much less himself."

"You may be right on both accounts, but what if Mayne turns out all cockeyed for good? He's gonna be sitting on one of Bella's stool's and drool in his drink!"

"Serves him right!" she declared.

"It doesn't serve me right. I have to clean that bar!"

When he finally began to tell her what happened between her father and Dovie, she didn't interrupt. It was good for her to hear it from another, unbiased, perspective.

"It was his damned pride that got him, Annie."

Gus told her how devious Dovie was in insinuating herself in Newman's affections *and* business affairs. He folded his arms across his chest and tucked his chin at the thought. Annabella nodded. It *had* an impressive victory. What had once been prideful man had gradually mutated into an enormous hulk of rotting misery. Even Newman realized that he was a half-step from ruin. Admitting his situation was one thing—it was clear that he flatly refused to accept that it was his own fault. Gus didn't tell Annabella how Newman had cried on his shoulder.

He had wailed, "She is committing acts of indecency with any man who can produce the proper change—under my very nose. Why, *Mrs.* Newman Chase is nothing but a Whore of Babylon!"

Gus reminded him, "According to your own whys and wherefores, she is actually a "freelancer." Like mercenaries in the Middle Ages. You know—the ones who are unaffiliated."

Newman sputtered for a minute, but he knew he was beat.

"No fool like an old fool," Gus muttered.

He knew first hand that proverbs had held no weight with a middle-aged man in lust. Newman *should* have known better. He was a *business man*. Dovie had chasséd about the *Bella* twiddling him under the chin until she had him panting like a hound. Gus had held out hope that the affair would run its natural course. So he was flabbergasted when Newman announced their betrothal. Gus shook his head at the memory and continued his diatribe to Annabella.

"It's one thing to hoodwink a man out of his money, but it's another to humiliate him in the process."

Here, Gus took a breath. Annabella squeezed his arm—both in comfort and encouragement.

He continued, "She fixed a room upstairs as their *honey-moon* suite and had it all decked out like a Spanish bordello. Then she started pouring booze down him with one hand and massaging his... ego with the other. When he found her servicing customers in *his* bed, he was too drunk to protest properly. I suspect she doctored his drinks with absinthe. He stayed in that state so long we thought he'd gone batty."

She asked, "Absinthe—is that the horrid green liquid?"

"Yeah, the "green serpent" the johnnies call it. It's a wicked drink. It's the stuff that used keep Patrick laid up."

Suddenly, Patrick's fits and fevers made sense to her. That must have been the sickly sweet smell that used to follow him wherever he went.

"Does Patrick still...?"

"Naw," replied Gus. "Either you lick that stuff or it kills you."

It was a relief to know Patrick had escaped its grasp.

She asked Gus softly, "What can be done?"

Cupping his hands around his coffee, he looked deep into the piceous liquid as if the answers were there. He knew what was needed. He just didn't know how to go about getting it.

"Cash," said he. "There's one thing that female understands and that's money. Now all Dovie talks about is going back to New Orleans. That's why she came out here in the first place—not just to whore. Well, to whore until she can make enough to go back home and live grand—in that she no different than these miners."

Suddenly minding himself, Gus said, "Beg pardon for the language."

"And what else would you call her than a whore?" she asked. "Cleopatra, Queen of the Nile?"

A flick of his brows proved him in agreement. Neither of them spoke for some time.

Finally, Annabella said, "I just don't see why Poppa thought he had to marry her."

"You might say it was a triumph of hope over experience," Gus said. "A lot of men—and women—keep trying until they get it right."

They both laughed. That felt good. It spurred Annabella into action.

"I'll make the rounds tomorrow. How many banks are in town now?"

"Three," said Gus. "That is, not counting First National—Asher Price's place."

"I'll skip that one, if you don't mind."

"I don't," replied Gus. "But him having some familiarity with Newman might give us a leg up."

"In his case," Annabella said snidely. "Familiarity may not exactly breed contempt, but sure takes the edge off of admiration."

If he recognized one of his maxims, he didn't show it.

Instead, he said, "Just remember that a bank...."

She interrupted, reciting, "A bank is a place where they lend you an umbrella in fair weather and ask for it back when it begins to rain."

"Well, it *is*," he said. "I'm just warning you is all. It's not like you've got any collateral."

"I take your warning with all due gravity," she patted his arm again. "I am grateful for your kindness."

Placing his pipe in the corner of his mouth, he smiled approvingly that his little maxims were making a dent. His smile lasted until he thought again about the lack of collateral. Newman's half interest in the *Bella* might not be worth what it once was. Annabella was just impudent enough to pledge something that she might regret.

Because he was pondering that possibility, she was out the door before he realized it.

"When are you going to tell me about Jose Carrillo?" he called after her.

But she had already gone.

50

Newman Chase's great fall shouldn't have surprised everyone like it had. Years of bachelorhood had made him ripe for the plucking. Yet it wasn't just physical deprivation that drove him into Dovie's arms. His daughter's departure had left him a truly lonely man. It was a common affliction in mining towns. However, Newman's case was a bit different than those of prospectors. He was living a loveless existence long before the gold strike. Annabella's reappearance had reminded him that he had once been an affectionate man. When she left, his newly rejuvenated heart was the worse for it.

Years of working men for money meant Dovie knew just what comfort to supply.

Compliments were only the first in her repertoire of wiles. She admired Newman's strong arms, trim figure and manly charms to high heaven. She batted her provocative eyes and stroked his ego until he was mad to have her. It was all part of her grand scheme to insinuate herself not only in his bed, but at his right hand as well.

She purposely set out to have him catch her with another man—and in their marital bed. That cruelty hadn't been really necessary. If she had asked, Newman might've even forgiven her for it. Gus never would. Nobody deserved that kind of humiliation. Gus never had much stomach for vengeance, but some acts just begged retribution.

Gus wanted to believe that if Dovie hadn't caught Newman at such a vulnerable time that he wouldn't have been such a fool. Gus wasn't the kind of man who deserted a friend in a time of need. He even clung to the hope that once Newman was sobered up he'd be as good as new. After his talk with Annabella, he chewed the cud on it a bit before deciding it was time for him to ante up. He didn't have much, but what he had, he was happy to put it in the kitty to save Newman from himself.

To make his grand endowment, he sent Patrick to get Annabella from the hotel. (She had been keeping to her room so as not to have a run-in with Dovie.) Annabella didn't much like having to sneak into her father's saloon—it reminded her of her father's idiotic dictum over the teak doors. However, stealth was all-important if they were to win out over Dovie. Gus grabbed her hand and made a beeline to the storeroom. Fishing beneath the cot he kept in the corner, he pulled out a strong box. By the time he had it set on top of the cot, she was breathless with impatience.

He said matter-of-fact "I didn't get a lot when me and Newman divvied up. But what I got I'll be glad to put back in the Bella."

She was so excited that she asked urgently, "How much do you have?"

Fumbling to unlock it, Gus shrugged, "A few thousand—five at most."

At one time, that would have been enough to retire on in grand style. But it wouldn't go far in the new San Francisco. So she made admiring noises, but both knew that wasn't near enough to tempt Dovie to give up her hold on the Bella. It was a great sacrifice nonetheless. How much Gus was willing to make to save her father's skin almost moved her to tears—but not quite. Instead, she put a reassuring hand on his shoulder and searched for the words to adequately thank him. He shushed her.

"But think of it, Gus," she insisted. "This will make you a partner in the *Bella* again!"

"I've been that," he said indignantly. "It's powerfully overrated."

Gus shut his treasure chest and pushed it back beneath the cot. Carefully, he replaced the keys in his waistband. As he did, they discussed whether or not Newman should be kept in the dark about their plan. They concluded that it was best that they not get his hopes up—and they didn't want his interference either. His managerial skills were not at their peak. He had begun to complain constantly how fortune had turned its cold, bleak back against him which was a considerable aggravation. Annabella was even more irked to see him snap his yap shut like some whipped pup whenever Dovie paraded into the room.

It was clear to everyone that Newman was a wounded beast. Beads of sweat formed regularly on his forehead and the tremor in his hand was so severe Gus didn't dare fill his coffee cup more than half full. Since Annabella came back, however, he hadn't taken another drink. Yet it was plain that it was going to take some time before he regained any semblance of the man he was. So much so that Gus and Annabella were satisfied with their decision not tell him they had a scheme to save him.

That was just as well. The Lords of Finance did not fall at her feet offering pecuniary assistance.

Annabella visited every bank in town wearing her most fetching bonnet, her finest dress, and most responsible expression, but without success. The first two bankers laughed in her face; a third pinched her bottom—then laughed in her face. It fell well apparent that financial institutions owned so much real estate—and were making so much money—they had little interest in making a loan that had any kind of risk.

"Little lady," said the first banker (and the second and the third), "why would I loan money to you to purchase a saloon? Why wouldn't I buy it outright from the owner myself?"

For that, she had no answer.

Forlornly, she reported to Gus, "If I was one of those blessed bankers, I wouldn't loan me any money either."

It took her several days to admit that Asher Price was their only hope. Because she had made herself particularly disagreeable to him, she stalled as long as she could. Overcoming personal mortification took time. But in the end even she admitted that Mr. Price should have been who they had gone to first. He was, after all, one of the richest men in town, and he and Newman had an amiable history. If anyone was to be their benefactor, it would be him. That is if Asher Price didn't throw her and her bonnet out the door.

It would take renewed determination—and allurement.

She had worn her best finery when she visited the other banks, but she knew she had to go a step further before visiting Mr. Asher Price. In going to such lengths, the possibility that her own ego was as much at stake as the *Bella Goode* should have troubled her. But it didn't. She despised being laughed at more than she despised Mr. Price. Every fiber of her being was bent on winning him over.

She had decided to embark on the nasty job before her by employing an oblique assault. Instead of asking for a loan outright, she would ask for Mr. Price's advice on a monetary matter. If he was any kind of a gentleman, a fluttering of her eyelashes and a few heaves of her bosom would have him and his financial wherewithal in a heap at her feet. She trilled at the thought of the triumph.

She was right to feel confident. Miss Chase was the owner of a stunningly handsome face, a striking figure, and a bushel of charm. She did lack one thing—a proper corsetière.

Her bosom was unrivalled. It had been her habit to keep such charms under wrap in rowdy circles. Time had come for her to employ the big guns. Any woman (at least any who had an ounce of sense) knew that real seduction began with the proper foundation. There was no one around to get this captive-taking enterprise going. If that was to happen, she had to call Patrick to find someone to come and tighten the laces on her bosom-lifting (and very naughty) Parisian corset.

51

To most men, getting a public whopping by some bit of skirt would have been a huge embarrassment. But Rutledge Mayne didn't have much dignity to start with, so he wasn't much bothered about it. That didn't mean he couldn't put on a big show of outrage.

"I'll bring Hell-fire down on you all!" he screamed once he was beyond anyone hearing.

After his little conniption, Mayne wilted. He spent the remainder of that night face down in the alleyway. Like most San Francisco nights, it was pretty chilly. Fog made it worse, leaving Mayne wet as well as unconscious. He was lucky that he woke up. More than one drunk didn't. If he didn't get taken by the elements, a man with a knife might cut him a second smile.

Rutledge might not have survived either if fortune hadn't taken an odd turn.

Alternately sniffing and peeing as he sought out familiar haunts, Stewpot happened along Clay Street. Having mistaken Mayne for a rodent carcass (a completely understandable misapprehension), the dog curled up next to him for the night. Both of them woke up thirsty.

Of the two, Mayne's tongue was driest and he staggered over to a watering trough. Stewpot trotted along fast on his heels. The trough was full and both dog and man drank from the pungent water side by side. But the moss-covered sides were slippery and Mayne had the shakes. Almost immediately, he lost his grip on the side and plunged in head first. It was just as well. He needed a reviver. After he held his breath as long as he could, he came up for a big gasp of air and threw himself over the side. He fell on buttocks and sat splay-legged in the mud. Flews wet and dripping, Stewpot came over to Mayne and nuzzled him. Mayne was uninterested.

"Get away you mangy cur!" he lashed out.

Immediately, Mayne regretted yelling—but only because of his head. He had a horrific headache. Stewpot tucked his tail and headed for the Bella. The teak doors were still closed. With patience only known to dogs, he sat down in front of them. Seeing him there, Mayne recognized him as the dog that Miss Chase had fostered. The dog had disappeared about the same time Miss Chase left for Boston. Mayne's powers of deduction were slower than usual, but Mayne finally realized who had smacked him the night before.

Snapping his fingers, he spoke her name, "Annabella *Chase*!"

And there before him was her *dog*. Revenge was at hand.

"Here pup, nice, pup," Mayne crooned.

Looking warily at him, Stewpot didn't budge. Continuing to call to him, Mayne searched his mind for the whereabouts of the nearest mineshaft.

"Here, puppy, come here you sorry cur!"

"Leave him!" said a voice. "That's my dog. Leave him be!"

That was not Annabella Chase's voice. To see just who it was, Mayne had to steeple his hands over his eyebrows from the glare of the morning sun. He immediately recognized the kid that had survived Yellow Jack.

Falling to one knee, Tucker McFee called the dog, cooing, "I been looking all over for you. Where'd you go off to feller? Where you been, huh?"

"I tell you this," Mayne said, taking out the makings for a cigarette. "If you're expecting that dog to answer, you might be in for a wait."

Mayne pushed himself up the side of the building until he was in a standing position and tried to tap a line of tobacco into a paper, but his hands were too shaky and it scattered to the ground.

"Your makings are too dry," Tucker said.

"Thanks," Mayne said gratefully, waiting for Tucker to offer some of his.

He realized a tad late that Tucker offered only the observation, not a smoke. He was too busy scratching the dog's belly. To Mayne, it was just as well. He didn't want to owe Tucker a favor—at least not yet. A poor gambler, Mayne was always on the lookout for an advantage. It occurred to him that in surviving Yellow fever and what not, Tucker McFee was a veritable talisman of good fortune. Legend had it, that luck rubbed off—usually by means of a head-rub. Given a chance, he decided to try to stroke Tucker's forelock.

As Tucker rose from petting the dog, Mayne managed to knock off his hat. In retrieving it for him, he rather artlessly brushed his hand across the top of Tucker's head. Fortunately, Tucker didn't seem to notice. (More than one man would've taken mortal offense at such a liberty.)

"Whatcha doin' in town, kid?" Mayne asked innocently.

Tucker said that he had come into town to re-supply his camp. Before Mayne could ask more, Tucker told him that he'd come to San Francisco rather than just travel up to Sutter's Fort because gold is bringing more here just now.

"I need every penny," he explained.

"Things that sorry up there, huh?" asked Mayne.

"Not any worse than anywhere else. Veins of gold thick as a man's thumb are everywhere. I just got to give it time."

"Yeah," smirked Mayne. "It's just a pan of creek-rock away."

Totally unwitting of the sarcasm, Tucker agreed amicably. Noticing his complete lack of guile, Mayne began to wonder if Tucker had any money left from his payoff from Asher Price. If the boy had played his cards right, he could made plenty trading his story. Lots of people would have liked to hear him to particularize the telling, but he wouldn't.

As Mayne's normal expression was one of slack-jawed incomprehension, Tucker should have noticed the gleam in his eye. Being the guileless type, Tucker was oblivious to it. He was just happy to have someone to talk to and he chatted on, telling how he used the money from the wreck to buy a gold claim.

"It had been averaging $300 to $400 a day," he said earnestly.

"Who told you how much it was bringing?" Mayne asked.

"Why, Harvey Rooker—the man I bought the claim from."

Stifling a laugh, Mayne listened without comment as Tucker talked. It was as if someone had pulled their thumb out of his verbal dike—words poured out of him like a river.

"A hundred mile swath of gold-bearing quartz begins on the Calaveras River and runs all the way down the Sierras just shy of Stockton. Gold were so plentiful that pulling up a tuft of grass a man can find nuggets clinging to the roots. Mr. Rooker said the foothills were still full of gold—nuggets as big as a man's fist. His claim was one of the richest."

"Is that right?" remarked Mayne mildly.

Tucker nodded his head vigorously.

Mayne asked, "If that was true, why was Rooker selling it?"

"Oh, we wouldn't have dreamed of it, excepting that his wife was sick," explained Tucker.

"Loving spouse, was he?"

"Very good husband I'd say," said Tucker. "She was ailing back in Kansas City and he had no one there to see to her and his three small children."

"Poor man," opined Mayne.

"Two boys and a little girl," Tucker said. "His claim was plumb in the middle of a band of gold ore. All it would take to make a fortune was a strong back and perseverance. Grit, that's the key to everything."

To Tucker, it was as if providence itself had directed Harvey Rooker to sit down at his table. True, Mr. Price had told him to be cautious with his payout. But he didn't think twice before handing every dime of it over to Mr. Rooker. Lucking into sure proposition so quickly was a good omen. Still, Tucker didn't think it would be right not to admit up front that he knew nothing whatsoever about panning for gold.

"But Mr. Rooker told me how to do it right there at the bar. He even gave me a little nugget so as know what he was looking for. Placer mines—those are the road to riches."

As Tucker began to relate just how back-breaking and slow it was, Mayne had second thoughts about how much luck he rubbed off of Tucker's head. He wiped his hand on his pant leg as he listened.

"Sunup to sundown," said Tucker, "I scratched out a creek bed at the bottom of a ravine, both wet-digging and panning. I bent over a shallow washing pan so much I couldn't hardly stand back up."

Then, off-handedly, Tucker said that he had actually found a nest of marble-sized gold nuggets. That perked Mayne up.

He interrupted, "I hear more and more single miners are teaming up with others—combining their efforts."

But Tucker turned up his nose at the thought, saying, "I didn't much like the camps I passed on the way down the mountain. One had a sign calling their claim "Jackass Gulch." I took a night with them. They did nothing but drink, gamble and brawl. Claim jumpers are everywhere, but I'd rather sleep with Stewie here than those boys. I've dug this little cave into the side of the hill..."

"Sounds enchantin'," said Mayne.

Sighing, Tucker said, "The one comfort I have is in knowing that Miss Annabella went back to Boston and is out of harm's reach. This is mean country now."

Spent of words and emotion, Tucker turned and walked away. Deep in semi-thought, Mayne didn't hear him. Without asking, he lumbered along beside him. He figured Rooker to be a crook, but it sounded as if Tucker could be close to striking it big. That was the way to prospect. Let the dumb ones do all the work and then join 'em when they hit pay dirt.

"As for me," Mayne offered unasked, "I'm looking for a good opportunity."

Met with silence, he continued, "I don't have much ready cash, but I know how to rig up a slough."

That seemed to interest Tucker.

"Four hands are better than two, eh?" Mayne prodded.

Tucker seemed to be weighing the offer and, seeing Gus opening the doors to the Bella, Mayne suggested they get a beer and talk about it. Tucker thought it was a bit early, but said he wouldn't mind a cup of coffee. Gus stood just inside the door eying them. Stewpot apparently passed the muster. At least Gus didn't stop the dog or Tucker at the threshold. However, he put out a hand in front of Mayne.

"You here to cause more trouble, Rutledge? Where's your cutter?"

"I got it stowed," claimed Mayne. "I'm good."

Gus let him pass and nodded to Tucker.

Tucker asked Rutledge, "Did you start trouble?"

"It wasn't nothing," Rutledge said, giggling. "I just got a bit worse for the wear and was playing the pian-er. Young Miss Annabella took exception to it."

As if struck by a thunderbolt, Tucker stopped and whirled around, facing Mayne. "Miss Annabella? She's here in town?"

"To be shure," said Rutledge, suddenly impressed that he held some information valuable to someone else. He touched his forehead. It was swollen and tender. Tucker could see the welt.

"She whacked me right here in her daddy's saloon last night."

With exaggerated nonchalance, Tucker said, "I have her dog."

52

Once again to be without a maid became the bane of Annabella's young life. Not having servants to wait on her hand and foot was one of the few regrets she carried with her from Boston. Right then she would have been thrilled to have Lupe annoying her. San Francisco had grown so rich; it had been a surprise how difficult it was to hire help. The wealthiest residents were forced into importing people from Europe. That was proof enough that the changes that were in progress when she left had run wildly out of control.

The lack of maids wasn't the half of it.

Much to her chagrin, the madness that had infected the prospectors had spread to all its citizens. The price of everything—which had once just been exorbitant, now was unfathomable. Cooks now called themselves chefs and porters weren't to be found at any price. Not only had Mrs. Gottwald quit servicing men, but she was no longer was a laundress either. She still did clothes, but the sign on her door now read "Clothing Refreshed" and had a menu of prices to match. Some found it cheaper to send their linen underwear and boiled shirts on a clipper ship to Honolulu and back than pay someone local.

It heralded a new era insofar as fastidiousness was concerned. If you were only of middling means, you washed out your unmentionables yourself. That included Annabella. But an emergency like hers required emergency measures. Patrick hurried across to the hotel as soon as he got the message that she needed him. Her request was a bit odd.

From behind her newly acquired Japanese screen, she ordered, "Find me a female and send her here."

"Beg pardon?" he asked.

Her explanation was terse, "I need help with my under-things."

"Under-things" meant Patrick didn't question her request. He was simply happy not to be corralled into tending to her himself. (Having been chief wrangler of his mother's corset strings harkened memories he'd just as soon keep buried.) He headed down the steps fast in case she changed her mind.

Annabella called out after him, "And make certain she's sturdy!"

Soon, a young woman rapped on her door. Annabella was half-dressed and peeked out to give her a quick inspection. The girl didn't look all that strapping. Still, Annabella waved her into the room. Beggars couldn't be choosers. She stepped out and immediately turned her back to her.

Introducing herself, she said, "I am Miss Chase."

"I am Miss Mosley," the girl responded. "I am called Gaby the... Gaby."

Annabella recognized the girl from as one the harlots that hung around the *Bella* like so many jackals. At least she wasn't one of Dovie's string of girls. Annabella had never been absolutely alone with a real prostitute before. She was wildly curious, but she didn't have the time just then to ask the myriad of questions swirling in the back of her mind. All her thoughts had to be on the task ahead of her. Perhaps that was why she didn't realize that Gaby Mosley had completely misunderstood her mission. The girl was in a quandary whether to throw off her clothes or curtsy.

Annabella turned her back to her and commanded, "Proceed."

With a bewildered expression, Gaby hesitated a moment before stepping forward. Then she reached around Annabella and placed a hand on each of her breasts and tweaked them. Whirling about, Annabella was both impatient and offended.

"If you *please*," she yowled.

Gaby leapt back several feet, clearly happy to not have her hands snapped off.

"What the bloody hell you want then?" she cried out indignantly.

"I need furtherance in my corset laces!"

"You want it *on*, not *off* then?"

"Yes. *On*, not off."

Scolding, Gaby said, "Well if you needed some highfalutin maid, Patty should have said so."

With that, Annabella turned back around and Gaby warned her, "This will cost you a dollar."

Nodding her head at the price, Annabella dutifully grabbed the bedpost and hung on for dear life as Gaby put her knee in her back and tugged and pulled her back and forth with every tug. As she did, Annabella wondered how she was going to get back out the corset once it was properly secured.

"Can you come back later?" she inquired tentatively.

"For this," Gaby nodded at the laces. "Or for that," she then nodded towards the bed.

"God in heaven above!" Annabella fumed.

"Well, I'm only sayin'—it'll cost your more than a dollar if it's *that*."

Truly curious just what *that* was, Annabella remarked, "When I have more time I'll pay you a dollar for a little enlightenment on your trade."

Crinkling her forehead, Gaby continued to lace and tie, but mused as she did, "However you get your jollifications don't matter to me. I seen it all, I have."

"No doubt," Annabella agreed under her breath.

Rarely did Annabella admit defeat, but she then realized that some conversations were better in the listening than participation. Therefore, Gaby prattled on without interruption.

"Yessir, I have seen it all," she said. "You'd be surprised what inspires some folks. Sometimes something as light as a feather; sometimes a bucket of.... Well, you get my meaning. Some men like it mean and there's plenty of mean women to give it to them. Me, I can draw a splooge in sixty seconds and have no complaints. It's all in the technique. Tongue action really. I give it the ol' tongue and they spout like one of them volcanoes in the Sammich Islands."

Taking a breath, she asked Annabella, "Tighter?"

Still dazed with astonishment at her reverie, it took Annabella a second or two to respond. "Yes," she said, "A bit more."

"I say so," Gaby agreed. "No sense doing something if not doing it right—that's what my mama used to tell me. Of course, she had six husbands, so she should know something about pleasin' a man, now shouldn't she? We don't go squeezin' the life out ourselves to impress other women, now do we?"

"No, we don't," agreed Annabella on both accounts. "Help me with my petticoats."

"All of 'em?"

"All of them."

Drawing her favorite bisque-colored gown down over her mound of petticoats, Annabella looked into her looking glass.

"You look just like a...," Gaby fumbled for the proper comparison, "a dandelion!"

Pleased with the appraisal, Gaby smiled blissfully. Annabella didn't see her; she was busy plumping her bosom. Happy with those results, she took out her powder puff and dusted herself. Then, she pinched her cheeks. Even happier, she preened just a bit.

"It don't hurt to dress the window a little, now does it, Miss Annabella," said Gaby.

"No," Annabella said agreed again, "it does not."

Fixing her ribbon at the neck of her short cape, she almost headed out the door in her usual queenly fashion. Suddenly she saw Gaby eyeing the silver hand mirror on her dressing table. So instead of going out herself, she held the door open and waited for Gaby to exit. Gaby, however, seemed in no hurry. Her finger trailed across the silver dresser set and then a bonnet hanging from a hook.

"Don't take me for a fool, Miss Mosley," she said curtly.

If Gaby was casing her belongings for a later robbery, Annabella thought it best to squelch the notion in its infancy. In return, Gaby only shrugged her shoulders—as if Annabella and her possessions were simply fair game. Annabella, however, was surprised at herself. A year before she wouldn't have confronted someone like Gaby. But then, a year before she wouldn't have recognized a thief if he had his hand in her pocket.

Taking her parasol jauntily on her shoulder, Annabella locked her door. Gaby flipped her coin as she trooped down the stairs. When they reached the front door, Gaby headed across to the *Bella* and Annabella the opposite direction.

Both, however, bore remarkably similar expressions.

53

As soon as Annabella started up the walkway, Patrick fell in behind her. Because he adored her and was quick with compliments, she usually enjoyed his company. But Patrick wasn't good at keeping secrets, so when she had something up her sleeve she liked to keep him in the dark.

"Where are we going?" he asked jovially,

"*We* are not going anywhere," she said pointedly. "I have business to tend to. I promise to tell you everything when I am finished."

With that, she blew him a kiss and skipped on ahead of him. He looked perplexed, but didn't follow her.

It was a fine San Francisco afternoon. For that Annabella was happy.

She didn't want to worry about soiled skirts and a red nose. It was imperative to be as appealing as possible without seeming contrived.

Until she was actually on her way, she hadn't decided just what she would say to Asher Price. Usually such things flowed out of her mouth like honey. It was an innate talent, but one she had honed in her grandfather's parlor. Dozens of men had flocked to her and because she had cared no more for them than they had for her, it was easy to toy with them and their affections. Truly, they were all after the same thing—some were just more subtle than others. That was what she had come to learn—it was all a big game. Of course there was an art to it. One had to be flip without appearing inelegant. The key was to keep one's emotions in check. Once a man had your heart, he held sway over your being. But she had no fear of that anymore. She reminded herself—a heart was given but once.

At one time, by just stepping out onto the walkway she could stop traffic in its tracks. There were plenty of women in town now. As she looked up each street, she took a gander at her competition. To her mind, there still wasn't all that much. If a woman wasn't married, she was a wage earner of some sort. And there were few occupations for women in San Francisco that were reputable. No wonder Mr. Price had remained a bachelor. What was more apt? All he cared about was money. Some reckoned him a cold fish, but she thought that was a misapprehension. His eyes flashed too quickly to be unfeeling. If his wife met a brutal end, it was possible the opposite might be true. More than one wife in San Francisco saw the back of their husband's hand.

Her sociological reverie didn't put her in a charming mood, so she tried to make herself think about what lay ahead as something other than a chore. By the time she entered the First National Bank, a smile came easily. However, such radiance was wasted on the man who sat at a desk just inside the door. It was Mr. Butler.

Momentarily Annabella considered asking Mr. Price where he got such a gem of an assistant. Perhaps he knew where housemaids were to be had as well. But she decided that was neither here nor there and must stick to the business at hand. Fortunately, the bank wasn't busy. Two men were at the other end of the room. They were separated from the front by a glass partition and looked to be weighing gold dust. The brass weights glinted even in the dim light. She was startled when she turned back to Mr. Butler. His eyes bore into her the moment she looked at him. As always, he was wearing a suit, tie, and a black felt hat so far down on his head that his ears were bent.

"Mr. Price?" she asked Mr. Butler.

Butler grunted, "I'm not Mr. Price. I'm Mr. Butler."

She nodded patiently, explaining, "I would like to speak to Mr. Price."

Mr. Butler nodded to a door with a glass pane behind him. Gold-lettering said "President."

"Shall you announce me?" she asked even more patiently.

With a show of great displeasure, Butler dragged himself to his feet and rapped on his employer's door. He then went in and Annabella could hear only muffled voices. She practiced looking both carefree and fetching. When it came to pretense, she believed she was more talented in affecting great distress. As she waited, she pondered the possibility of a life on the stage.

"Miss Chase?"

Asher Price broke the trance she had fallen into. It was a mild irritation that she had lost her beatific expression for one that was simply vacant. He might mistake that for stupidity.

He asked, "You asked for me?"

Asher seemed surprised. That was a good sign. It was always best to catch one's quarry off guard.

"Yes," she said in a soft, breathy voice that sounded nothing like her own. "If I may have a private word."

"Of course," he responded.

He held his hand out in the direction of his office.

As she entered she heard him tell Mr. Butler, "Take your hat off, Henry."

A comfortable chair sat in front of Asher's desk and he went around and placed his hand on the back of it while she took her seat. It was a nice gentlemanly touch—one she rarely saw in San Francisco. It was apparent that he had either forgotten their contretemps or forgiven it. How gentlemanly of him. Perhaps this would be easier than she had expected.

"I thank you," she whispered.

Even she didn't believe the sotto voce she was employing. So she cleared her throat and tried to look business-like. They spent several minutes commenting on the lovely weather, the abominable cost of vegetables, when the next opera might arrive, and then, fortuitously, the volatility of the local economy. She was startled when Mr. Price asked her a very direct question.

"If I may inquire," he asked politely, "as to why you decided to return to San Francisco?"

Taken aback, she wasn't certain how to respond. On the spur of the moment, she couldn't come up with a plausible answer so she decided to be truthful—or at least a variation of it.

"My father has been...," she hesitated, "unwell. His business affairs are in...." Here she hesitated again before finding the right word, "Disarray."

"Unwell?" he said thoughtfully. "Disarray, you say?"

"Yes," she answered.

It wasn't hot, but she withdrew her fan and began to fan her powdered bosom.

Her eyelashes fluttered almost as fast as did her fan.

"I fear that is so."

"It was my understanding," said Asher Price. "That he has become a sot due to marrying a whore who stole his business from him."

Annabella stood, "*Sir!*"

Suddenly, all Mr. Price's good manners left him. He did not stand when she did. In fact, he leaned back in his chair and propped his feet on top of his desk. He twiddled his thumbs and very nearly smirked.

In a tone that was at complete odds with his coarse display, he said (fluttering his own eyelashes back at her), "My dear Miss Chase, am I laboring under a misapprehension?"

"Yes!" she replied.

"And what have I misunderstood? That he has become a sot, your new step-mother is a whore, or that she is stealing his business?"

"My father is *not* a sot!" she replied, tears of indignation stinging her eyes. "He has been *unwell*."

Her last remark was hushed—and a feeble lie.

If he took pity on her, it was short-lived.

He asked, "Why have you come to my door? The refusals of the other three bankers in town were insufficient?"

Mortified and suddenly tired of the charade, she sank back to the chair. Her skirts caught the air and billowed around her like a mushroom. But she turned her head away from Asher until she was certain that the tears that threatened her had passed. However when she turned back, two huge red blotches on her cheeks were her most significant features. Because he was clearly aware of every humiliating detail or her father's situation, she made herself prevail over an intense desire to flee—possibly back to Boston.

But she gathered herself. Mustering every bit of courage she had, she made herself ask him for help.

"Since you are so well-acquainted with our affairs, might I prevail upon you—you who have been a friend to my father—to help us?"

"If I am such a friend, why did you not come to me first, not last?" he said pointedly.

Annabella looked at her lap. Her fingers were twisting the strings of her reticule into a knot. She watched them as if they were a separate entity for moment before realizing she must give an answer if she was to have any hope of obtaining his cooperation.

Finally, she said, "You cannot pretend that we have an amiable association."

"If we do not, I cannot see where I have any part in it. I have not said more than a few words to you. The single time I tried to assist you, I was assaulted."

As his words poured out, the timbre of his voice rose ominously. That might have been the reason why he abruptly stopped talking. His temper was barely in check. Having her own actions thrown back at her from a different perspective was a disconcertion. Annabella almost accused him of conspiring with her father, but suddenly thought better of it. That *could* have all been her father's doing. When she had initially wanted to despise Asher Price at all costs, she realized that he may have had no part in her father's scheming.

"If I was rude, I am sorry," she replied civilly. "I was most troubled at the time."

Without ado, he said, "Apology accepted."

That, she believed, was that.

But it was not so simple. As the inflictor of the wound, she was far happier to have it healed than her victim. Asher Price and Annabella Chase were nothing if not well-matched in conceit. But neither recognized arrogance in themselves. They were, however, highly aware of it in the other. There was a standoff—and not a particularly noble one.

Annabella took a moment to draw a deep breath and attempt to reinvent the confident woman who had just come into Mr. Price's place of business. She told herself that any ill-feelings had been expunged from their relationship and Mr. Price should look with favor on any proposal she suggested. She withdrew a set of papers from her bag. Because it was small, they were crunched around the edges. She smoothed them.

"Now that we have dispensed with unpleasantries, may I put my proposal to you, Mr. Price? The terms, I believe, are quite clear."

Smiling, she handed the documents to him. He took them from her, but did not remove his feet from his desk. As he went through them one by one, point by point, he was flippant. It wasn't until he had read it all that he put his feet back on the floor and looked at her properly.

"I cannot accept these terms," he announced.

"If your acceptance of my apology was sincere, may I ask why not?" she asked haughtily.

"Your offer me no collateral."

"The collateral is the *Bella* itself!" she replied tartly.

"I already hold the mortgage on the Bella."

"Beg pardon?" she asked incredulously.

"Your new mother has already mortgaged the Bella," Asher replied dispassionately.

"But it is not hers to borrow against!" she very nearly bellowed.

"*Au contraire*," Asher replied. "Her name appears on the deed. She and your father both signed the loan papers."

"Was this instrument signed in your presence?" she demanded. "And since when does a lady's name appear on property documents?"

Here, Asher paused. Then, with great hesitation, he admitted that he had not seen Newman sign the papers himself.

"Such niceties are not the custom in present day San Francisco."

"My father knows nothing of this loan. She forged his name!" she gasped. "Even in San Francisco forgery is a crime—is it *not*?"

"It happens twenty times a day."

"*That* is not the *point*! She must be arrested!"

Asher wasn't convinced. "Can your father say unequivocally that he did not sign them? He has, after all, been 'unwell'."

"He would never, *never* do such a thing!" Annabella insisted. "Even you know that."

"No, I cannot say that I do. Your father and I are not that intimately acquainted."

Annabella's voice rose, "You must see that woman is arrested! She plans to take all the Bella's assets and then sail for New Orleans. It is your duty to stop her!"

"Why do I care if Newman Chase was duped or not?" he asked mildly. "My duty is to the bank. It would be in the bank's favor if the loans are called in. We would obtain the *Bella* at quite a good price."

"I am shocked at such callous behavior!" Rising in her chair, she said, "I thought you were my father's friend!"

Raising his eyebrows, Asher's gaze was both cold and direct as he reminded her, "We are but business acquaintances."

"At one time," she said, "you were meant to be more! Does that mean nothing to you?"

Asher Price stood. They were very nearly nose to nose. He smelled quite nice. Teeth alarmingly white. No nose hair.

"I don't take your meaning, Miss Chase."

Startled, she remembered herself, asking bluntly, "Did you, or did you not have an understanding with my father?"

Asher's expression altered ever so slightly. She couldn't quite gauge its origination.

"Your father and I talked of many matters."

"I will give you five-thousand dollars to file criminal charges against Dovie Gaspard."

"She borrowed twenty-five."

"You can carry the note on the rest."

"Why would I do that?"

"My proposition will make you five-thousand dollars ahead. You know that the *Bella* is good for the rest—so long as that woman is out of the picture." Trying to sweeten the bargain, she said, "If we come to an agreement, August Gerlache will be part owner and overseer—should you fear my father's indisposition would be a burden."

Asher sat back down and leaned back in his chair. First he steepled his fingers, then he tapped them together thoughtfully.

Finally, he said, "Let me recap our conversation. You will bribe me five thousand dollars to file charges on a woman for fiscal misconduct without proof that wrongdoing was done?"

"That sounds about right," Annabella sniffed. "She will leave my father, the *Bella* will be saved—and your bank will get its money."

"If I don't do it, she will still leave and the bank will own the Bella—all quite legally," he replied. "I am an ethical man, Miss Chase."

"Ethical, Mr. Price? What of morals, I ask?" she said angrily.

"It is not I who married in haste and is repenting at leisure," he said.

Upon summoning the subject of matrimony, a quiet descended over the two combatants. It wasn't as Asher would recall it, but Annabella blurted an unrehearsed plea.

"Is there no other arrangement we can make, Mr. Price? There is nothing that I will not do to save my father."

54

The time between when Miss Chase had entered Asher's office and when she left twirling her parasol was life-altering—for them both.

✧

At one time Asher Price had been one of the most sophisticated men in San Francisco. But the continuing affluence had lured true cosmopolitans. Some of the men swaggering up the walkway had been recently domiciled in such metropolises as New York City, Philadelphia, and even Paris. Unlike Sutter's Fort which remained a rough outpost, San Francisco had aspirations to urbanity. Finely tailored men and well-dressed women walked the thoroughfare. Granted, few of them were what would be considered upright citizens. Almost everyone in town had the same hungry look. They were either sniffing out their next victim or looking to become one.

The *Bella Goode* had been a respectable place, but its reputation had taken a beating when that Gaspard woman was in charge. With her gone the place could be turned around, but competition was growing with each passing day. More and more of such establishments around the square had pretensions to grandeur—what with fancy fixtures, orchestra pits, and lady singers.

Finery wouldn't fool any but the least discerning of customers. All the Persian carpets and chandeliers didn't make them anything but brothels. The lack of ladies in town meant even god-fearing, disease-dreading men of means were reduced to paying for female company. So far, he had chosen celibacy. Anything was better than have one's genitals shrivel and fall off with syphilis. If aroused, all he had to do was think of the line of men outside Doc Walters' clinic waiting to be tortured by his "Miraculous Mercury Cure."

The fault was entirely his own. Asher Price admitted that. Had he not behaved like some high-muck-a-muck to Miss Chase's financial proposal, the entire marriage business would have been nipped in the bud. They would have gone about their merry way without rancor (or at least without visible wounds). As a businessman, he knew it was unacceptable to let personal feelings to intrude. Nothing good came of it.

From the very beginning she had annoyed him—standing in his

office coquettishly peeking over her fluttering fan. No doubt it was an effect she had employed countless times on countless men before him. Had he not been such a keen judge of human nature, he might have been taken in by her exquisite blue eyes. He didn't let them sway him. Without comment and wearing his most sedulous expression, he allowed her to have her say.

He knew it all.

Newman Chase's humiliating situation was the talk of the town. Asher had even heard that Miss Chase was shopping for a loan. So when he saw her in his bank he expected some sort of financial petition. He hadn't really decided beforehand whether he would help her or not. But what with her sitting there all haughty, he couldn't keep himself from reacting in kind. When he refused her first proposition, she scarcely missed a beat before proclaiming that she had deigned to reconsider *his* suit for her hand. He didn't know if he was more shocked or angry. His reaction was an honest one. Perhaps, he scoffed. He might have even snorted.

He did not blame himself at all. Miss Chase's ego looked as if it needed to be taken down a peg or two. If she thought she could just flounce in his bank and demand him to marry her, she was most seriously deluded. He wouldn't marry such a tart for all the tea in China.

It was a toss-up whether to admire her spirit or fear for her soul. Lolling about a saloon could sully the most earnest girl's leanings. True, Gus Gerlache seemed to have good sense. But what was one man against a cast of drunks, whores, and plain ne'er-do-wells? Lord knew her father hadn't been a decent influence.

In what he considered his most civilized tone, he pointed out to her, "A great deal has come to pass since your father and I last spoke."

She had agreed, "So it has."

It both pleased and irked him that he had not provoked her. He gave it another try.

His voice pinched, he said, 'Your father may not have scruples against a wife with a disreputable past, but I am not so inclined."

Her voice was raised a near-decibel, she squawked, "*A disreputable past,* you say?"

Such incredulousness meant nothing to him.

"Would you care to explain yourself before I take a swat at you with my bag?" she offered.

He raised his voice in kind, "Did you not spend six weeks in the throes of wild abandon with a *sailor*?"

He said the word so disdainfully that it was an offense in and of itself. She registered the insult completely.

"In the throes of... I beg your pardon!"

He answered, "As well you should!"

Flushed with rage, she announced, "You are impugning my honor."

"For that you don't need my help. You did a good enough job of that on your own."

"Not only do you defame me, you ridicule the man I loved."

He didn't note her use of the past tense. It was a significant oversight—one that continued even in his recollections of the conversation.

Instead, he scoffed again, "The man *you love*—what a bunch of twaddle."

By then, both had leaned across the desk. They were once again nose to nose and she looked ready for war. He should have been prepared when she whapped him hard on the cheek with her closed fan. A red spot was immediately evident on his cheek, but he didn't register her attack beyond a very fierce glare. He took his time before he stood back, his hands at his side. His fingers twitched.

"I dare say," he intoned, "that who ever does take you off your father's hands had better own a suit of armor. You are a prickly girl indeed."

"In case you haven't noticed, sir, I am no longer a girl."

"Yes," he said quietly. "I have noticed."

He *had* noticed that. It was difficult not to. She had changed from a pretty girl to a handsome young woman. In fact, she was quite beautiful despite her face having turned to an unattractive shade of crimson. He didn't see that. He only saw that the color had spread to her bosom. He tried to avert his eyes, but lost the battle. Fortunately, she was busy fumbling to open her fan. In this she failed. Her fan was broken and crumpled; she had crushed it when she whacked him. Quickly putting it behind her, she stared hard at the floor. At that point, a gentleman would have helped her down from her high-horse. But Asher wanted to make her do that herself. As a seasoned businessman, he was of the opinion that once blows were administered, a business meeting was concluded.

Miss Chase, however, was prepared to take it a step further.

"It is imperative that we rid my father of this woman, do you *understand*?" Raising her chin, she said, "If we don't, I am certain that he will die."

Asher tried to remain untouched by her candor. Lips closed, he ran his tongue round his teeth.

When he didn't speak, she continued, asking bluntly, "If you will not take cash money, what consideration will tempt you?"

That confounded him more than getting walloped.

His expression must have alerted her to the ambiguity of her question.

She made herself clear, "I believe at one time you wanted my hand in marriage."

He realized then just how desperate she was. But just then his own conceit distorted his perception. Having the upper hand, he intended to keep it. Few locales had as many fools per square foot as San Francisco. No man wanted to be the laughing stock. Her infatuation with Aaron Ainsworth was very public. Asher was wary—and more than a bit terse.

"What will tempt me?" he snorted. "Certainly not 'used goods."

"Is that what loving another man makes me?" she demanded. "Did you not love your dead wife? Are men and women not governed by the same God?"

"I was married," Asher said stiffly.

"As if love draws that line," she hissed.

He cleared his throat. Only moments before he had been so in control of the conversation, it had been a test not to gloat. Suddenly, he was struggling to maintain his composure. But he couldn't help being curious just how far Annabella Chase would go to get her way. She was fetching when she was angry. As a wife, however, he had grave doubts—the more by the minute. At that moment, however, all he had to do was to escort her to the door and bid her on her way. He could have returned to his own business with only a fleeting interest in the doings of Newman Chase and his daughter.

But he didn't.

He had been leading a very uneventful and solitary life. That was the only rationale he could find to defend what he said then. It was either that or he had totally lost his mind.

"I will make you this proposition," he announced. "On the day you take my hand in marriage, I will file criminal charges of misappropriation against Dovie Gaspard Chase."

"And follow through with that prosecution?" Annabella asked with a raised eyebrow.

Most likely that eyebrow sealed the deal.

"Agreed," said he.

"Agreed," she repeated.

With that, she flounced out the door, only pausing long enough to say over her shoulder, "Tomorrow, then?"

"Tomorrow," he said firmly. "Two o'clock sharp. Which church shall I reserve?"

"Under the circumstances," she said snidely, "I think that would be a sacrilege. Here in your office will do nicely."

With that she was gone. Asher stood with one hand at his waist, the other in fingering his watch. A small tinkling sound could be heard, but he didn't see initially where it came from. When he did, he closed the cover to his watch to make it stop. That silenced it, but his hand still trembled. The only thing that settled him was that in all probability, Miss Chase wouldn't go through with it.

But then she just might.

Reminding himself that arranged marriages were the most common type on the frontier, he decided to would worry about it when and if the time came. He would don a clean shirt regardless. One must be prepared for all events.

The actuality of marrying such a lovely creature suddenly hit him. He began to take a more personal accounting. His nightmares *had* declined. They had begun to dwindle about the time she threw her shoe at him. They had dwindled to the point that he was reasonably certain that he wouldn't scare the living daylights out of anyone sharing his bed. The cessation of his night terrors and Miss Chase's proposal coalesced precisely. He didn't recognize the full significance of that, but he thought it a good sign.

Granted, finding himself so suddenly betrothed took a bit of adjustment. He had not intended to marry her. He had merely intended—admittedly for reasons of vanity—to determine whether or not that scruffy seadog Aaron Ainsworth had his way with her. That was truly none of his business. And he had been abominably direct. Being freed from the bond of courtesy had been a rather liberating. Still, he was a bit ashamed. No doubt his own sensibilities as a gentleman had been polluted by the wretches that had overtaken the town. He feared that he owed Miss Chase an apology.

Even he admitted, "I've made a pig's ear of everything."

"What'd you say, boss?" answered the ever-vigilant Mr. Butler.

"Nothing," said Asher. "Nothing."

Asher considered all aspects of his looming nuptials and his bride-to-be. Whether it was a sacrilege or not, he didn't really believe a woman was immoral if she engaged in congress with her lover. Living just beyond the rules of man had made him believe that. It wasn't the public vows that we important, but the private ones. He just didn't want to look the fool—in that he was no better than any other man. If Annabella Chase had given more than just her heart to that whaler, he didn't want to be the last to know.

If he believed in love without nuptials, he knew plenty of men wooed their wives after they were married as well. Although he was relatively unlearned in love, he had the conceit to believe that given time, he could win her. Her complete lack of sentiment *was* troubling. One would have thought that a prospective wife would have at least pretended some affection. That concerned him. Perhaps her travails had hardened her heart. That would be understandable—what with her lover's demise and her father's disgrace. Only heaven knew what occurred on her journeys. The thought of it inspired all his protective instincts. He had to fight against them.

Negotiating complex agreements was his stock and trade. Clearly he should have obtained assurances to her situation before he had agreed to marry her. But when she flashed her big blue eyes at him, all reason took wing. He wanted to have her—good sense be damned.

As a banker, he of all people should know that it wasn't the price to consider, but the cost.

55

Having sealed her deal with Asher, Annabella was initially gleeful—so much so that she had to make herself not skip down the street like a little child.

All was well. Dovie would be run out of town, her father would recover, Gus would run the Bella, and everyone would be happy once again! She couldn't keep the smile from her face. As she passed knots of town-folk, they smiled in return. A few of the men tipped their hats. Normally she relished such attention. This time, however, was different.

The smiles weren't the amiable addresses of admiring gentlemen, but leers. Several men made suggestive remarks. One absolutely cackled. As she tried to escape, a trio of prostitutes camped in her way. Arm in arm, they were too busy casing their marks to move out of her way. Without begging anyone's pardon, she elbowed herself through them.

Catcalls followed her up the walk. Her cheeks burned. Holding her parasol low, she tried to deflect further stares. But with every gaze she excited, her shoulders shivered with mortification. By the time she neared the Bella, her teeth were almost chattering. It was late and she had planned to return to her room at the hotel, but she didn't want to be alone. Irony was an ugly roommate. She hit the Bella's teak doors at full steam.

Patrick was blissfully tinkling away at the piano when Annabella walked in the door. That meant Dovie wasn't prowling the room. Patrick both despised and was frightened by Dovie. It had taken considerable gumption for him to have crossed her like he did when he wrote to Annabella. As she headed towards him, she had to shrug one man's hand from her shoulder. She looked back at the man crossly, but he only laughed. The *Bella* wasn't all that crowded—or any more rowdy—than usual. That impudence was, she supposed, just the tenor of the times. She was just one shriek away from Gus rescuing her, so she wasn't scared. Still, she didn't want to have to depend on him at every turn. It occurred to her that it might be wise to start carrying her father's trusty pistol again. Clearly, her fierce reputation was already fading.

Within seconds of reaching Patrick, she had an urgent question.

"Do I look like a tart?"

Patrick had perked up when he saw her heading in his direction, but her question took him aback. Without a pause in his playing, he glanced up to gauge whether she was joking out of good humor or bad.

Determining she was not making merry, he answered her straight up, "You look like an angel."

"Where's my new mother?"

"Upstairs—with a special friend," he answered.

Knowing the truth and hearing of it as it was in progress were two very different things.

"Bless me," she intoned.

Patrick said, "Hear, hear.

"No wonder Poppa stayed drunk," she said. "What was that song you played the other night—the pretty, sad one?"

Suddenly, Patrick stopped mid-song. He began to play "Blue Julianna."

It was a sweet, searing tune and she smiled wanly.

"I wish I had been named Julianna," she mused.

"Annabella suits you," insisted Patrick.

Leaning against the piano, she began to tap her foot to the music. A group of men behind them began to hum along. Suddenly, Annabella wanted a drink. A frowsy blonde carrying a tray of drinks like they were the crown jewels passed by and Annabella liberated one from her. The woman looked at her angrily at her, but Annabella cut her off before she could set to cussing her.

"Tell Gus to take it off your tab."

Giving it a second thought, Annabella grabbed another one off the tray to boot. The woman went on her way without noticing. Struck by fit of silliness, Annabella stuck her tongue out at her.

Thinking better of behaving like such a child with a glass of liquor in each hand, she quickly looked to see if Patrick had seen her. He was too busy being unhappy at the first drink she took to have noticed the second. All his concentration had moved to his piano's sweet notes. To him, she was an innocent flower. Drinking intoxicants didn't suit his notion of who she was, so he preferred not to see it. She turned away from him and, as she had seen others do, threw back first one drink and then the other. Unused to more than a sip of wine, she quickly put the back of her hand to her lips to keep from gagging. As she did, she saw Gus looking hard at her from behind the bar. She was nearly moved to stick her tongue out at him, but figured one act of foolishness a night was sufficient.

Finding a chair, she sat there sullenly for a moment, her eyes sweeping the room for something of interest. In an odd twist of fate, the thick cigar smoke that always clung to the ceiling and walls like grey, velvet drapes, meliorated before her very eyes. She saw an enormous painting. It was so large that she marveled how she could have not seen it before. This work sported voluptuous female figures, supine, erotic, and very, very naked. A few wisps of smoke snaked over and around their bodies like translucent sheaths. It was the most jarringly sensual piece of art that she had ever laid eyes on. It was also absolutely breathtaking in its vulgarity.

Directly beneath the painting sat Tucker McFee.

He was sitting alone at a table. A woman had been sitting with him, but having seen a more lucrative client, she stood and left. Annabella hadn't seen Tucker since she had returned to town. For that matter, she hadn't thought of Tucker since he had told the story of the demise of the *Mary Thayer*'s crew. Seeing him again gave her a pang in her stomach (either that or in conjunction with the liquor). So much had been happening that she had devoted very little time to mourning Aaron's memory. Tucker reminded her of that.

The drinks were already beginning to make themselves known, but she walked in his direction without weaving. It gave her a lovely sensation of floating. Tucker's eyes bulged when he caught sight of Annabella and that pleased her. She took it as a compliment. He neither blinked nor spoke. He also seemed unable to decide whether to stand or remain sitting. She waved him to sit down putting an end to his puppet-like bobbing.

"Tucker," she marveled. "Dear Tucker."

His eyes receded a bit, but he still looked a bit incredulous as she seated herself next to him. A small drink sat half-full on the table. His neck was rubbed raw and he was dusted with talc. Tucker McFee had had a bath.

"May I," she asked, picking up his drink.

He nodded. She downed the drink in one swallow, but didn't gag this time. Rather, she burped like a sailor. Suddenly, flushed, she began fanning herself with one hand.

"Ooh! Is it warm in here to you?" Without waiting for his response, she answered herself. "Of course it is. Too many people I suppose... or is it just me?"

If Tucker entertained an answer, she didn't wait to hear it. A barmaid walked by and she grabbed two more drinks. Her first drinks had been rum. These two were gin. His tongue had been paralyzed with astonishment, but he finally was able to speak.

"I don't think you're supposed to mix your liquors like that."

"Oh, what do we care?" she said.

Suddenly she saw two coal eyes twinkling at her beneath the table.

"Stewpot!" she called out.

As if waiting to be noticed, the dog leapt on to her lap and began to excitedly lick her face. He didn't settle down until she put a stop to it by petting his head. The fabric of her gown was slippery and he slid back to the floor. Yawning and licking his snout with excitement, he finally laid his nose against her thigh. She continued to pet and coo at him. Another time she would have beside herself at the claw marks in the fabric, but she didn't see it just then.

"Miss Annabella," Tucker said, successfully vying for her attention.

She looked at him, which made him remember his manners. He grabbed his hat from his head and wadded it in his lap. Catching sight of his hat, she recalled Aaron's striped one. It made her sad.

Disconcerted, Tucker stated the obvious, "You've come back."

"Ye-e-s." She made the word three syllables. "And you look as pink and clean as a newborn babe."

"I had a bath. It cost three dollars."

Suddenly, Annabella grasped Tucker by his shirt front. Shaking him, her words slurred, "You won't believe it, Tucker dear. You won't believe it."

"What?" he asked dumbly. "What won't I believe?"

"My poor Aaron's dead," she responded, tears welling in her eyes. "And I am to be wed."

Then she giggled, "I made a rhyme."

With a tenuous smile pulling at the corners of his mouth, Tucker agreed, "So you did."

Annabella swayed slightly in her chair, but he suddenly realized what she had said.

"You're to be wed?"

Heartbroken and incredulous, his voice was a bit higher-pitched than usual. He cleared his throat, but waited for an answer. Annabella leaned forward conspiratorially, shushing him with a finger to her lips.

"No one knows yet," she whispered. "It's a secret. A secret bargain."

"Who? Who're you to marry?" Tucker asked in the same stage whisper she used. "And why is it a secret?"

"It's a secret because I don't want anyone to *know*," she replied.

Clearly exasperated, he almost snapped, "Who? *Who*?"

With a look of exaggerated hurt, she stuck out her lip, "I don't think I can say."

Seeing the conversation wasn't improving, he said, "You are too young to marry."

"What do you know of it?" she barked.

She had crisscrossed between Boston and San Francisco three times. He had come but once. And that, no doubt, was in the company of his family. Aaron told her that Tucker had come by prairie wagon. Even she knew that they were always filled with refugees from Missouri or the like.

"I am twenty years old," says he.

"I am too," says she. Then she added, "Next autumn."

Annabella laughed at her truth-telling. Tucker, however, was stiff with indignation.

"See, I am older than you and I am no boy," he announced. "If you would have me, I'd be proud to marry you."

He still looked like a boy—although crouching over a stream and digging in the riverbank for twelve hours a day had given him a lean and wiry look. But his hair still looked wet from a bath and he smelled of cheap, scented soap. When loose women passed by and waggled their wares at him, he crimsoned. Annabella wasn't any more experienced than he, but at least she had quit blushing at every turn. Perhaps he was not a boy, but he was in no way a man. In a town where women could be bought for a dime, she doubted that he had been with one. Just her gaze made him so uncomfortable that the tips of his ears burned red. Just then, his innocence seemed the sweetest, most adorable feature imaginable.

"Oh, Tucker, dear, I am promised to another."

She wished she was free to marry whom she chose. Tucker wasn't half the man that Aaron was, but he was a sight better than the likes Asher Price. He had been married before. There was nothing pure about him. Like all prospective grooms, he coveted his bride like a prize heifer. Men wanted to own their women, not love them. She knew why too. They wanted to make certain there wasn't someone else's bun in the oven. What lechers. Men could hump half the whores in Christendom, but his wife had to be a virgin.

The hypocrisy was unbearable. And she knew that she would soon be a part of it.

It was only just dawning on her that in agreeing to marry Asher Price, she would have to share his bed—and submit to loathsome acts perpetrated upon her person. What little she knew about intimate activity was that a woman bled her first time. She had no idea how much blood there would be, but talk was that it was enough for the husband to know. It was an abominable thought. Mr. Price would learn her most private of secrets. Whether she and Aaron Ainsworth had been lovers in all senses was none of his business. If their entire arrangement hinged on giving in to Asher Price in that, she thought she would rather die.

Die!

There had to be way to keep such information to herself. She racked her befuddled brain for a way round it. The thought worried her—so much so that she forgot Tucker was sitting there. Chin in her one hand, she struck her other fist hard against the table in frustration. The table shook when she did, but she didn't notice. Looking into the near distance, she tried to concentrate. That was difficult what with the liquor she had drunk and Tucker continuing to look all moony at her. Suddenly, a magnificent idea struck her.

She and Tucker would enter the realm of amatory rites together.

What a beautiful notion. She was surprised that she hadn't thought of it before. If she wanted to give herself to a man, what better way than two pristine beings hand in hand. It was as God intended—well if one discounted the marriage part. It would all work out perfectly. Asher Price would believe that Aaron had deflowered her. Watching the arrogance drain from his face when he learned that he wasn't her first would be bliss itself.

"Come," she demanded.

When Annabella left, Tucker followed her out the door like a puppy. Stewpot was too busy licking his privates to realize they had gone. But Patrick saw them. Allowing the band take over, he went to the door. From there he watched Annabella staggering towards the hotel with Tucker eagerly behind.

56

When it came to illicit embraces, the streets and alleys of San Francisco were quite handy for most fornicators. One probably worked just as well for Annabella since she just wanted to be done with the business as quickly and efficiently as possible. However, Miss Chase considered herself in a class far above that of most fornicators. Therefore, the environs for her amatory act must be elevated too.

It would have served her father right if she had marched Tucker up the stairs at the *Bella* then and there. But someone might see her and tell Gus. Word would get around for sure, and this was one union that Annabella wanted to keep private. Although it was entirely for his benefit, Mr. Asher Price was to remain unwitting of it. All he was to know was that she had her privates docked before he got there. He would be left to surmise that it had been at the hands of the dashing Aaron Ainsworth—not an unfledged boy like Tucker McFee.

In wanting to get the thing over with as fast as possible, she headed for the Deluxe Hotel. The streets in San Francisco were still alternately rivers of mud or choked with dust. That night it was a river of mud. To get to her room, they had to traverse the slats of boards laid out across the street for pedestrians. Navigating the slats was difficult enough without being tipsy. Giggling, she weaved a bit and Tucker tried to grasp her elbow. She shook off his help.

"I'm alright," she said. "I can *do* it!"

All the rooms in the hotel were let, so no one was manning the desk. Annabella motioned for Tucker to follow her up the stairs and got another case of the giggles. He was too worried about getting a scolding to laugh. Unaware that she was who was making all the noise, Annabella put a shushing finger first to Tucker's lips and then to hers.

"You're loud enough to wake snakes," she cautioned.

The one thing good about Lupe being gone was that she didn't have to worry about waking her. She would have propelled herself across the street as fast as her feet could carry her to blab it all to Gus. Nothing pleased Lupe more than tattling. She could imagine Lupe right then, arms folded and fire in her eyes. The disapproval made her a little titillated.

When they got to the landing, she shushed Tucker again. He didn't mind, his eyes were bright with excitement. She knew that it was a memory the dear boy would keep with himself forever. Hers was the ultimate gift. She vowed to be gentle.

The key to her room was tucked into her bodice. Digging for it made it slip deeper into her bosom. Tucker watched this procedure closely. It was infinitely more arousing to him than watching those women make tortillas. After several tries, however, she was unable to get the key in the keyhole. Several keys and several keyholes swam before her.

"Here," she commanded, handing it to him.

As he fumbled with it, she leaned against the door jamb trying to keep from sliding to the floor. (That they were both having so much trouble with so simple an insertion should have cautioned them.) When the door opened, she stepped into the room, but he didn't.

"Come," she commanded. When he didn't respond, she demanded again, "Come in!"

That got him moving—but just far enough into the room for her to close the door behind him. She tossed her cape in the direction of a chair. It slid to the floor, but she was too busy turning up the light to care. When it illuminated them, she could see that Tucker had picked her cape up from the floor and held it with both hands. His eyes, however, were transfixed on her bosom. She whirled around and showed him her back.

"I can't do this by myself, now can I?"

"Wha-a-t?" he stuttered.

Her mind had leapt ahead, already calculating the fact that with Tucker doing the duties, she wouldn't have to fork over another dollar to Gaby Mosley to undo her corset.

Pointing to her laces, she demanded, "Undo me."

Then it occurred to her that she was commencing a seduction.

So she said sweetly, "Please Tucker, dear."

Puzzled, it took him a minute to respond. He did so only under the conclusion that she simply needed a favor. He was well-intentioned, but having never undone anyone's clothing but his own, his fingers fumbled with the delicate little hooks. In a scholarly tone, she encouraged him, explaining each step.

"Yes, that's good. Now the laces—just loosen them one by one."

Once he got most of them undone, she finished the job herself. He stood back in awe as she tossed the contraption aside and leapt playfully on the bed in just her chemise and petticoats. They flounced out prettily around her and she reached out her hand.

"Come," she bid.

Once again, Tucker stuttered, "Wha-a-t?"

"Don't you want to kiss me?"

"Wha-a-t?"

Employing her most fetching mock-pout, she said, "You will hurt my feelings if you don't."

Closing her eyes and pursing her lips, she leaned towards him. Wanting very much to kiss her, Tucker was extremely careful not to touch any part of her person but her lips when he did. Then he leapt back as if she was on fire.

"Please, Miss Annabella," he begged. "I want to kiss you bad, but can't I just kiss your cheek first?"

That seemed like a reasonable request, but as time was a-wasting, she refused to take a step backward.

"Please, try again."

Again, she pursed her lips. With trembling hands held fast to his sides, he leaned forward just enough to brush her lips with his. She couldn't help but compare him to Aaron. Pitiable Tucker had much to learn. First of all, there was the matter of saliva—Tucker didn't seem to have any. Aaron's kiss was wet. Hot. Passionate. This recollection of Aaron upset her.

Suddenly woozy, she fell back on her bed. The mattress was of the finest down and it enveloped her. At the sight of her up-ended limbs, Tucker was suddenly lost to lust. Without warning, he lunged on top of her. She shrieked, but he didn't hear her.

All his corporeal knowledge was obtained through stories traded aboard ship and in the light of mining campfires. They were both lurid and explicit. He had heard of hidden slits, wet and wanting. Commingling those frank images and the fanciful tales of the Arabian Nights meant Tucker was so randy he couldn't speak. Finally, his throbbing member understood what Annabella wanted of it. He scrambled madly to find the bottom layer of her petticoats.

She shrieked with surprise. At that very moment, Tucker very nearly shrieked himself. Having uncovered the mother-lode of sex, he did what any lusty young man would have done when presented with his first whiff of the female scent. He buried his face in it.

Unleashing a man's libido, Annabella realized belatedly, was a bit cataclysmic. Unknowing how to get him redirected, she sat up. That sent him sliding head first to the floor. She was not sympathetic.

"*You*," she announced, "are not doing it correctly."

The lump on his forehead was exceeded by the one engorging his crotch. He was powerfully grateful to be given another go. But before he set to climbing the skirts of Mount Annabella again, she leapt onto the floor and loosed the ties and kicked her petticoats aside. Quick as that, she was back on the bed and as seductively as she knew how, began to roll her stockings down one leg then the other.

Her procedure was uninterrupted.

Tucker sat with surprising patience and watched. His chin rested on the edge of the mattress. One corner of his mouth collected a small puddle of drool. Having his full attention, she curled her forefinger in his direction. Thinking it was better to corral the beast, she straddled him. A look of incomprehension passed over his face before instinct took over. Fumbling with the buttons of his pants, he finally loosed himself. The information Annabella had about male anatomy, however, did not include an erection. She was alternately shocked and curious.

"How big does that thing get?" she blurted out.

Tucker himself couldn't really say at that point and merely shrugged. Annabella kept a watch on the thing just in case she changed her mind. Tucker also wanted to watch and turned her over, grabbing her by the ankles like a turkey wishbone.

"No!" she kicked his hands away.

By then Tucker had gotten a gander at her pudenda, but come to the realization that an erection didn't have a honing device. It may have been stiff, but it flopped about without a free hand to guide it. He grabbed hold of himself and aimed in the general direction of what the boys called the "Promise Land." Then, he felt the ferocious quiver of release. He fell to the side, breathing like a spent rabbit.

"Did you do it?" she asked. "Did you *do it*?"

Somewhere in the back of his mind, Tucker supposed that if she had to ask, he had failed in his manly duties. The boys called that "shooting in the bush."

"I-I-I'm not sure," he said. Ambiguity seemed a safe harbor just then. "I might have."

"If you didn't do it, we'll have to have another go," she announced.

Given a few minutes that would have seemed like a good idea, but at that point it looked highly unlikely to him.

"I did it," he said reassuringly, for he did not want to let her down.

"Is there blood?" she asked with increasing concern. "There is supposed to be blood."

"Blood?"

The idea horrified him. He wanted to know what blood, where it came from and why, but he was too embarrassed to ask. The man was supposed to be the most knowledgeable in these matters. Pushing him away, she climbed off the bed. As soon as she did, she felt a wetness making its way down her legs. At first she thought that might be blood. She turned her back to Tucker and lifted the edge of her chemise. What ever it was, it wasn't blood. It was some other bodily fluid—and she knew who to blame.

"What have you done?" she asked accusingly.

Floundering for an answer, he wracked his memory, searching out every barnyard fornication that he had ever witnessed. "I think it might be my seed."

"Your *what*?"

She was suddenly reminded that the goal of such behavior was fertilization. It was a comfort to know that it was on her legs and not inside her. She didn't tell Tucker that. She didn't want to talk about it at all—to Tucker or anyone else. Moreover, the very notion of Tucker and what they had done suddenly repulsed her.

Tucker still lay on the bed. His flaccid member was exposed and it looked very much like a salted slug. Seeing her eye him, he quickly covered himself. But it was too late. She had seen it. Smoothing her chemise, she went to the door, unbolted it and then held it open.

In a pinched voice, she said, "Thank you."

Like a whipped dog, Tucker trudged towards the door. On the way he saw one of his woolen socks on the floor. He pressed it into his pocket and walked out of the room carrying his shoes. Just outside, he turned around and opened his mouth to speak. Before he could, she shut the door in his face.

"Goodbye, Miss Annabella," he said weakly. Then with a bit of bravado, "Will I see you tomorrow?"

Although she pretended she didn't hear him, she did. She leaned back heavily against the door until she heard his footsteps padding down the stairs. The entire affair seemed sordid and ugly. Quickly finding a basin, she cleaned his semen from her thighs. The smell of the stuff was repugnant. A wave of nausea overcame her. Perhaps it was the liquor. She hoped it was the liquor. If it wasn't, it had to have been her conscience.

If it was, why hadn't it made its presence known sooner?

57

Like most ladies of the night prowling the San Francisco walk-boards, Dovie Gaspard wasn't all bad. She was a long-distance mother of two boys who were enrolled in New Orleans's foremost military academy. Although it served in all other aspects of her life, her preeminence as a courtesan had come at considerable cost. Her sons believed their mother was dead. In order to keep it that way, she needed money—and lots of it. She relished that money, not for just what she could buy, but with power that came with it. In that, she was no different from most men.

As they suspected, once Dovie got wind of Annabella's return, she was on the lookout for an ambush. Newman continued to stay out of her way and acted cowed when she came round. However difficult it was for his friends to watch, she regaled in his fear. It had been relatively easy to get him under her thumb, keeping him there was a little more trying.

The one thing Newman dared to refuse her was when she demanded that he fire Gus. (She had tried to fire him herself, but Gus had ignored her.) At Newman's one rebellion, Dovie had grabbed his coffee cup from him and threw it against the wall.

"There, you bleedin' eunuch," she hissed.

When that daughter of his arrived, someone hid the cashbox. Although she threw her entire repertoire of threats at Gus, he refused to produce it. That made her panic and the panic made her meaner.

Gus won the coin toss to be the one to tell her that her luck had changed.

She was easy to find. Newman had taken to sleeping in his office again, so she had the room upstairs to herself. Gus picked his time carefully. Knowing an audience might invite her to violence, he watched until he was sure she was alone before he ascended the steps. The door was half-open. She stood at the window looking down at the street. The dressing gown that she wore was so loosely tied that a fair amount of what had so beguiled Newman was on display. Gus rarely ventured up the stairs. He had spoken to Dovie even less. Therefore, he expected her to be surprised to see him. She was.

"Well, August Gerlache is at my door," she said without emotion. Then she gave a half-smile, saying, "Not locking in my tits don't mean I ain't struck with wonder."

"Dovie, my love, always the charmer," he responded.

She harrumphed.

Gus went on, "Now that Newman had devoted his life to coffee, he is questioning the business decisions that you made on his behalf."

As he spoke, he watched her bristle. Dovie wasn't easily spooked. With quick purposeful steps, she walked in his direction. It took considerable willpower on his part to keep from backing up.

But she didn't confront him. Instead, she sat down at her dressing table and motioned for him to sit on the bed. The mattress was bare, exposing the stains of innumerable ejaculations. He declined her offer (both real and implied) and stood just far enough away from her to have both a running start if she took after him and room to duck should she chunk one of her potion jars.

When Gus didn't accept the bait of the bed, she only shrugged.

He didn't wait on ceremony before producing the leather pouch full of "persuasion" money. Opening it just far enough for her to see what was in it, he extended the bag and told her what she had to do to earn it.

"You have decided to leave San Francisco and divorce your husband. Should you think otherwise, I must advise you that as of today, there have been several charges of a felonious nature filed against you with the constabulary. Only your swift departure will forestall your incarceration."

Few citizens of San Francisco would be unhappy to see Dovie Gaspard in jail. That ill will was due more to her being a woman of commerce than a lady of the night. Arresting her would set a precedent for any other uppity female. Of course, there was little chance Dovie would actually be thrown in prison. To San Franciscans, she would have to have done murder to merit that. Female fraud meant banishment.

Dovie took the bag and plunked it on the table without counting it. A deep, rasping sigh emitted from the back of her throat. Her dressing table was heaped with ribbons and boas. Reaching beneath the mound, she produced a slender cigar. An oil lamp sat flickering atop the table, but she ignored it.

Instead she asked Gus, "Give a lady a light?"

Gus always kept a few matches tucked in his belt for his pipe. As they were hard to come by, he was parsimonious with them. It annoyed him a bit that Dovie knew something that privileged about him. Still, he dug one out and walked over to her. Snapping it across his thumbnail, it lit with a hiss. Because it threatened to fizzle, he cupped his hands around it as he held it out to her. With surprising softness, she placed her hands over his and leaned forward. (That was a distasteful intimacy for him and he wondered if she knew it.) After several deep inhalations from her, it lit.

Once it did, she quickly leaned back and crossed her legs. In doing so, Gus was provided with a generous look at Dovie's muff.

"What do you think, Gus?" she said breathily.

"Think of what?" he responded.

Rubbing one knee against the back of the other, she said, "What do you think of having me?"

Gus pursed his lips. "Not much."

With that he turned and headed for the door.

It was prudent that he closed it quickly. He heard a thud and crash as some sort of porcelain object as it hit the door and fell to the floor.

Dovie's pique was fortuitous for Gus. Her little show had caused a longing in his loins that he didn't much want her to see. He couldn't quite stomach giving her that satisfaction.

For whatever reason, Dovie packed up immediately. Sporting a two-handled bag and three-feathered hat, she trooped regally down the stairs. She stopped at the bottom and looked around the room searching for a specific face. To a man, everyone cowered—most of all Newman. Certain she was after him, he shrank back into the storeroom doorway. But she wasn't looking for a man.

She put her hands on her hips, she bellowed, "Annie Chase! I want Annie Chase!"

Fortunately—for the sake of all involved—Annabella was no where to be found. Dovie gave soon gave up.

"Tell her," she said to Gus, "that I was lookin' for her."

Gus said that he would.

Patrick became ashen-faced the moment she bayed for Annabella. His bug-eyes, however, almost bulged out of his eye-sockets when she turned and leveled the long, pointed nail of her forefinger at him.

"You, Patrick Coffin," she demanded.

Patrick pointed his index finger at his own chest and mouthed, "Me?"

"Yes, *you*!"

He cringed.

She dropped her bag at her feet and sniffed, "See to this."

He was visibly relieved. But he didn't move towards her. Rutledge Mayne was slouched at the bar. Patrick snapped his fingers at him. Rutledge didn't budge, however, until Gus flipped a quarter on the bar. Everyone held their collective breaths until she was out of sight. Newman slipped back into the room, sipping his coffee like he had been there all the time.

"I swear, Mr. Chase," said Patrick. "Before you marry again, please do recall what Mr. Gus tells us all."

"What's that, Patrick?"

"Marry in haste, detest at leisure."

Merry with relief, Gus guffawed and so did Newman.

As for Dovie, once her malefaction was exposed, her friends were happy to inform on her. According to them, Newman was not her first husband—he was her fifth. That wouldn't have mattered except that she had not observed the nicety of divorcing any of the others. In theory, bigamy wasn't as unsavory as fraud involving money. Those whose hearts were involved might have disagreed.

Newman took it all in stride. He still didn't accept fault for any of it, but he didn't claim the credit for extricating himself either. For that Annabella was grateful.

As for Gus, he quit worrying about Newman's affairs. Annabella's gave him fits enough.

58

Simon Goodenow had made certain that the failure of Miss Perry's Academy for Young Ladies was reported in the newspapers. Usually such things were left to be spread about informally. But under his influence, this unfortunate event was entered into history riddled with inaccuracies and rife with innuendos. It left Adelaide Perry no avenue for rebuttal. Mr. Dutton told her that demanding a retraction would do nothing but spread the slander further.

That wouldn't do.

There might be an inquiry. And if there was an inquiry, someone with a shovel might start probing the soil in the bottom of her late father's root cellar. That was to be avoided at all cost. Having spent all of her adult life in a productive and decorous manner, she felt victimized again. She also felt the cold hand of divine retribution too.

✧

Her innate stubbornness kept Adelaide from retreating from Boston for some time. Eventually, however, she was convinced that nothing was left for her there.

Where she would go was a well-considered decision. New Orleans was deemed too humid, St. Louis too pedestrian. A palazzo or chateau sounded wonderful, but regarded as unattainable. Only California sounded both doable and desirable. It was wild and wide open. Her reputation wouldn't matter there. Its greatest disadvantage was it largest attraction. Such an untamed land wasn't a plum destination for an unmarried woman.

Her lawyer, Mr. Dutton always had a calm reasoning. She sought his advice then. He reminded her that unescorted and without resources, she might well fall to the wrong influences. She didn't remind him that it was too late—her virginity and naiveté were only a distant memory. Besides, she had already decided that she intended to go west and do what ever she had to do to make her way.

Seeing her decision irrevocable, Mr. Dutton asked, "Do you know anyone there?"

"Yes and no," she said. "The father of one of my students—one of my most incorrigible students—lived there. I do not know him personally," she said.

Although last she believed he was still there, she had no intention of looking up Newman Chase. San Francisco was barbarous, but a teeming Metropolis too. She doubted that their paths would cross. No fears of seeing his daughter either. Adelaide had it on good authority that Annabella Chase had returned to Boston. There was no one in San Francisco to remind her of her past.

Mr. Dutton said, "I can't allow you to travel alone."

She was hesitant to be short with a man who had come to her rescue so many times. So she said, "I cannot stay here, and I have no one to travel with me. I have no choice but to go it alone."

"If you choose not stay here, then I shall accompany where ever you decide to go. No doubt there is a need for lawyers in such a lawless place as California."

She looked at him incredulously.

That embarrassed him, but he said softly, "I find that being your protector is my favorite profession. If you go, so must I."

It occurred to her that he had a point.

Timidly, she asks, "There is no one who will miss you?"

She didn't ask him about his business affairs and he didn't offer. In all the years that she knew him, he had told her little about his private life.

"No," he said quietly.

Suddenly shy, she said, "I have managed to put away enough to pay for my own passage."

His cheeks had flushed at the beginning of their conversation and with that declaration, grew redder. Seeing that she had embarrassed him, she immediately regretted it. But she wasn't altogether certain what he was he was proposing. It was necessary to be blunt.

"Do you mean for us to travel as a couple?"

"Shall we *be* a couple, Miss Perry? I should not like to lie."

"Nor should I, Mr. Dutton."

"Under the circumstances, Miss Perry, you should call me Loyal."

He took her hand and kissed her knuckles. Never was there a finer knight in shining armor.

A friend of Loyal's married them the morning they sailed. She announced then that she wanted to be called "Libby" after her mother. Adelaide Perry was no more.

"A new name for a new life. I am now Libby Dutton! Mrs. Loyal Dutton! Loyal and Libby!" she veritably crowed.

That suited her new husband fine.

They took their wedding night staring out at sea as the moon sprinkled it with a thousand twinkles. It truly was a new life.

It wasn't a large ship, so they were happy to have obtained a cabin for their wedding night. The bed had a thin feather mattress on it.

Loyal told her they would have probably been more comfortable in a hammock in steerage.

As she was completely in the dark about his past, she couldn't help but ask, "How would you know that?"

"The way that you would expect, my dear," he said gently. "I traveled in a variety of circumstances. On some of these travels, I incurred the most luxurious accommodations—and on others there was nothing at all."

"Some day you will have to tell me about all your adventures."

Kissing her on the cheek, he said, "My greatest feat has been winning you."

Until that moment, she hadn't realized that he had—or that she could be a prize. She had considered herself just another spinster schoolteacher.

Impulsively, she said, "I love you."

"You don't have to say that," he gently.

"I know I don't," she replied.

She meant it—although at first there was no grand passion. Her one lover had been everything Loyal wasn't—quick to grab her and even quicker to satisfy himself once he did. Still, he often left her breathless—and a bit wanting. It took Loyal longer to become aroused and longer still to finish. But that meant there was about twenty minutes of sheer bliss for her in between.

For that, she thanked him.

"The pleasure, my dear, is all mine," he assured her.

She stretched her limbs, saying, "I have never been so surprised in my life."

"What?" he replied a bit testily, "That I am not quite ready to be put out to pasture?"

"No," she said laughing, "Not at all." Grasping a bit of the red hair beneath his lower lip, she said, "To think this bit of red hair used to kindle my spirit."

"It doesn't any longer?"

"Not as it once did," she said solemnly.

"I am sorry to hear that...."

She interrupted him, "When once I had admired this little russet tuft, I have now have uncovered... a scarlet meadow!" At that, she tossed back the covers. Both looked down at the crimson ruff of hair surrounding his male apparatus. They both laughed.

Twirling the chin tuft between two fingers, she asked, "Is there a name for this?"

Thinking a moment, he answered, "I believe it is called an imperial."

"If this is an "imperial," she said, "Then that below must be lordly indeed."

Proof then did abound that the adage about old dogs not learning new tricks was written by a youngster.

It was the next morning when he surprised her by bringing out some photographs of San Francisco. It showed a rudimentary town with a bay of sticks in the distance. They looked at each one closely.

Pointing to the masts of sunken ships, she asked, "What are those?"

"Those are abandoned ships," he answered. Explaining, "Vessels have been left to rot in the harbor while the crew and passengers go pan for gold."

"I am not only surprised these gems exist so much as there was a photographer there to take them," she marveled. "Still, it doesn't look like much of a city."

"I hear that of late it has improved. Opera singers, jewelers, and undertakers have all set up shop. Grand hotels and French restaurants are on every street. By the time we get there, it may well be as refined as Boston."

"All that civilized?" she said sarcastically.

He took her chin in his hand and had her look at him. "All will be well."

"So long as you are by my side, I believe that," she said.

"All *will be* well," he told her. "I give you my solemn *promise*."

Loyal Dutton was, if nothing else, a man of his word. His reassurance quieted her in an abiding way. She was so reassured that she never once worried about the trip ahead of them. Loyal had traveled so extensively, he anticipated every setback. Holding up a small leather bag, he withdrew a small, brown bottle.

"See here? Quinine. Malaria won't touch us."

They dropped anchor at Colon and prepared themselves for the trip across the Isthmus. It would be rough, but they were assured they could make the trip in the comfort of a wagon. They both saw it as an exciting enterprise. Loyal assured her that there were far worse jungles along the Amazon River. He extolled her with tales of monkeys and piranha the entire forty miles to Panama City.

The natives there didn't much like the quarrelsome Americans streaming into their village, and Americans despised the lackadaisical ways of the tropics. It was only a matter of time until hostilities erupted. Teeming with men impatient to get either home or to the great Mecca, street-fights broke out nightly and gunfire stung the air. It was getting worse by the day.

Although the town was under the aegis of the Republic of Nueva Granada, it wasn't a strong influence. Loyal decided not to wait for a ship to take them north. That might take six weeks. Instead of purchasing passage, he bought a sloop.

"It is a fast one, Libby dear. I have named it *Miss Liberty*!"

He was like a boy with a toy. His excitement was contagious.

She cried, "Oh, Loyal!"

She wasn't sure why he had purchased it in the first place. She asked him that straight out.

"Why pay outrageous fares to sit in someone else's ship?" he replied.

His point was well taken. He told her that staples like rice and sugar were sitting on the shore rotting while waiting for chance to bring a returning vessel. Ships had been abandoned all up and down the Pacific coast—their captains and crews long gone to the Southern gold fields. He had already hired a crew among the men who wanted passage to San Francisco. It was all arranged before she could catch her breath.

They were gone with the tide.

They worked out their plan together. She tallied the figures as Loyal enumerated them. After they had secured a source of fundamental supplies, they could begin a regular transport between the isthmus and San Francisco. One way he would bring cargo hopeful miners and on the return, he would ferry deflated passengers heading home. If prices held, they would clear three thousand dollars each way.

Chucking her under the chin, he said, "Don't you worry, my dear. Together we can take on the world."

She saw that her husband was as daring as he was brilliant. They would be supported in style in for as long as they wished. The gold would eventually play out. But in the mean time, they would profit from it. If they were cautious, they could be well-set for life.

The sea air had a bracing effect on them both. Loyal wasn't a young man (he wasn't a handsome or graceful man either she supposed—but that didn't much matter to her). His face and hands grew tanned. He was still white as chalk beneath his clothes and she teased him that he looked like a native plunked in a glass of milk.

The chills and fever came after. He became so ill that he couldn't leave his bed. Yet, he insisted that it was just a recurrence of malaria.

"We have quinine. I shall be well in two shakes."

But it wasn't malaria. He had dysentery. He grew weaker and weaker. She wiped his forehead with a wet cloth and changed his bedding when it was soiled. Mortified, he kept apologizing for that indignity, insisting he didn't want to be a burden to her. When he finally died, it was her father's death twice over. She refused to allow anyone to tend to his corpse. Knowing that they would throw his body overboard, she kept refusing until the crew knew that she was out of her mind with grief. It fell to the ship doctor to hold her at bay while first mate and two others wrapped Loyal's body in canvas and hauled up onto to the deck. They committed him to the deep as fast as they could. No one could bear Libby's wails, so when the doctor administered a fair sized portion of opium; it was a relief to all concerned.

Lying in a haze below decks, Libby Dutton finally knew the God's honest truth. Men were not to be trusted. No one kept their promises, not even Loyal Dutton.

59

The wedding ceremony uniting Annabella Chase and Asher Magellan Price was spare on accoutrements and completely absent of sentiment.

Although Asher presented her with a small bouquet of blue columbine, she tossed it into the muck of a road after the rites. This was just prior to an awkward conversation concerning where they would chamber that night. Annabella made it clear that she would come to Asher only after she witnessed Dovie Gaspard's departure on the evening tide.

She told Asher, "I will report to you to do my duty only after I watch Miss Gaspard sail."

By that time, Asher was having serious misgivings. Observing the crushed columbines, he worried just what kind of a lady would do such a cruel thing to innocent flowers. He wondered was she just that heartless, or did she suppose him so?

Had they followed convention, he would have asked Mr. Chase for his daughter's hand in marriage first. Annabella insisted that was unnecessary. She went on her way seemingly without a worry to bother her pretty little head. That was curious to him. Newman hadn't been shy about wanting Asher to marry Annabella. Perhaps that meant they had Mr. Chase's tacit approval. He had believed that she had been acting of her own volition. Nothing made sense to him anymore.

As for the chambering part, Asher had suggested that they take a room at one of the grander hotels for the night. Annabella was against it as an unneeded expense.

Prim as Sunday morning, she replied, "Your house is quite adequate, I am sure."

It was just one more of many cold responses that she had given to his attempts at extending an olive branch. Asher wondered if she was just that mercenary. Or did she mean to kill him in his sleep and needed privacy to do so? He was a rich man. He toyed with the idea of writing a note to his family that if he was to die under mysterious circumstances, his young bride should be a primary suspect.

As he began to frame it in his mind (Should my life be taken in an untimely fashion, please look to my new wife...), he was struck by the unadulterated absurdity of such and idea. Instead, he went home and set to making his austere bedroom more appealing. A bachelor for so long, his imagination for such a project was limited. But he brought in a potted plant and placed a lace doily on the back of his armchair. It was one that he had purchased himself. It had been an inexplicable purchase. (He disliked frippery.) The bedding was relatively clean. Beyond that he couldn't see where improvement might be made.

When the new Mrs. Price arrived on his doorstep, he had been busily washing his armpits. The ceremony and upcoming marital rites had tried his nerves to the saturation point. By the time he bounded down the stairs and opened the door, he had put on a fresh shirt. Too late he discovered that it was a night shirt and it hung to the middle of his calves. If his new bride hadn't already been having qualms, he figured the sight of him greeting her in his night-clothes was reason enough.

Mortified, all he could think of to say to her was, "I take it all is well."

Looking him up and down, Annabella responded, "Until this very minute I would have agreed."

Asher couldn't help but chuckle. He did so behind his hand. Somehow it just didn't seem like the time to laugh. Still early, he inquired if she cared for a glass of wine. When she shook her head, he was at a loss what to do next. She spared him the decision by asking where she was to place her things. Just outside on the stoop were two trunks and a bag. It looked as if she meant to stay.

"I'll send for the rest tomorrow," she answered before he could ask.

He took one satchel and stiffly extended his hand towards the stairway. She ascended the steps as if she was going to her doom. He was torn between comforting her and sending her home to her father. But when he reached out to put a consoling hand on her shoulder, she indignantly shrugged it away. She continued to march up the staircase and when they reached the landing, she turned to him with such an expression of disgust, that he gave her no quarter. He had intended to lead her to a room of her own. But instead, he opened the door to his bedroom.

In doing so, he thought meanly, "Let's just see how far you will take this, Missy."

At any moment he expected her to renege.

"I'll only be a moment," she said and quickly went into the room and closed the door behind her.

That was perplexing.

"You are a hard one," he whispered as he returned down the staircase.

Seeking reassurance of hard wood, he sat down in a straight-backed dining chair and pondered his situation. He wondered, not whether, but how long he could perpetuate the illusion of a marriage. If it lasted through the night, he would be surprised. He fully expected her to bring him to the brink of coupling and then laugh in his face. That thought did nothing to whet his sexual appetite. Not being able to perform had never troubled his thoughts until that moment.

Agonizing over such possibilities just made matters worse. So he headed for the stairs, but stopped at the bottom. He would not let her get the best of him. Thereby, his feelings had done a flip-flop. No longer did he worry whether he would could perform, the tingling of excitement was awakening his long-dormant manhood.

He was also guilt-ridden.

Because he had never quit loving his Cora, he felt as if he was betraying her—again. No doubt more than a few widowers had suffered their consciences when they remarried. This didn't seem quite so simple. If his new wife wasn't so bloody fetching it might not have seemed so bloody wicked. It was no secret that sinful love was more impassioning than others. The combination of conflicting emotions all but electrified him out of his socks. He tried to settle himself. If he didn't, he was afraid that he might leap on the new Mrs. Price, ravish her, and be done with it. If she wasn't an innocent, he damn well didn't want to give her the satisfaction of knowing that he desired her. If she was inexperienced, he didn't want to scare the bejabers out of her either.

His indecision was lucky in one sense. By the time he came back up the stairs, it was good and dark. His ascent was miraculously similar to hers. It was as if the nuptial bedroom was the scaffold, the bed a noose. Upon entering room, he went directly to each window and drew the curtains. This was to settle his nerves rather than protect their privacy. He wondered if she suspected that.

One fortune was that he already wore his nightshirt. The thorny business of disrobing in front of her was avoided.

The wick of the lamp was turned so that it barely glowed. There was just enough light to see that Annabella was beneath the covers. Her hair was in braids which disappointed him. He hadn't realized how much he wanted to run his fingers through her yellow tresses. Her hair looked nothing like Cora's. That was a comfort. He wasn't certain his nerves could bear such similarity.

He sat cautiously on the opposite side of the bed. He always slept in the middle of the mattress and the outline of his body in it was clear. It suddenly occurred to him that he should have had put in new batting. (Another unanticipated problem gave him a new admiration for long engagements.) It was curious how she managed to keep from sliding into the deep a canyon in the middle of the bed. She must truly want to keep her distance.

These were not any more comforting than his previous musings—particularly for a man who was about to make love.

Through sheer will, he made himself stop fretting. He put every effort into first pulling off his boots, then removing his trousers. He kicked the boots aside and tossed his trousers atop them. Looking at his white, bare feet, he came to a momentous decision. He refused to be some insipid husband holding the feeble hope that his bride would grant him marital favors. Physical congress was his right as a husband. He had no intention of forcing her, but he wouldn't make it easy for her to ignore him either.

Instead of crawling meekly beneath the covers, he walked around to the side of the bed Annabella had staked out as her own. Her tiny, pink slippers lay next to the bed exactly as she had removed them from her feet. He marveled at how small they were. Her hands were small too. He could tell that because she had knotted them into tight little fists and crossed them at the wrists across her bosom. Her eyes were shut tight in what looked to be a wince.

He wasn't above peeking beneath the covers. There was little chance that would disturb her—she lay still as a corpse. Her gown was a surprise. It was muslin without a single frill on it. Since she flounced around all day decorated up like a Moroccan princess, he supposed her plain nightdress was on his account. He might've dropped the cover and left it at that but for the fact that she took a peek at him.

"I thought you were supposed to be pretending to be asleep," he said.

She heaved a great sigh, "I *was* asleep. You woke me is all."

"Move over, please."

As she complied, she ended up in the cavity in the middle of the mattress. That displeased her, "How do you sleep like this!"

"Alone," he replied simply.

"Well," she huffed, "to have any chance of this arrangement to work, we need a new mattress—nice goose-down one."

Without over-thinking it, he quickly climbed beneath the covers.

"Your feet are cold!"

"What do you expect, the floor is bare," he answered defensively.

"This room needs a nice carpet too. Robinson's Emporium had some nice Persian ones made of silk."

He responded, "Wool is best. It's more durable."

It occurred to him that they were already sounded like an old married couple. Apparently, she had an opinion on everything—including the proceedings at hand.

"If you rest your weight on your hands, it should be more comfortable for us both."

He had barely had the courage to inch one leg over hers, so it took him a bit aback that she was anticipating him climbing aboard. For the life of him, he couldn't figure whether she just had a practical side, or she was an old hand at love-making. But she was right. It was better for him to rest his weight on his arms.

"Let me clear my gown," she said. "It's in the way."

Oddly enough, after being so cooperative, she once again crossed her arms across her bosom and tightly closed her eyes. She looked as if she was waiting to be executed. He truly didn't know how to approach her. But he knew that he wasn't about to make love to a woman wearing a grimace. So with great care, he took her right wrist and gently laid it on the pillow next to her head. There he clasped her hand. Her eyes didn't open, but they flickered.

He kissed her.

At first her mouth was unyielding. But he kept kissing her softly, until she finally responded. After that, he forgot that she meant to hate him. Cora didn't come to mind either. He felt it when her left hand quit guarding her bosom and grasped the placket of his nightshirt. It was just dumb luck that he found the back of her knee. It was truly more for his pleasure than hers when he drew his fingertips up her leg. Her skin was so soft that he flattened his hand and began to stroke her thigh with great, long caresses. He didn't even realize that her legs had enveloped him. Nestling against her, she seemed resistant. But once again he drew the back of his fingers the length of her thighs.

This time, she laughed.

But it wasn't a derisive cackle—it was possibly the most delightful sound he had ever heard. Her delight opened the floodgates of... what? Passion? It could not yet be love. Desire, yes that was what it was. He desired her and, quite possibly, she desired him. He kissed her deeply and she kissed him in return.

For a few—far too few—moments it was unmitigated bliss. However, he couldn't hold back. She gasped and clutched him.

It was done.

The moment was unfeigned, unforced, and pure.

Was it the beginning... the possibility... of a true union? A great sigh escaped his lips.

Still in the well of the mattress, she turned her back to him.

In a moment she said, "I will submit to your intrusions, but I won't like it."

When he left the bed that next morning, he tried not think about Aaron Ainsworth. Although he knew it would tell the tale, he vowed that he would not be so crass as to inspect their sheets for signs of her virginity. It was a difficult—and possibly momentous—decision. He ruminated over his decision while he steadied the mirror above his bachelor chest. Splashing his blade in the cold water, he raised his chin to make the first pass of his razor. He stopped before he pressed it against his flesh. His eye was caught by something odd.

On his upper shoulder was a red mark that he had never seen before. He couldn't see it well because it was more to the back than the front. Running his finger across it, he saw it was a contusion. At first he attributed it to a scrape of some sort. When he placed the blade against his throat, he stopped again. The realization that it was a bite mark gave him a slight shiver.

Had she done it in a fit of pain? Or did it occur from pleasure? Either way she hid it from him. She uttered no moans, no groans. Other than that one exhilarating laugh, she had remained silent as the grave. He didn't know which possibility bothered him most.

Not realizing that it was the first time he had spoken to God other than to curse him since Cora died, he said, "Lord, please help me."

And he meant every word.

60

When Annabella awoke in Asher Price's bed that first morning, it was daylight. It took her a moment to realize where she was. She looked across the bed sheet and recognized the figure of her new husband. For some reason, he feigned sleep.

"No doubt he is ashamed of himself," she thought. "One would think that he could have had the decency to do his business and be done with it. After all, she had performed her wifely duty. All that peripheral activity had been unwarranted."

At least that was the position she intended to maintain intellectively.

When she let her mind wander, however, the recollection of all the stroking and kissing was quite... nice. She had little doubt that was why she had experienced that curiously intense frisson down there again. She had felt a similar sensation when she was in the arms of her true love, dear Aaron. Perhaps such events occurred through sufferance. It mattered not. Even if she had enjoyed her husband's ministrations, she wasn't disposed her to like him any better.

After her disappointing round with poor Tucker, it had been her intention to kick Mr. Price out of her bed the first chance she got. She had supposed that married couples scheduled their physical rites like beating the rugs. After her marital initiation, her tolerance of intercourse improved dramatically. If Asher absolutely insisted on such business on a more regular basis, she just might allow it. If she closed her eyes and envisioned Aaron, she believed that such repeated acts could be considered a glorification of his memory.

Having a groom who wasn't quite as odious as she supposed allowed her conscience to get the best of her too. Getting piss-faced drunk and bedding the first man she saw the night before she took her wedding vows didn't seem quite the grand idea that it had. In fact, it was a great big fat sin. Insofar as morals were concerned, pining for another man while making love to one's husband was a bit muddier. So she tried not to think of any of it at all.

But she did harbor one more foolish notion.

Now fully enlightened about the whole love-making procedure, she had half a mind to go to Tucker McFee and explain to him the short-comings in his technique. In the end, she decided against that. Innate, if struggling wisdom convinced her that critiquing a man in such a delicate matter would not be well-taken. It wasn't that the boy hadn't tried. If memory served, he had taken instruction in stride. She was content to know that he would figure it all out in time. Once he was married to some fine girl, he might please her too.

If she could figure out just what to do about all the mess, she would have the entire procedure in order herself.

Drawing on her bed coat, she retrieved her pink slippers and tip-toed from her new bedroom looking for her things. Her mirror and combs were where she had left them in an adjoining room. After the night she spent, it would take some doing to get her hair in order. One of her braids had come loose. She pulled the ribbon from the other one and began to brush it out, first at the ends and then working upward. As a married woman she intended to insist on a maid—she didn't care if Asher had to send to China for one. Peering into the mirror, she checked to see if she looked any different. The eyes that looked back at her didn't appear to be any wiser—or any happier for that matter either.

One thing she knew—love-making made one's hair a mess. She also knew that all the lessons Miss Perry's school had forced on them about protecting their virginity was a holy bunch of hogwash. The only thing to protect wasn't chastity, it was getting pregnant. She did not want to bear Asher Price's child.

When she figured out just who to ask, she would look into that.

✧

She slipped out the door to his house without facing Asher Price. No doubt word would be getting around that she hadn't spent the night at the hotel. Gus might already have a search party out looking for her. And if she wasn't first to tell her father that she up and married Asher Price, he would be fit to be tied.

She made her way directly to the *Bella* to announce the news.

Even then, Newman wasn't too happy. After it dawned on him that he was getting exactly what he wanted—Dovie gone and his beloved daughter safely married to the very noble, the very rich, Asher Price, he still continued to bluster. But then it was his fatherly obligation to oppose any decision she made independently.

"We don't even know if the man is a wife-murderer or not," Newman intoned.

Bringing up Asher Price's history startled her. Of her many concerns the night before, she had never worried once that she might be tied to the bed and torched.

Regardless, she said, "Oh, Poppa, don't be ridiculous."

She hoped he was being ridiculous. She prayed the possibility that her new husband was a murderer *was* ridiculous. Suddenly, she felt very contrite that she had been fantasizing about lying in the arms of Aaron Ainsworth. Good Lord, wild as San Francisco was, adultery (even in one's imagination) was probably justifiable homicide. If Asher learned of it, at the very least he might toss her out. Being a divorcee was only mildly more socially acceptable than a prostitute.

Gus didn't have much to say when she announced her nuptials. No doubt at the first opportunity, he would scold her for being so hasty—if nothing worse. It was important to her that wouldn't happen anytime soon. She could bear just about anything better than Gus being disappointed in her. Patrick, as always, applauded her.

"Our sweet Annabella, a married woman! I can hardly believe it!"

She shushed Patrick. There weren't many people in the place, but she didn't like anyone knowing what she and Asher had been up to (and she and Tucker, too, oh dear). She blushed at both recollections. As she glanced around to see if anyone was staring, she was startled at one set of eyes on her.

Tucker McFee didn't just stare, he glowered.

It was a mean stare, not like the simple, adoring expression that she had always enjoyed. It was obvious that he had overheard the news. He had no reason to be jealous. In Boston, a dozen gentlemen had vied for the honor of sitting next to her on the settee. Their freshly shaved faces, eager with determination, made her believe that rivalry was just a frivolous game. She hadn't really lied to Tucker. She told him straight up that she was to be married to another.

No matter how she rationalized it, her conscience troubled her. It troubled her even without Tucker giving her the evil eye. Because of that, she made herself a promise. She had now crossed an invisible bridge. On yonder shore she had made misjudgments. On this side, she would be an honorable woman. After all, Asher Price promised to build her a house. So, she most certainly didn't want Tucker—all muddy and morose—pointing a finger at her and making a flap. He had no right to be put out. He should be grateful to her. No doubt he would have had to pay good money to enjoy such a favor otherwise.

Besides, he didn't even know how to do it right.

Tucker's eyes burned into her so relentlessly that she decided it would be necessary to talk to him. There hadn't been a man yet that she couldn't charm. (Didn't she walk into Asher Price's office and come out engaged?) It was a point of pride. She would smooth things over with Tucker too. Wearing her finest smile, she pranced over to where he sat and rested a hand on his shoulder. Stewpot lay at his feet, but perked up when he saw Annabella. She petted his head.

Only then did she look up at Tucker, saying, "Tucker, dear, you look as if you swallowed a toad."

His eyes flickered in her direction then down to the drink in his hand. He took a sip.

Without looking at her, he asked accusingly, "Where's your *husband*?"

"He is tending to business," she chirped.

"Is he now?" he said with false airiness.

Taking the glass from his hand and holding it up, she clucked, "How many of these have you had?"

"Not enough."

"Do not try to drown your sorrows, for they can swim," she repeated from memory.

His hackles rising, he said, "Don't be telling me what to do, and gimme back my drink."

Not knowing what else to do, she sat it back on the table.

With her voice at its most cajoling, she asked, "Why are you so angry? I thought we were friends."

He spat back at her, "Friends is it now? Night before last we vowed eternal love!"

"We did no such thing!" she said, her voice rising. "I don't love you any more than you love me!"

"You *do too* love me, and God in Heaven knows I love you," he lowered his voice to just above a whisper.

"We love each other, else we wouldn't have *done what we done*."

She hushed too, but said, "In this town people fall in love for twenty cents a go!"

Indignant, he countered, "That is whoring! Did I pay you? "

Reluctant to agree with him, she still shook her head.

"There are three ways of having a woman," he said. "Either by paying her or making her—and the other is when both parties are willing."

He seemed pleased with his deduction.

Gritting her teeth and speaking to him as if he was a simpleton, she continued, "Sometimes people just fall together because they have nothing better to do."

Tucker wasn't buying it. And his resolve didn't falter.

"When a man and lady come together like we did, that spells l-o-v to me."

With a harsh laugh, she said, "Try spelling 'unpremeditated' or 'spontaneous' or, better still, 'inebriated'..."

Her conversation took too sharp a turn for him to follow and he looked at her blankly

"Oh, Tucker," Annabella sighed. "You are a sweet boy..."

"I am not *a boy*!"

Quickly, Annabella put a calming hand on his forearm. She was desperate for his silence. Then suddenly she became very worried less about what people might overhear and more concerned that Tucker might have already spilled the beans. Tiny beads of sweat appeared on her upper lip.

More abruptly than she meant to, she hissed, "You didn't *tell* anyone did you?"

Squaring his shoulders, Tucker answered, "I am a *gentleman*!"

Knowing that he had genteel scruples reassured her.

"Thank you for that. It is important that our association remains just between us."

"I understand." Tucker said suddenly conspiratorial. "You gotta do what you gotta do."

Annabella patted his arm again, content that he was no longer angry and appeared to be agreeable to keeping quiet.

"I must go," she said. "Farewell, my sweet Tucker."

Her goodbye was a bit theatrical, but she was disposed to allow Tucker to believe theirs was some star-crossed affair so long as he kept it to himself. She stood. He looked longingly up at her as she returned to Gus. Out of the corner of her eye she saw Tucker as he walked unsteadily out the door. She breathed a great sigh of relief. With any luck, he would wander off and not bother her again. Did he say he was prospecting? Whatever his pursuit, she wished him well. What she didn't like, however, was that Stewpot followed him. She went to the doorway and called to the dog. Although she had traipsed off to Boston without a moments thought of him, she would have thought a pup would be more loyal.

"Here, Stewpot! Come here, Stewie."

But the dog kept walking, his head low, ears back. Such disloyalty incensed her. She stamped her foot and called to him again without any luck. He followed Tucker step for step.

She comforted herself with the fact that Stewpot was Tucker McFee's dog to begin with. But she had put a lot of time washing and petting him. She would have liked to have a friend with her when she took her place in Asher Price's home. However, if taking Stewpot quieted Tucker's wild hair, she was happy to let him have the dog.

As she walked over to the bar, Gus pretended not to be looking at her. His brow, however, was furrowed.

She didn't have to pretend that she was unhappy, saying, "I guess my dog has jilted me."

"Yes, they are a cussedly fickle sort," he replied.

Before he could ask about Tucker, she asked, "Did Dovie leave with all her belongings?"

It was a surprise to see that Gus didn't like the subject. He growled, "How would I know?"

"Just making conversation," she replied in a hurt voice.

"If you want to talk, how 'bout us talking about what was stuck in that kid, McFee's craw?"

In a pinched voice, Annabella replied, "I'm sure I have no idea to what you refer."

She could have kicked herself for being defensive. There was no chance in Hades that she would to admit to Gus that she had been wafted away on the wings of inebriation, much less that she dragged a farm boy back to her room for the sole purpose of engaging in carnal congress—and just to spite her groom. The thought of all her blunders of the passed few days made her glum. She had reason to be a bit uncomfortable perched atop her usual barstool. They didn't call it getting 'pricked' for nothing. Having two different men rubbing on her in two days made sitting a misery.

Gus looked hard at her, but didn't say anything

She confronted him, “What? *What?*”

He shrugged.

Happy to change the subject, she said, “I never did tell you about our stage being held up Jose Carrillo.”

“There was an account in the papers,” snorted Gus. “Every time anyone gets robbed this side of the Sierras they claim it’s that reprobate.”

“It was him,” she said excitedly. “It *was*!”

“And he introduced himself to you?” he asked.

“No, of course not,” she snapped. “But I saw him plainly....”

“So, was his wife and Three-Fingered Jack with him?”

“I’m sure I didn’t take a finger count—there was hardly time. But one could have been a woman. They all wore big hats and covered their faces.”

“Then it could be any of a dozen bandito gangs that go marauding in the camps.”

Having seen his work up close, Annabella believed she knew Senor Carrillo better than Gus.

She told him authoritatively, “Jose Carrillo isn’t like that. He didn’t rob us nor interfere with us in any way. All he wanted was our valuables. They say he only is trying to make those men pay who dishonored his wife.”

“All I can say is that if it was Jose Carrillo, you can count yourself lucky to have survived with your life.”

“No other words of wisdom?” she sniffed.

“Yeah,” he answered.

Turning on her heel and making for the door, she asked over her shoulder, “What?”

Before she cleared it, he called out, “*Don’t ride a gift horse to death.*”

61

Miss Chase shouldn’t have worried that Tucker McFee might let word of their affair escape. His lips were sealed like a tomb. Spies were everywhere. No telling what an evil man like Asher Price would do to them both if he knew the truth. When his poor Annabella left him that day to go to her damnable husband, it ripped his heart from his chest. But he knew what he must do. He hardened his resolve to find enough gold to buy her away.

Once back at camp, he would relived the union of their mortal bodies again and again. (Truth be told, in his mind's eye he was a much better lover—and she was much more appreciative.) Theirs was a betrothal of the heart—as good as any taking vows before a preacher. Annabella knew it too. It didn't matter to him what she said to him in front of others. Those were not her true feelings. She had to say what she said because of her father. It was him who forced her into marrying that wife-murderer. She was sold to Mr. Price like a bucket of nails.

As harsh as it was, it would have been easier for Tucker to see his pure little dove dead than have to hand her over to someone else. At some point umbrage overtook despair. Fortunately, he had kept his head about him. If he was to have any chance at rescuing sweet Annabella, cunning would win the day. No man would tear their love asunder—not Asher Price, not Newman Chase. God help him, Mr. Gus better not try to stop him either. He would do whatever he had to do to save her—even if he had to do murder.

He *would*. He would do *murder* if he had to.

Tucker wasn't one for hand guns. Besides if he took one and killed Newman Chase and Asher Price dead in their tracks, the law wouldn't be on his side. (Without the proper groundwork, Annabella might not take kindly to him killing her father, either.) Justice in San Francisco was mostly of the vigilante sort. Killing taxpaying citizens would get him a noose from the nearest pole. So when the time came for blood to be shed, it was best not to parade it around. Above all that, Tucker had a more urgent concern. For time was of the essence. It was said that husbands have the right to insist on their conjugal rights. No telling how long she could keep Mr. Price at bay. The likes of him might even force himself on her.

"Bastard!" he whispered harshly. "Rotten bastard!"

At the first opportunity, he took out his skinning knife and cradled it. He sat and thought about Asher Price having province over his woman, his Annabella. He held the knife before him like a chalice, admiring the tip. As he did, he imagined it slicing Mr. Price's throat. The thought of that man's warm, sticky blood seeping down his hand pleased him no end.

Although it hurt like hell to leave Annabella with her husband, he knew he was in no position to take her with him. It would be best to return to the hills, gather his gold and when it was least expected, swoop down and rescue her.

The sheer urgency of his plight was the only reason that he made the decision he would come to regret.

He only threw in with the like of Rutledge Mayne and his cohort, Ezekiel Hardy because he thought they would triple how much gold was pulled from his claim. As it turned out, their combined resources didn't amount to much.

They had gotten a leg up on things when they came across a prospector with a broken arm and bartered the rest of Tucker's gold dust for his mule. Procuring the mule inspired a bit of gold fever in them. The foothills beckoned the three of them. Their excitement lasted the entire trip into the hills and only let loose of their vitals when they were faced with actual labor.

Initially Tucker admired Rutledge and Zeke's enthusiasm. That didn't last more than hour, which was about ten minutes longer than Hardy ran around like a madman searching for that illusive vein. Then he lay down and took a nap. Mayne didn't even make a show of working until Tucker reminded him that he had claimed he was an expert in sloughing and a hard worker.

"Yeah, I love work," he guffawed. "I can sit and watch you do it for hours!"

With Tucker prodding him, they did manage to build a slough. It took finding a little gold to get them to actively pan. Getting through the rock was made a sight easier with Lolly, the mule. All they had to do was load the sled and she would pull it without batting one of her long, black eyelashes. Tucker saw to it that she got fed before anyone else.

He also clung to the fiction that he was in charge of his claim.

At first Mayne and Hardy allowed him think that. But after a while they quit the pretense. They didn't do much work either. The only thing Hardy was good for was bagging the occasional rabbit. For Tucker, such hunting trips were a waste of time and gunpowder. Traps were easy to set. He could have caught more than Hardy shot by using a box, a stick, and some string. The only good was that hunting kept Hardy out of camp. When he was there, all he did was bicker with Mayne.

Mayne slept until the sun was beating down on him. Then he groused because the coffee was cold and declared that he could not bend over to pan, saying it aggravated his back. Both Mayne and Hardy were content to watch as Tucker scraped the bottom of the creek for gravel and skinned his fingernails to the quick grubbing through the river rock.

It was hard to come by, but Tucker finally had to admit to himself that instead of bringing help with the mine, he had brought two enormous leeches—and uncompanionable ones at that.

If not a particularly good judge of men, Tucker's new partners taught him to keep what nuggets he found tucked in his shirt. They were notorious thieves. The further he stayed from the camp, the easier it was to keep what gold he found stashed from them. That was why he had been a bit up river shoveling fill into the slough when he first heard their worst fray.

The high-pitched squeal that echoed down the creek didn't sound human. In fact it sounded like a hog being butchered. Back home that always meant cracklings for supper. Their meals had been so spare that the thought of bacon sent him running. Javelinas weren't generally found this far north. It was good luck if one wandered into camp. He would much rather face a wild boar than a bear with just a knife. He wondered why Hardy didn't shoot him.

All these questions plagued the short sprint to their campsite. As he came to a skidding stop, he was appalled by what he saw. It came to him, however, in increments.

There wasn't a javelina. There would be no pork for supper. There was no bear either, but there was lots of blood. All of it was from Mayne who was holding his hand, howling and hopping around on first one foot and then the other. Mayne's amputated finger squirted blood everywhere and quashed Tucker's appetite right away. There had been a squabble again and Hardy ended it by cutting off Mayne's middle finger.

Hardy wasn't even a little sorry, "I'll take another if you don't shut your mouth."

"With my own knife!" Mayne squawked. "That ain't right! What kinda feller does such a thing?"

It was getting late so Hardy plopped down on his bedroll and threw his blanket over his head, muttering, "See that you don't get blood on my traps."

Before anybody else thought to do it, Tucker took the last swig of gin. He supposed he should have let Mayne have it, but there really wasn't enough to do him any good and Tucker figured he needed it more. It took some fortification to doctor a severed finger—especially on the likes of Mayne.

Prepared for all eventualities, Tucker pulled out his trusty tin of bear grease. As it was known far and wide and as an all-purpose cure, no self-respecting prospector would be caught without it. It took the sting out of a cut and protected it against festering. Getting Mayne to be still long enough to daub it on was the biggest problem. With Tucker hollering at him to be still, he finally collapsed by the fire and, whimpering, allowed Tucker to slather on the grease.

Nobody seemed to notice where the finger had landed but Stewpot. The dog quickly sneaked in and stole it. Tucker didn't realize what happened until he saw dirt flying near the edge of the camp. At least Stewpot had sense enough to hide the thing and not to gnaw on it out in the open. Tucker wasn't inclined to scold the dog. Nobody in camp was getting enough food. The law of the wilderness was that when somebody's starving, anything is up for grabs. Tucker knew that above all else.

After the fight, Mayne continued to wail. Without any liquor to soothe his own nerves, Hardy cursed him for that too. When Hardy up and left camp, Tucker didn't know—or really care—if he was coming back. He didn't reappear until the next evening. When he did, he had several bottles of liquor with him. Tucker was too happy to have it to make inquires as to where it came from.

The liquor settled everybody down for the night. Tucker was glad. They needed to have a powwow about continuing their affiliation. So far the claim wasn't even profitable enough to tempt claim-jumpers. The whacking off of Mayne's finger pretty well convinced Tucker that he was better off alone. His only pleasure had been daydreaming about rescuing Miss Annabella. With each passing day, that seemed even farther away.

The turning point was when, flogged and earless, Ernie Braithwaite turned up.

62

By the time Libby arrived at San Francisco, the ship's opium was gone and she was in great need of more. If she could find a doctor and complain of female trouble, she could secure some quite easily. But she didn't want to go through that subterfuge unless she had to. She knew the most direct source was through the Chinese shops. There were always such places in port towns. South Boston had a Chinese marketplace where everything was sold from goose livers to pearls. She stopped the first person she saw and inquired.

"Them celestials set up shop up there towards Union," the man said pointing up the Street. "But I wouldn't go there alone, ma'am...."

Ignoring him she began to walk. It wasn't far, but it was uphill. Stomach cramps plagued her every step of the way. Stopping to catch her breath, her stomach began to heave. Mortified, she retched. There wasn't much on her stomach, but what there was splattered onto walkboards—and her shoes. She wiped her mouth with the back of her hand and search in her bosom for a handkerchief. Before she could be on her way, a tiny, almond-eyed woman took her hand and led her around the corner to a shop. It was held up by large, sanded posts, but was really just a canvas tent. With fluid grace, the women slid behind the counter. Huge shelves surrounded her, all stocked with a variety of colored bottles. Libby didn't have the wherewithal to dicker.

She said weakly, "Laudanum, please."

Before she finished the word, the woman had a bottle of opium in her hand.

"I've been sick..." Libby began.

Without changing expression, the woman said something in Chinese.

Libby shook her head, uncomprehending.

"You pay," the woman said, holding out her hand.

Libby handed her a bag of coins. The woman dug through them one by one until she had enough to cover the price. Only when she had the right amount did the woman hand over the blue bottle. Thanking her kindly, Libby eyed it. She would've given anything not to be compelled to take a drink of it before she left the shop, but she knew she had to drink it before her stomach turned on her again.

After downing a generous swallow, she turned and gave the woman a wan smile. The woman looked at her with dispassion. Libby took that as a lack of censure, thanked her kindly and went outside into the bright sunshine. Shielding her eyes, she stood for a moment, allowing the sunlight to fall down upon the remainder of her face. Then, the all too brief rush of euphoria overtook her. Swaying like a drunk, she waited for it to pass. Then she carefully descended the hill. The wharf was rife with rude people and squalling animals. She had noticed any of the mayhem before. That, she supposed, was unhappy testament to her priorities.

Now with all four corners of her mental bed tucked in, she looked for someone to bear her trunks up to a hotel. She had to play the helpless female to garner some assistance and then it cost her two dollars. It was just a guess as to where she wanted them taken. She could see a sign for the St. Charles Hotel, so that was where she went.

With its brick facade, the St. Charles looked quite respectable. Once inside, however, it was bedlam. Remodeling was in progress and sawdust covered every inch of the lobby. The hammering alone was deafening. She had to scream to be heard above it. The weary-looking desk clerk told her that the St. Charles was known far and wide for its comfort and luxury, but, unfortunately, they were short of rooms. Could she see herself sharing?

She looked at him incredulously.

His unctuous manner remained, "I see you do not care to share."

Her head was swimming. It was important for her to find a place to lie down. If she didn't she was afraid she might swoon. She had retched on the street once. Another public display might seal her fate. "You must have *something*," she insisted, laying her bag on his desk.

"Alright, ma'am," he said. This time his tone was more direct, "One hundred dollars for tonight, eighty for each day after."

She nodded her head and he said, "Follow me."

For him to tote her trunk up the stairs to a room cost her another dollar each. As he handed her the key, she saw that the rooms were divided by nothing more than the thinnest board partitions. She could clearly hear expletives and the efforts of sexual congress. Bowing curtly, he left without looking her in the face.

Calling after him, she asked, "May I have some fresh water?"

"Water will cost you extra," he replied. "You can get it down in the restaurant."

"I thank you," she said to his back.

The room looked reasonably clean. She went to the window. Across the way, a sign identified the building as the Ward House. A band played on the balcony. Next to them stood a variety of women in various degrees of undress waving their lacy under-things at prospective clients.

In the other direction was a post office. It would prove to be the single establishments in town busier than the brothels. Hundred of men stood in line—one that didn't appear to be moving. A shriek from the next room startled her. It sounded as if someone was being killed. That was quickly followed by feet pounding down the hall. A shot was fired. Putting her fist to her mouth to keep from crying out, she put a chair beneath the doorknob and tried the knob to be certain it was locked. Her hands trembling, she carefully laid her cloak across the bedding and lay down on it. Lifting her head, she took another swig of laudanum. She stuck the cork back in the bottle and lapsed into sleep.

✧

She had no idea if the *Miss Liberty* was still in port or if it had been looted and sunk like so many others. But she made herself not think of it yet. The first thing she had to do was to regain her senses. And the second was to grieve for Loyal Dutton.

63

Mrs. Asher Price was not a happy wife. In fact, she was fit to be tied. She could barely contain her outrage until she got all the way to Gaby's room on the second story of the *Bella Goode*.

"How could this happen!" she screeched at Gaby.

Gaby put her finger to her lips, trying to get her to shush. Suddenly wary of eavesdroppers, Annabella hushed herself. She was mortified and determined not to let the news out of her present catastrophe until she was ready. Gaby looked so frightened, Annabella tried to speak civilly.

"I followed your instructions precisely."

Like a half-dozen other women, Gaby Mosley kept a steady room on the second story of the *Bella*. Gus didn't like them there, but the women were so thoroughly entrenched that he gave up trying to rent the place out to what passed for upstanding citizenry.

In the months since her marriage, Annabella insisted upon visiting the *Bella* regularly under the ruse of seeing to her poor, old father. And since she generally came in early afternoon and often did actually converse with Newman, Asher didn't seem to mind.

More often than not, Annabella sneaked upstairs to talk to Gaby (her conversation was far more entertaining than Newman's). Indeed, the girl was a wellspring of fascinating information. Not all of it, Annabella came to learn, was unimpeachable.

To Annabella's mind, she had good reason to be angry with Gaby. The vile liquid Gaby sold her was purported to bring on one's menses like clockwork. Gaby's advice on such matters should have been impeccable. The town was teeming with women who had sex for a living and there wasn't a baby to be seen anywhere. Perhaps sporting women were not known for their integrity, but their contraceptive methods should have been gold. Annabella had taken the tansy root semi-religiously. Despite such precautions, she was pregnant—and very, very irate.

Tapping her foot impatiently, she waited for Gaby to answer for it.

"Tansy don't always work," Gaby stuttered. "I'm sure I told you that."

"Not always, you say?" Annabella gasped. "No you did not!"

Actually, she may have said that, but Annabella wasn't about to concede the point.

Hesitantly, Gaby offered, "I don't suppose you want to bring on the curse now."

Annabella looked at her, uncomprehending.

"You know...." Gaby whispered.

"No, I don't believe I do know."

"A lady up the street has a special stick....."

"You're not talking about killing it are you?" Annabella gasped.

"No," Gaby sniffled.

"I won't do that!" she hissed.

Annabella was startled at her own vehemence. The nebulous yearning she had about wanting a baby when she was back in Boston had suddenly returned.

She repeated, "I could never do *that!*"

"You don't know what you'll do if you're pushed into that corner," Gaby said softly.

Annabella looked at Gaby thoughtfully. She hadn't asked Gaby about herself.

"Have you ever done that? You know, got rid of one?" she heard herself whisper.

Looking back at Annabella just as thoughtfully, Gaby told her what she wanted to be true.

"No."

Pleased not to be troubled by undesirable information, Annabella patted Gaby's hand, "Good."

Gaby changed the subject and Annabella didn't protest. She didn't want to hurt Gaby's feelings. She felt a sisterly affection for her and enjoyed bringing her trinkets and ribbons. After all, she could afford to be generous. She was married to one of the most prominent men in San Francisco. It was a position she had grown to enjoy. She had a carriage and driver at her disposal while Asher was busy seeing customers at his bank. His whalers were still lucrative, but his thriving bank took up more and more of his time. She liked that. Whale ships were often moored in the harbor and the mere sight of one gave her a knot in her stomach.

After confronting Gaby, Annabella wasn't certain what to do next. The finality of her situation hit her, and Annabella's mood wilted. She reluctantly bid Gaby goodbye and trooped back down the stairs. As she descended, she decided that she should tell those closest to her about her condition before she told Asher. Practice would be helpful, for she wasn't eager to give him the news. She wasn't all that anxious to tell her father either.

Not knowing where to turn always meant she went to find Gus.

As if on cue, Gus walked in from the back. The ever-present bar rag was once again tossed over his shoulder. He had seen Annabella go upstairs and planned to have a frank talk to her about visiting Gaby in her room. He didn't relish that idea, knowing Annabella would argue back, no doubt employing euphemisms too frank for a lady just to rattle him. Menial chores soothed his nerves and he began to wipe down the bar in preparation for their tangle.

The moment Annabella saw Gus—just as he was every day of the week, something, perhaps sentiment, caused her to begin to cry. Seeing the expression on her face, he was taken aback. He immediately came out from the bar and walked to her.

"Come, darling girl," he said, leading her away from prying eyes.

Even sequestered in the back room she was unable to form coherent sentences.

"What's the problem," he asked softly. "Do you and your man have a fight?"

Annabella rolled her eyes at such an innocent presumption.

"I wish it was only that!"

With his arm still comforting her shoulders, he nodded his head, encouraging her to say more. But tears of self-pity had begun to flow for real and when she tried to talk, she blubbered.

"Take a breath," he said. "Take a breath."

She did. In a moment she blurted out the truth.

"I am to have a baby!"

"Well, that's wonderful!" he exclaimed. "No news would make your Poppa happier."

She shook her head. "I don't know if I want it, Gus."

He waited a moment before responding. "I don't think you have that choice."

"That's just it! I don't have a choice. I want a choice. I want to sit down and think it through before I make that decision. It is a big decision—one that will change my life forever!"

It was clear that she was just blathering, but she couldn't stop. Without a change in his sympathetic expression, Gus reminded her of what she chose to ignore.

He said, "When you married Asher Price, you made not only a promise to him, but to God."

Gus didn't talk much about God, so that remark surprised her. She opened her mouth to speak, but he put up a hand and stopped her.

"Your motive for marrying him wasn't selfish, but that doesn't absolve you of that promise. You must think of your child and not yourself now. If you are truly miserable and a misery to Asher Price too, you can always return to us. You know we'd be pleased as punch to have you and your baby here."

She began to cry again.

"Of course we couldn't let the young'un to run around here. We'd have to find a nicer place for you to raise him."

"I won't go back to Boston, I *won't*!"

"Don't worry," Gus said.

Then, he uttered *her very favorite* promise, "You won't have to do anything you don't want to do."

She brightened at the thought.

"Come," Gus said, taking her hand. "We must go tell your Poppa that he is to be a grandpa."

For that performance, Annabella plastered on a most convincing smile. Newman wasn't one to want to hear of unhappiness. Having seen him at his worst—drunk, disheveled, and delusional, Annabella had been treating him almost like a child. The old Newman would have pitched a fit if he even suspected condescension. Not anymore. Gus said all the whiskey he drank had addled his mind. Annabella believed it. He looked older than his years and she meant to coddle him as much as she could.

He was absolutely tickled to laughter with her news.

"It is my dream, little girl," he burbled. "I saw in my mind you married to Asher Price, living in a grand house, with me sitting in your parlor bouncing a grandchild on my knee—and it has all come true!"

"Yes," she repeated. "It has all come true."

64

Annabella was resigned to her fate.

After trying to blame Gaby for her condition, she didn't immediately take responsibility for it herself. She shifted the blame on her husband. He was the one who impregnated her.

It wasn't until the solitude of the ride home that she finally admitted to herself that she had only herself to blame. A nagging little voice kept reminding her that woman wasn't supposed to get a baby if she didn't take pleasure in the act. Gaby had told her that. Even under that caution, she had taken pleasure from their lovemaking—not a lot, but some. Maybe sometimes more than others. Oh, alright. She liked it quite a bit. Not that she let him know it. She'd never allow him that. She wanted him to believe that she merely endured him. It was the only way she knew to have a hand over him in their marriage.

By disposition, she was both candid and curious. (Asher seemed taken aback by that. She supposed it was because his first wife was a Quaker.) First chance she got she took a big long gander at her husband's doodads. Her interest was purely for comparative purposes. Not knowing that she saw Tucker's manhood in its less-than-resplendent glory, she thought she had seen all there was to see. As Asher suffered an erection the minute he spied her in her nightgown, it wasn't a fair appraisal.

What stumped her was why Asher Price didn't try to gawk at her. She thought men lived for such trivialities.

It was good that she looked at him when she had a chance, for they had fallen into a pattern of lovemaking that made visual inquiries awkward. Each night before they both slipped beneath the covers, Asher doused the light. Then, they met in the middle of the bed and did the deed. It was quick, passionate, and silent. When it was over, they turned their backs and slipped into the deep sleep of satisfaction. He didn't have the opportunity to worship her worldly temple and she did not have to hide her revulsion at his red-scarred hands. In fact, she barely noticed them.

At breakfast, he sipped coffee and read whatever newspaper happened to be nearby while she nibbled at some bread and raspberry jam. To an outsider, it might have passed for wedded bliss. Adoring glances were nonexistent. After a while, she rarely glanced in his direction. After all, he was a just a bookkeeper. Perhaps he was a rich bookkeeper, but a bookkeeper all the same. Seeing him in his bare feet and nightshirt convinced her that all that talk about him murdering his wife was a load of hogwash. He was mild as a summer's breeze.

Having little else to do but allow her imagination to run wild, she had little to spark her interest. Everything about her life was static. There was only one aspect of her life she dared antagonize. So she embarked on a series of inflammatory seductions—all against her husband. She told herself that it was boredom that moved her, perhaps that had a hand in it. In truth, she was attempting to rekindle the sparks that had flown in his office the day they made their agreement. That little exchange had stirred her more than she ever would admit to anyone.

What she did know was that by snuggling her backside next to his privates, nature took its course. After all, the nights were cold even in the summer in San Francisco. Before she knew it, she was on all fours and he was... quite happy for her to be there. Thankfully they didn't have live-in help, she heard from Gaby that such doings were quite the scandal.

After these exciting encounters, she suffered fits of guilt.

She made excuses for it. It was easier to pretend that Asher was Aaron when she didn't have to look at his face. In truth she really wasn't thinking of Aaron Ainsworth when Asher Price slipped his hands beneath her gown and caressed her. Those inward strokes dandled some part of her innards that inflamed her no end. She muffled her cries of pleasure by burying her face in her pillow. Plain stubbornness made her refuse to let him know that he conquered her in that way.

By the time she arrived home after her little confrontation with Gaby and her talk with Gus, she was unhappy and unsettled. She knew that if she wanted to, pregnancy could give her a long vacation from her marital bed. If she truly despised Asher, that should have improved her disposition. She didn't care about that just then. All she could think about was that now that others knew of her condition that she would have to tell him he was to be a father. She looked on that duty with unadulterated dread. It might well ignite a show of bathos that would be uncomfortable. Sentimentality was her enemy. She had to guard against soft feelings for him at all cost. She would never love him.

Her one and only love was dead and gone.

Theirs was a marriage of convenience. Simple as that.

Asher had kept his word about building her a fine house overlooking San Francisco and its blossoming society. Her house wasn't grander than anyone else's (which was the only reason to have a fine house), but it was the finest built by honest money. She went about decorating it with unfettered abandon. For a Quaker (even a failed one), he tolerated her spending rather well.

Although they sent their laundry to Ruby Gottwald, Asher balked at hiring unnecessary help. He allowed her a day maid, but his name was Chester and he owed Asher money. Her carriage was fine as any other in town although Chester served as her driver too. She held her ground when it came to wardrobe expenses. There, she refused to compromise. After a while, Asher rarely complained about her more exorbitant purchases.

Such freedom was addictive. If bearing a child was the price she must pay for living such a life, she supposed it was a small one. A baby would be a lovely diversion. She would devote herself to him.

When Asher arrived home, Annabella was waiting for him.

They had not had marital relations for several weeks. She had begged off, claiming female trouble. As time went on, Asher began to look at her as if she was shirking her responsibilities. It was clear that the time for frankness was at hand. They rarely engaged in small talk and she didn't see any reason to start then. That didn't mean that she hadn't given her stage great thought. She had gone to the trouble of seating herself on the parlor settee, her finest frock billowing around her.

Once she had settled, she hurriedly wet her fingertips so they could daub at the new little kiss curls escaping from beneath her red barrette. Her hands were then placed gracefully atop her ever-present pink shawl as it lay in her lap. Picking at it, she saw that it was getting threadbare. Why was it that just when something was broken nice and comfy, it fell all apart? Perhaps she would learn to knit. A cap for the coming baby would be nice. It would be small enough article so as not to overwork her fingers, but large enough a task to give her hours upon hours of not having to pay attention to her husband.

He was surprised to see her there all primped and attentive. When he came into the room, she stood immediately. She was so anxious about giving him the news that she just blurted it out.

"I am to have a baby."

He neither rejoiced nor expressed dismay. Since she believed him to be disinterested, she decided to go for broke.

She announced primly, "Due to my condition, I will be unable to perform my marital duties."

He replied, "Of course."

"I do hope this will not inconvenience you."

That was a bald-faced lie. It was also rubbing it in. She hushed herself. It was best not to burn one's bridges. If she couldn't gloat verbally, she did the next best thing. Employing the regal bearing of Cleopatra on her barge, she marched from the room.

She was quite pleased with their chat. It was informative, succinct, and dispassionate. Easy as one, two, three. Unburdened, she could now dedicate her time to her coming child. The first matter of business was to locate proper medical aid—someone who knew what they were doing. She had listened to a poor woman who lay in labor out on the prairie for what seemed like days. Women ran to and fro wringing their hands, but no one seemed sure what to do to help. The mother and her child survived, but the woman never looked quite the same after the birth. She had an odd haunted look—not unlike the empty-handed prospectors trickling back from the gold field. Her poor, dusted husband didn't look much better. Perhaps it ruined their intimate conduct. That was understandable.

Annabella fully intended to have a competent physician to attend her—and a baby nurse. She must have a real baby nurse—Chester be damned.

65

Having thought the matter behind her, Annabella was taken aback when Asher cornered her in the corridor the next evening. Clearing his throat, he made a formal request for her to join him in the back parlor.

Although he called it that, it was not actually a parlor, but a sitting room—her sitting room. He had his study and she did not intrude there. The same went for her sitting room. It was her retreat. There, she nestled in the down pillows on the daybed. Wrapping herself in her shawl, she read sad novels, wrote bad poetry, and ate sponge cake. Indulging herself seemed the most apt way to moon about Aaron Ainsworth. So rich were her dreams, his essence permeated every pillow and drape. For that reason Asher Price wasn't welcome.

Since it was an unspoken rule that he was forbidden to invade her private space, she couldn't come up with an alternative quickly enough to stop him. With considerable reluctance, she followed her husband into the room that was dedicated to her lover.

Moving quickly, she situated herself in a high-backed chair. Before she was ready, he thrust a velvet box in her direction. She knew a box such as that would most certainly contain jewelry. She had to make herself not snatch it out of his hand. For a Quaker, Asher had exquisite taste in such things. She was so overcome with curiosity that she didn't realize that the box was only half his gift. The rest was a little speech—one that sounded as if he had been practicing it all day. Managing to wrest her eyes from the box and what it contained, she made herself listen. His tone was so soft that she had to lean forward a bit to understand what he said.

"I must confess that I was so taken aback by your happy news," he said barely above a whisper. "I did not respond properly."

He kneeled awkwardly, saying, "I hope you will accept this gift."

It was as if he was proposing to her—this time properly. She was mortified for him. Had he run mad?

Hesitantly, he cleared his throat and said, "Perhaps we can begin again... as husband and wife... to be the mother and father that our child deserves."

Her brow furrowed as she tried to follow what he was saying. But the gift box still sat on the palm of his extended hand and that was all she could think of nothing else. Her attention so rapt, he didn't wait on ceremony before removing the top, thus unveiling an exquisite opal brooch.

"Oh," she crooned. "So lovely."

Her enthusiastic approval made him smile. It didn't occur to her that he thought part of her admiration was for his little speech. Thoroughly engrossed in taking a caret count of the diamonds circling the broach, she forgot that they were in the middle of her snug little shrine to The Ghost of Lost Love. If she had given that any thought at all, she might not have prattled on exactly as she did. But in that comfy chamber, she looked at the broach and spoke dreamily.

"If it is a girl," she murmured. "Her name shall be Amy."

Asher looked down at her lovingly and nodded amicably at her choice.

"If it is a boy," she continued, "I will call him Aaron."

At the very moment she said the name, she realized what an enormous blunder she had made. Not that it was a bad idea; just that she shouldn't have mentioned it just then. She did not have the courage to watch her husband's expression alter as the name she had just uttered registered on him. She knew it what was coming all the same. No doubt she cringed.

"Aaron?" he repeated as if hadn't heard her completely. When he realized that he had, he gasped, "As in Aaron-*God-damned*-Ainsworth?"

She nodded defiantly, but she gave a great gulp as she did. Because he had not actually handed the brooch over to her, he did not have to yank it back.

"You suppose that I would approve of naming my son after my wife's lover?"

Granted it sounded much worse when he said it, she did not back down.

"It is a fine name. He was a fine man."

"Fine? You call him *fine*?"

"Yes, I do," she answered, matching him in pitch. "I wish he had fathered my baby instead of *you*!"

In answer to that, he upped the ante. Taking the brooch in his hand, he cast it with all his might against the floor. It missed the carpet. But then he wasn't aiming for the carpet. He was aiming for the wood floor so the opal would shatter. It did. Annabella burst into tears—and was highly agitated to have done so. It must be her condition. Otherwise she would never have let him know she was upset.

Suddenly solicitous, Asher forgot himself and reached towards her.

Contemptuously, she hit his hand away, saying, "I'm not afraid of you... you wife-murderer!"

The expression on his face changed several times. He opened his mouth as if to respond, but then he didn't. Instead he walked out and, with careful precision, closed the door behind him. That frightened her. At that moment she was more frightened by Asher Price than twenty Jose Carrillos.

She cried herself to sleep on the daybed. When she was awakened by Asher calling her name, it was still dark. He stood in the doorway. The lamp had been turned down in the room, but the one in the hallway was burning brightly. That was why all she could see was the taut shadow of his lean frame. She gasped, fearful once again.

She needn't have been.

His voice was soft, almost consoling, "Annabella."

"What?" she answered crossly.

"There is something you need to know."

When he put like that, she was quite certain however she might *need* to know it, she didn't necessarily *want* to hear it. She turned away, but that didn't stop him from speaking.

"In the days after the *Mary Thayer* crew was reported lost, it fell to me to write to their families telling them of the tragedy."

Because she remained silent, he continued, "I am most sorry to be the one to tell you that Aaron Ainsworth had a wife and three children in Baltimore. I issued them their benefits myself."

66

Tucker had quickly learned that arguing with a couple of drunks was about as profitable as the gulch they were digging. He began to hope that when they ran out of liquor that both Mayne and Hardy would pack up and leave. They sure as heck weren't any help panning. Instead of sitting around the fire talking at night, he usually dragged his bedroll upwind and away from them and their raucous laughter.

Even sober, their conversation wasn't worth listening to. Mayne yammered about women in general; Hardy talked specifics. His specialty was delineating the attributes of any given woman. Tucker didn't want to hear any of it. The only lady who interested him was Annabella Chase. (Never—*never*—was she Mrs. Price.) He thought of her incessantly, oftentimes enflaming his lust to the point of embarrassment.

Although Mayne whacked away at his manhood on a regular basis, Tucker didn't dare touch his privates where they could see him. The ridicule would have been unbearable. Alone in his bedroll he could enjoy such pleasures unmolested. For months it had been a point of pride that he had not spoken of Annabella once. Her memory was too dear.

In the first weeks at the claim, he had told and retold them the stories from *Arabian Nights*. Eventually, Hardy grew impatient with their storyline.

Hardy groused. "They ain't got enough about snatch in 'em."

Tucker refused to doctor the stories to suit Hardy. His favorite remained that of Scheherazade. He felt a bit like her himself, telling stories each night so as not to get murdered. After launching into her story again one night, Hardy stopped him.

He hollered, "No, you spud! Not one of those stories! We want to hear *your* story, a *real* story!"

Confused, Tucker stuttered a moment.

Mayne said to Hardy, "That's all our Tucker here knows is fairy tales. He don't know nothing about real women!"

Tucker pulled himself up, saying, "A real gentleman doesn't speak of such things."

"Yeah, right," said Mayne. "You're just a cherry-boy with nothing to tell."

Tucker responded indignantly, "I ain't either! I have acquitted myself quite ably on the field of *amour*."

"The field of *amour*?" Hardy looked to Mayne for translation.

Mayne explained, "He says he ain't a cherry."

With that, Tucker threw himself down on his bedroll, covered himself with his blanket and closed his eyes. Stewpot waited patiently until he had, then curled up next to him. Tucker was only half-asleep when he was hit square in the head with Mayne's empty cup. Startled, he sat back up and Stewpot crept away.

Mayne said, "Me and Hardy have been up-front with you about our 'a-moors,' you gotta do the same."

"A gentleman never...."

But before Tucker got further, Mayne cussed him. "Goddammit, Tucker, you ain't no gentleman!"

It wasn't what he was, but what he aspired to be, but Tucker wouldn't tell them that.

"Ferget him," barked Hardy. "Let's go over the bluff. I heard they got a couple of whores over there doing business."

For a moment, that was a consideration for them. They soon realized that they didn't have enough gold to pay for that. Besides it was dark and Mayne was afraid of snakes. At night, he strung a rope around his bedroll to keep them from slithering in with him. In a general funk, a recollection came to him.

Mayne announced, "Annie Chase! That's what Tuck here is so high and mighty about."

Tucker leapt to his feet, fists up.

"Don't you speak her name, you *skunk*!"

Hardy looked at Mayne and Mayne looked at Hardy. Clearly they had hit a nerve. Neither was particularly intelligent, but they could be cunning. Uncovering Tucker's love for Annabella Chase wasn't all that difficult. As hard as they tried, however, they couldn't get him to admit to any outright indecency. When pressed, all Tucker would tell them was that he intended to rescue her one day.

"After her marrying another man, I'd of thought you'd be soured on that girl," said Mayne. "She's rich now. What does she need you for?"

"*Love*!" Tucker all but shouted. "Don't you see, it's true *love*. She'll come with me one day, you'll see! It's me she loves—*me*!"

Both Mayne and Hardy were taken aback—but very interested. Exchanging glances, they encouraged Tucker to talk more. He was wrong about them not knowing about love. They had a deep and abiding love of money and what it could buy them—and they weren't very particular about how they came about getting it. Even they could see they weren't going to get rich off of Tucker and his claim. They didn't have their next scheme lined up.

Giving it thought, both realized that the pot of gold wasn't on the American River. It was sitting in a bank in San Francisco and Asher Price held the key. So when Tucker meticulously began to map out his plan to rescue Annabella, they listened closely.

"I know just how I'll do it," Tucker intoned.

Night after night they listened to him talk about how he would find a fortune of gold and go find the Price woman. To them, his conviction was laughable. Mayne almost gagged stifling himself. Hardy only smirked. In the flickering firelight, it was easy to ignore his prattling. Lulled by whiskey and the warmth of the fire, they often dozed. When Mayne suddenly emitted a high-pitched howl and pointed into the near distance, it flabbergasted them all—including Mayne himself.

"What the hell..." breathed Hardy.

A figure came staggering into what was left of the firelight. Drunk as they were, Mayne and Hardy both came up with weapons remarkably fast. Tucker's knife was lying on the other side of his bedroll and he leapt for it. Still on his knees, he had it by the blade, ready to throw.

But his voice quaked when he asked, "Who goes there?"

The man had kept walking, but sunk to his knees with his forehead less than an inch from the barrel of Hardy's carbine.

"Do me in. I'm no good for this world! Do me in, goddamnit!"

In the dim light all Tucker could see was the dome of a man's head. He was covered with either tar or dried blood. Who could be walking around in the Sierras at night, he hadn't a clue.

Turning to Tucker, the man said, "Don't you know me, McFee? It's me, Ernie."

Realizing that they hadn't been beset by bandits, Hardy uncocked his gun, but kept it out.

Mayne asked Tucker, "Who the hell is this?"

Putting his knife back in his belt, Tucker leaned in to get a closer look. It was an ugly sight, but he could discern Ernie Braithwaite beneath whatever covered his head. He said so in an aside to Mayne.

Then to Ernie, he asked, "What the hell-fire happened to you, Ernie?"

"I got no ears!" Ernie howled, pointing to the rag that was wrapped around his head like a partial turban.

"Jeez, he looks like a feller in one of those A-rab stories," Mayne marveled.

Begrudgingly, he grabbed a piece of jerked beef and gave it to Ernie.

"This story better be worth the grub," he grumbled.

Ernie hungrily gnawed on the beef—it wasn't easy on the teeth, but it was nourishing. While he chewed, he told them that he had been in a camp a few bluffs away.

"We was attacked by, I dunno, a hundred banditos—all armed to the hilt. They killed everyone else and stole our provisions. We didn't have no gold, but he didn't believe us."

Hearing of bandits that nearby made them all sit up and pay attention.

Hardy asked urgently, "Who was it? Where'd they go?"

Ernie kept talking, "I know who it was. It was Jose Carrillo! I saw the man who tied me up. He had one less digit that you." He pointed at Rutledge.

"Three-fingered Jack," he said in a hushed tone.

"Was there a woman with 'em?" asked Rutledge. "They say he rides with his wife—and that she's meaner than the rest put together."

"I didn't see no woman. But then they were all dressed alike. They spared me and Willie to get us tell 'em where we hid our gold. They tied me to a tree..."

Here Ernie had to spit out a piece of gristle.

Then he continued, "Then they flogged me. I was hollering pretty good, but Willie couldn't tell 'em what he didn't know. They commenced to cuttin' off my ears. I was screamin' and beggin' and pleadin' for my life. Willie tells 'em that there's gold hid above the ravine and they throw'd a rope around him and drug him off up the hill. That was the last I saw of him, but I heard him screamin' something awful—worse than me I think—but I didn't go and look."

At this point, no one spoke a word. Ernie continued.

"So I ran like hell. I didn't even stop to look for my ears—what good are they gonna do me now anyhow? I hid in a ravine for better'n a day. You boys got a blanket I could use?"

Since Mayne and Hardy didn't jump to give him theirs, Tucker jerked his off his back. Stewpot had retrieved the gristle Ernie had spat out and was making short work of it. Stewpot had always been an easy keeper.

"I got some bear grease for... those... your wounds there," Tucker said. "You're the one who always did this stuff on board ship."

With a short crew, it usually fell to a ship's cook to doctor wounds. That being so, Tucker didn't bother to ask him for advice. However, Ernie was so covered with blood from the flogging and being de-eared, he wasn't sure where to start. Unscrewing the tin, he got a large gob on his middle finger of his right hand and tried to gauge where to begin daubing it on. Suddenly, the blood drained from his face, his eyes rolled back, and he fell over in a dead faint. Everybody stood there looking at him. Stewpot began barking.

With a shudder, Tucker regained his senses and sat up.

"Fer Christ's sake, this place is turning into bleedin' circus!" complained Hardy.

He marched off to sulk and Tucker steeled himself to have go at Ernie's wounds. Before he did, he couldn't help but exclaim, "Hell-fire, Ernie, you got no ears!"

"I was tellin' you that fergodsake! Weren't you listenin'?"

"Hearing it and seeing it is two different things!"

"Bloody girls," Mayne muttered.

Mayne poured himself a cup of coffee and turned away. After doctoring what was left of Ernie's ears, Tucker peeled the rags off of his back. The wounds there were deep. The blood had congealed, but there was debris imbedded in it. Tucker tried to pull a few leaves off, but when he did, it started bleeding again. Tucker had always heard that bleeding was a good way to cleanse a wound, but the days Ernie spent laying low didn't help with that. The flesh looked as if it was putrifying. Tucker knew they needed to take Ernie to a doctor. As he tore the leg off a ragged pair of old denim trousers, the problem was addressed. What doctors weren't diggin for gold themselves were absolute quacks. Even those charged a dollar to look at someone's tongue.

Immediately, Mayne started to whine, "Why do we have to do for him? He ain't our kin."

Resigned, Tucker replied, "Well, he can't make it on his own. I'll make a litter for him in the morning."

Ernie hollered from the pain of the bear grease.

Tucker told Mayne, "We need to head for San Francisco. Ernie's got a payment due him. Asher Price was paying out indemnities. He gave me extra for bringing the ship in. Could be he'll give Ernie his, too."

A glimmer of a smile tugged at Ernie's mouth. Tucker patted his shoulder. Perhaps the impromptu trip would mean he was to be rid of Mayne and Hardy.

Remarkably, that was what Hardy had in mind too—at least a variation of it.

67

In the days that followed Asher's revelation about Aaron, Annabella tried to convince herself that it had nothing to do with her. If Aaron was married, it was in another time and place. Their love had been in the present—or at least what *had* been the present. No doubt it had been years since he had seen his wife. Bigamy was nothing to a whaler. Some bragged of wives in several different ports—especially in the South Seas. Those bare-breasted maidens were tantalizing to men whose wives at home were the pinched-faced, unloving sort. Aaron hadn't asked her to marry him exactly. Perhaps he intended to seek a divorce and return to her a free man. Rectitude may have caused his retreat. It was a wonderful explanation for something that had always plagued her.

Try as she might, she couldn't make herself believe that he was that honorable. He flirted and wooed her like a free man. Even shined up as bright as a copper penny, a cheating spouse was nothing but a cheating spouse—whether his wife was ugly or not. In truth, had she learned he was married before he died she would have slapped his face.

Putting her own face in her hands, Annabella tried to weep. All she could manage were dry heaves, yet the pain was searing. When she settled herself, she wondered why it hurt so much more to lose, not the man, but the man she thought he was. The only thing she concluded was that the both of them were fools—he for serving her up such a boat-load of drivel. She was guilty of being so bloody gullible. She feared some where in the mix was a basic lack of character—and she wasn't certain it was all Aaron's.

Muddled and morose, she knew who would set her straight. In matters of morality and love, Gus's seemed always to the only voice of reason.

✧

When Annabella first arrived at the *Bella*, she didn't see Gus. However, Gaby was sitting at a table with Patrick and raised a hand to say "hello" to Annabella before she remembered to pretend they weren't friends. Just then, pretenses seemed rather pointless and Annabella walked over and put a hand on her shoulder.

"Where's Gus?" she asked them both.

Gaby was too disconcerted to answer. Patrick pointed at the bar. He was there, just hidden by the box of liquor he unpacking. He hated to be interrupted in the middle of a chore. She couldn't help it. This was a dire emergency. If Annabella hadn't been so distraught, she would have noticed that a woman sat on the stool that used to be reserved for her. The woman—a lady really—looked vaguely familiar. But then there were so many new people passing through town or moving in, it was difficult to keep tabs on them.

"Gus," she called out. "Might I have a private word?"

"Of course," he said. "In the liquor closet or the storeroom?"

"Storeroom, please."

Seeing she was in a state, Gus didn't ask questions—or offer introductions. After shutting the door behind them, he upended a pair of crates.

She grimaced, "Once again I come to you for help."

Only after they sat did he ask, "Now, what's this all about?"

"What do you know about Aaron's family?"

Taken off guard, Gus asked, "Aaron, as in Ainsworth?"

"*Yes*," she said impatiently. "Please don't patronize me."

Clearing his throat, he said, "Now let's see, I know what you told me. I don't recall it all. He was from back east, his father was dead..."

"I don't mean *that* family. I mean family—like a wife and children."

"Oh," he said cautiously. "I don't believe I recall you saying."

Her expression said that she already knew the worst. That made telling her the God's honest truth a little easier.

"He was married, Sis," he said gently. "Married at least three times and supporting five children—or so his mother said. She told Asher to send any money to his first wife in Baltimore."

Stunned into silence, her hands formed fists and she pressed them against her mouth as if to stifle a moan. A tear appeared in the corner of one eye and began a slow descent down her cheek. Angrily, she wiped it away with the back of her hand.

Smoothing out the skirt of her dress, she marveled, "Three wives, you say? And to think that I thought it was merely one."

Not knowing what else to do, Gus patted her hand.

Half-plaintive, half-angry, she demanded, "Why didn't anyone *tell* me?"

"I can't speak for your husband or your father, but I could have lived all my days without seeing you this disappointed."

Annabella put her head in her hands, saying, "Oh, God."

"What have you done, Annie?" Gus said urgently. "You didn't go and do anything foolish, did you?"

"If you don't call telling my husband that I wanted to name our baby son after that sorry bastard Aaron Ainsworth foolish, then I didn't."

For a moment, they sat in identical poses—each with their hands resting on their knees. The silence was broken by Gus.

"Look on the bright side, m'love. You could've taken that wretch as a lover."

Annabella looked alarmed.

That alarmed Gus too, he asked—almost pleading, "You didn't, *did you*?"

A little hesitantly, she replied, "No...."

"Don't you *know*?"

"Well, we were more lovers of the *heart*."

"Thank God," said Gus.

"What?" she demanded. "*What*?"

Reluctantly, he said, "There are lots of names for it. It's a disgraceful disorder—the kind a man gets from loose women."

Without hesitation, she asked, "The clap?"

"Where in blue blazes...," he began. Then he decided he didn't want to know where or how she heard about such a thing. "No, it's worse than that...."

"The *pox*," she whispered.

He nodded and said "syphilis," just to make certain she understood completely.

Hearing the word, the corners of her mouth drew down and she said, "Eew!"

"More than 'eew,' I beg you," Gus lectured. "Do you know what that does to a man, or for that matter, a woman?"

She allowed that, in truth, she did not.

"Well," he continued, weighing just how to put it. Concluding he didn't want to be explicit, he said, "Just know that you don't want to know. You sure wouldn't be able to have a baby if you caught it. It eats up all your privates."

"I've done a terrible thing," she announced.

"Worse than saying you wanted to name your baby after that bastard?"

Her mouth screwed up, but she didn't cry. She did, however, bite her lip so bad it bled.

Increasingly apprehensive, Gus said, "What you did—it can't be all *that* terrible, can it?"

"Yes," she squeaked out, "it can."

His eyes almost bulged with anticipation. She gulped hard.

Then, she blurted out, "I told Asher that I wished our baby was *Aaron's*!"

"No!"

"*Yes*!"

Annabella saw Gus's fingers dig into his knees and his face turned red as a cherry. She wondered if it was possible for a man to explode.

"Jeezus, girl!" he did explode. "You can't keep trouble from visitin', but you don't have to offer it a bleedin' chair!" Then, helplessly, he whispered, "I never once believed you was stupid as all that."

"But I am, Gus," she cried out. "I *am*!"

With his usual practicality, Gus asked, "Has he left you?"

"Not officially, if that's what you mean."

He raised his eyebrows. Both knew that might not be the last of it. But while Gus was in a forthcoming mood, Annabella decided to see what other secrets he held.

"Do you know how Asher's wife died? I mean, did he really kill her?"

"I dunno, little girl," Gus said wearily. "Have you asked him how she died? I would think, as his wife, you would have the right to know."

Cowed, she said, "You would think."

She didn't, however, tell Gus that she called her husband a wife-murderer. In the heat of their argument the night before, she had felt smug about the accusation. While eating a huge portion of crow, she didn't admire her candidness all that much.

Gus was quiet.

In the silence, she said what she finally realized, "He told me about Aaron in a kindly way, Gus. He didn't say it to be cruel."

"Sounds like a decent man to me."

"Yes, he does." She sighed. "Why is it that you never know what you've got until you lose it?"

"Because we're all fools, the whole great big lot of us. But don't give up, Sis. I've come to think we can redeem poor, worthless souls."

"You think so?"

Gus nodded.

"Go on, now. You have some fence-mending to do."

68

Chester usually drove Annabella into town. She had been so upset when she called for her gig to be readied that afternoon, she didn't want to have to keep her face straight for the likes of him. So she climbed in and took off in it on her own.

Chester had stood there for a minute looking a bit testy. No doubt he figured that Mr. Price would blame him. Annabella knew Asher would be peeved at her too—especially in her delicate condition. Or at least he would have been concerned yesterday. Today might be a different story. He might hope that she fell out of the gig and bashed in her head. At that thought, a twinge of guilt tickled her stomach. Asher had been quite protective of her well-being despite how coldly she had behaved to him in return. He would only put up with that for a certain amount of time. He might have already reached the end of his rope.

Hunched over with the reins in her hands, she could feel the bulge in her abdomen. Every chuckhole made the wagon seat ever less comfortable. Stretching her back, she realized that before long, she would be wearing smocks. Some women went into hiding until the baby was born. She had heard of women preening about their condition in the comfort of their homes. So far the only thing she could brag about was a thick waist and sour stomach.

The thought of new dresses usually cheered her. Unfortunately it reminded her of another pressing problem. Cooks and maids were still scarce. What little she knew about running a household had worn thin. In lieu of actually cooking herself, she was sent Chester down to town each day to bring them supper. That had become her culinary specialty—Hotel DeLuxe's warmed over lunch special. Although he wasn't fooled, Asher always managed to choke down what she fed him. Newly determined to be the wife he deserved, she vowed that if he forgave her, she would learn to cook. Failing that, she would at least find someone who could.

Thinking of the mundane was convenient. It kept her from having to think about what she dreaded. She had to go home and serve up an enormous helping of humble pie. It would go nicely with her plate of crow.

She hadn't really known anything about the man that she had married—nothing at all. But the past days revelations had improved her opinion of him. She wanted to try to make amends. What worried her most was that she wouldn't have that chance. There was a very good possibility that he was already done with her.

✧

It was really all Tucker's own fault. If he hadn't gotten to talking about how he was going to rescue Annabella Chase away from her husband, Hardy and Mayne might not have ever got to talking about it themselves.

Without Tucker knowing, they had hatched a plan to steal her outright. Even they knew that a scheme like that required money for supplies to hole up while they waited for their ransom demands to be met. The many ways they would spend Asher Price's ransom money had just been an excuse to pass the time. They had all but given it up when Ernie fell into their laps.

Tucker was so determined to get a good night's sleep that he went a ways off and didn't hear Mayne and Hardy talking conspiratorially. Unfortunately, they kept Ernie awake. Into the night, his mind took a dark turn. He began to rant and rave. They just figured that blood poison had spread to his upper story. That wouldn't have troubled them if it hadn't been urgent to keep him alive long enough to collect his payout.

Putting a bottle of rum in Ernie's hands, Hardy said, "Here you crazy coot, drink this and shut the hell up!"

It had been a consideration to kill Ernie as soon as he cashed out and go on a bender until their liquor ran out. Hardy, however, talked up them going after Annabella Chase. Ernie would still have to be killed of course. So would Tucker. He was the blabby type.

Ernie was the blabby type too. The more stewed he got, the wilder he talked. His voice in a raspy whisper, he railed against everything—but primarily at Tucker McFee. As Tucker was the only one willing to help him, Hardy thought that odd. Catching Mayne's attention, he motioned for him to listen. As they did, Ernie began to tell why he hadn't come ashore with Tucker when *Mary Thayer* returned. He claimed to know why Tucker burned what was left of the ship.

"He wanted to cover up what he did!" Ernie insisted.

Hardy and Mayne were both uninterested in the ravings of a lunatic. He kept talking until he finally got their attention.

"It's true, its *true*. Them savages stole our vittles. We was a week out to sea. No food, no water—nothing. Not even a dog. Them that died of the yeller fever we throwed overboard. Them that died of thirst, Tucker did the hacking. He was the one. Nobody else would do it. The blood, the gore—it was worse than any whale kill...."

Hardy said. "You're full of crap."

Ernie hissed, "He'll cut out yer heart and eat it for dinner if yer don't watch!"

That spooked Mayne. Hardy wasn't so sure.

"A kid like that?" marveled Hardy.

"It's the way of the sea, ya know," Ernie maintained. "If nobody dies, you draw straws. I didn't want to. It was Tucker. He's the one. He'll eat ya if you ain't lookin'."

"It's true," Mayne agreed. "I heard about that business in '46 with them Donner people! Castaways too! Dammit, they do it!"

In the face of that reminder, Hardy gave a half-hearted nod of agreement, pointing out, "It ain't against the law."

"Notice how Tucker don't look straight?" Mayne contended. "He's cock-eyed."

It was a first for Hardy and Mayne. They were in a state of wide-eyed disconcertion. Content to have finally gotten his sordid tale off his chest, Ernie fell into a deep, dream-free sleep.

Mayne wondered, "Maybe we oughta chunk that kid in the head while he's sleeping?"

"You said we'll need him for the girl."

Hardy didn't look like he entirely bought that connection. Mayne told him Annabella liked Tucker's dog too. Who knew what made young girls wet.

In the early morning hours, they went on to fine-tune their plans. It would be dicey. Asher Price didn't look like a pushover. Neither did that feller with the hat that he always had with him. But horses were in sort supply and it would take a while for them to gather a posse. They could have the girl and be hid in the hills before Price even knew she was gone. Tucker didn't need to know any of it. No telling what a lunatic like that might do. Of course, they'd have to keep Ernie from shooting his mouth off in the mean time. Price might not give him his money if he thought he was touched.

The next morning, they were slow to get up. When they smelled coffee, Tucker was already readying a cart for Ernie. Mayne went over and kicked him.

"Get up, Earless."

"Leave off, Rutledge. Ernie's got trouble enough," Tucker had said.

"Aw, even if his ears weren't chewed off, he's deafer as an adder with that bandage you've got on him," Mayne said.

To prove the point, he hollered, "Hey ya, Earless. Can ya hear me!"

Gradually coming round, Ernie looked up at Mayne and answered, "I can't hear ya, Rutledge. I ain't got no ears!"

After he finished rigging Lolly to the cart for Ernie, Tucker slapped her on the rump.

Hardy walked over and said, "Jesus on the cross, this ain't no fit conveyance for a white man!"

Tucker replied, "Well, white man, you can ride or you can walk."

Hardy kept his mouth shut. Tucker looked to have a bee in his britches. As they drank their coffee, Tucker told him why.

"After we take care of Ernie, I mean to go save Miss Annabella."

They nodded in unison. How convenient. Tucker believed it would all be his idea. They thought they would have to convince him. With a smirk, Hardy stood and poured his coffee onto the fire. It sizzled out.

"All right, my friend, me and Rutledge'll go too."

Tucker looked pleased. Holding out an arm, he helped Ernie over to the cart. Hardy and Mayne wondered if Ernie recalled his midnight ravings. Tucker waved them over, ready to go.

"Look at him," snorted Mayne. "Tucker thinks the girl's sitting there in her fancy house pining away for him."

Hardy laughed.

Their agreeableness should have been a tip off to Tucker that something was up. He was too hell-bent on his mission to realize it.

The cart pitched about as they descended from hills. It was Tucker's job to keep Ernie from falling out the back. Hardy sat up front with his carbine propped on his knee. Mayne held the reins. Occasionally he looked in the back. Mostly he was checking to make sure Ernie didn't turn toes up before they could steal his pay.

"You keep him alive back there, Tucker," Mayne hissed.

Every once in a while, Hardy would say something about Annabella being Asher Price's woman just to keep Tucker riled. So he spent the trip getter angrier and angrier.

It didn't take much to fan the fire. Tucker thought obsessively about what he had to do to rescue Annabella. It would be much easier if Mr. Price wasn't at home. He speculated that Asher Price spent his days at his stinking bank—no doubt stealing money from widows and orphans. If, by chance, he was home, Tucker wouldn't hesitate to do murder to get Annabella away. Some people might not have understood that Price had it coming so it would be necessary for them to make tracks. He was glad that his friends, Hardy and Mayne had thrown in with him. Somehow, someday, he would repay them.

He and Annabella might become famous like Jose Carrillo. After all, his wife rides by his side. Tucker could envision them riding together into the gold-laden hills. Any day he would find a vein so rich they could live high off the hog in any city in the world. He could even go to Arabia—with his own lovely Scheherazade.

It turned from a rescue int o a kidnapping long before Tucker realized it.

69

Because it coincided with complications in Annabella's marriage, she was too distracted to notice what would otherwise have been an extraordinary turn of events. The first hint of change came when Gus began to alter his daily rituals.

It took the complaints from a couple of their habitués that the doors to the *Bella* weren't opening on time to bring it to Newman's attention. He could have just asked Gus why he was late with the doors, but he didn't. Instead, he asked Patrick.

Enigmatically, he replied, "You just wait until lunchtime, Mr. C. It'll be clear as a bell what's up."

Annoyed, but curious, Newman came out front at straight up noon. With a majestically extended forefinger, Patrick pointed out the front window. On the opposite walkway, Gus could be seen with a lady on his arm. He was escorting her to the Hotel Deluxe's restaurant.

"It has happened every day for a week," Patrick announced.

Clearly, more than a friendship was underway.

Newman chomped angrily on his cigar, fussing at no one in particular, "Well, why didn't somebody tell me? Who is she?"

Patrick had made it his business to find out all he could, but truth was, he had little to tell.

"She's a lady—a recent widow—from back east. Mrs. Dutton's her name. Been here a few months is all."

Patrick and Newman both raised an eyebrow. Neither of them disapproved. Both of them were pink with curiosity. That eager interest was rewarded when Gus finally accompanied Libby to the Bella that afternoon. His timing was purposeful, presenting her when the fewest onlookers would be gawking.

Except for a small, nervous laugh, Mrs. Dutton seemed quite collected despite Newman, Patrick, and Gaby. They knotted together, each silently taking measure of her while Gus tended to the first wave of customers. It was notable that Gus saw that she was seated at a table near the iron stove and kept her cup filled with a highfalutin blend of English tea. He joined her and they sat there all alone.

In the cold, wet evenings, that was a prime table for customers.

Newman pursed his lips and hissed to Patrick, "Tea! English bloody *tea*! What's this place coming to? Are we gonna put out lace doilies on the tables next?"

"Doilies," mused Patrick. "They might be a nice touch."

Newman glared at Patrick, believing him possibly the most obtuse person on the face of the bleeding world.

As for Patrick, he was happy at Gus's new love interest. He also thought he saw sparks of the old Newman returning. It was quite a welcome change.

It took several visits before Gus actually introduced Mrs. Dutton to Newman.

✧

San Francisco, which had seemed so intolerable at first, had improved on Libby since meeting Gus. Still, when anyone had the gall to ask, she didn't elaborate on her status beyond stating that she was a widow. Reminisces of Loyal were not yet a comfort. Everyone always said that some day that they would, but the pain she still felt begged to differ. She had come to feel sympathy for her father and his ill-advised remarriage. Any port in a storm, she supposed.

She was most pleased to have her elbow taken by Mr. Gerlache. If he had not been there to rescue her, she might have thrown herself off Clark's Point.

The foggy evening she had gotten lost, it had been sheer luck that she stumbled in to the *Bella Goode*. Mr. Gerlache had come to her rescue immediately, even overseeing her move from the St. Charles to the Hotel Deluxe. It was upon moving there that she realized that the *Bella* was Newman Chase's establishment and it was his daughter's room they intended for her let.

"Won't she be in need of it?" she asked. "Like visits?"

Gus smiled and shook his head, "Annabella's married to Mr. Price now, so she has no need of it."

Well, thought Libby, that wasn't a great surprise. No doubt she had a sea of suitors back in Boston. Whoever her intended was, she wished him well. He would need it. Annabella Chase was a pistol. Perhaps as Mrs. Price she will settle down.

When the room charge was quoted as thirty dollars a week, Libby put a restraining hand on Gus's forearm and demurred. The going rate for a room in a nice hotel was far more than thirty dollars a week.

"That's all right," Gus smiled. "I know the proprietor."

She was a bit flustered. It wasn't ladylike to accept favors—especially monetary favors—from a man she barely knew. But Mr. Gerlache was so kind that she couldn't bring herself to protest. No fool, she did not suppose for a moment that he was the second coming of Loyal Dutton. Quite inexplicably, however, she trusted him. His entrance into her life also convinced her that she had to rid herself of opium addiction.

Once she was ensconced in the DeLuxe Hotel, she weaned herself off the stuff gradually. She pleaded stomach upset for several days (for it was) and was let alone. It had been a severe test to keep her trembling from Gus Gerlache. (If he noticed, he had the good manners not to say so.)

She remained reluctant to meet Newman Chase. He was a connection with her past life—the one where she was the scandalized Adelaide Perry who had been run out of Boston. Once she met him, she saw that he was not the ogre that Simon Goodenow made him out to be. In fact, he was quite charming in that "aren't you a pretty little lady" kind of way.

At least he knew enough not to pull up a chair when she and Gus sat down for a cup of tea. Of this, she was happy. She had business to talk with Gus and needed privacy.

Some way, some how, she had to secure the *Miss Liberty* and its cargo.

Upon hearing the particulars, Gus looked alarmed. He hardly seemed a hysteric, so that frightened her. He patted her hand reassuringly and told her that help was at hand.

"Time is, however, of the essence," he said, placing his hat on his head. "We must see Mr. Price straightaway. He is a banker now, but he was a ship owner first. He will know what must be done."

As they strolled briskly up the street, she hoped that Mr. Price didn't ask her too many inconvenient questions. Making herself finally address her very sticky situation left her a raw bundle of nerves. Under her breath she prayed that *Miss Liberty* hadn't been sacked and sunk. Then, she really would be financially adrift.

Addressing her anxious expression, Gus soothed her, "You seem to have a head for business. When you see Mr. Price, I trust you'll use it."

That time, she recognized the name and deduced this Mr. Price might well be Annabella's husband. She had supposed that she had married, and lived, in Boston. If he was Annabella's husband, their paths would no doubt cross. Annabella would recognize her and she would be exposed. Gus would think her just another San Francisco cheat. (That she had changed her identity was accusation enough.) Libby's inclination was to flee—and when she did, she would stop by a shop and buy a store of laudanum.

Before she had time to actually make that decision, they were in the bank's door.

After introductions were made, Gus told Asher, "I appreciate what you can do for Mrs. Dutton—so newly widowed and all."

Asher looked surprised. Gus seldom involved himself with the affairs of others. His motto had been, "You'll save yourself a heap of trouble if you keep in mind where your business ends and someone's begins."

"I'm happy to be of service," Asher said ceremoniously.

Gus said, "There certainly aren't enough ladies hereabouts. We ought to encourage them to stay by accommodating them when we can—not to say they're always easy to please."

As Libby didn't know that Mr. Gerlache had been giving marital advice to Mr. Price's wife, she thought that he was referring to her. She wondered what she had done or said to make Mr. Gerlache think she was difficult to please. Her look of puzzlement caused Asher a fit of candor.

"I'm newly married," he explained.

Yes, it was true. Asher Price *was* married to Annabella Chase. That look of worriment could not have been engendered by any other creature. He had her complete sympathy. Mr. Price opened the door to his office, and led her inside.

Before he closed the door, Asher said, "Take your hat off Henry."

Gus didn't follow them into Asher's office. Her business was not his. He also didn't think she was the sort of lady who would need a supervisor. He took a seat next to Mr. Butler's desk and settled in for a wait.

With both hands, Mr. Butler removed his hat. He set it on the corner of his desk. Gus had been spinning his own hat around by the crown. Spotting the hat rack standing in the corner, Gus took a measured toss. It hit a hook, but made a revolution before it caught. Mr. Butler smirked. Gus raised an eyebrow. Taking his derby, Mr. Butler threw it carefully towards the hat rack. It hit the top, twirled around then bounced on the floor. It landed on its crown. Both Mr. Butler and Gus looked at Mr. Butler's hat lying like an upturned turtle on the floor. Gus stood, walked over to it and picked it up. As he walked back to Mr. Butler, he dusted it off with the cuff of his shirt. Mr. Butler, he snatched it from his hand, dusted it himself and then sat it back on the edge of his desk. Taking up the newspaper, he buried his nose in it.

Gus began to whistle. After a while, Asher re-emerged with Libby.

"Mr. Butler," said Asher, handing him a folded piece of paper. "See to this."

Plopping his derby back on his head, Mr. Butler saluted, "Yes sir!"

As Mr. Butler headed toward the wharf with his cigar tucked into the corner of his mouth, they all filed out on to the walkway. Libby was pleased with the meeting.

Watching Mr. Butler head down to the wharf, Libby heaved a sigh of relief. Having someone competent in the shipping business to advise her was a godsend. In such a frontier, it was almost startling not to be treated with condescension. Mr. Price was quite civil. She thanked him.

Asher extended his hand to Gus, but before they parted company, someone called out.

70

"Mr. Price. Mr. Price!"

The call came from an unholy heap sitting in the back of an oxcart tied to the post. Asher had no idea who or even what it was.

"Mr. Price!"

The man who kept calling him was covered in mud and blood. Gus seemed to think he looked familiar but he couldn't put a name to him. He did, however, recognize Rutledge Mayne and Ezekiel Hardy.

Gus called to Mayne. "Rutledge, who's your companion back there?"

"Don't you know me, Mr. Gus?" Ernie Braithwaite cried out plaintively. "Am I that ruint?"

"Pretty much," snickered Hardy looking back at Ernie.

All Gus could see was a blood-caked, blue-denim-clad dome. The cart was up to its axle in mud, so he walked as close to it cart as he dared in order to get a look at the man who knew him by name. Up close, he recognized him.

"Aren't you the cook from the ship crew that got done in by yellow dog?"

"That's right!" Ernie chirped happily. Then, with lip protruding, he admitted, "I've had a run of bad luck."

"I'd say you had," agreed Gus.

Sitting cross-legged in the back of the cart, Ernie had a near-empty bottle of rum—no doubt the reason for him being in such good humor. Without waiting for him to ask, Ernie started blabbering out his story of banditos and mayhem in the mountains. Bottom line was that Ernie knew he had money coming and the other boys were there to help him collect.

Ernie said, "I'm told I got some pay owed me."

Gus turned and looked at Asher. Asher looked at Ernie and asked his name.

"Ernest Braithwaite, ship cook, the *Mary Thayer*, may she rest in peace," intoned Ernie.

If he didn't recognize the man in his present circumstances, Asher knew his name and occupation.

He nodded his head, "I've been holding it for you. I was going to send it to your next of kin before long."

"My mama's passed and the rest of my kin would just fight o'ern it," Ernie reported.

Asher held up his hand. Mr. Butler trotted over to the walkway. Seeing the cartload of miscreants, he stopped his trek to the wharf. At Asher's command, he grabbed Ernie by the scruff of the neck and herded him into the bank. Hardy and Mayne didn't wait to be invited, trooping proprietarily inside along with Ernie.

Thinking it was over; Gus started back to the Bella with Libby. Then he caught sight of Tucker McFee still sitting in the deep bed of the cart. He had been hiding behind Ernie. Gus might not have noticed him if Stewpot hadn't escaped and scrambled over the cart's side and straight to Gus's feet. There he began leaping and yapping with excitement.

Resisting the desire to escort Mrs. Dutton away from such doings, Gus crouched over the dog, saying, "Well I thought you'd been wolf-bait long before now, you mangy cur."

He began to tousle the dog's head, but his fur was stiff with dirt and the scents of a hundred dead animals.

To Tucker, he said, "You might want to dunk him a trough a time or two before you leave."

Tucker didn't have anything to say.

Gus tried again, "Were you there when Ernie got waylaid?"

Tucker shook his head. He was only moved to speak when Gus took Mrs. Dutton's elbow and turned to leave.

Then he asked, "Do you mind me asking if Miss Annabella's still here?"

Gus stopped and turned around. Tucker's face and clothes were the same color of grey-brown.

Ignoring his question, Gus inquired, "You had any luck at your mine?"

Uncertain what to admit to, Tucker said, "Some." Then he asked again, "Is Miss Annabella here 'bouts?"

Thinking what a determined little cuss he was, Gus answered, "If you mean is she still in San Francisco, yes she is. She is married to Mr. Price and he built her a pretty house up the way."

Tucker's expression was a mixture of envy and anger. A subtle look of worry crossed Gus's face. He didn't want Tucker throwing any sparks into what was already a tinderbox of a marriage. He certainly looked as if he was ready to make a fuss. Gus took a moment to decide just what to tell him. Finally, he decided on the truth.

"Yes, she's married and expecting a baby, Tucker. You best go on now and leave her be."

A scowl took over Tucker's expression before he sunk out of sight. He didn't respond to Gus's advice one way or the other. Gus would rather have had a document from him, signed, and sealed, vowing never to darken her door again. But the lack of any outright threat, all he could hope for was the best. That and the hope that Tucker's young love was of the abbreviated sort. The longer it lasted, the greater chance for damage—of all kind.

Looking through the bank window, Gus saw Hardy and Mayne standing on either side of Ernie. Mr. Butler had tucked his coat around back of his side arm, exposing it. Gus knew that would keep them in line. He took Mrs. Dutton and left them to their business.

The punctilious Mr. Price glowered at the trio—but mostly at Hardy and Mayne. Ernie was weak and swaying when he tried to walk. It was reasonable for him to need someone to escort him to town. They didn't much look like good Samaritans. He told them to leave their firearms outside.

No one saw that as a request. Reluctantly, Hardy set his carbine against the doorjamb. It was Mr. Butler who retrieved a chair for Ernie. As soon as they let go of his arms, Ernie sank into the seat. His hands were shaking, and it was all he could do to sign his name to the papers.

Mayne and Hardy didn't smell much better than Ernie, but Asher didn't blink. There were worse offenders walking the streets every day of the week. Hygiene was usually the first thing to lapse when money was short. Self-respect often wasn't far behind. What concerned him was the rotting odor emanating from Ernie.

Asher told him, "Mr. Braithwaite, if you would like to have a doctor tend you first, please do so. Our business can wait."

"Huh?" replied Ernie.

Hardy stepped forward. "No, we've come this far, we ... he needs his money."

Asher ignored Hardy, "Mr. Braithwaite, I'll send for a doctor now. He can see you here."

"Huh?" said Ernie. "Speak up! I ain't got no ears!"

Asher looked at Mayne and Hardy. "I suppose that you have accompanied him due to his infirmity?"

"Yeah," said Hardy. "That'n he's had his ears lopped off."

Only a slight twitch above his left eye registered Asher's repugnance. The likelihood that Mayne and Hardy had Ernie's best interests in mind grew even more remote with each passing moment. In fact, he saw them as outright malevolent. Realizing that Asher was a half-second away from calling the authorities, Hardy decided there was a need for clarification of just how Ernie met with calamity.

"Banditos accosted Ernie and his camp. They flogged him until he near dead and cut off his ears to try make him tell where the gold was buried. They didn't have no gold. He came to our camp and we doctored him up."

"I see," said Asher.

"They didn't have no gold," Mayne repeated. "Else Ernie would've told 'em."

Mr. Price exchanged looks with Mr. Butler—who casually rested his hand on the butt of his gun. Asher ducked into the back to retrieve Ernie's indemnity papers. Hardy and Mayne were on their tiptoes trying to watch. A scattergun sat right next to the door of the safe, but they didn't know that.

Just in case they were stupider than they looked, Butler said, "That safe came all the way from Philadelphia."

"Mmm," said Mayne appreciatively.

Mayne wanted to brag that he and Hardy didn't need to bust Mr. Price's safe. They were gonna have Mr. Price beggin' to give them his money. But for once Mayne kept his mouth shut. But he hadn't control over Ernie's loquacity. If he started talking about Tucker being a cannibal and all again, it'd foil their whole plan. Asher returned with a piece of paper around a roll of bills. He unfurled it and began to count out what he was owed onto Ernie's outstretched palm. Excited to see so much cash, Ernie began to blabber again.

"I'd never known about this if I hadn't come across my good friend, Tucker McFee. My camp was beset on by Jose Carrillo and his banditos. He cut off in my ears and flogged me within an inch of my life. He didn't believe we didn't have no more'n we had."

"Do you want to report the incident?" asked Asher.

"Naw," interrupted Hardy. "Those rats hit everybody sooner or later. It ain't worth bothering with."

"If men were killed, their families should be notified and their effects gathered," said Mr. Price.

Then he spoke directly to Ernie, "That is your decision, Mr. Braithwaite. Shall we get you a doctor to see to your wounds—you said you were flogged? We could make a report on your behalf."

"Huh?" Ernie replied putting his hand up to the vicinity of where his ear had been.

"Just give 'em *the money*," spat out Hardy. Then, thinking better of it, spoke more calmly, "You can see he just wants to get back to the claim."

Hardy's hand had been resting on Ernie's shoulder and Asher could see his fingers begin to dig in. Ernie winced. If the man had been flogged, Asher couldn't imagine how tender his wounds must have been.

"Careful," he said reaching out.

Hardy released Ernie, but said, "We need to get goin' a-fore it gets dark."

"Yeah," agreed Ernie. "It's a long haul back to the camp. It's on the south fork of the Feather River. Not that there's any gold left. The miners have tapped it all out and the banditos stole if from the miners." He was rambling then, "The only gold is in banks like yours Mr. Price. They spend it in Sacramento, and Sacramento sends it to Frisco. That's where everything ends up—shit don't run uphill."

"Come on you nitwit," said Mayne, dragging Ernie to his feet.

To Asher, he tipped his battered felt hat.

Ernie was still talking, "They're gonna see that Tucker McFee don't get at me."

As they turned to leave, an engorged tick fell to the floor.

When they were gone, Asher looked down at the tick. He knew what would happen when he stepped on it, but it was something he had to do. It exploded beneath the pressure of his foot. He looked at the sole of his boot. For some reason, the blotch of blood reminded him of Ernie Braithwaite.

71

When Annabella rounded the drive in front of the house, she saw a horse tied to the post. It was dusk so she didn't notice right away that it wasn't Asher's mare. When she got closer, she realized that it wasn't even a saddle horse. It was a grey mule and it was hooked up to a primitive-looking two-wheeled cart. From the looks of it, she sincerely doubted that it was company come to call.

She sighed, "No doubt it's some down-and-out prospectors hoping for a handout."

Beggars come down from the hills—that was the last thing she wanted to deal with in her state of mind. Maybe Chester was giving them some food and would run them off.

As she approached the house, it was bathed in darkness. There wasn't a light glowing anywhere. She wished she hadn't left without speaking to Chester. He was the sort looked to have his feelings hurt and then console himself with whiskey. He was probably laid out in the barn juiced to the gills instead of at the house seeing to her. A vision of Chester pushing their baby carriage down the city street both irked and amused her. This nanny business would have to be sorted out as soon as she had set things right with Asher.

Without thinking more about it, she trotted her gig around to the back. She had never learned how to properly hitch and unhitch her carriage, which had relieved her of the inconvenience of doing it herself. So she slung the reins around the hitching post and walked up the steps. If Chester didn't show up soon, Asher would come home and see to the rig himself. That would put off their little confabulation. She was anxious to put her apologies behind her.

No light in the window meant no smoke from the chimney. Without Chester, she was left to do that as well. The evening air had left her cheeks and fingers cold as ice. That would teach her to drive without her gloves. Her grandmother's admonishments rang in her ear. No doubt she was right. If she didn't follow her advice she would be sporting calluses in no time. She hoped the wood box was full. It would be a nice homecoming for Asher if his wife had a roaring blaze to warm his toes.

That wish was as far as she had gotten when it came to eliciting forgiveness from him. She hadn't decided exactly what she wanted to say. One thing she did know was that they would consummate their renewed love in bed. Now that this idiotic infatuation with Aaron Ainsworth was over, she could finally admit that making love to her husband was the greatest pleasure of her life. It was time that she told him that—and showed him too. Poor Asher only thought he had tasted all the delights she had to offer. (Her little confab with Gaby taught a thing or two about that.) The big question was whether or not she dared inquire about his former wife and her death. Before she turned the door knob, she had concluded that it was better to give that a little more time.

Although she knew that their house was much safer than any nearer to the town square, it always unsettled her to home to deserted house at dusk. She would rather it be pitch dark than see everything in gloom of twilight. Knowing that a lamp and matches sat on a small table just inside the back door was reassuring.

She struck the match against the door jamb and then the wick. As she replaced the chimney, it illuminated the room. And with it came a small exhalation of relief. Tightening her shawl, she carried the lamp with her as she crossed the kitchen and headed for the fireplace. To her great dismay, there was only one small log lying orphaned in wood box.

"Curse you, Chester!" she complained. "You have blessed little to do around here but keep the wood box filled...."

Maneuvering down the narrow steps leading to the wood pile was not what she wanted to do just then. However, it was essential that she have a cup of hot coffee sitting next that nice warm fire she planned to have waiting for Asher when he returned. Making it with her own, pampered hands would be the beginning of her penance. Turning the flue up on the lamp, she steeled herself for that chore.

"I am pregnant; I really shouldn't have to do this," was an empty observation.

Just as her grumble echoed against the walls, she heard scratching at the back door. It had a small window with a shade over it near the top. She tried to peer out to see who was there, but it was too dark. At first she thought it might be a wild animal, but she couldn't imagine one digging at the threshold like that. She opened the door a crack, if need be, she was ready to slam it shut. Peering down, she saw something furry.

"Stewpot!"

Throwing back the door, she bent to pick him up.

"Where did you come from you silly pet?"

Suddenly, a shiver of apprehension snaked down her spine. She knew Stewpot could not have come on his own. Tucker had to be nearby. Knowing that spooked her. Had he come to confront Asher? Perhaps he already had. She had apologies enough to make about Aaron and the blasphemous remarks she had delivered because of him. Admitting that she took Tucker to bed had yet to been added to her already lengthy list of crimes. The last thing she needed was a lovelorn Tucker McFee stirring up things. Narrowing her eyes, she peered out into the darkness.

Sure enough, there stood Tucker. He was leaning back against the porch railing at the far end of the steps. She didn't dare ask him in; she wanted him to leave—as quickly as possible. Stewpot whined in her arms, so she set him down.

"Why are you here?" she asked him bluntly.

If he expected them, no words of welcome were in the neighborhood of her lips. She was highly irate. But before he could answer or she could scream, a hand reached out and caught her wrist. She was yanked forward and onto her knees. They hit hard on the porch boards, but she kept from falling on her face. A splinter stuck in the palm of her hand, but before she could complain about that, a burlap sack was thrust over her head. Infuriated, she screamed and fought wildly against it. A blow to the back of her head made everything go black.

72

By the time he headed home, Asher began his ritual of divesting himself of his business façade. While he was at the bank, his thoughts were entirely financial. For a man in his position, it was essential that he not fret over the immutable during the working day. Ernie Braithwaite and his companions were nothing extraordinary—albeit they smelled a bit more than the average bank patron. Although he was sympathetic, he tried not to worry about poor Ernie. He was as good as dead. Putrefaction would take him if foul play didn't get him first. No matter how certain he was that Hardy and Mayne were up to no good, the law didn't make a move on crimes that *might* happen. They had their hands full apprehending felons running at large.

When Asher got on his horse and breathed some fresh air, he finally cleared his head enough to address his many concerns. The most important was not his chimerical wife or their mockery of a marriage. It was the poor, innocent child that was to be born into the wreckage.

It was his own fault. He had been lonely and longed for a family. Because of that, he had allowed his head to be turned. All bewitching and radiant, Annabella confounded him in ways he never thought possible. And what had that gotten him? As it stood, he was married to a woman-child who cared more for her bonnets than she cared for him. A baby wasn't likely to improve things. Annabella's head was so empty she might mislay the poor thing. He would have done better if he had gone down and ordered a wife out of one of those catalogs they have at the dry goods store.

They were a mismatch from the very beginning. He lived simply. She had more baggage than a harem. It took twenty wagon trips to carry her trunks to their new house. Never in his life did he imagine one woman could have that much paraphernalia. His lovely Cora had but three dresses—one for Sunday and two for weekdays. Annabella owned enough gowns for her to change three times a day, every day for a month. When he dared make that observation, she had laughed. She told him that in her grandfather's house, she did, indeed, change three times a day—as if that made it right. Each and every one of her gowns was exquisite, but that certainly wasn't the Quaker way. He couldn't imagine bringing her and her hundred-count of petticoats home to meet his mother.

On the other hand, he couldn't accuse her of shirking her wifely duties. True, she made a flap about mussing her hair and such. But her little tirades were long on volume and short on content. He thought that she made a fuss just because it was expected of her. It was said that ladies weren't supposed to enjoy sexual conduct. Despite that presumption, their mutual passion was undeniable. With her knees nestled behind his every night, it was easy to believe that she might actually care for him.

Annabella had no right to complain. He had kept all his many promises. First and foremost, he had rid the Chases (and the town of San Francisco) of Dovie Gaspard's and her many malefactions. He had built a fine house overlooking San Francisco and the ocean beyond. She had filled it with carpets, upholstered furniture and a crystal chandelier so elaborate that it would have suited the ballroom at the El Dorado Hotel. He allowed her to have her way with every room. His only contribution was to the wide porch that stretched around three sides of the house. He placed a pair of tall-backed rockers on the west side thinking they might one day watch the setting sun together. Annabella never even noticed them. That disappointment should have prepared him for others.

In all ways save beauty, Annabella paled in comparison to his first wife. Cora had been warm, sensible and loving. She had come to his bed pure as the driven snow, her body unsullied by another man's touch.

A flash of distant memory disturbed his snit of self-righteousness.

After that first agonizing revelation about her death, he had thought that he had managed to stamp it from his consciousness. But it returned to him then—a sun-baked hand against her porcelain skin. He closed his eyes and shook his head. Again his mind's eye saw the knife point and Cora's eyes wide with fright. He shook his head again and recollection was gone as quickly as it came. Overcoming such a forbidding memory made him feel all-powerful again—ready to take on his wife, her condition, and her past lovers.

If there had been no baby, they might have continued on their way, alternately despising and delighting in each other. He told himself that her affair with the sailor had been just a youthful infatuation. Clearly, it was not. She refused to let go of it.

Well, if she was so puerile that she preferred pining for a fantasy, he wouldn't stand in her way. There was, however, no way in hell that she would name his child after that contemptible bastard. Rather, he would offer Annabella her freedom. She could name the amount. He would fill her coffers with gold and send her on her way. Unless she wanted to be free to marry again, he wouldn't even seek a divorce. Plenty of wives lived happy lives a continent away from their spouses. But if she chose to leave San Francisco, she would leave alone. Their child would stay with him. There might be a battle, but he didn't care. He would do what he had to do, pay what he had to pay, and fight who he had to fight to keep his child. He would then have his family without the bother of an unloving wife.

Until she threw her lover in his face, he had held out hope that love between them might blossom. Regardless, he knew he had been right in exposing Ainsworth's character. He should have told her before it was too late. And there was no doubt that it was too late. She revealed her true feelings. The harm was irreparable.

As he approached the house, he could see the rockers on the porch bathed in last glow of the late afternoon sun. They swayed gently and for a brief moment he thought he saw Annabella seated there. But it wasn't Annabella at all. It was only the wind.

Turning up the collar of his coat, he steeled himself for the confrontation that was to come. He was in such a state of temper about what might happen, when it did it nearly escaped him.

73

Annabella had no way of telling how long she had been unconscious. When she awoke, it took her a minute to find her bearings. All she smelled was the odor of oats and cat urine. It was a strong enough odor to have made her gag, pregnant or not. Not only was she queasy, the roughness of the burlap sack was rubbing her cheek raw. She also had an enormous headache. Her aching head made her recall, if not how it happened, who she was looking at when it did.

Tucker McFee—that damnable little runt! Never in all her born days had she been so angry. How dare he manhandle her like that? Had he totally lost his mind?

Her arms were bound at her sides so tightly her hands were numb. Her legs were tied at the ankles too. She wriggled and tugged, but her bindings wouldn't budge. She wanted to scream, but she couldn't do that either. There was a nasty gag was in her mouth. All her flailing and squealing had only managed to knock dust loose from the sack over her head. That caused her to sneeze repeatedly. Being unable to get loose or even scream for help made her to reassess her situation.

It wasn't good.

Never in all her life had she been made so powerless. Even the ferry bandits didn't truss her up like Sunday's chicken. If she hadn't seen Tucker, she might have been more worried than what she was. Tucker adored her. He was hers to command—or at least she thought he was.

"Tucker, *Tucker McFee*! You let me go right this minute!"

Her words were muffled, but certainly understandable. He didn't answer her, however, so she screamed again.

A swishing sound was heard and with it came a slicing blow across her shoulders.

A man's voice—both harsh and unapologetic—told her, "Shut yer yap if you don't want another lick!"

The sting of the whip lasted long enough for her to know that she didn't want another. She hushed—but she wasn't cowed. The guffaws erupting above her angered her more than the whip did. Now insulted and injured, she tried to make sense of her predicament. It dawned rather quickly that she was being kidnapped. Tucker was obviously involved, but she had no idea who his cohorts might be. Were they helping him or was he helping them? If it had only been Tucker, she would've been sure that it was just some harebrained scheme of his to try to win her over. (That would be problem enough explaining away to Asher.) Since he had accomplices, money had to play a hand in it.

As she hadn't heard Tucker say anything since she had been first knocked in the head, she wondered if he had been just a pawn and was now dead. Poor Tucker. Poor *her*!

If they would kill a boy like Tucker, no telling what kind of brutality they had in store for her. She prayed they merely wanted her for ransom, not to enslave her. Yellow-haired women fetched good money in bad places. Her one hope was that she was worth more alive than dead. Her second greatest hope was that her much-abused husband would be willing to pay to get her back. And even if he would pay a ransom, she couldn't count on not being murdered anyway. Dead men—and women—don't tell tales.

Over the rattling of the wagon wheels, she strained to see if she recognized any of the voices. So far as she could tell, they weren't speaking Spanish. That ruled out Jose Carrillo and his band. Then she was suddenly struck by the possibility that Dovie Gaspard might have returned to town to settle old scores. The last she saw of Dovie, she was fit to be tied. She would rather take her chances with slave traders than be tortured by a pissed off woman.

Damn that Dovie.

They were traveling a bone-rattling speed which wasn't very helpful in theorizing. The only padding between her and every chug hole was sides of the cart and the burlap bag. It was also getting colder so knew they were heading into the hills. When her teeth began to chatter, Stewpot scrambled in with her. His warmth was a godsend.

Stewpot had whined restlessly the entire ride. When they stopped at a stream, she heard his claws against the boards as he leapt out of the back of whatever their conveyance was. It had no springs and every rock they crossed was an agony. Someone climbed up onto the bed and tightened the rope around her body. With the sack still on her head, her gag was loosened. She was far too thirsty to risk screaming.

Her mouth was full of dust and she could hardly speak, she gasped, "Water. *Please*!"

If she only had herself to consider, she would have sooner died than beg her captors for anything. But some instinct had begun to instruct her that took not only her wellbeing into account, but that of her unborn child.

She choked out again, "Water. I need *water*!"

A male voice said, "Well, give her some!"

Suddenly a knife tugged a hole in the oat sack and a metal cup was thrust against the hole. She drank deep and long. It spilled down her chin and to the front of her dress. She didn't care about her dress, only that the water would last.

The fresh air revived her—both physically and mentally. She kept quiet lest she got another whipping. She did think that them giving her water was a good sign. They didn't intend to do her in—at least not right away. One thought nagged her though. She wondered if they knew she was pregnant, or would it be a device she could use in her favor.

Soon enough, they began their struggle up into the Sierras. The terrain was even more savage and the wagon careened over rocks and lurched down trails.

In her misery, she wondered if she would have the opportunity to add one last chapter to her memoirs. But fine words and phrases didn't come. Rather, an old ditty rang over and over in her mind.

This road ain't passable.
Not even jackassable.

74

At the last crossing before the road to his house, Asher had seen fresh wagon ruts, so he stopped his horse to get a clearer look. It had been too dark to tell much except that what ever made them left wide tracks.

However, it brought to mind something that he hadn't paid attention to earlier. He recalled that Ernie hadn't been in a regular wagon. They were in an odd sort of cart with rough wooden wheels. Asher also recollected that Mayne had turned around and spoken to someone in the back. At the time he had supposed he was talking to Ernie.

The vignette plagued Asher again as he rode on towards his house and saw the rocking chairs swaying on the porch. He was still trying to make out why he was so bothered by it when he saw that as the front of the house was aglow from the setting sun, the back porch glimmered too. Surely it was the fireplace or perhaps, a lamp. Try as he might, he couldn't quite convince himself of that. No fireplace raged that hot, no lamp that bright. Kicking his horse in the flanks, the mare lunged forward. As he reached the crest of the hill, he leapt off and sprinted through the yard and to the front door. It was locked.

Not again. No, not *again*!

"Annabella!"

Looking in the windows, he could see that the fire hadn't spread. Running around the enormous porch, he jumped over the banister to reach the back door. Out of the corner of his eye he saw her carriage and horse tied to the post. The horse was wild-eyed and pulling at the reins. He was just moments away from spilling the carriage and tangling himself in the rigging, but Asher couldn't take time to turn him loose.

He called out, "Fire! *Fire*!"

Looking through the kitchen window, he could see flames licking across the floorboards. The fire hadn't started in the chimney. It must have been a broken oil lamp. A God-damned *oil lamp*!

Placing his shoulder against the door, he took aim and hit it with all his might. It splintered on the first try. As if waiting for a gust of air to feed it, the smoke belched out the door, knocking him to the ground. That was fortunate since the only breathable air was at the baseboards. Head down, he crawled around the flames towards the hallway.

"Annabella!" he cried. "Annabella!"

How could a good and just God allow this to happen twice? His hands found a heavy curtain and he grabbed it loose, using it to beat back the flames. Again and again he beat the floor until his strength was spent. Coughing, his lungs and throat burning like fire itself, he wrapped the fabric around his arm and used his elbow to break out the windows trying the release the smoke.

All the while, he called out again and again, "Annabella, *Annabella*!"

Smoke, he knew, killed more quickly than fire. He searched every inch of the house until he was satisfied that she wasn't there. Only then did he go outside to try to catch his breath. Seeing that the horse had managed to get loose without getting caught in the harness, he called to her. The horse pricked her ears, but was too spooked to come closer. Giving up, he fell to the ground. He lay there for only a moment—just long enough to catch his breath. Then he sat up and looked back at the house. Black soot covered the eaves and doorway, but the house was intact.

He stood. He had just decided to try to go back through the house for reassurance that Annabella wasn't hiding somewhere from the fire, when something on the on the ground caught his attention. A wagon wheel had crushed it into the ground. He recognized Annabella's favorite pink shawl immediately.

Everything came to him at once. Ernie. Hardy and Mayne. The wooden cart and Mayne's furtive look in the back. And peering over the side was the baneful face of Tucker McFee.

75

Gus was ready to take a bit of a rest after the tumultuous day he had.

He escorted Mrs. Dutton to the hotel then returned to the *Bella* and poured himself a cup of coffee, then settled in for some time to himself. It didn't take long before Patrick intruded.

"So, Patrick simpered. "How is the lady?"

"What lady?" Gus replied evenly.

Alerted that he had introduced Mrs. Dutton to Newman, Patrick gave him a you-don't-fool-me grin. Gus looked away.

"I've seen you with her over at the Deluxe Restaurant. She's a handsome woman."

Knowing full well Patrick was not going stop until he told him what he wanted to know, Gus gave a groan of submission.

"You really want to know why I like her?" Gus asked.

Patrick nodded his head, enthusiastically waiting for the answer.

"She doesn't ask impertinent questions."

That wasn't good enough for Patrick.

"What's her name, where's she from, who are her people...?"

Flabbergasted, Gus demanded, "What do you mean asking 'who are her people?' This ain't bleedin' St. Louis. Every person in San Francisco hales from whores, murderers, miners, or fools of some kind—now don't we?"

Awed, Patrick asked, "Her people are *whores*?"

Impatiently, Gus said, "I was speaking metaphorically, you idiot."

Unchastened but a still hurt, Patrick's face fell. Gus tried unsuccessfully to appear that he didn't care whether he hurt Patrick's feelings or not. Rather than apologize, he told him what he wanted to know.

"Actually, she's from Boston—from good people no doubt. Her name is Mrs. Dutton and she had a school there."

After returning from the bank, Gus and Libby talked for some time. She had startled him with what she had to tell about how she came to San Francisco. She also related under what circumstances and by whose auspices she left Boston. That only proved the old adage about small worlds.

She hadn't stopped with just the ruination of her name. She went deeper into her past. Indeed, she had told him all of it. Her telling of Eduard Stackpole's demise was particularly chilling. Gus's sensibilities, however, were quite able to weather mere murder—especially when the bugger had it coming. As a man who was abstemious for good reason, he admired her for freeing herself of opium.

Bearing an expression untroubled by all that she said, Gus reassured Libby as emphatically as he could.

"We all got stories here, darlin.' Some day I'll tell you one."

After hearing of her dead stepbrother and how she kicked opium, being run out of Boston seemed pretty piddling. Here he had thought she was just a lady. He was damned glad to learn that she was a lady with some gumption.

The only thing that surprised him was the coincidence.

"Get this," he said to Patrick conspiratorially. "Mrs. Dutton came out here because her name was ruined back home by none other than...."

Before Gus could finish his story, he stopped mid-sentence. He was interrupted by a confusion of sounds. First came the baying of dogs; then came the nerve-shattering clanging of the fire-wagon.

Grabbing Patrick by the shirt front, he said evenly, "Get everyone out of here and lock the doors behind you."

Patrick motioned to the other two members of his three-man band. They were waiting patiently for Patrick to grill Gus before beginning their evening show. Frantically waving towards the door, Patrick began shooing people out of the place.

He called upstairs, "Gaby! *Gaby*! Clear out the house—*now*!"

There was a great deal of grumbling while every one trumped down the stair case. Men were tucking in their shirttails and a few girls wore only wrappers.

Gus told Patrick, "I don't know where the fire is, but you know how fast flames can whip through town. Tell everyone to go to the hotel and stay there—it's brick. Tell Boomer to lock the doors after you and see to Mrs. Dutton."

Newman was usually at the door when the fire-fighters went by. This time, he had been in the place of convenience out back. He had begun to find great solace in food, and the fare around them was, by turn, lardy and full of starch. His physique was getting stubbier by the day. Despite Gus's encouragement, he was moving slow.

At least five major fires had ravaged San Francisco in a two-year period. The city council had banned the use of canvas as a building material. Despite that decree, soft-sided buildings popped up faster than the constable could tack up ordinances on them. Any fire was considered a disaster in the making, so assisting the volunteer fire department was compulsory. Business owners were also mandated to keep six barrels of water next on their premises. When a fire threatened, Newman always stood by his proprietarily. They were right outside his office door and he didn't want anybody messing with them without good reason.

As devastating as fires were, the organized gangs who pillaged during the confusion were added grief. Anyone suspected of arson or caught looting was hung on the spot. Fires, therefore, were big on entertainment value for some citizens. All was needed to start a near riot was the clanging of the bells on the water wagon.

This time the fire was within easy sight of half the balconies in town.

Newman only got to going when Gus hollered, "Kick it into fast mule-speed, partner! They're heading up the hill."

Despite the vague destination, Newman knew that he meant that the Price home was on fire or in danger of it. Patrick and Gus scrambled aboard a gig commandeered by Newman. Loaded with men, their horse struggled up the hill. Gus jumped down and ran the rest of the way. When Newman arrived, his breathing was tortured. Seeing that he was on the verge of collapse, Gus told him to wait in the gig. He refused. Gus couldn't blame him.

Even in the melee of firemen, horses, water buckets, and barking dogs, Asher was easy to find. He was still standing in his yard wearing a dazed expression. Much to the disappointment of the onlookers, the fire was announced officially out before they could start pumping water. A good portion of the town had gathered and they were milling discontentedly, unhappy that more excitement wasn't afoot. Newman Chase remedied that.

He ran up to Asher and grabbed him by his lapels.

In near hysteria, he cried out, "Where is my daughter? Is she dead? Did you burn her alive too! Did you? *Did you*?"

It took Asher a moment to recognize that it was his father-in-law who had a hold of his coat. When he did, he looked at him without comprehension. The crowd quieted menacingly. Someone produced a rope.

"What?" Asher finally said. "What did you say to me?"

Seeing that the crowd was hungry for blood and Asher was a hairsbreadth away from smacking Newman, Gus intervened.

To Newman, he said, "Have you lost your bleedin' mind?" Then he asked Asher evenly, "Is our Annabella all right?"

"I can't say," said Asher. "She's safe insofar as the fire. I made a thorough search inside and she was no where to be found."

Newman looked heavenward, "Blessed be to God."

Just then, Chester came up. He was full of excuses and explanations as to how it came about that Annabella was driving by herself. Before he was half-through his enumeration, a man tackled Chester to the ground. He landed with a grunt and immediately covered his face to keep it from being pummeled. Straddling Chester's middle, Henry Butler beat him for all he was worth. Asher and Gus caught Butler under the armpits and drug him off of Chester before he did real harm.

Asher gasped, "Mr. Butler, remember yourself!"

Mr. Butler contritely donned his hat, mumbling, "Sorry, Boss. I just can't abide a man who don't do his job."

Shaken, Chester got to his feet, brushing himself off as he did. He was given a brief but intense interrogation. In the end Asher was satisfied with his story and, disgusted, waved him away.

Noticing the muddy rag Asher held in his hand like the crown jewels, Patrick curled his lip and asked, "What, pray tell, is that?"

"It was once pink," Asher said. "It is Annabella's beloved shawl."

"You sure?" Gus asked.

Although he recognized the design, Gus wouldn't have known it if Asher hadn't told him. Immediately, he saw its significance.

Anticipating the question, Asher told them, "Her gig and horse are *here*."

"Well, where the bloody hell is she?" demanded Newman.

Asher said with great profundity, "*I don't know*."

"Why don't you know?" Newman was becoming belligerent again. "Why don't you know where your *wife* is?"

"Hell-fire, let him talk," Gus snapped at Newman.

He looked at Asher and gave an encouraging half-nod of his head.

"I doubt she's *wandered* off," Asher told Gus pointedly.

Gus stroked his chin. (He needed his pipe for proper rumination, but didn't have it.) He disliked being the bearer of bad tidings, but he thought it was only fair for him to tell Asher of a few coincidences that had occurred that very afternoon.

"I talked with Annabella this very day, Mr. Price," he said barely above a whisper. "She told me that you two were experiencing... a bad patch."

Heaving a great shuddering sigh, Asher said, "Yes, she has indicated that she is unhappy. Here. With me. "

Then Gus added, "That McFee boy, he was in town this afternoon with Hardy, Mayne and that other feller."

Patrick chimed in, "Young Tucker has always been sweet on Annabella."

Gus glared at Patrick, who then declined to offer any more extraneous information."

"Tucker *did* want to know where she was," said Gus. "He was sweet on her—like half the town I might add. I don't think she felt anything for him...still, it was an odd business all around."

Asher was very quiet.

Newman raised his voice, joining in on the conversation, "Her mind—it's never been quite right since that sailor met his fate. That's what made her run off to Boston last time! Maybe she ran off again!"

Asher didn't appear to entertain that possibility. Gus didn't really either, but knowing how upset Annabella had been, nothing could be discounted. It was possible that her pride wouldn't let her face Asher. Her little tryst with Tucker the night before her wedding had been fodder for the local gossips for weeks. Gus had worked hard at Newman not learning about it. He had no idea what Asher did and didn't know. He hoped he was ignorant of it too. His only hope was that people were too scared of Asher to say something like that to his face. One thing had to be considered though—Tucker had been handy foil against Asher before, maybe he would be again.

In a clipped voice, Asher said, "We must proceed with the assumption that she has been stolen."

Gus didn't bother arguing. Remembering how she made a grand announcement when she went back to Boston, he knew Annabella wasn't the type to just go away without an uproar.

He asked Asher, "Can I bother you for the loan of a horse?"

Asher didn't hear him at first. His mind was busy plotting their strategy. Mechanically, he untied his own horse and only then pointed towards the horse still hitched to the gig.

He told Gus, "There's a saddle in the stable."

Crouching, Asher's fingers touched first one rock and then another. He walked a bit, and looked again. When Gus came leading a horse over to him, he had crouched again, but one hand covered his mouth.

"Do you see any tracks?" Gus asked.

"Yes," Asher said. "There are lots of them. If there had been a trail leading away, it has been obliterated by these sightseers."

He stood looking thoughtfully into the distance, possibly weighing which might be the most likely direction to look. Gus tried to be logical too. It took a moment for Asher to realize that Annabella's shawl had a wheel track across it. That meant she lost it before the conveyance left. He sincerely doubted that she dropped it on the way to the house.

He told that conclusion to Gus.

Struck with that probability, Gus tried to gather his wits, suggesting, "Perhaps we should wait to see if there is a ransom demand."

"What if they have stolen her for another reason?" Asher said, "I pray money is all they want."

Gus reasoned, "If they were gonna kill her they would've already done it."

Asher disagreed, "Not necessarily."

No one wanted to recall how many rapes and murders had taken place in and around San Francisco. There was certainly no shortage of cutthroats in town. It was critical to determine not only who took her, but which way they went. Because Asher didn't say, it fell to Gus to point out that the wharves must be checked. A ship escaping into the night wasn't the possibility any of them wanted to ponder. Stealing women for the slave trade happened regularly. A golden-haired girl like Annabella would be especially prized.

"Shall I ride with you?" Mr. Butler asked Asher.

Asher just shook his head and mounted his horse. Gus nodded towards Mr. Butler. Asher understood immediately what he meant. Before either could tell him to go, Mr. Butler anticipated them.

He announced, "I am on my way to the ships even now. I'll have men fan out up and down the shore. No one will escape our notice."

Patrick watched as Mr. Butler headed back down the road to town.

"You know, she has been friends with Gaby," he offered. "Perhaps...."

"Yes," Gus said before he could finish his sentence.

Without hesitation, Patrick ran after Mr. Butler.

Standing in slope-shouldered despair, Newman stuttered, "But, but... what about me? A time like this, a girl will need her Poppa."

76

"Can you believe it," crowed Mayne. "Nobody was even around. Easy pickings!"

The partnership of Hardy and Mayne was full of ambition, but short on sense. With the girl tied up in the back of their cart, they had stopped at bustling mining camp on the way up river. Then they peeled bills off Ernie's roll to buy whiskey, biscuits, and dried beef. Mayne wanted to buy a beaded Indian bag to stuff the remainder of the money and he and Hardy bickered over the purchase. The only caution they took was to leave the cart and their hostage below the rise and out of sight.

After they killed Ernie and kidnapped Annabella, he saw no reason to keep Tucker alive.

"Just looking at him turns my stomach," Mayne growled.

Hardy still thought that Tucker might be needed to keep the girl in line. If not, they could get rid of his body up in the mountains. Leaving more than one corpse too close to town would be asking for trouble. Besides, he had an affable, honest face. He was easily manipulated and easily believed. Yeah, Tucker was better alive—for now.

While his fate was discussed, Tucker sat in the back of the cart watching lovingly over his sweet Annabella. Although she was unconscious, she was moving about and he didn't think she was badly hurt. If she wasn't, it wasn't for Mayne not trying. Tucker had specifically ordered that she was not to be frightened or harmed. He told them that if he could just talk to her a moment, she would come with him willingly. Although she *had* put a brave front, she had to be horribly unhappy living with that heartless money-monger. Perhaps it was best that a decision was made on her behalf. When left to their own devices ladies' minds went all willy-nilly. A man must be the strong one.

If Mayne and Hardy had thought he was blowing smoke about Annabella loving him, they was showed—they was showed good. Who did she ask for the minute she came to? She didn't want her husband, no. She called for him. Hardy had to go a lay a whip on her. It was terrible hard to keep from giving him what-for. But after what they did to old Ernie, Tucker didn't dare raise a fuss.

Sometimes being strong means laying low.

✧

When they finally arrived at their destination, it was dusk again. Annabella couldn't recall how long she had been tied up or how far they had traveled. In due time, they removed the bag over her head. Hoping to get a good refreshing intake of air, she got a generous whiff of the rancid air instead. The stink permeated the camp. She immediately vomited.

She was very disheartened.

It hadn't been as squalid on the leaking ocean tub—and certainly not with the wagons crossing the prairies. Those caravans had been bastions of civilization. Men relieved themselves discretely behind a bush. The women all used a pot. Never once did she see anyone behave an indelicate fashion. The men were courtly and the women, refined—well, mostly. (Granted, from the retrospect of captivity her other travails were seen in a kinder light.)

What did she expect from a bunch of craven kidnappers? If she had her father's Pauly, she'd put them in their place! Using a poor dog as a lure! And Tucker McFee! Either he wasn't the gentle soul she thought he was or he had been used as bait too. She had heard about these wretched mining camps. They were lawless places. Kidnappers weren't the half of it. Bandits of all sort ran at large.

Still bound hand and foot, she lowered herself onto the ground and tried not to breath. It was black as pitch so she couldn't make out who was part of this particular gang. All she could see was ominous shadows. Given some thought, the only thing she was reasonably certain was that Dovie Gaspard wasn't with them—if only because she had watched that woman set sail herself.

After some time, she hadn't heard Dovie's voice (which was quite distinctive), she finally let that particular fear go. One less villain didn't mean her mind was comforted. The cold grip of dread attached firmly to wherever she kept her nerve and rendered her, at least temporarily, helpless.

As her eyes adjusted to the night, she made out a two-wheeled cart and realized that was what they rode. Someone began a fire and before long, she discerned the sound of grease sizzling. Dear God, they were cooking something. The smell was horridly familiar. Ah yes. It was bear grease. Enough trappers had come to the *Bella* stinking of it. They used it for everything—especially their hair. It was as ingrained in her very being as firmly as her mother's voice.

When a man came over with a plate of beans, he took out a knife and cut her binds. His hat fell over his eyes, so even if she dared look, she couldn't see his face. She stared at the plate instead. The beans looked like a mound of rabbit pellets. It was impossible to gag any down, but she used the excuse of eating to sneak a look around. If she was to escape—or even survive—it was imperative she knew who took her. Was it Dovie? Slave traders? Or Jose Carrillo? In a moment she recognized, if not the man, then the muskrat coat.

Rutledge Mayne!

Good God in heaven! It was all she could do not to choke. This was an extraordinarily bad turn of events. What the bloody hell did Mayne think he was doing? She had half a mind to give him what for. He couldn't be the brains behind this particular plot—he was evil, not devious. She looked around for the head culprit. It wasn't obvious. Then she saw Tucker sitting on a rock with his back turned to her.

"Good," she thought. "I don't want to see your worthless face."

To her captors in general, she said brightly, "So what is your plan here? Or do you have one?"

"Oh, yeah, sister, we have a plan," one man replied.

It took her a moment to recognize Zeke Hardy. He stunk too—worse than Mayne's coat. Nausea washed over her, but she tried not to retch again. Seeing her with her head between her knees, Mayne walked back over to her.

"Remember me?" he asked mildly.

She said, "How could I forget?"

"I owe you this," he replied.

Without further warning, he slapped her hard across the cheek.

When he did, Tucker leapt to his feet. She could see then that his hands were tied. He tried hard, but all he managed was to kick out impotently in Mayne's direction.

Annabella glared at Mayne, "Are we even now, you *pig*?"

Mayne put a finger to one side of his nostril and blew a wad of snot on the ground in front of her.

"Honey, we ain't close to being even."

Refusing to let him see how terrified she was, she looked away. Her eyes watered, and she could feel her cheek begin to swell. Being hit was becoming a huge annoyance. She wondered again if they knew she was pregnant. If they did, would they care? She decided to keep that information to herself until she knew it would be useful.

Mayne went back to the fire and sat with Hardy. They began taking turns drinking from a jug. The deeper they got into it, the more they began to argue.

Hardy told Mayne, "We should've bought a proper wagon."

"I like the mule," replied Mayne. Calling to Tucker, he asked, "What's that mule's name, McFee?"

"Lolly," answered Tucker sullenly. "Her name is Lolly."

"That's right," said Mayne. "Lolly and Ernie."

"Shut up!" hissed Hardy.

"Why?" asked Mayne. "She don't know Ernie."

Hardy shook his head with disgust. "You don't know when to shut yer pie-hole do ya?"

Mayne seemed uncertain how to answer that. So he took one more slug of brew. It must have been the topper because he keeled over, dead drunk. Hardy leaned back on his bedroll and tipped his hat over his eyes. Pretty soon both men were snoring the deep bombination of the inebriate.

After Mayne and Hardy started snoring, Tucker hopped over to Annabella. Sitting on an opposing rock, knee to knee, he was very apologetic. But she wouldn't listen.

"Get away!" she hissed.

"I don't blame you. This isn't the way it was supposed to go. They said they would help me rescue you."

"Rescue me? From what? From who? Who are you to decide that I need rescuing?"

Her voice rose and she immediately lowered it. She didn't want to wake the yellow villains. She might get hit again.

Tucker insisted, "It is our destiny to be together! We are as one. I am a king and you are my Scheherazade. We sealed our love with a mortal union. No man can put us asunder!"

"Where the devil did you learn to talk that way?" she wondered.

He looked deeply in her eyes, as if trying to possess her from the outside in.

"Miss Annabella," he said huskily."

She looked away. His eyes repulsed her. He no longer looked like the adorable, innocent kid. He looked like a snub-nosed piece of trash—and he stunk. Tucker, however, was unaware of her revulsion. All he could see was the degree of her delicate condition. She was springing like a heifer. It made him feel smug—even indomitable.

"Tell me, my sweet," he whispered, "how long until our baby is to come?"

Startled, she said, "*What*?"

"You can confide in me," he whispered. "I will protect you and our child."

"*Our* child? What are you talking about?" she gasped.

He smiled at her lovingly, repeating, "I will protect us."

She didn't know what delusion to protest first—that he was the father of her child or that he was in any position to protect anyone, much less her. But he looked at her with such devotion, she tried to be patient.

"Tucker," she began, taking a deep breath, "Do you know what month it is? Or what year?"

"Not really."

"I know that you can count."

He nodded his head agreeably.

"Well, count."

"What?"

Impatiently, she said, "*Months*."

"Months?"

"Do you know how long it takes to have a baby?"

He pursed his lips thoughtfully. Then with hope in his voice, he volunteered, "A cow takes nine months."

Slowly, so he would be sure to understand, she said, "It takes the same time for a lady."

"You don't say? I would've thought as complicated as a person is, you know, in their thoughts and fingers and all and cows just have hooves, it would've been more."

Her voice flat, she said, "Well, it's not—and I've been married going on a year."

He was very solemn for a moment, taking in the full extent of what she was saying.

"Surely you didn't lay with a man that you hate?"

The look of disappointment on his face was so excruciating that, for a moment, she couldn't be mad at him. But their predicament was just too dire. If Hardy and Mayne were in cahoots to ransom her, they didn't need Tucker to do it. She wasn't sure he realized that he was dispensable. As he had a hand in it all, she was torn between feeling sorry for him and wanting to kill him with her bare hands.

"I don't hate Asher—I mean I didn't. Well, I kind of did, but I don't now."

Tucker looked confused and angry.

"You did what we did with *him*? How *could* you?"

"He's my husband," she said. Then with more conviction, she repeated, "Asher Price is *my husband*."

Suddenly, she realized how true that was. She began to cry. All was lost. Asher would never know her true feelings. She would die at the hands of this murderous bunch and be buried in a common grave with Tucker McFee. She would never learn whether she was carrying a boy or a girl. A girl named Amy or a boy named after his father, Asher.

Tucker didn't know why she was crying. His hands were tied, so the only way he knew to soothe her was to put his head on her shoulder.

"There, there," he cooed.

Unfortunately, the odor from his hair was so pungent, it made her gag.

"Please, please," she begged. "Don't."

In order to get Tucker's greasy head off her shoulder, she asked, "Who is this 'Ernie' they were talking about?"

Slowly, Tucker sat upright.

"Ernie was my mate on the *Mary Thayer*. We brought him into town to get his indemnity from Mr. Price."

In the back of her mind, she recalled that there had been a second crewman who had survived with Tucker. She nodded that she recalled him.

"After he collected his pay, Mayne sliced Ernie's throat and Hardy kicked his body in a ditch."

He added, "Varmints are feeding off poor Ernie as we speak."

Until then, Mayne and Hardy had been just a pair of ruffians bent on easy money. She was beginning to see that they would slit her throat the minute it suited them. She swallowed hard, trying to settle her stomach.

"Dear God."

77

Ernie's body had been found while he was still identifiable.

That was because the commotion and furor of the fire-wagon attracted every loose hound in San Francisco. A few of them tired on the way out to the Price house and turned back. Those that woofed and yelped all the way up the hill were soon underfoot and had to be shooed away. Thwarted, they meandered homeward through the sand hills and low weeds along the road. As always, their noses were alert for an interesting scent. Sniffing out a carcass as big as Ernie was easy. Once the corpse was uncovered, they began to bay. When they couldn't rouse any interest that way, they went one better.

A flop-eared scent hound of questionable parentage came to the smoldering Price house and sat at Gus's feet. He and Asher were still trying to determine just which way to approach the hills when Gus noticed him. The hound was gnawing on a blue denim rag. It smelled to high-heaven.

"I recognize that," said Gus, catching the dog behind his ears. He petted him until Asher could get the dog into releasing the fabric. Holding it up with two fingers, Gus nodded knowingly.

"I swear that was on Ernie Braithwaite's head not four hours ago."

"The question is—where is Ernie Braithwaite's head right now?" said Asher. "Do you know whose hound this is? Let's get him get back on the scent."

That was relatively easy. The dog led them straight to poor Ernie's body. He was lying not a half mile away. His throat was slit ear to ear.

"Now why doesn't that surprise me?" said Gus.

They didn't really need the lanterns to identify him. Still, they thought it a good idea to make sure. A couple of volunteers went down the hill and tied a rope around him to drag his body to high ground. His identity certain, his murderers were easy enough to figure out. It didn't take much cogitating to divine that whoever killed Ernie was almost certainly behind the kidnapping too.

If the grisly sight of Ernie's dead body unnerved Asher, Gus didn't see it. He watched with silent intensity as the growing assembly of men crowded around the corpse. Some were fresh from wanting to string Asher Price from the highest tree, others were just curiosity seekers. A number of men were on horseback. When Asher spoke, it was primarily to them.

"A man has been murdered. My wife has been stolen. We can do nothing now for Mr. Braithwaite. My wife's situation, however, is desperate. I need volunteers to help find her. I will give ten-thousand dollars for her safe return. I'll also give one thousand dollars bounty on the head of each of her kidnappers."

"For Hardy, Mayne and McFee—each of 'em?" somebody yelled.

"For each of them," Asher said through clenched teeth.

Having caught every man's complete interest, those with a horse to beg, borrow or steal gathered nearer to hear the particulars. Stern-faced, Asher gave orders.

"We will assemble forthwith and leave from the ferry crossing. Bring your guns and plenty of ammunition. All due care will be taken so that Mrs. Price isn't harmed. That is *imperative*!"

"Shall we wait for morning?" a man asked.

Asher's glare was unambiguous. He and his money would not wait for anything—man, beast, nor nature's stage.

78

Heads pounding and eyes bleary from the previous night's drunkenness, Hardy and Mayne began squabbling early. The argued over who would ride down and find a way to deliver their demands and wait for payment. Hardy ended the disagreement by announcing that it was his idea and, Mayne-be-damned, he would go collect. The only concession to his cohort was to throw a bottle of rum in his direction.

Mayne wasn't really satisfied with the arrangement, but appeased himself with a swig from the liquor.

"I hate mules anyway—give me a horse any day."

The dollar amount for the ransom took more consideration. They had no idea how much Asher Price's wife would be worth to him. Ten thousand seemed too little, fifty too much. They decided on twenty-five thousand even. Neither of them had ever had more than a few hundred dollars at a time. Anything more was pretty much beyond real comprehension.

While pretending indifference, Annabella listened to their negotiations carefully. She couldn't begin to gauge how long it would take for Hardy to get to San Francisco, deliver the ransom demand, get paid—or not—and return. Try as she might, she couldn't help but think about the real possibility that Asher wouldn't pay to get her back. There was no one else to ask. Gus used all his money to bail out her father. Every dime Newman had, Dovie stole. If Asher didn't pony up, she was good as dead. He was her only hope.

Hardy rode off muttering and cursing at Lolly. Mayne hollered after him, "Don't beat that mule, Zeke! She'll throw you and then kick you dead!"

As he set into drinking in earnest, Annabella's thoughts became increasingly pragmatic—and therefore, pessimistic. As she saw it, her goose was cooked whether the ransom was paid or not. They could still kill her—or even sell her like a piece of livestock. Stories were everywhere about women being forced to work in some godforsaken whorehouses. That was why her daddy warned her about gallivanting around unescorted. He told her blonde hair would bring a premium to slave traders. The very thought of that repulsed her—almost as much as watching as Mayne laboriously picked his nose.

Catching her looking, he winked at her.

She decided then that hell or high water, she'd try to escape. She'd rather take the chance of being molested fifty times a day by men she didn't know than even once by Mayne.

Considering how to do it took concentration. She knew that she'd better make her move before Hardy got back. Her time spent in the *Bella* watching men drink themselves into a stupor wasn't entirely wasted. She knew that sooner or later Mayne would pass out. Then she would have time to wriggle free. What to do after that was a bit of a problem. Bears and bandits were behind every bush in the Sierras. Without provisions or protection, she would be easy pickings for predators of all variety. If she didn't become dinner for some local wildlife, the best she could hope for was to happen on to a ruthless mining camp and be taken in as a concubine.

Looking at Mayne eye what he found up his nose made prospective flight evermore attractive. Then, she heard Tucker began to talk to Mayne. Instead of trying to sooth him into unconsciousness, he seemed bent on riling him.

"You can't trust Hardy. He's a drunken fool. He'll lead a posse right to you."

Mayne ignored him.

"Mayne!" he called out again. "*Mayne!* You don't have to stay here and wait for the law to come get you. They'll hang you for kidnapping, you know. They don't even take you to court. They'll find a way to hang you right here in this ravine."

Mayne was crouching by the fire and kept poking at the coals of the fire with his knife.

"You heard of the Blackwell Cut-off?" he asked. "Well, I know it. That's how I got through the Sierras."

Annabella only looked at Mayne out of the corner of her eye and couldn't tell if he was listening or not. Regardless, Tucker kept talking.

"I was with a wagon train. They were stranded in the pass—early snow and all. Folks died. Before they did they buried their valuables so the Indians wouldn't get at them. I left them all behind. There is a treasure buried there. Who ever finds it will be rich. *Rich*!"

That garnered Mayne's attention. His eyes glazed over just a bit.

"The whole bed of a wagon was packed with guns, silver, jewelry and the like was buried. Then they covered it with boards and spread dirt over it. We'll have to look around some since grass has probably grown over it by now—but its there."

By then, Annabella was awestruck. She had no idea whether Tucker was telling the truth or not. The rational side of her thought it highly unlikely that he spent as much time as he had searching for gold if there was a cache of riches waiting for him up in some mountain pass. (She wondered if Mayne would come to that conclusion too.) Tucker had to be lying. For such an open, unassuming soul, however, lies slithered from his tongue with extraordinary ease.

As he contemplated what Tucker was telling him, Mayne's tongue made a slow rotation around his mouth. He was primed. Tucker's bait had worked.

"Undo me," Tucker said, sticking his bound hands out. "I can draw you the map."

Instead of whipping out his knife to cut his ties, the unexpected happened. A recollection emerged from Mayne's rum-saturated brain. His brow furrowed and his eyes narrowed. Lost in his own scheme, Tucker missed the signs.

Mayne shook his head, saying, "Ernie told me and Hardy about you, McFee."

Rising, Mayne walked over to Tucker and crouched. His lips were next to Tucker's ear and he whispered, but Annabella could hear what he said.

"I *know* about you McFee. Ernie told us it *all*."

An odd expression colored Tucker's face.

He stuttered, "Wh-a-at?"

"Don't act all innocent, boy. You been found out."

Withdrawing his knife from his scabbard, he put the tip of the blade under Tucker's chin.

"How'd you decide, huh, Tucker? Where'd you make the first cut?"

Annabella didn't understand the conversation at all—just that it had to do with that poor Ernie.

"Well," repeated Mayne. "Where's the first cut?"

All was quiet for a moment before Tucker responded. When he spoke, it was in a voice entirely unfamiliar to Annabella.

He said, "You hang 'em up and dress 'em out just like a deer."

Mayne gulped. Annabella, however, was stumped by this exchange. So she just chalked it to the ways of the wild. No telling what these men do up at the camps.

Mayne remained incredulous, "Ah, you're pissing in my pocket."

"The treasure is all that matters, Mayne!" Tucker said, "We could go in partners on it. There's way too much for me to carry alone."

Suddenly, Mayne made a decision. He sliced through the leather strap wrapped around Tucker's wrists and let him loose. Then he looked hard at Annabella.

"Don't think I ain't watchin' you, missy."

Annabella didn't speak. A keen sense of self-preservation told her not to have any part in whatever Tucker was scheming. Unfortunately, she didn't have an alternative on hand. If Tucker meant to take Mayne off on some wild goose chase, she might have to go with them. There was little pleasure in that thought, but sitting on the hard ground waiting for some fools to decide whether you lived or died wasn't much of an alternative. She wanted some say in how she died. Given a choice, she'd take a knife to the back—if that meant she was running hell-bent-for-leather in the other direction.

After Mayne cut Tucker's ties, she held out her wrists, hoping he'd cut hers too. Instead, Mayne and Tucker walked over to the fire. Tucker looked back her. All she could do was to bug out her eyes and then roll them. Tucker, however, remained expressionless. That irritated her no end. She was getting very cranky. Her condition made being consigned such an uncomfortable position all the more unbearable. She had tried sitting cross-legged, knees together with her ankles to first one side then the other. It was all agony and indignation at her plight was fast supplanting fear.

And she certainly didn't much like the sidelong glances Mayne was giving her. They weren't particularly cryptic. They were absolutely obscene. It was time for her to play her ace in the hole.

"I'm expecting a baby," she announced haughtily.

To her great dismay, that merely aroused his interest. He wiped the back of his hand across his mouth.

Making little kissing noises, he said, "Yeah, sweetheart. Come to daddy,"

"Ew," responded Annabella. "Ew."

She looked at Tucker. He was busy with his map. Perhaps convincing him that he wasn't the father of her child was a bit premature. He might defend her honor. If Mayne made more advances, she'd tell Tucker. Maybe they'd kill each other. Setting a confrontation up like that time would take some finagling and a lot of deceit. She didn't know if she was up to it. It had recently dawned on her that she just wasn't much good at lying. It was a talent like singing or embroidery. Deception, equivocation, and tergiversation were skills essential for a true lady.

And Lord knew she was no lady.

79

The day was spent with Tucker trying to talk Mayne into going on a treasure hunt, and Mayne giving Annabella long, lascivious looks. Annabella both yearned for and loathed the thought of darkness. It would either cloak their escape, or shelter Mayne's foul deeds.

Tucker tried to convince Mayne that Hardy meant to betray him. The more he said that he would be hanged, that they had to strike out on their own, the wilder Mayne became. He twirled around like he was dancing, but clawed at his face and jabbed out at Tucker with his knife.

"Stay away from me," Mayne cried out. "I don't like the look in your eyes."

Mystified, Annabella looked at Tucker. He did have an odd look about the eyes. It made her shiver. Tucker ignored Annabella and concentrated on Mayne.

"Even if Hardy gets that money, he wouldn't bring it back here. He'll head for Jalisco."

Emptying another bottle, Mayne threw it against a tree. Without so much as a twitch, Tucker stood up and brought Annabella a plate of cold beans. They were highly uninviting and she shoved them aside. He didn't notice that. Sitting down next to her, he began to whisper urgently in her ear about some plan he was hatching.

She didn't care to listen to anything he had to say. If Tucker didn't quit sniffing around her, he was going to make Mayne jealous. Having Tucker and Mayne vying for her affections was just too disgusting to contemplate. They were both deranged.

"Once Mayne is good and drunk, I'll cut you loose and we can get away."

Initially so unfalteringly determined, Annabella had finally had enough. She began to whimper and then cry outright.

"I want my husband," she said. "I want my husband to come and take me home *right now*!"

Never in her life had she meant anything more. A black look crossed Tucker's face, one she didn't like. She had quite enough of him too.

"Get away, you lunatic!" she hissed.

"Now, now," he began to coo. "You don't mean that. You're just testy because of your state. My mama had ten babies. Just let me know when our baby is to come and I'll help you."

Drained from anxiety and fear, she said dully, "You'll be the first to know."

Clearly, Tucker was back to believing it was his baby and she didn't have the energy to argue with him. He was truly living in the land of fairies and sprites. Looking first at Mayne as he pared his nails with his enormous dagger, then to Tucker's beatific smile, she truly didn't know who was more dangerous.

"We need some more wood, McFee," decreed Mayne. "This fire's going out."

Tucker dutifully wandered off gathering wood and Mayne experienced another tickle of mucous. Finger to one side of his nose, he blew hard through the other. He looked at the dirt and seemed pleased. The minute Tucker was out of sight, Mayne astonished her by initiating a conversation. His tone was as conspiratorial as Tucker's. Despite his repugnance (which was only slightly below that of a spotted skunk), she listened to what he had to say. Perhaps he would help her escape without carnal insult.

Speaking barely above a whisper, he said, "I know you been friends with McFee and all, but he ain't who you think he is. We heard the straight of it from Ernie."

Her face remained placid as she replied, "We each have our own shortcomings?"

He snorted and then gave his nose an upward swipe with his index finger. Having no idea what he was getting at, her eyelids barely flickered.

Playing a solitary game of mumblety-peg, he threw his knife into a log at her feet.

He said, "I guess you don't care then."

She didn't want to ask, but couldn't help herself, "Don't care about what?"

"That he ate your sweetheart."

"*Beg pardon*?"

"That's how him and Ernie made it back. They ate their dead mates."

Her lip curled involuntarily. She had heard of such business. When faced with starvation, castaways resorted to partaking of the flesh of the dead. That wasn't possible with the *Mary Thayer*, however. The crew died of yellow fever. Tucker told her so.

Tucker told... her... so.

Her mouth formed a question, but she couldn't quite get it out. It was just as well, Rutledge Mayne was busy filling in the details of his story.

"Yellow fever killed the captain and some of the crew, but they lost their provisions to them natives. They drew straws at first. Then they started killing people in their sleep. It was down to him and Ernie when they finally made land. That's why Ernie deserted and why Tucker scuttled the ship. He didn't want to be found out."

As coarse as Mayne was, she didn't think even he could make up a story such as that.

"I don't believe you," she lied.

Mayne grinned, "I wouldn't either if I was you. But it was in Tucker's blood. His family died up in one of those mountain passes. Winter hit early and snowed them in. It happened before. Those settlers, the Donners and the Reeds, they...."

The first report of gunfire wasn't very loud.

The second bullet came whizzing by and ended with a soft ping. The third hit Mayne right in his belly. Blood spilled out between his fingers as he clutched at his wound. She didn't care whatsoever; rescue was at hand! When the riders came rushing into the camp kicking up debris, she stood and smiled her welcome. Mayne recognized that it wasn't a posse long before she did. By then he was lying on the ground leaking blood like a geyser—but he was still alive. The interlopers were hollering in Spanish.

"*Alto*! *Alto*! *Los manos arriba*!"

It didn't take her long to realize that it wasn't the posse, they were being pillaged by banditos. Frantic to escape, she screamed at Mayne to cut her loose. To his credit, he managed to toss her his knife. It landed blade down at her feet. Holding the hilt awkwardly between her ankles, she frantically sawed at the straps. When she finally cut them loose, she had no place to run. So she rolled in a ball, desperate to avoid the gunfire and horses hooves. Dust was everywhere, including in her eyes. Covering her face, she could see through her fingers. Every one of them had guns—some of them held their reins in their teeth so they could shoot two pistols. In the ravine the echo of the gunfire was deafening.

As quick as it began, the din stopped. It wasn't, however, quite over.

Several *pistoleros* stepped down from their horses and kicked through the belongings on the ground. One man picked up Mayne's half-eaten apple and pared off a slice for himself. Annabella stayed down, her face halfway in her plate of beans. She didn't dare move, figuring that as a supplicant, she was in proper position.

When all was quiet, she finally got nerve enough to take a peek at what was going on.

Gun smoke hung in the air so thick it looked like fog. She didn't see Tucker anywhere. He must have run when he heard all the shooting. The slough had been knocked from its braces and water trickled back towards them, encircling Mayne's body. He lay very still. When she stood and turned around, she was looking up at the hardened faces of a dozen men.

They had formed a half-circle around her as if they had never seen such a being before. A half-dozen beans and their residue stuck to the side of her face.

A man's voice called out, "*Se tiene el pelo de oro*!"

She would have liked to stand before her slaughterers and ask for no quarter. However would gladly trade her dignity for her life. She also would've given anything to have better command of the Spanish language. All she knew that "*oro*" meant "gold." If money was what they wanted, she wanted to tell them that if they treated her well, there would be a great reward in it for them. Unfortunately, she didn't know how to say it.

"*Mi esposo*," she racked her brain for a translation. "*Mi esposo es muy*..." she couldn't think of the word for "rich." She sought their assailants' help, "*Como se dice*, 'rich?"

"*Rico*," said one man as he kicked his horse to the front of the group.

"*Mi esposo es muy rico!*" she all but shouted. "*Muy, muy*!"

Her new captors burst into hearty laughter—the significance of which remained a mystery to her. Trying not to appear as terrified as she was, she laughed back. Another man walked his horse over to her and slid to the ground. She faced him, but without belligerence. He cupped her chin in the palm of his hand, turning her first one way and then the other, clearly assessing her value.

She had no idea which she wanted to be—too valuable to kill, or not valuable enough to bother with.

He patted her cheek, saying, "*No esta mal*."

It was abundantly clear that the man who held her face in his hand only had three fingers. Next to him was the muscular figure of Jose Carrillo himself. She wondered if he remembered her from the ferry. Before she had a chance to ask, the three-fingered man grabbed her about the nape of the neck and put the barrel of his gun to her temple.

As he did, she closed her eyes.

80

Asher Price had never been much of a talker, so his silence while on the trail of the mysterious oxcart and its excursionists was unextraordinary. Lost in his own thoughts, Gus certainly didn't notice. When any of the dozen or so men following them tried to talk, Asher raised a gloved hand to shush them. Their horses were raising enough commotion as it was. As he saw it, surprise would be the only way to avoid bloodshed.

During and after his furious fight to save his home from burning, it had been all Asher could do not to leave it to God. If he had to identify another charred corpse, he thought he might run screaming into the sea. With his history, that might have been taken as a sign of guilt rather than despair. Had Newman Chase not brought him back to his senses in time to defend himself, the mob of onlookers would have been happy to string him up in the nearest tree limb.

It was only after the horses began their upward ascent that he finally allowed himself to think about what they would find at the end of their search. He was extremely apprehensive—as much for what he did know as for what he didn't.

Despite what Newman Chase thought and Gus Gerlache hoped, Asher Price had learned about what his bride was up to on the eve of their wedding. The dutiful Mr. Butler had told him just that very afternoon. Asher had been temporarily dumbstruck by the information, so much so that he didn't even ask Butler why he had waited until half-year after to fact to tell him. He could only strike it up to the man's personal discomposure over the subject. Ultimately, Asher dismissed the whole sordid episode. He had been far too distracted by Annabella's more recent disaffection to be bothered by those in the past.

As the day progressed, he had come to realize that all these events were intertwined.

Only time would tell if Annabella had gone with McFee of her own accord or not. Mayne and Hardy were the loose cannons in the mix. Even if Annabella had decided to escape her marriage, he couldn't believe she would have any dealings with them. McFee was just a farm boy; Hardy and Mayne were evil personified. Those contemplations made Asher more anxious by the moment.

He gave a nudge to his horse's flanks and the bay's chest heaved as they took the incline. Having never taken the horse out for more than a brief exercise, Asher had no idea how long he could keep such a treacherous pace. As the horse labored on, he let up on the reins. However anxious he was, a felled horse wouldn't close the ground between them and Annabella any faster.

The wagon horse Gus rode had a broader chest than the bay. He was bred for stamina. With Gus on board and laden with iron, he needed it. Although Gus wasn't much of a horseman either, he managed to look like he knew what he was doing. The majority of the hired guns had never ridden together before. It was important that they stay orderly.

Asher fondled the pistol in his belt. He had never felt so far from his faith in his life. To close the gap, he felt the need to talk. When the trail allowed it, he pulled back on the reins a bit to ride next to Gus.

"These men behind us look well-armed," he noted. "One claims to have shot a man at sixty yards measure. I suppose that means they will make a good showing if it comes to a clash."

Gus laughed, "My mama always said that it's the best swimmers who drown."

Asher smiled, "I like your mother's hypothesis. That means that I have a better chance than anybody to survive a gunfight."

Gus pointed to the Pauly in Asher's belt. He recognized it.

"Do you know how to use that thing?"

"I used to carry a sidearm before I married."

"That isn't what I asked."

Gus had a huge rifle tied to his saddle. Instead of answering, Asher asked Gus how well he could shoot.

"Good enough, I suppose," mused Gus. "It depends on the circumstances. I've found that if someone's shooting back, it marshals a man's concentration miraculously."

Because Asher didn't say anything, Gus tried to change the subject.

"They say that the whales are giving out."

"I've heard that. I've heard lots of things," Asher replied cryptically.

Gus ducked his chin, but Asher kept talking.

"No one needs to avoid speaking about Annabella's dalliance with that boy, Mr. Gerlache. I understand what might lay behind this present situation."

Startled, Gus fiddled with one of the stirrups. Then he resituated his hat. When he spoke, he was direct.

"Do you mean to exact revenge?"

It was Asher's turn to be surprised.

"How do you mean?" he asked.

"Well, either you blame Annabella or you blame McFee."

With unaccustomed candor, Asher replied, "Why, I blame no one but myself."

"If you don't mind me commenting...," Gus prefaced.

Asher didn't.

"If anybody's to blame, it's Rutledge Mayne and Zeke Hardy. There'll be time enough for finger-pointing about other things later."

Asher was defensive.

"Do you speak as my reprover?"

"I only know that if you marry a high-stepper, you better not complain about the bumpy ride."

After a moment of thought, Asher replied, "Point taken."

Gus then added, "One of the greatest frauds perpetrated against mankind is the pretense that virginity is a virtue."

Asher wasn't used to such plain language and he blushed. Noting his discomfort, Gus hushed. In the silence, Asher thought of the circumstances surrounding his marriage. He hadn't behaved nobly. His primary concern had been his own reputation. He had accused her of immoral conduct with her sailor. That was reason enough for her to want revenge. Whether they had actually consummated the act or not was beside the point. Whatever she did, she did it just to spite him.

No doubt she tossed Ainsworth's name in his face for the same reason. Of the two, he had believed that the dead man posed a greater threat to their marriage. He couldn't say the same thing today.

Given time to mull it over, he decided that the timing of Mr. Butler's disclosure had been quite fortunate. Several months ago, he might have left her. Several months ago, he wouldn't have known about the child.

Several months ago, he hadn't realized how very much he loved her.

81

Just as Annabella felt the cold barrel of the gun against her temple, she was knocked from her feet. Someone had tackled her. She fell hard on her back, the wind knocked from her. Lying across her was a serape-wearing bandit.

"*Mi amiga!*"

That was one of the few Spanish words she understood.

"My friend."

Immediately, a flurry of Spanish was exchanged. Annabella wondered if perhaps Jose Carrillo had remembered her from the ferry—and whether or not that would advantageous. Before she could come to a conclusion about it, gunfire erupted again. She had no idea who it was or why it was happening. To her great fortune, the Mexican still lay on top of her, giving her cover as bullets flew overhead. That meant that all she could see of what was happening was a shower of dirt and rocks.

At least that was all she could see until Three-fingered Jack's body came rolling towards her. He landed face up, just inches away from her. An enormous black-rimmed hole was in the middle of his cheek, but it didn't bleed. Instead, a pool of blood formed beneath his head. Horrified, she could see the crimson fluid as it began to ooze in her direction. Pinned to the ground, she could do nothing but stare into the man's huge brown eyes and watch as the life drained out of them.

Squeezing her eyes shut, she screamed, "No, no, no, no!"

Invectives of Spanish and English both were heard between the scatter of gunfire. She still didn't know who was shooting. As the shots dwindled, she managed to get a gasp of air. A familiar voice echoed across the ravine.

"Annabella! *Annabella?*"

Wheezing and grunting, she finally wriggled out beneath her new *compañera*. Wild to be free, she came to her feet too fast and a spell of dizziness brought her back to her knees. She saw Gus, carbine in hand.

Kneeling, he asked, "Little girl, are you all right?"

Blinking wildly, she was beyond reassurance. She wanted blood. Jerking the rifle from his hand, she tried to level it first one way and then the other. Fortunately, it wasn't cocked. So Gus grabbed it back and aimed it directly at the Mexican she had just thrown aside. Before he could pull the trigger, however, Annabella astonished herself with a realization.

"Don't shoot, Gus!" she gasped. "Don't shoot!"

Gus's head jerked in her direction. "What?"

This is my friend," she explained pulling off the bandito's hat.

"What the hell...?" said Gus. "It's Lupe!"

Past being dumbfounded, Annabella wrapped her arms about Lupe's neck. Lupe withstood Annabella's fit of affection with brave impassiveness. Not surprisingly, Gus wanted further explanation.

"Who is who here? Is Lupe a bandito or a captive?"

Annabella didn't really know that. She did know, however, that Lupe saved her.

She said, "Three-Fingered Jack had a gun to my head and was going to kill me, but Lupe saved my life!"

Before she could say more, Lupe said, "His name was Manuel. He murdered a priest near Lake Tulare. He cut out his tongue and fed it to the hogs."

Annabella recoiled. She thought she was beyond being shocked by such malefactions. Worse outrages were a fact of life in the gulches and gullies of the Sierras. The lust for gold turned bullies into cutthroats and the temperate into thieves. So beautiful from a distance, the mountains were infected with their own kind of Yellow Fever. The more she heard of other treachery and depredations, the easier it was to believe Mayne's tale about Tucker. She also knew that she was very lucky to be alive.

Gus caught sight of a huge splotch of bright red blood on her dress. When she saw it, she felt sick. Her thoughts were in a jumble, one minute thinking that she was to die only to have Lupe come out of the blue and save her. She scarcely had it straight in her own mind, never mind trying to explain everything to others. She didn't think, however, that she was hit by any bullets. Then she looked at her blood-stained dress and then at Three-fingered Jack lying at her feet.

Pointing to him and the hole in his face, she said solemnly, "Leakage."

Gus surmised, "So, it was Carrillo's banditos that stole you, not Mayne and his bunch?"

She shook her head. Before she could explain though, she saw Asher just thirty feet away. Making no move to come to her, he was nervously slapping his horse's reins across the palm of his gloved hand. His eyes had been tense with concern, but when he saw that she had seen him, his expression altered the slightest bit. Invisible to her, a sigh of relief escaped him. When it did, his hands dropped to his sides.

Bodies littered the ravine and Lupe had begun to walk them, kicking one corpse and then the other.

"Where's Carrillo?" asked Gus.

Lupe almost laughed, "He's long gone. Nobody will get Carrillo."

Walking a ways, she called to whoever was listening, "Here is Mayne."

Annabella saw him too. He lay on his back, his eyes staring vacantly toward the sky. Gun smoke hung in the trees like cobwebs. It infused her hair, her clothes, her nasal passages, her throat—and quite possibly her womb. In the middle of the carnage, she fell to her knees and retched. As waves of nausea hit her again and again, Asher came to her and held her hair back from her face. That was as sure an act of love as she had ever imagined.

She gave him a wan smile and said, "I didn't think you would come for me."

"You are my wife," he said, knowing that wasn't what she wanted him to say.

The gunmen who had just chased the banditos out of the camp had returned, Asher's reward much on their minds. One of them saw Mayne and took out his rope. Another climbed down from his horse, pulled his knife from its scabbard and walked towards Three-Fingered Jack's dead body. Gus waved them both off.

"Carrillo's on the loose, I reckon these two will stay dead for a while yet."

The lead man wore a broad hat. His eyes were red-rimmed and determined. As the man with the money, he looked to Asher for corroboration. Asher nodded and reached into his coat pocket, producing a pay note.

"I'll pay you for Mayne now and verify this 'Jack' fellow's death to the proper authorities."

With a single-fingered salute, the gunman snatched the note from Asher's hand. Digging his heels into his horse's flank, he led the posse over the hill and out of sight. Gus didn't like to second guess another man's decision, but couldn't help himself.

"Marvelous employees, Asher," opined Gus. "Still, don't you think they'd be handy if Carrillo and his bunch come back for another round?"

"Paid guns aren't going to stand and fight," Asher replied.

Gus saw the wisdom in that. He turned to Annabella.

"As our people seem so eager to mete out justice on the dead," he said. "We need to know what happened here, Annie."

Annabella wasn't entirely certain what had happened, so she related that which she knew as fact.

"Rutledge Mayne and the man called Hardy knocked me in the head and carried me here in the back of an oxcart. Hardy went down to demand a ransom. Did you see him?"

"No, we didn't," Gus said. "What about Tucker McFee. Last I saw of him, he was with the other two and Ernie Braithwaite."

Reluctantly, Annabella agreed that Tucker was with them. She stared at the ground, trying to find the words to properly characterize Tucker's participation. She certainly didn't want anyone to know why Tucker thought he needed to rescue her. That would take quite a bit of explaining, none of which would be favorable to her.

So she said, "Tucker didn't mean to ransom me. That was the other two. Tucker's crazy, you know."

Gus was less worried about Annabella's marital problems than she was. He wanted to know not only who was behind the kidnapping, but who was responsible for Ernie Braithwaite's murder. To him Tucker was just as culpable as Hardy or Mayne.

He snapped, "They murdered poor Ernie Braithwaite for his pay, Sis. As for Tucker, crazy don't give anybody a free ride."

Annabella didn't know what to believe about Tucker. Not daring to look at Asher lest her guilty conscience be seen on her face, she held out her hand to Lupe for moral support. Lupe came and stood next to her but wouldn't take her hand. Gus and Asher looked at Lupe warily. They weren't near as certain as Annabella that given half a chance she wouldn't turn on them.

"We need to get packing or ol' Jose'll swoop down on us again before dark," Gus said.

Annabella asked Lupe, "What in the blazes are you doing with Jose Carrillo anyway? Did he steal you too?"

There was a pause as Lupe took out a cigar and lit it. Through a puff of smoke, she remained mute. It reminded Annabella of Lupe's surprising little night-time rendezvous. It seemed like that had happened in another lifetime. The truth struck her in a flash.

"You are Carrillo's *esposa?*"

Lupe shrugged.

Gus said, "Don't let those gunmen with us know that. There's probably money on her head too."

"People say I rode with him," she said. "But I stay mostly in San Francisco. I tell him he kill enough. It is time to go home, but he says no."

Annabella patted her hand. She could see the bottom of Lupe's trousers. The edges were frayed. At one time, that had flabbergasted her. No more. She understood that wearing his trousers kept her husband near. That didn't mean she and Carrillo weren't both crazy—crazy as Tucker McFee. They'd all gone loco. As she pondered that, it dawned on her that she hadn't seen Tucker—alive or dead.

"Gus, have you seen Tucker?"

A voice called from the hill just above them.

"I'm right here," he announced.

Tucker sat atop a tall horse and had a five-shot pistol in his hand. He was cool as the sunset and pissed as a newt. .

82

It took Newman Chase a while before he finally accepted that his dear little girl was snatched by kidnappers. When he did, his knees buckled. He felt faint. Squatting on his heels, he inhaled deeply several times. If he had been a woman he would have blamed corset strings. But he simply hadn't the time to cater to such nonsense.

Standing and shaking his head, he muttered, "Gather yourself you old fool! Your daughter needs you!"

"Come again, Mr. C?" called Patrick.

Newman shook his head again, but didn't say anything else.

He really didn't want to partner up with Patrick. But then, every hired gun in town had ridden off with Gus and Price. Beggars certainly couldn't be choosers. At least Patrick was willing—he'd give him that. He couldn't say the same for the rest of the town's inhabitants. When it came to find men to pony up for rescuing a lady, the new San Franciscans came up a bit short on sand.

It wasn't that way in the beginning. Back then it was still called Yerba Buena and was populated by trappers, traders, and cutthroats. There was no American flag and no real law. If a man was to survive he had to hang onto his *cajones* with both hands. Before these fast-talking speculators and open-minded women choked the landscape, it took real guts to eke out a living.

Of course, he had even greater obstacles to overcome than most—what with him being gentrified and all. Back in Boston he had courted the most beautiful lady in the world. Bella had exasperated him, but he never so much as raised his hand to her. He hadn't struck anyone—man, beast, or highfalutin woman. Now that someone had gone and stolen his little girl, he was ready to shoot every one of them. Not only would he kill the bastards that got her, he'd keep each of their heads in a pickle jar at the end of *Bella Goode*'s teakwood bar.

Newman didn't have many regrets, but he did wish he had kept his mouth shut up there at the Price house fire. He didn't have any business telling people Asher Price was a murderer. Thankfully, that had blown over. It had just been his fear talking. Once his blood had cooled a bit, he realized that alienating the only man who had the financial wherewithal to pay to get little Annabella back from her captors wasn't a good idea. However, he couldn't help but be miffed about how Asher and Gus had gone off and left him in the dust. After all, he was her father.

He understood why they did it. Everyone had consigned him to the trash heap, gauging him barely a notch above dead Ernie Braithwaite.

He'd show them. Just knowing that calamity threatened his dear daughter birthed stirrings of his early audaciousness. He felt bold and intrepid again. Girding himself for battle, he knew he had to marshal all his manly acumen. His every thought must be disciplined. Under such dangerous circumstances, a man needed to be well-armed too. Therefore, his precious Pauly pistol should have been a great comfort to him.

Next to his daughter and his teak doors, the Pauly was his most prized possession. He had brought it with him all the way from Boston. Although it was Swiss made and very innovative, he had initially disliked how it had ruined the line of his coat. Traveling clothes had been very important to him back then.

The present state of his collar and cuffs made that notion laughable. He was sobered by the thought that Annabella didn't have the Pauly anymore though. She had taken it without so much as a by your leave and returned it the same way. Had she kept it with her, those woman-stealers would've never got her. After all, she had her father's grit. But then, if she didn't have Bella's yellow hair, nobody would have thought to steal her in the first place. It was his worst fear—played out just like he predicted.

Being right wasn't near the pleasure he once imagined it might have been.

The Sierra foothills were dangerous when they weren't swarming with banditos. Newman hadn't set foot in the hinterland since he landed in town. That first day he took a stroll up to the Presidio and had been surprised by a bear. Actually, it wasn't a bear that scared him, but bear droppings. It was the biggest pile of dung he had ever seen. It was also very fresh. He had made tracks and didn't feel cowardly for doing so either. It was merely a prudent retreat. Sometimes that *was* the better part of valor.

But not at present.

He wouldn't let his daughter down again. He had quit his blubbering right off, determined to follow the posse as soon as he found an animal to ride.

Because of the fire brigade and general melee, there were several beasts of burden running at large. With Patrick's help, he managed to corner a wore-out, half-blind old horse still dragging someone's harness and a good-sized donkey. Given that Patrick was less of a rider than he was, Newman let him use the tall Mexican saddle. However, he was not so magnanimous about the mounts. He made Patrick take the donkey and he rode the horse. Despite Patrick's loud protestations about that and their lack of weapons, Newman stayed the course.

"Time is of the essence. I can't be standing here arguing with you. Either get on the jackass or stay here."

As each warily climbed aboard their steeds, Patrick said, "I'd feel better if we had guns."

"You'd just shoot yourself in the foot—or shoot me," Newman said testily. "Our job is primarily investigatory. A scouting party, if you will."

You know what Gus would say, don't you?"

Newman tied a knot in the reins to keep them from dragging the ground and pretended not to hear.

Patrick continued anyway, "He'd say, 'If you find yourself in a hole, quit digging.'"

Although he wouldn't have admitted it for the world, Newman was glad for Patrick's company. He didn't know his way around in the foothills. At least Patrick had traveled overland to get to San Francisco. Neither of them could follow a trail in the dark though. Newman decided it would be best to leave at first light.

As they waited, Patrick thought to take their minds off Annabella by bringing Newman up to speed on the latest gossip.

"I heard that Jose Carrillo came to California as a horse trainer for a traveling circus."

Newman didn't really want to hear about Carrillo. He was scared enough. He thought to frighten Patrick instead.

"Well I heard," Newman countered, "that he is followed by eighty riders—all having good reason to hate American miners."

"He has no reason to harm us," Patrick quavered. "We aren't miners."

"Yeah, but we're Americans—or at least I was an American the last time I looked. I don't know what you Missourians call yourselves."

Sniffing, Patrick replied, "I guess I was speaking against my own interests when I said I'd not let you go alone."

Newman grunted.

Despite Patrick's attempt at small talk, Newman still fretted obsessively. He had become convinced that Mayne and Hardy weren't behind Annabella's disappearance. They weren't that cunning. Now, Jose Carrillo, he was sly as a fox. If anyone had his little girl, it was Carrillo and his pack of desperados. If it was Carrillo, Asher and his dozen men would be outmatched. Those banditos knew the Sierras like the back of their hands. They'd know how to ambush a posse.

"You know, Patty, Price's reward isn't the only one out there. There's plenty of money on Carrillo's head too. Three-fingered Jack is worth ten thousand all on his own."

Patrick replied, "I Whoever he has killed, Carrillo thinks of himself a champion of the Mexicans. I heard folks say the politicians are less interested in his pillaging than him and his band being called revolutionists."

"I once saw a man kiss a goat on the mouth too, but that don't make it right," spat Newman.

For the next six hours, Newman never said another word. After a few feeble tries at conversation, Patrick concluded that he was just worried about Annabella.

Newman Chase was so worried that for the first time in years, he prayed. He prayed for Annabella's safety above everything. But he also prayed that he had done right when he handed Asher Price his precious Pauly pistol.

He tormented himself about it up to the moment they came face to face with Ezekiel Hardy.

83

The Tucker McFee who sat on a horse at the top of the escarpment looked nothing like the farm boy he had been. He didn't sound like him either.

"Annabella is mine, goddammit!"

The horse he rode was tall. The saddle was festooned with silver and braided with black pigtails. Most likely the horse and its saddle belonged to Three-fingered Jack. Nobody noticed that. All they saw was the five-shot pistol in Tucker's hand. It looked to be two foot long and its bore as wide as a fist. The gun had belonged to someone else too. Ownership was unimportant just then. What mattered was who had it.

Tucker screamed, "Annabella's mine and you sorry bastards ain't taking her from me again!"

To Tucker, the stunned faces looking back at him were uncomprehending. He reddened with indignation and hollered again.

"She's *mine*, do you hear me?"

That didn't ignite any action either, so he fired a warning shot into the air. With a stinging sound, it spat straight up through the treetops. Leaves floated to the ground like snowflakes. Everyone stood still, stupefied by the report. Tucker tossed his right leg over the tall Spanish pommel and slid to the ground so easily it was as if he did it every day of his life. Walking purposefully down hill, he called for her again.

"*Annabella*!"

Exasperated, she spat back, "What? *What*?"

Tucker held out his hand. His voice was soft now, but his words were chillingly wrong.

"Come Annabella dear. I'll save you from your tormentors."

Holding the gun level, he inched his way towards her until he caught her by the elbow. As she tried to squirm away from him, his gun barrel waved erratically keeping Asher and Gus twitching with alarm. Lupe, however, was unimpressed. Fed up with the whole business, she plopped down on the ground to wait out the impasse in comfort.

When Tucker made the grab for Annabella, Gus put a restraining arm in front of Asher.

"Not yet," he whispered.

Annabella saw no such caution. Impatiently, she jerked from Tucker's grip and tried to get beyond his reach. He caught her by the skirt and gave a tug, causing her to stumble to the ground. Still waving his gun, he hooked her by the neck and drug her to her feet. Before Asher took more than a step, Tucker aimed the pistol at his mid-section.

He screamed, "Don't you do it, Mr. Price! She doesn't love you. She loves me! *Me!*"

Caught in a chokehold, Annabella couldn't speak. She couldn't say anything. She would have given her life to have shut him up. She couldn't deny it—nothing. All she could do was thrash about, gagging and drooling like a mad woman.

"She was mine first. That's my baby, you hear? *Mine*!"

Flailing helplessly, she began to wilt from lack of air. With her last breath, she let out a gurgling wail. When she did, it startled Tucker. At the same moment he looked at her, a shot rang out. It knocked Tucker off his feet.

Finally escaping his grip, Annabella lay sprawled on the ground. Thinking of nothing but her next breath, she continued to cough and gasp for air.

Gus ran over to Tucker and kicked the gun beyond his grasp. Crouching, he took an objective appraisal of the shot.

"Through the heart," Gus pronounced. "As prosaic a wound as I have ever seen. Precise. Clean and economical."

It took a moment before Annabella could talk. When she did, the first thing she asked was, "Is he dead?"

Nodding his head, Gus said, "He's dead alright. Deader'n Abraham's ghost."

Bathed with relief, she tried to stand. No one, however, rushed to help her up. Gus was emptying the remaining bullets from the pistol Tucker had. Lupe puffed away on her cigarillo, studying the clouds. It was only when she looked towards Asher that she saw the Pauly on the ground next to him. Smoke still curled from its barrel.

It dawned on her that Gus didn't kill Tucker, Asher did.

He did not appear to enjoy Gus's admiration of his shot. In fact, he looked down right sick. A wife who held her husband's well-being foremost in her heart would have moved to comfort him then. Annabella, however, had seen more blood that day than she cared to think about. Her worries were far dearer than anyone's squeamishness. If she didn't set things to right with Asher then, her compassion wouldn't be accepted anyway.

She said evenly, "You didn't believe him, did you? Did *you*?"

He looked as if he had been slapped. She was immediately ashamed to have asked.

"It was all a pack of lies. I never, *never* loved Tucker. He has no part in anything."

"You misjudge me," he said quietly.

A double-edged sort of guilt pierced her. She was silent for a moment—long enough to realize just how catastrophically wrong she had been. In that time, she also realized that she might not have another chance to make amends.

"Yes," she said quietly. "I have misjudged you. I have misjudged almost from the very beginning."

It was shamefully obvious that her rescue did not come without cost beyond those who were merely dead.

84

As they descended the Sierras, Annabella's contrition increased exponentially. Being freed from the hands of murderous cutthroats and obtaining her husband's semi-forgiveness (for he had come for her) should have elated her. However, she couldn't quit thinking of Tucker's body lying in the clearing. His dead, unseeing eyes stared upward through the treetops. No doubt wolves were circling him even then. She looked overhead. Turkey buzzards were circling too.

Asher had insisted that they take time to bury the dead. Gus was against it.

"Carrillo's not gonna let us get away with running him off. He'll get around our posse and come back. When he returns, I doubt he'll be in a good mood."

Asher looked at Lupe and asked, "Do we have time to see to the dead?"

From beneath her faded serape came a wisp of smoke. Lupe shook her head.

Gus said with finality, "I expect she would know."

Annabella wanted to ride a horse, but she was overruled. Due to her condition, she was once again relegated to the oxcart. This time it was hitched to a horse. Silently, she wondered where Lolly was. When last seen, Hardy was riding her.

Asher took the reins and helped her on the seat next to him. Lupe climbed wordlessly in back. Annabella expected her to make more of a fuss. She certainly didn't envy her. It wasn't a comfortable place to ride.

Gus was already looking ahead, telling Annabella, "Your Poppa's gonna be glad to see you."

She hadn't thought about how worried her father might be. That was just one more sin to bear. Because no one literally pointed a finger at her didn't mean the whole thing wasn't her fault. She had lured poor Tucker to his death sure as she had been a siren from the shore. She had used her womanly (if drunken) wiles to do her selfish bidding. Perhaps his mind was addled, but if she hadn't toyed with him, he would have still been alive.

Rationalizing Rutledge Mayne's death was a little dicier. On the one hand, it death should have evened the score some in her favor. He may have had it coming a hundred times over, but when the gauntlet was thrown down, he saved her life. She didn't tell Gus that. One day she would though. It'd give him something to put in his pipe to puff on.

As Asher didn't have much to say, Annabella talked to Gus. He rode along next to them, but was plenty grumpy. He wasn't a man to complain about what had to be done, so he grumbled about a more acceptable annoyance.

"If I never get on the back of another horse, it'll be too soon."

"We shouldn't have left them back there, Gus," she said.

"We'd have spent all day and all night trying to dig holes big enough to keep the varmints from digging them up. As soon as we get back, we'll have the undertaker go collect them."

Believing that they'd all get buried properly gave the entire incident a more fitting end. Sitting crouched over, however, plagued her midsection. The pain that seared her just below her ribcage wasn't mistaken for anything other that what it was. Her conscience had set up shop in stomach and wasn't about to turn loose. If there was any truth to the tale that the unborn is scarred by any horrors the mother experiences, she had doomed her child too.

Groping for a reason for Tucker to be crazy that didn't include her, she asked, "Do you think the yellow fever made a lunatic of him, Gus?"

"I'd say Tucker arrived in San Francisco short of straw."

The possibility that she hadn't driven Tucker insane settled her some. It was a hard lesson to learn, but larking about with the gods was never a good idea. She couldn't decide if she had saved Lupe or not. She sat in the back as if she had not a care in the world, but she had have feelings for Carrillo. He was a plundering murderer, but who in this life was perfect?

"Will you stay in San Francisco?" she asked Lupe.

Lupe shrugged.

Holding out her hand, Annabella called to her, "Please ride up here with us."

Instead, Lupe tightened her hat strings and leapt out of the cart. She scrambled atop of a boulder and then stood up.

"What are you doing?" Annabella asked incredulously. "You must come *now* before Carrillo returns with more bandits."

Almost as if she had summoned him herself, a tall man wearing a sombrero and an irate expression appeared behind them. He and a dozen men had guns leveled at their heads. Gus was riding with the butt of his carbine perched on his right thigh, but he didn't have time to cock it.

"*Alto!*" demanded Carrillo.

Annabella dug her fingernails into his Asher's arm.

No one breathed—save Lupe. With a skip to her step, she leapt from one rock to the other until she stood next to Carrillo. He lowered a hand. She took it. With one motion, she was lifted onto his horse behind him. Without another sound, they disappeared as quickly as he had come.

Gus, Asher, and Annabella were silent for a moment as well. None of them questioned why Carrillo didn't kill them. They were just thankful to be alive. Without ado, Asher flicked the reins. With every rut hit on there downward course, she recalled every bump, bang, and rattle that was she endured with the sack over her head. When they reached flatter land, the splinter she had picked up began to annoy her. Putting her palm against her lips, she tried to suck it out but with no luck.

"Here," said Asher handing her the reins.

Peeling off his gloves, he picked at with his fingernails until he got it out. As he worked, it was the first good look she had of his hands. Running her finger along the blood-red gouges, she winced.

Mostly to herself, she whispered, "How could such scarred hands be so tender?"

Regaining the reins, he flicked them again. He gave no indication he heard her. His gaze remained on the trail before them.

Like Gus predicted, they met Newman on the way back down the trail.

85

Gus kept looking over his shoulder, seeing bandits behind every rock. As they came through a steep pass, he was especially watchful, knowing that if he was to ambush someone that was where he would do it.

Looking back, he admonished them all in a low voice, "Vigilance!"

A figure shadowing their movements from the ledge above caught his attention. It looked more like a cougar than a bandit. Either was a threat. Gus raised his carbine and took aim.

Annabella shrieked, "No!"

Just as the rock was even with the side of the wagon, Stewpot took a flying leap. He landed in the middle of that cart bed, scrambling to stay upright. Whining, the dog turned in a few circles in the bed of the cart before curling up on a burlap sack. He was asleep so fast that he didn't even lick Annabella's fingers.

"That dog has more lives than any three cats," marveled Gus.

Annabella began convincing Asher of what a good ratter Stewpot was. Asher had already given in to the idea when Gus spied Patrick coming up the trail. Annabella had never seen him in such a state. He looked terrified, somber and determined all at once. It was an odd combination of emotions for him, so it was understandable that the severity of the situation wasn't obvious.

Their interpretation of his plight was compromised further by the fact that he was struggling to ride a jumpy one-eyed mare. Behind him came a docile grey mule and a reluctant donkey. When Patrick caught sight of them, he pulled the reins back with all his might. He slid to the ground, landed with a thud and immediately doubled over.

"Dear Mother of God," Patrick moaned. "That saddle horn has brought me to unspeakable grief."

Immediately Gus saw something ominous. Annabella did too.

"Oh, dear God!" she gasped.

Slung over the back of the mule was a rolled up blanket. It wasn't empty.

Before Asher could help her, she scrambled down. She didn't run to the mule, however. She stopped at Patrick and fell to her knees. He didn't look at her at first. Slowly, he raised his face. Huge tears filled his eyes and began to run down his cheeks. Annabella sat back, drawing her knees to her bosom.

"Poppa, *Poppa!*" She wailed.

"I didn't know what to do," Patrick whimpered. "I couldn't leave him for the buzzards. I had to bring him to you."

Gasping, Annabella made herself hush. She placed her hand against Patrick's cheek.

"Thank you," she said. "You did right."

In the first moments of anguish, it was easy to be magnanimous. After all, Patrick did nothing wrong. The blame for this tragedy was hers too. Newman Chase had been perfectly happy before she came to town. She came into his world, turned it upside down and then left him to it. No wonder he turned to Dovie and then to drink.

These had been her thoughts alone. Although she was certain he blamed her, Gus was too overwhelmed with shock and grief to think of anything but Newman. After all, Newman Chase had been his best friend since God was a boy.

As Annabella brought herself clumsily to her feet, Gus climbed down from his horse. He stopped next to Patrick and watched as Annabella walked over to the blanketed body and lifted one corner. She slipped her hand beneath it and stroked her father's hair.

When, oh when had it become so white?

Although he wanted to, Gus couldn't look at Newman's dead body. If someone had been so impertinent as to ask why, he would have said that he had seen too much death that day. But that wasn't true. He just didn't have the courage. Asher didn't either. He still sat on the seat of the cart. He felt as if his limbs were made of lead. Neither of them dared to tempt the fates, lest they be overcome by an attack of unmanly weeping.

Finally, Asher stumbled down from the cart. Unable to speak, Gus took Annabella by the shoulders and steered her towards her husband's arms. Moaning, she began to beat impotently against Asher's chest. He took her in his arms, (the gesture awkward from disuse) at last giving her the comfort that he had a long denied himself.

Clearing his throat, Gus tried to gather himself. In order to take it all in, he needed to determine what had happened.

Before he could ask, Patrick said, "We came across Hardy in the pass." Then began to recite what had befallen them without his usual embroidery.

"Mr. C didn't have his Pauly, you see. I said we shouldn't have come without guns. But Mr. C told me I would just shoot myself or him. We were just a scouting party. Hardy had a gun though. I don't think he would have shot at us if Mr. C hadn't have jumped on him like he did. They fell to the ground, flailing and hitting each other. Hardy had a gun and I didn't know what to do.

Then Patrick turned to Gus and said, "I didn't know what to *do*!"

Squeezing his shoulder reassuringly, Gus told him, "You did fine, Patty, you did fine."

Patrick wept when Annabella wept, but knew better than to push Gus. He withdrew his handkerchief and blew hard into it. After a sniff or two, his discomposure was squared away.

"Where is Hardy now?" asked Asher. "I promise you, Annabella, that I shall hunt him down...."

Patrick interrupted, "Why, he's dead, Mr. Price. I bashed him in the head with an axe handle."

"I say that's well done," said Gus. "One less bastard to worry about."

"Well, Mr. C said I shouldn't have a gun, not be unarmed altogether."

Perhaps it was because they were largely incompetent when it came to expressing sentimentality in other ways that the three of them threw themselves into the masculine duty of securing the earthly remains of the dead. Heaving the portly remains of Newman Chase off the mule and into the cart, however, was an exhausting procedure.

"Damn you, Newman, I told you to quit eatin' so many potatoes," groaned Gus.

Standing to the side holding Stewpot, Annabella didn't miss the affection behind Gus's words. His hat was pulled down low on his forehead so not to expose his devastation.

Gus retrieved the Pauly he had put in his waistband and handed it back to Asher. Asher in turn, gave the Pauly to Annabella. They both knew it should be hers.

"We've run out of soap here," Gus said evenly. "We need to vamoose if we don't want a similar fate."

Annabella cried silently and her snuffling made her blistered nose even more obvious. Without a word, Asher removed his hat from his head and plopped it on hers. That bit of thoughtfulness meant more to her than a half-dozen opal broaches. She wanted to tell him so, but it was difficult to talk in the jouncing cart. Knowing bandits could beset them again at any turn didn't encourage conversation either. It also took the edge off of grief.

The silence gave Annabella time to think. She resolved never to tell Asher about what she had done with Tucker. She knew that they hadn't actually consummated the act, but that hardly mattered. Whether Aaron Ainsworth ever did more than kiss her didn't matter either. She would've done anything he asked of her. If she came to her husband pure in body, it was a complete accident.

She reached out and touched Asher's scarred hand. He took hers.

When Gus went back to looking for assassins, Asher decided it was finally time to talk.

"Just so you know, he said. "I didn't murder my wife—not actually. But then one can cause a death without actually doing the killing."

"Yes," she said.

When it came to honor, neither of them had a stranglehold on first place. Many a marriage had been made happy on far less.

86

1851—San Francisco

The blanket was warm from the sun hitting it through the window pane. She drew her finger lazily across its lattice shadow. When it reached the edge of the bed, it would be time to leave.

Her hand was delicate, her fingers long and pliant. His easily engulfed hers. She turned on her back, stretching like a cat.

He said, "You are the most fetching woman on earth."

With a gentle hand on her shoulder, he encouraged her to turn on her back. She complied, but crossed her wrists, and allowing her cupped hands cover her breasts. That didn't matter. There were other places that interested him.

He put his hand palm down on her stomach. A hint of panic widened her eyes made her innards flutter. Seeing that, he quickly grabbed her waist and, before she could stop him, began tickling her.

"You beast!" she laughed.

She laughed so hard, she emitted an unladylike snort which only made her laugh harder. He laughed too, but only stopped tickling her when she slapped at his hand like a toddler's. He caught hold of her hand and kissed it like a knight. To her, he was more than that.

At first it had been difficult to differentiate gratitude from infatuation and infatuation with love. When trampled—whether through betrayal or loss—the heart isn't infinitely resilient.

His big hands clasped hers and held them fast above her head. She allowed him that and let his lips trace down her neck and across her breast.

"It's late," she said.

She was smiling, but he turned serious.

"No," he whispered. "It's love."

She tensed. It was the first time that word had been used. They had always said that they would only have today. There would be no promises made. No promises made, meant none to be broken.

"For, you see," he said, "each day I love you more."

Pressing the back of her fingers against his cheek, she said, "I love you today more than yesterday and tomorrow more than today."

"As for now, a man's duty calls," Gus said.

"Must you go?" Libby cooed.

"Those teak doors won't open on their own," he replied. "That Annabella's damn particular about them."

He didn't mind at all. It was only fitting that she have run of the place with him. After all, the *Bella Goode* was named after her mother.